LORI FOSTER

TOUGH LOVE

HQN™

ISBN-13: 978-0-373-78848-4

Recycling programs
for this product may
not exist in your area.

Tough Love
Copyright © 2015 by Lori Foster

The publisher acknowledges the copyright holder
of the additional work:

Back to Buckhorn
Copyright © 2014 by Lori Foster

www.HQNBooks.com

Printed in U.S.A.

Also available from Lori Foster and HQN Books

The Ultimate series

Hard Knocks
(e-prequel novella)
No Limits
Holding Strong
Tough Love

Love Undercover

Run the Risk
Bare It All
Getting Rowdy
Dash of Peril

Men Who Walk the Edge of Honor

"Ready, Set, Jett"
in *The Guy Next Door* anthology
When You Dare
Trace of Fever
Savor the Danger
A Perfect Storm
What Chris Wants
(ebook novella)

Other must-reads

A Buckhorn Summer
(ebook novella)
All For You
Back to Buckhorn
(ebook novella)
Heartbreakers
Charade
Up in Flames
Turn Up the Heat
Hot in Here
Animal Attraction
(ebook anthology)
Love Bites
All Riled Up
The Buckhorn Legacy
Forever Buckhorn
Buckhorn Beginnings
Bewitched
Unbelievable
Tempted
Bodyguard
Caught!
Fallen Angels
Enticing

Don't miss the next book in the Ultimate series

Fighting Dirty

Dear Reader,

My newest Ultimate series, with books that each stand alone but are connected by characters who know each other, involves mixed martial arts (MMA) fighters *and* falling in love. The sport brings with it some hunky, capable alpha heroes so that all I need to do is add in the romance. Superfun for me and, given the reaction to the first three stories (*Hard Knocks*, an e-prequel novella, and the full-length novels *No Limits* and *Holding Strong*), readers are enjoying them, too. I'm thrilled with the feedback I've gotten so far, and now I'm pleased to introduce readers to Stack and Vanity's story!

Their romance starts with a sexy proposition from Vanity. Seems simple enough. But every time Stack thinks he has a handle on things, Vanity throws him for a loop—in a good way. Vanity knows she's playing a tricky game, but she's playing to win. I loved writing their romance—and I hope you'll love reading it!

If you're not familiar with MMA, no worries. You don't need to follow the sport to understand the books because the core of these stories is romance— sexy, fun, one-on-one romance. They're about the fighters—not fighting.

With every new Ultimate book released, I receive reader letters and emails asking which of the fighters will be next. Judging by readers' reactions, I'm guessing you'll be excited to learn that Armie's getting a book of his own! I saved him for last because let's face it, Armie has some things to work out before he plays the role of romantic hero. But if you've read the other books, you'll have a pretty good sense by now of the woman who just might give him everything—even those things he didn't know were missing.

Just for fun, at the end of this book you'll find *Back to Buckhorn*, a novella from my reader-favorite Buckhorn Brothers series, in print for the first time. While Garrett Hudson is a firefighter rather than an MMA fighter, I think you'll find he has a lot of qualities in common with my Ultimate men.

I hope you enjoy the reads. And of course, you're always welcome to reach out to me. I'm very active on most social media forums including Facebook, Twitter, Pinterest and Goodreads, and my email address is listed on my website at lorifoster.com.

Happy reading to all,

Lori Foster

To Whitney Price,

You know I think of you as a daughter, and lil Ruby as a granddaughter. You're both very special to me.

And because you're so endlessly sweet (and because of the private joke we started on Facebook) it was extra fun to give your name to the coldhearted fictional character in this book. Yes, you finally get to be really bad!

Love you much,

Lori

CHAPTER ONE

VANITY BAKER TRIED not to look, but she felt the intensity of his stare tracking her every move. She was pretty sure she felt simmering lust, too, and when she peeked at him, sexual heat glimmered hotly in his eyes.

Pretending to dance, she put a hand to her heart to contain the rapid tripping.

Yummy Stack Hannigan, with the steel biceps and rigid abs, the charm-your-pants-off smile and smoky, gray-blue eyes. Whew. She supposed weeks of teasing could hone the interest of any red-blooded man.

But she didn't want just any man. She wanted this particular light-heavyweight mixed martial arts fighter. The offer she'd given him—be her escort for their friends' wedding and she'd take the guesswork out of his post-evening sexcapades—had been pretty daring. But then, she'd needed an edge to get what she wanted.

In the fight world, they called him The Wolf. Since she soaked up everything that had to do with Stack, she'd naturally listened to the rationale for the name. Men claimed he got the handle because of the way he stalked his fight opponents like prey.

Women said he'd earned it in the bedroom—by making the ladies howl.

Vanity shivered, just thinking about it.

She'd known him for months, and other than being

polite, other than treating her like one of the group, either flustering her or making her laugh—and often making her hot—he hadn't made a move.

So she had.

And now, finally, the big day had arrived.

Laughing, the bride and best man danced around her. Yvette, her very best friend, now happily married to her own fighter, looked beyond stunning. Love did that for a woman, Vanity guessed, took away all the shadows and doubt and filled in every empty space with joy.

Love. Yes, anyone who looked at Cannon or Yvette saw it.

In fact, she saw love on the faces of a lot of the guests. The wedding had been *the* anticipated event with most of the town attending. Yvette had married a very popular guy; everyone adored and respected Cannon, from local shop owners to police detectives and a wide range of fighters, amateurs and pros alike.

All around her their friends talked, laughed, danced. Usually Vanity enjoyed people-watching, but now she barely noticed them as she concentrated on not looking at Stack.

When Yvette announced it was time for her to throw the bouquet, the single ladies all lined up. Cherry Peyton, currently very involved with one of the bigger fighters, Denver Lewis, sidled up next to Vanity.

As part of the wedding party, their dresses coordinated. But as the maid of honor, Vanity's had a sweetheart neckline instead of spaghetti straps, and where the others were a richer rose color, hers was a paler blush.

Smiling and indulgent, the men all clustered around the bar, looking very fine in their tuxes.

When her gaze met Yvette's, Vanity knew what her

friend would do. Laughing, she played along, her arms up as if she hoped to catch the flowers.

Yvette let them fly—right for Vanity.

But commitment wasn't what she wanted right now, not while Stack stood there watching her so intently. No way would she chance scaring him off before they'd even had a chance to get together. Not when she was this close to finally knowing him intimately.

At the last second she dipped to the side, and the bouquet hit Cherry's impressive breasts instead.

Everyone laughed, and when Vanity peeked at Denver, she saw his smug smile. Huh. So maybe matrimony didn't scare *him*. Maybe he and Cherry had already made plans.

While the room broke out in catcalls, applause and laughter, Cannon scooped Yvette into his arms, whirled her in a circle, then shouted his farewell and took his smiling bride out a side door.

That made it official—an end to the wedding, allowing her to wrap up her duties as maid of honor. She, too, was now free to leave.

With Stack.

Her heart started pumping harder. An insidious warmth expanded inside her. She drew a careful breath, looked toward Stack, and got caught in his piercing gaze.

For weeks now she'd been tormenting him, kissing him when he least expected it, while also encouraging him to continue his bachelor ways. She'd deliberately confused him with her insistence that he see other women, that it should be "business as usual" for both of them.

Not that she'd been seeing anyone else. But Stack

didn't know that. Since she'd left him free and clear
to play the field, she wanted him to think she'd been
doing the same.

But no more. After an excruciatingly long wait, tonight was finally their night.

Smiling at Stack, she crooked her finger to beckon
him.

As if he'd been waiting with the engine revving, he
shot toward her, reaching her in only a few long strides.

The breath she held came out in a gasp as he pulled
her against him, locked an arm around her waist and
took her mouth with hot, incredible greed.

Whoa. And here she thought *she'd* been on the ragged
edge.

He was so much bigger than her in every way, he
made her feel tiny and feminine and fragile. In all other
situations her independent soul might have rebelled, but
not now. Not with Stack. She trusted him 100 percent,
and wanted him even more than that.

Flattening her hands on his chest, she smoothed over
the solid wall of his pecs, up to those rock-solid shoulders. Heat poured off him, and—*oh, God*—he smelled
so good. With his big hands opened on her, his mouth
eating at hers, she forgot…everything.

The music and the conversation of other guests faded
away. She tunneled her fingers into his hair and tried
to get closer still.

Someone bumped into them; Stack didn't stop kissing her. If anything, his tongue became bolder, exploring, tasting.

Laughter, probably from his friends, sounded nearby,
and still he didn't stop. He gathered her closer.

Jarred back to the here and now, Vanity pressed against him. A true gentleman, Stack immediately eased up.

Her lips tingled. Shoot, her whole body tingled. She drew in a shaky breath. "Wow."

Proving he hadn't, in fact, forgotten they stood in the middle of the floor at a friend's wedding, he whispered against her lips, "Let me get you someplace private." A softer kiss of persuasion. "I'll give you reason to be wowed."

Such a tempting promise.

Oh, how she wanted to haul him to the nearest quiet closet. But that would be dumb. What she wanted, what she hoped he ultimately wanted, would require hours, not a few frenzied minutes.

Voice filled with regret, Vanity explained, "I can't go just yet."

His rough growl proved his impatience.

"Very soon, I promise." Adjusting their embrace, her arms around his neck, his hands at her waist, she put some space between them. "Let's dance while you cool down and I—"

"Dream on." But he eased his hold and fell into step with her. Gaze burning over her, then lingering on her cleavage, he asked, "How much longer do I have to wait?"

Vanity didn't pretend confusion; she knew exactly what he meant, exactly what he wanted. "One dance. Then I need to get the bouquet out of the fridge and gather up some presents and—"

He groaned again, prompting Vanity to laugh.

"Let's talk." Maybe casual conversation would help cool his jets and give her a needed opportunity to regroup.

"Okay." He leaned in. "I can't wait to taste you—all over."

All over?

"And to get you under me. Or over me. Your preference."

"Stack." Her shaky voice sounded weak. "Let's talk about something that isn't provoking."

"Like what? Because honest to God, darlin', after weeks of your verbal foreplay, I'm feeling pretty damned provoked."

The smile came slowly. Teasing Stack was a true pleasure.

She wouldn't mind teasing him for the rest of her life.

"Verbal foreplay?" she asked. "Is that what we've been doing?"

Holding her gaze, he pressed his hand lower to the small of her back...and beyond. When her eyes widened, he stopped, and his mouth tipped in his own small smile. "Yeah, you play with words, saying just enough to get me firing on all cylinders." He ducked his head to steal another quick kiss. "Tonight your playtime is over."

"I like playing," she protested. With any luck she'd soon have uninterrupted hours with his naked body.

"I know you do. But now it's my turn." Stack tucked her closer and said softly near her ear, "I'm going to love playing with you."

"Stack." She hid her warm face against his warmer throat. She'd drunk very little, but his touch, his scent, intoxicated her. "Everyone is watching us."

"Wrong." His lips grazed her throat. "Denver is zoning on Cherry. Armie's trying to figure out how to dodge Merissa, Miles and Brand are hooking up with some locals, and Leese is surrounded by three young things actively trying to convince him they're not *too* young."

It was the last that had her leaning back to take a look. She and Leese had grown close. She thought of him as her pal, and he accommodated her as long as he didn't have other plans. Whenever she needed an excuse to be in the same area as Stack, or a platonic date to one of the fight competitions, Leese stepped up for her.

True enough, Leese currently stood off to the side, one shoulder to the wall and an indulgent smile on his handsome face as three remarkably gorgeous girls, probably no more than twenty years old, hung on his every word.

A soft bite to her shoulder regained Vanity's attention. "Hey!"

Stack licked the spot, then opened his mouth on her, sucking until her toes curled in her shoes and she moaned, entirely forgetting that they were on a dance floor with other people around.

"Better," he whispered, kissing his way back to her mouth. "Attention on me tonight, darlin'. Me and only me."

Incredulous, she reared back to see him. "You're jealous of Leese?"

Blue eyes darkened, turned smokier. "No reason to be, right?"

"None at all." Being as honest with him as she could, she admitted, "Leese knows I want you."

Stack missed a beat before resuming the sway of their dance. "You told him about tonight?"

"No." How much should she admit? She considered it, and decided, why not? "I get hit on."

That made him laugh.

Feeling her face go hot, Vanity lifted her chin. "Well, I do. So whenever I go to watch one of you fight, Leese goes along with me—as long as he's not the one fighting and he doesn't have a date."

"Using him as repellent, huh?"

She wrinkled her nose. "That sounds terrible." And true. "I like Leese. We get along well. Random guys think he's a date, and Leese understands."

Cocking a brow, Stack stated, "That you want me."

"Yes." Deal with that, she thought.

Before tonight, before this very moment, Vanity would have clarified that she wanted him *just* for tonight. She'd lured him in with a no-strings-attached promise in hopes that once they hooked up, he'd enjoy himself enough to insist on a replay.

Then another, and another.

Devious, yes. Manipulative, sure. But her deception wouldn't hurt anyone. She would have sex with Stack. And if, despite her best efforts, he decided they were one and done, she wouldn't harass him. She'd be disappointed. *She'd be devastated.* But she had her pride.

Tilting his head, Stack studied her. "So Leese throws other guys off the scent, because…what? You don't date?"

Mmm, no. She didn't, but she'd prefer he not know that. Not just yet, anyway. "Let's just say I'm choosy. When I want a man, I let him know."

Now Stack looked irate. "The way you let me know?"

She tried not to smile but lost the battle. "You're the only man I've made a deal with."

"The deal being a date for sex?"

Yes, that was the deal she'd offered him. But it wasn't

that simple. "Not just any date," she insisted while looking at his mouth. "It's not like I'd make that offer for a
date to a movie or a dance or anything lame."

"You're saying the wedding is special?"

Vanity bit her lip and slowly shook her head.

His gaze held hers. "So you're saying *I'm* special."

The teasing look in his eyes warmed her from the
inside out. "As the maid of honor, I needed a date. And
this wasn't just any wedding. It was *the* wedding." Just
about everyone in Warfield, Ohio, knew Cannon. As a
top fighter for the SBC, he was a hometown hero. Actually, he was such a great guy that he'd been a hero before the SBC signed him on. But now, with fans around
the world, the locals totally revered him.

Being a fighter on the fast track and one of Cannon's
close friends, Stack had his own share of admiration
from near and far. "You were the perfect choice."

He nodded slowly. "So I'm not only special but perfect." He nudged her closer. "Careful or you'll make
me blush."

Vanity doubted such a thing was possible. "I know
I've teased you."

"Yeah, but most of the time I enjoyed it."

"I'm glad." Going on tiptoe to brush her mouth over
his, Vanity stared into his eyes. Timing was everything,
she reminded herself. And now seemed like a good time
to share a truth. "You're the only one I considered for
this particular bargain."

For the longest time he stared into her eyes and said
nothing. Finally, when she thought she couldn't take it
a moment more, he cupped a hand to her neck, moved
his thumb over her jaw. "I'm glad it was me."

Without her realizing it, he'd danced them over to the

entryway. Now he took her hand and tugged her away
from the ballroom. "What do we have to do before we
can get out of here? And don't make the list too long,
because I swear, I won't make it."

No, she wouldn't either. "Five minutes, tops."

"I'll help and we'll make it two."

EARLY NOVEMBER IN OHIO brought colder temps but,
thankfully, no frost. A good thing, since Vanity's dress,
shoes and matching wrap weren't designed to brave
the elements.

As the car quickly warmed, Stack watched her relax.
Her shivering subsided, and she allowed the wrap to
loosen.

He liked her in that fluffy dress, how it showed off
her tiny waist and cleavage, how feminine it looked.
But he'd like her more out of it. So many times he'd
imagined her naked, waiting on him, accepting him.
Moving against him.

Coming with him.

It hadn't taken much to work up the visual, given that
the clothes she wore often left little to the imagination.
Especially at the gym. Her fitted bike shorts and sports
bras left every guy in the place stealing looks.

Stealing, because even if Vanity didn't realize it, the
others knew that Stack had laid claim, so they thought
twice about outright ogling her.

Vanity liked to think she had all the control.

Didn't bother Stack any. When it came to women,
he was pretty easygoing. Some laughs, lots of sex, a
friendly fare-thee-well, and everyone stayed happy. No
reason for drama. Definitely no reason for getting all
tensed up.

But even as he thought it, he flexed his shoulders to work out the stiffness in his muscles. Tense? Hell, yeah. Lust had him tied into about a hundred knots, all thanks to Vanity Baker.

The light of street lamps flashed into the car, giving him glimpses of her pale blond hair, her high breasts nearly spilling out of her dress, and those longer than long legs that had filled his dreams for too many nights.

He also saw the banked excitement in her eyes and the flush of anticipation in her cheeks.

"Hey." Driving one-handed, he laid his other hand on the seat between them, palm up.

After a small smile, she put her hand in his—and he felt her trembling.

"Still cold?" Lust had him on fire, but he could adjust the heat for her.

"No."

Other possibilities skated into his mind, filling him with protectiveness. Was she uneasy? Maybe a little worried?

It'd make sense. For a while after they'd first met, she'd been polite but not openly interested. By small degrees she'd warmed up, started paying more attention to him. Then out of the blue she'd propositioned him, and every day since, she'd been deliberately toying with him, hyping up the attraction until he could think of little other than hearing her scream with a climax.

All their friends knew he was ready to detonate. Vanity knew it, too.

Brushing his thumb over her knuckles, he asked gently, "Nervous, then?"

She shook her head. "No."

"You're shaking."

Lifting his hand to her mouth, she lightly bit a knuckle, then kissed the spot. Gaze sincere, she whispered, "Because I'm eager."

Well, hell. She'd just done it again, made him taut with her words. Needing to explain to her, just in case he jumped the gun, he said, "The first time..."

"Fast and hard," she finished for him. "I know." Her smile slipped into place even as her eyes darkened and her voice went all breathy. "It'll be worth it if I get to watch you. I've been thinking about that forever."

Jesus.

"After that," she murmured, "then it can be my turn."

Trying to give a little more room to his growing erection, Stack stretched out one leg. If she kept that up, he wouldn't make it to her place. Hell, he was so close to losing it, the idea of pulling over for a quickie in the car appealed in a big way. It should have embarrassed him, how she stole his control. But knowing Vanity pushed him on purpose only made him more determined to blow her mind with sex.

Reaching for long-lost patience, he drew in a deep breath and put both hands back on the steering wheel. "You're playing with fire. You know that, right?"

"I'm playing with *you*, Stack Hannigan, and it's the most fun I've had in a very long time."

He liked her like this, so open about what she wanted— namely, him. "Like I said before, you'll pay for the play."

"I'm hopeful." She laughed, and even that turned him on.

Vanity was the one of the sexiest women he'd ever known, but she was also real. Bold. He didn't have to wonder at her thoughts, because she spelled out what she wanted and how she wanted it.

She also made it clear that their time together had a short time frame, and after they'd settled the lust, she fully expected him to mosey on out of her life.

Should've been perfect, only…it nettled him that she didn't push for more.

Both of them now silent, he turned a corner onto a dark street—and immediately saw the collision. Two vehicles, one in a ditch, the other overturned. Headlights cut the dark of the night at odd angles. Even as Stack slowed his car, searching the scene, the overturned car ignited and flames licked into the air.

"Oh, my God." Vanity sat forward to stare. "There!" She pointed to the side of one car. "There's a body!"

Stack jerked the car to the curb, slammed it into Park and released his seat belt at the same time. "Call 911."

She already had her purse in her hands, digging through it. "Be careful," she called after him as he hurriedly left the car.

He'd only taken one step when Stack heard a woman's weak screams.

Breaking into a run, he headed toward the burning SUV. The body Vanity had spotted was a man. It appeared he'd been thrown free and half sat nearby, dazed and confused, blood trickling down his face.

The heat grew nearly unbearable as Stack got closer to the mangled vehicle. Following the voice, he bent to look under the heap of twisted metal and found the woman frantically trying to free herself. Soot covered her face, along with some blood and bruises. Hysterical, she reached toward him. "Help me!"

Stack caught her hands, but some part of the SUV pinned her legs, and he couldn't free her. *Fuck, fuck.*

He looked around again. From the other car a man staggered out. Drunk or injured, Stack wasn't sure.

"Give me a hand," Stack told him.

Instead the man backed up and started nearly incoherent babbling. Drunk, then. Stack watched as he took a lopsided step and fell to his ass.

Suddenly Vanity was there. She'd left her wrap behind, and now her arms and shoulders were exposed to the cold.

She paid no mind to that, asking quickly, "What can I do?"

Ah, hell, he didn't want her anywhere near the burning car.

"Please, oh, please, help me!"

Grabbing his shirt, Vanity hauled him closer. "*I'm helping.* Now tell me what to do!"

Clearly she couldn't ignore the woman's screams any more than he could.

"Grab her hands. Soon as I rock it back, see if you can pull her free." He knelt to see the woman. So far the flames weren't near her, but she'd still feel the heat, and she'd have to know the fire was spreading. "We're going to try to drag you out."

"Yes, yes, hurry!"

Shit. "Your legs—"

"It's okay," she screamed. "Hurry!"

With her dress dangerously close to the hot flames, Vanity knelt down and locked hands with the woman. "Tell me if I hurt you."

Putting his shoulder to the SUV, Stack dug in his feet and pushed with all his might. He felt it give, lifting just a little. Not much, but hopefully enough.

"I've got you." Vanity also dug in with her dressy

heeled sandals, her bare arms straining, her face high-lighted by the red glow of the fire. The panicked woman moaned, but Vanity didn't relent. "Shh, shh," she said around her efforts. "Almost there. Almost."

Making not a sound, Stack strained to keep the ve-hicle in position and just watched, impressed by her, grateful for her lack of hysterics. Sweat popped on his brow and his jaw locked, but he stayed focused on Van-ity.

Finally, the woman's legs cleared the wreckage, and Vanity relaxed. Jerking back, Stack let the vehicle drop forward again. The hot metal scattered sparks that floated into the darkness.

He didn't trust the situation at all and went right back to work.

"Move to the curb," he told Vanity. "Now." Urg-ing her away from the wreckage, Stack took her place, scooping his hands under the woman's shoulders and, being as careful as he could, dragging her farther away.

Once he felt they were at a safe distance, he shrugged off his now-ruined tux jacket and put it around Van-ity's shoulders.

She'd already knelt by the woman, talking to her, trying to calm her, but she took a second to smile her gratitude.

Stack smoothed her hair, overwhelmed for reasons he couldn't understand. It wasn't the wreck or the dan-ger of the situation.

It was Vanity, her quick thinking and her grounded attitude, her fortitude and her ability.

With a loud *whoosh*, flames consumed the SUV, making Vanity jump and the woman scream anew.

"Stay with her," he told Vanity, then jogged back for

the two men who seemed incapable of thinking clearly. Given his sluggish reactions, the first guy had a severe concussion, or worse, Stack was pretty sure. The blood covering his face probably came from a head wound, but with so much gore he couldn't be sure. Also looked like he might have a dislocated shoulder and probably a broken leg.

It wasn't easy to move him without causing him more pain, but he was so out of it he only grunted as Stack put an arm around him and half lifted, half dragged him to the side. He didn't take him near the women, thinking they might react badly to all the blood.

The other guy—yeah. Only superficial wounds, but flat-out drunk, which probably explained the wreck. Stack urged him a safer distance away, but the idiot didn't stay put, and he wasn't about to babysit a drunken fool, not when the others might need help.

Luckily, seconds later, both police and paramedics arrived. While the injured were tended, Stack explained to the cops what he'd found.

"Hang around a minute," the cop said before he and two others went to talk to the drunken man.

Breathing hard through an adrenaline dump, Stack looked around for Vanity and found her sitting on the curb, his coat wrapped around her like a cape, her face in her hands.

Fresh alarm ripped into him and before he even realized he was moving, he found himself next to her. Parts of her dress were scorched, the material all but melted. Soot blackened her long beautiful hair, now a tangled mess. He saw a small burn on her forearm, maybe where she'd bumped into hot metal.

Heart clenching, he crouched down and took her wrists. "Hey. You okay?"

She resisted his attempt to uncover her face and merely nodded.

"Vanity?"

"I'm sorry. I'm just…rattled." Her shoulders lifted with a deep breath, but she didn't come out of hiding.

"Are you hurt?" Had she been burned anywhere else? Maybe pulled a muscle while dragging out the other woman? She was so slim, so delicate and female and—

"I look like a disaster."

So Vanity was being…vain? He smiled. "Naw." After smoothing her hair again, he put a finger beneath her chin. "C'mon, darlin'. I need you to look at me now."

Her hands lowered, and Stack got caught in her big blue eyes, framed with smudged makeup.

He'd expected tears, or at least residual fear. He saw neither.

Tipping her head, she smiled at him. "You only recently started calling me darlin'. Is it because we're finally going to have sex?"

Behind them, a cop coughed.

Closing his eyes, Stack took a single moment, then stood and faced the officer.

Both worried and amused, the cop said, "She's okay?"

"She will be." He'd see to it…not that she appeared to need his help with that.

Coming to her feet, Vanity shook out her skirt, tossed back her hair, adjusted his coat over her shoulders, and gave each guy a direct, rock-steady look. "She can speak for herself, and, yes, she's fine."

Chastising them?

The cop coughed again, chagrined.

Putting his arm around her, Stack drew her into his side. Whether Vanity needed it or not wasn't the point. Not for a second did he miss the way the other man looked at her. He got that. Even slightly singed and badly disheveled, Vanity could bowl a guy over.

But the cop needed to understand that, at least for now, she was taken.

When neither man said anything more, Vanity looked toward the ambulance and the woman being lifted onto a stretcher. Her husband was now at her side, still pretty dazed but much of the blood cleaned away. "That poor lady," Vanity said when they all heard her crying.

"She says the other driver came around the corner on their side of the road. The headlights blinded them. Guess her husband instinctively tried to veer away, but they got clipped anyway, he lost control, and whatever they hit caused the SUV to roll."

Stack stared toward the second driver who was now loudly complaining. "Drunk?"

"Totally shit-faced and driving on a suspended license. He's lucky he didn't kill someone." The cop eyed them both but settled on Stack. "Luckier still that you came along. You know, most people run from fire. Not to it."

Stack tugged at his ear. In all honesty, he hadn't thought about the fire. He'd seen the wreck, then heard the woman calling out…

"He's wonderful," Vanity said and leaned into his side. "The way that woman was pinned down… How badly is she hurt?"

"They're still looking her over, but I know she has several bad burns, maybe a few breaks."

"Oh, God," Vanity whispered.

"She's alive," Stack reminded her, and kissed the top of her head. The scent of smoke mixed with the softer scents of woman. He wanted to get her home, as much now to comfort her and ensure she was okay as for the sex they'd both been anticipating for months now. They needed showers, and he wanted to check the burn mark on her arm.

More vehicles pulled up, including a news crew complete with mics and cameras.

"And the circus begins," the cop complained. "Get ready for an interview."

The last thing he wanted. Given how Vanity had stiffened, she felt the same. "Mind if we skip out on that?"

Nodding in understanding, the cop tapped a notepad to his thigh. "I have your info. I'll be in touch if I need anything else."

"Thanks." Avoiding eye contact with the reporters, Stack got Vanity moving.

In a whisper, she said, "I feel so conspicuous in this dress with your tux jacket. I hope they don't notice us."

Nice to know she wasn't one of those people who preened for attention. Stack opened her door and got her in, taking one quick look to see two reporters clustered around the injured woman and her husband.

They got out of there before anyone tried to talk to them.

For five minutes they rode in silence. Using his coat like a blanket, Vanity tried to smooth her hair, lifted the skirt of her dress and grimaced, then turned down the visor mirror and blew out a breath at her reflection. "I'm wrecked."

"And brave."

"Mostly wrecked." She flipped the visor back up. "What that nice officer said? It's true. You literally ran right up to that fire. You didn't know if the car would explode—"

"Cars don't explode. Or at least, not very often. What you see in movies is just for drama." She still looked shaken, so he tried to reassure her with bland facts. "The wreck probably sheared the fuel line. Totaled as that SUV was, I'm guessing some metal might've punctured the gas tank, too. Hard to know what happened, but once everything catches fire, yeah, it can look like an explosion."

She leveled a look on him. "You're debating semantics. It was dangerous. Very dangerous."

"And you were right there." He white-knuckled the steering wheel, still hating how close she'd gotten to that danger. "I thought you were going to stay in the car."

"If you hadn't needed my help, I would have." She wrinkled her nose. "I'm not great in a crisis."

"That's a joke, right?" When she just stared at him, he added, "You were perfect. Steady, calm." He thought of how she'd struggled to get the woman free, and added, "Strong."

"So why are you frowning?"

"You could have been hurt."

Her brows went up. "You were worried about me?"

Stack didn't answer that. Did she really find that idea so surprising?

"Ahhh…" Vanity stroked his shoulder. "You were. That is so sweet."

Annoying, but what he noticed most was the continued trembling of her hand. She put up a good front, but obviously she had been affected.

He chanced a glance at her, then at the time on the dash. One in the morning. It choked him, but he knew he had to make a noble offer. He had to be considerate.

He had to be fucking *sweet*.

His balls protested, but he made himself say, "Listen, it's late, and things have gone sideways. If you need some time, we can put this off—"

"What?" Rearing back, for the first time looking truly upset, Vanity watched him. "You're backing out on me?"

"No." Hell, no. "We're definitely getting together. I'm just saying, if you're hurt or upset, it doesn't have to be tonight."

Her eyes flashed at him. Leaning toward him, her voice firm, she growled, "Yes, Stack Hannigan, it does!"

CHAPTER TWO

STACK FROWNED OVER her raised voice. "Calm down." Her quick glare befuddled him. "Look, all I'm saying is that you're shaking. And your arm is burnt and—"

"And you made promises." While looking at her arm, she added, "Sexual promises, so don't even think of dodging out on me." She winced when she saw the burn. "Damn it. It wasn't hurting, but now that you've pointed it out, it is."

"I wasn't…" All her attention remained on her arm, so he gave up trying to explain that he'd only made an attempt at nobility. No way was he "dodging out," as she'd accused.

The burn on her arm didn't look serious. Slightly bigger than a quarter, it was red, angry, but only slightly blistered. "I can take care of that for you once we get to your place."

"What will you do?" She held her arm to her chest protectively.

Stack felt the crooked grin pulling at his mouth. The woman would brave a car fire, dismiss any danger, but at the thought of him patching her up, she grew wary. "I have a first-aid kit in the trunk," he explained, hoping to soothe her. "We'll put some ointment on it and wrap it, that's all. You can take some ibuprofen for pain."

Her shoulders relaxed. "Oh, good. Nothing too awful."

"Nothing awful at all," he promised. But the way she continued to study him prompted him to add, "You know I wouldn't do anything to hurt you, right?"

"It's not that, it's just…" She looked at her arm again, then deliberately dismissed it. "Before we do that, I need to shower." She licked her lips. "And so do you."

A hint? "You're sure you're okay?"

"Positive."

Thank God. "Then how about we shower together?"

As if she'd just been waiting for him to offer, she smiled. "That would be wonderful, thank you."

Thanking him? This time Stack couldn't choke back the laugh.

"What?"

He shook his head. Telling her she was the first woman to thank him for sex wouldn't be a good idea.

She scowled and repeated with more insistence, *"What?"*

Again he took her hand, then lifted it to his mouth and kissed her palm. "Like your enthusiasm, that's all."

"I am enthusiastic." She shifted her hand so her palm cupped his jaw. He'd shaved before the wedding, but now, as her thumb moved back and forth, he heard the rasp of new whiskers. "It seems like I've been waiting for this forever."

Yeah, no kidding. "You're the one who set the stipulations, darlin'." Hell, the second she'd propositioned him, he'd been ready. But she'd spelled out the rules—most importantly that they had to wait until the night of Cannon's wedding to seal the deal. Something about her not wanting to take the chance that they'd get together, hit a snag and she'd end up without a date to the wedding after all.

As if she expected him to annoy her right off. As if having him as an escort to the wedding was more appealing than having sex with him.

What had burned his ass the most was her assertion that in the meantime, they should both carry on as usual, dating others, sleeping around, as if they hadn't made an intimate deal.

What woman did that?

"So," she said, trying to be all businesslike despite her breathiness. "Quick shower first, you can take one minute to wrap my arm, and then, *finally*, sex. Yes?"

God help him. "Sure." He'd do his best to behave until then. And maybe after the shower she'd stop shaking and settle down. Because even now he could see the slight quivering of her shoulders. He didn't bring it up again, though. Why bother? She'd deny being affected by the wreck and fire and the injuries she'd witnessed, and for him it didn't matter anyway.

Nothing mattered except finally having her.

"Turn right here."

Stack slowed the car. "Where are we going?" He knew her apartment was straight ahead.

"My house."

"Your...house?"

"Yes." Clearly pleased, she told him, "I moved in last week."

Impossible. She'd only recently relocated to Ohio and settled into an apartment. But a house? He hadn't heard anything about her moving, and no way could she have moved on her own. Women had a lot of stuff. Clothes, makeup, toiletries, not to mention furniture and drapes and everything else she'd have needed.

"Who helped you move?" If she'd asked others, but not him, he'd—

"I hired a company." She shrugged. "All I did was pack up my most personal belongings, and they took care of everything else, including the setup in my new place."

New tension invaded his muscles. "You could have asked me."

"I didn't need to."

No, in so many ways she was the most independent woman he'd ever met.

"Stack." Indulgent, her smile small and knowing, she stroked his shoulder. "I appreciate your willingness, but you're always so busy, I didn't want to infringe on your free time. I told you, I can afford to hire the help I need."

Yeah, that bugged him, too. "You said you're well-to-do." She'd mentioned it only once, sort of matter-of-factly when explaining why she wanted him to be her date to the wedding. According to her, guys hit on her because of her wealth.

Stack knew it had a hell of a lot more to do with her looks, as well as her sweet personality, than anything as mercenary as supposed wealth. Besides, the fact that she neither acted nor lived like the pampered rich made him doubt her claims. Wealth could mean many different things to different people, depending on what they were used to.

She turned her head, studying him. "You sound disgruntled, but I don't know why. We don't have the type of relationship where I'd impose on you. We're…"

"Friends with benefits?"

Lifting her shoulders, she said, "We will be—as long as you don't change your mind."

"Not a chance."

"You look awfully grim for someone about to have sex."

He flashed a glance her way, saw the teasing glint in her eyes and smiled at her.

"Better." They were only halfway down the street when she pointed. "There. That's my driveway. The little yellow house is mine."

Disbelieving, Stack pulled into the driveway. Electric lanterns at either side of the double front doors lit the area, showing some fall decorations, a cozy wicker chair, and pots of still-thriving, colorful mums. With the headlights of his car, he could make out much of the house. Small, but very tidy. Yellow with white trim, a curving walkway, large entry, and one-car garage. "Nice." In fact, it looked like something out of a storybook.

"Thank you. I saw it and knew I had to have it." She reached for the door handle, but he touched her shoulder, staying her.

Getting out and walking around the hood, he opened the door for her—and with each step, he wondered why a woman of means would buy such a small, cozy house instead of something more extravagant.

"Such a gentleman," she teased, as she went on tiptoe to kiss him.

And just that, such a simple touch, her lips barely brushing his, almost set him off. When she started to retreat, he drew her back, kissing her more firmly, a little longer, a lot deeper. The crisp, cold air swirled around them.

Snuggling closer, she clenched her hands on his shirt. They were too close to a bed for him to start this in the yard. Shower, treat her burn, then he could and would keep her in bed until neither of them could think straight.

Cupping her face, Stack eased up on the kiss, retreating by small degrees.

Overhead, the moon ducked behind clouds, and the wind kicked up, toying with her hair and making her shiver. Vanity had a lot more skin exposed than he did. Catching the lapels of his jacket that she'd wrapped around herself, he pulled it closed, kissed her soft mouth one more time and stepped away.

"Sorry. I should save that until we're inside."

The clouds parted, allowing moonlight to stroke over her face, showing off the slight tilt of her smile and the curiosity in her eyes. "I like kissing you, Stack. I like it a lot."

"I promise a lot more kissing—all over—but not just yet."

She sucked in a breath and nodded.

Stack started for the trunk of his car.

"I have a first-aid kit in my house."

"I know mine has what I need." He opened the trunk, and saw all the wedding gifts they'd collected for Cannon and Yvette.

Vanity put a hand on his arm. "We could unload later."

"We could." Did that mean she wouldn't be tossing him out the second the sex stopped? Because she'd pretty much hinted at exactly that.

The conversation had replayed in his mind many times in the weeks since it had happened. They'd been together at Rowdy's bar, sitting close, her tone, her look, her body language all suggestive enough to get his libido racing.

After some teasing banter, she'd hit him up to be her date for the wedding. He'd waffled, until she added a guaranteed follow-up of the carnal variety.

I'm open to using my place—bed and light provided. That way you won't have to worry about getting rid of me afterward. I promise to toss you out before you can even get nervous about it.

If she still thought to follow through on that promise, she'd be in for a surprise. It was late enough now that even if they stayed at it until dawn, he knew he wouldn't get his fill.

One way or another, he'd have to talk her into a full day.

Maybe a full week. Or...longer.

"So just leave it all in there for now. If you keep your car locked, it'll all be safe, right?"

"Right." He stared down at her, sexual chemistry arcing between them. "You don't plan to kick me out at sunrise? Because seriously—" he looked up at the sky "—it's going to be happening soon."

Time ticked by in silence. Watching him, Vanity licked her lips, then shook her head. Eyes big and soft, she whispered, "I'm going to need more than just a few hours."

That promise had his heartbeat thundering again. Moving things aside, he located the first-aid kit tucked into the corner of the trunk. He pulled it free, closed and locked the trunk, then put a hand to the small of her back. "C'mon."

With both of them walking quickly, she opened her small purse, dug out her house key and handed it to him.

He opened the door and stepped into her living room.

After slipping off her sandals, Vanity closed the door and flipped a few locks. Following her cue, Stack, too, removed his shoes. Usually, unless jogging, he wore boots. But the damn tux had come with glaringly shiny shoes. Luckily, unlike his boots, he could toe them off easily enough.

Until Vanity had removed her sandals, he hadn't realized that they'd each collected grass and mud while freeing the woman from the fire.

Taking his hand, Vanity got him walking. "Living room," she said, waving a hand toward a midsize couch and two stuffed rocking chairs. An enormous television hung on the wall above a shelf of books, and what looked like real paintings hung on the remaining walls.

"Nice." The decor and the artwork, which he tried to see better, but Vanity hadn't slowed to give him time.

"Thanks." By the kitchen she finally paused. "That door over there opens to the garage." Indicating the opposite wall, she said, "And that one goes to the unfinished basement with the washer, dryer and...stuff."

The kitchen looked newly remodeled, but he barely had time to see it before she got him walking again, this time down the hall. "Bedroom one, bedroom two."

She was in such a rush that Stack smiled. It was a nice thing to be wanted by Vanity.

"Hall bath," she told him, and then she tugged him into an open room. Dropping his hand and tossing his tux jacket to a chair, she said, "And this is my bedroom. The connected bath is over there."

"Pretty," was all he managed to say before she took the first-aid kit from him, set it on the floor, then plastered herself against him.

Arms around his neck, her gaze on his mouth, she whispered, "Stack?"

He held her waist as she slowly stretched up to reach him. "Yeah?"

"Kiss me, please."

"Hell of an idea." And given that she wanted him, maybe he could work on wresting the control back from her in the process.

A HUNDRED TIMES Vanity had thought about this moment, about playing it cool, taking her time.

Being in charge.

Not likely, not now that she finally had Stack in her house, ready, willing, even anxious. He smelled so good, a little like smoke mixed with the chilly night and his own, delicious scent of macho man. She tunneled her fingers into his cool hair. In warmer weather the sun bleached his light brown hair into a dark blond. Now, though, after a recent trim for the wedding, most of the blond was gone. The wind and the fire had left the wavy strands mussed. She loved it.

She loved his incredible body even more.

While he kissed her, she drowned under the feel of him, so tall and strong with fluid muscles that shifted against her. She trailed her hands down to his hard shoulders, then over his strong chest.

Stack freed his mouth and drew her close, her head to his shoulder. One of his hands knotted in her hair, and she felt his heartbeat knocking hard against his ribs.

"Stack?"

"Give me a second."

But…why? Levering back enough to see him, she started on the buttons to his dress shirt. When she had

four of them free, she slipped her hand inside. Crisp
body hair teased her palm; his skin was so hot, his
chest solid.

"Hold up." He caught her wrist and kept her still
while he sucked in air. "Shower," he said. "And your
arm."

"Take your clothes off." She didn't mind that idea at
all. "Then we can shower."

His rough, strained laugh made her smile.

"I like that." He touched her mouth. "I like how your
smile always twitches into place. One side kicks up
first, then the other, almost like you're trying not to
smile but you can't help yourself."

An apt description, at least whenever she was around
him. He made her happy. She loved talking with him,
laughing with him, looking at him.

Loved getting closer to him.

Would love loving him if he'd give her half a chance.

All the fighters were focused on their careers, but
Stack, more than the others, had always seemed disinterested in the possibility of a relationship.

And so she'd used underhanded tactics to get him
on board.

"Right here," she told him, "right now, you could
notice things other than my smile."

Hands on her shoulders, he stepped her back. "Yeah,
and I do, believe me." With some space now between
them, he trailed one fingertip over the neckline of her
dress, dipping low between her breasts before dropping
his hand. "Turn around."

That husky command curled her toes. "What will
you do?"

"Get you out of this dress."

"Oh." She swallowed, then slowly turned her back to him and tipped her head forward.

He lifted her hair over her left shoulder so that it trailed down over her breasts. She waited for him to open the zipper, but instead, after a few silent seconds, his lips brushed the back of her neck.

Sweet sensation caught her breath.

Stepping up against her, Stack opened his mouth on her skin, lightly sucking, every so often letting her feel his teeth, then tasting with his tongue.

Making a small sound of wonder, she let her head fall back against him. God, that felt good. So good.

When he reached around her and settled his hands on her breasts, she started.

"Shh." He caressed her through her dress.

Vanity looked down at how he held her, how he'd filled his big hands with her. His fingers were long and strong, curved under the weight of her breasts. She swallowed, then went still as he brought his thumbs up to rasp her now swollen nipples.

"So soft," he murmured against her skin. "Be still now." His hands left her, but before she could register disappointment she felt him searching over the back of the dress.

Despite being a big badass fighter with hands that could knock out an opponent in one solid punch, he had no problem tackling the tiny hidden zipper. Utilizing a painstaking lack of haste, he dragged the zipper down, and seconds later the bodice loosened, then the waist, until he'd opened the dress all the way down past the small of her back.

Still standing close behind her, he slipped his hands

over her hips, pushing the material down—until the dress fell in a colorful heap to her feet.

There was a moment of stunned silence, then Stack said in a gravelly whisper, "Great fucking dress."

Aware of how she looked in nothing more than her sedate jewelry, peach lace panties and thigh-high nylons, Vanity kept her back to him.

Both of his hands cupped her backside. "I've wanted to get my hands on this ass for a very long time."

Trying a laugh that sounded a little too high and thin, Vanity turned—and his hot gaze zeroed in on her breasts.

"Damn." His attention burned over her.

Pleased with that reaction, she stepped away from the discarded dress and went to work on the rest of his buttons. "At this rate, we're never going to make it to the shower."

His nose nudged her hair, glided along the side of her throat, breathed deeply near her shoulder. "You smell as good as I imagined."

"Like smoke?"

"Like a major turn-on." He tipped up her face, let his mouth play over hers before settling in for a deep, hot kiss.

His hands on her waist were firm, his palms calloused. He coasted up her back, down to her bottom, back up and around to her breasts. The second he made contact, he groaned.

She did her own touching, trying to get him out of his clothes.

Without breaking the contact of their mouths, he brushed away her hands and got to work on the buttons himself. He'd removed the tie and cuff links earlier, and now he tossed the shirt aside. Every so often his hands went back to her body, and now, with his chest bare, he pulled her in so that their upper bodies made complete contact.

Vanity tightened her arms around his neck and moved against him, loving the sensation of his chest hair against her puckered nipples. At her belly, she could feel his knuckles as he opened his pants.

Wanting to watch, she stepped back. Lacking modesty—and with no reason for it—Stack shoved his pants down and off, removing his socks at the same time. He stood before her in only dark tented boxers.

"You're perfect," she whispered with awe, unable to stop staring.

"Vanity." He shifted, his muscles flexing and bunching. "You've seen me before," he reminded her.

A little dumbfounded, Vanity shook her head. "Not like this."

He rolled a shoulder. "Without the boner, yeah. But you always see me in boxing shorts."

True. She'd seen him often, and fantasized about him even more.

Stripped down to nothing more than those low shorts, Stack always stole the show at the rec center where all the fighters worked out. Most days he went at it until sweat left a sheen on his perfectly sculpted body, until his muscles swelled and became more pronounced.

She'd fallen in love with Stack's perfect physique, but also his laid-back manner and quick smiles and utter dedication to his friends. Now he was hers—at least for a little while.

As if drawn to him, her hands lifted and moved over his chest. The light covering of crisp hair fascinated her.

Some fighters waxed or shaved their bodies; she was very grateful that Stack wasn't one of them.

His body hair, eyebrows and thick lashes were shades darker than the golden brown hair on his head.

Spreading her fingers wide to cover as much of him as she could, she slowly, oh-so-slowly, drew her hands down his body. Her thumbs touched in that center groove created by his washboard abs.

She breathed harder.

His stomach tightened.

The body hair softened as it swirled around his navel, then arrowed downward to disappear in his boxers.

"Keep that up," Stack rasped, "and we won't make it to the shower. Hell, we might not make it to the bed."

Helpless with need, Vanity looked up at him.

"C'mon, darlin'." With one finger he touched her bottom lip, then up to her ear where he tucked back her hair. "Shower first, then your arm."

"I…I don't think I can wait."

Going all big macho protector, Stack gave an indulgent smile, lightly kissed her lips, and whispered, "I'll see that you do, and then I'll make it worth the wait, I promise."

Damn it, she didn't need more incentive.

She just needed Stack.

Vanity waited as he retrieved the first-aid kit, then let him take her hand and lead her into the connected bath. She even let him turn on the shower, then stood there and watched while he rummaged around and found two towels.

"I have a breaking point," he warned her. "So no touching."

She didn't understand—until he stripped off his boxers.

Her heart tried to punch its way out of her chest.

She stared at his throbbing erection surrounded by that soft dark hair. His testicles were tight, and even as she watched, a bead of glistening fluid showed on the head of his penis. The sight of him like this, so turned on, *for her*, stole her breath.

She reached for him, but he caught her hands, put them on his shoulders, and went to one knee before her.

Holy smokes. "Stack…"

Briefly he nuzzled her belly. "God, your skin is soft and smells so sweet. I want to breathe you in all over." As he said that, he palmed her backside…and pressed his mouth against her sex.

The skimpy panties did nothing to blunt the impact of such an intimate kiss. She could feel his breath, the movement of his lips, and it wasn't until he had her nylons off that she realized he was rolling them down.

"You have sexy legs," he said as he helped her lift each foot.

"They're barely keeping me upright."

He smiled. "I won't let you fall." Then he stripped away her panties, too.

He stayed there on his knees in front of her until the anticipation tried to melt her bones. Finally, using the back of one finger, he gently brushed over her pubic hair. The touch felt so electric she gasped.

And Stack, the tease, stood again.

"In you go." He held the curtain back with one hand.

It took extreme concentration, but Vanity got it together. "One sec." She grabbed up her big alligator clip by the sink, flipped her hair forward, twisted it, then slipped in the clip. She made a point of facing Stack as she did it.

No reason to give him a peek show, especially not while he resisted her.

As if he'd read her mind, he grinned, then stepped into the shower behind her and again kissed her neck. Near her ear he whispered, "Five minutes. I promise that's all."

At the moment, that sounded like a lifetime. "Are you back to being the minuteman?"

His teeth on her shoulder made her yelp.

He kissed the spot from the bite, which had felt more sensual than painful, and started lathering the soap in his hands. "You remember that, huh?"

Turning to face him, she recounted the conversation from weeks ago. "You told me your usual route at weddings was a fast hookup in bathrooms and closets. Quick sex. Seriously, Stack, do you think I'm ever likely to forget that?"

"I was trying to dissuade you from asking me to be your date to the wedding."

"So it wasn't true?" He'd claimed he went to weddings solo, so if he got lucky, nothing would hinder him. When she'd pressed him for details, he'd claimed even the bathroom could offer enough privacy.

And instead of being dissuaded, she'd been…intrigued. Still was. Risqué sexual situations were not her forte. But with Stack, she wouldn't mind taking a few chances.

Grinning like a sinner, he shrugged. "True enough." Pulling her in close, he worked those soapy hands down her back, down, down, down… "I also told you that when the woman is hot for it, a few minutes is all it takes me to make her happy."

She gasped at the feel of his hands on the backs of her thighs. "Braggart."

"What about you, Vanity?" His slick fingers trailed higher. "You hot enough, darlin'?"

"Yes!" She pushed him back, snatched up her face wash, and quickly removed her ruined makeup.

As he soaped up his perfect body, Stack watched her. "Switch places."

"Okay." Taking the scented, moisture-rich soap from him, she moved out of the shower's spray and let him rinse. It fascinated her, seeing the soap suds trickle down the deep groove of his back, over his muscular behind and those long, strong thighs. When he finished, he turned to her again and ran both hands through his wet hair to push it back.

Blindly, refusing to take her gaze off him, Vanity did her own quick cleanup. It wasn't until she sent the lather over the burn on her arm that she remembered it and winced.

"Easy." Taking over, Stack gently slid soapy fingertips over the mark and, blocking the shower spray with his broad back, cupped his hand and poured water over her small injury. As he examined it, he asked, "Does it hurt?"

"Not really." Their heads almost touched as they both looked at the burn. "I don't even know how I did it."

He lifted her wrist to his mouth and kissed it, around the burn, up to her elbow.

How could the inside of a freaking elbow be so sensitive?

Taking her by surprise, he turned his head and brushed his jaw over her breast. "Do I need to shave?"

Shaking her head, Vanity tunneled her fingers into his wet hair and kept him close. "No."

His warm breath moved over her wet nipple. "You sure?"

"Yes…ahhh." The word turned into a moan as he drew her in, sucking gently.

Carefully backing her up until she bumped into the wall, he caged her in. Steam rose around them. He left one nipple to lick his way over to the other.

"Stack…" She was right back to having shaky knees. "Please."

He braced one hand on the wall beside her head, and cupped the other between her legs, his fingers lightly exploring, parting her…two fingers sinking in.

She stiffened with acute sensation.

"Yeah," he murmured, all cocky and confident. "You're hot enough." He took her mouth again, kissing her deeply while his fingers slowly worked her.

When she moaned, he eased up to say, "You're wet."

"We're in a shower."

He nipped her bottom lip for deliberately misunderstanding. "You're hot, too. And swollen."

Just as softly, she said, "I know."

Amazingly, tension began to build, and she wanted it so badly, she tried to hold him closer.

He stared into her eyes, searched her face, and kissed her again. "You're close already, aren't ya, darlin'?"

Why that embarrassed her, she wasn't sure. "I… you…" She inhaled sharply. "Stack, *please*."

"We're good together."

Her legs stiffened. "Yes."

"So come for me, Vanity. Right here, right now."

And damned if she didn't.

She clutched at his shoulders, awestruck by the powerful climax stealing through her, twisting tighter and tighter until she couldn't contain it, until she cried out roughly.

"There you go," Stack murmured. "Damn."

Head back, legs locked, Vanity gave herself over to the intense pleasure. Stack stayed with her, kissing her throat and her jaw while his fingers maintained that perfect rhythm until she thought she couldn't take it anymore.

Somehow knowing the right moment to ease up, he withdrew, but cupped his hand over her.

The pleasure faded, leaving behind a warm throbbing contained by the pressure of his palm.

"Damn," he whispered again. "I almost came with you."

Lethargic, awestruck, Vanity nonetheless reached for his erection—only to have him draw her up short. "C'mon. Let's get dried off."

Her protesting groan made him smile, but he wasted no time shutting off the water and snagging a towel. When he started to dry her, she resisted. A deep breath, then another, helped her recover. Leveling a look on him, she said, "Let's speed up the process, shall we?" She stepped out of the tub on trembling limbs and hurriedly whisked the towel over her body.

Stack halfheartedly dried himself, then wrapped the towel around his waist.

"Modest?"

"Prudent." He opened the first-aid kit. "Let me see your arm."

"It's fine." She didn't want to take time messing with it.

"Sure it is. It also needs to be wrapped."

Deciding it wasn't worth a debate, Vanity obediently rested her arm on the sink counter. "Here you go, doc."

"So now we're playing doctor?" He cupped her breast, moved his thumb over her nipple. "I could get into that."

Still supersensitive, she gasped and stepped out of reach. "No, I meant..." She saw his knowing smile and frowned. "Never mind. Just do what you need to do."

"Yes, darlin'." With exaggerated focus, he liberally dabbed ointment on the burn before wrapping it in gauze.

As he worked, Vanity watched him. "I'm not modest."

He glanced at her naked body. "Noticed that."

The damp towel did little to conceal his erection, so, yes, she'd noticed him noticing. "I'm not all that prudent either."

"You go after what you want." He was careful not to get the gauze too tight. "I like that."

She laughed. "You like it because it's you I want."

"There is that." He finished and closed the first-aid kit. Taking her chin, he tipped her face this way and that while examining her hair.

"What are you doing?"

"Your hair has factored into some hot fantasies. I want it loose." Frowning in concentration, he figured out how to open the big clip, and her hair fell free. He worked his fingers through it a few times. "Better."

Without another word he removed his towel, picked her up in his arms, and headed for the bed.

"We're finally doing this?"

"A minute more and I'd have been a goner."

"Funny." She leaned in to kiss his chin. "I did try to offer in the shower."

"I want to be inside you. I want to feel you squeezing me when you come again."

Wow, he made her blood burn. "Again, huh?"

"Definitely." He lowered her to the bed and straightened to stand over her. After studying every inch of her, he went for his pants.

Vanity watched until he pulled several silver packets from his pocket. "You have condoms in your tux pants?"

"Wanted to make sure I was prepared when you decided you were ready." He set them on the nightstand with two cell phones and his wallet, traveled his gaze over the length of her body, and slowly lowered himself down beside her.

CHAPTER THREE

THE WAY VANITY looked at him, with those big blue eyes all dark and consuming, it was a wonder he could think long enough to grab the condoms.

Soon as he settled on the bed, she reached for him. She did that a lot, and damn, but he loved it. There was something about the way she continually wanted him against her, as if her pleasure depended on it. She didn't just want the fast convenient fuck she'd first hinted at back when they'd started this little game of cat and mouse.

She went out of her way to play it off, to deny it by her attitude and actions, but she wanted *him*. Him, specifically.

What a turn-on.

Women had chased him before, women who were also hot—built, pretty, brazen.

Vanity was different in a dozen ways. He wasn't sure of the differences, just that they affected him a lot.

"What is it about you?" he asked her while again holding her back.

Her shoulders relaxed in his hands as she sank into the plush comforter on her bed, her gorgeous blond hair everywhere. She shook her head, and in a voice as sultry as her eyes, she whispered, "I don't know what you mean."

No artifice. The lady had to know of her own killer good looks, but she didn't show it, didn't expect men to fawn over her. Overall, she seemed to think it didn't matter.

And maybe that was part of it. She was somehow more real than other beautiful women.

"I can't put my finger on it yet." Stack's attention went back to her body stretched out beside his. "But there are other, better places for my fingers right now anyway."

"Stack," she complained on a groan. "No more teasing, okay?"

"I'm dead serious, believe me." Opening his hand over her lush breast, he cuddled her. Overall she had a light tan. But not here, not on her breasts. The contrast of her pale, velvet skin under his darker, rougher hand ramped up the fever.

He had large fists, his knuckles burly from punching the speed bag, the heavy bag—and the bodies of opponents. But everything on Vanity was smooth and sleek and sexy beyond all fantasy.

While he played with her, her breath caught in that same way it had in the shower moments before she began tightening with a climax. Hearing those sexy sounds now triggered something in him; impatience faded under red-hot determination.

"Even without makeup, you are so fucking gorgeous." He lightly trapped her swollen pink nipple between his finger and thumb, tugging gently, rolling enough to get her squirming again.

In a wisp of sound, she said, "Looks fade."

Odd reply, especially for a woman in her midtwenties, while in the middle of foreplay. "Maybe." No matter her age, he couldn't imagine Vanity being anything other than stunning.

"No maybe to it," she argued with her eyes closed, her head back. "Women get older and everything changes."

Sensing some hidden insecurity behind the words, Stack frowned at her. "Men age, too."

She turned her head away. "It's different."

For a single heartbeat, he forgot about sex, about the red-hot lust pulsing through his body. A butterfly kiss to her cheek brought her face back around, her lips seeking his. He obliged her with a kiss that felt both sweet and, because this was Vanity, molten hot. "It's nature's way," he explained, drawing her closer, "for two people to age together and neither notices because they're in love."

Her lashes lifted, and her gaze locked on his. He saw startled confusion, dark secrets—and he saw heat.

Stack waited, curious as to what she'd say. But when she finally spoke, it was with mild complaint and a change of subject. "I thought you were in a hurry."

The glide of his fingers over her abdomen made goose bumps rise. "Changed my mind."

Her eyes flared. "But—"

"I want to savor you. Now hush while I get back to it." Lightly dragging his fingertips back up her ribs, he teased around one breast, with each stroke getting closer to her nipple. She tried wrapping a hand around his neck to draw him in for a kiss. And he let her—to a point.

But instead of her mouth he bent to her other nipple, circling it with his tongue. Wet and pink, it beaded tight, spurring him to draw her in, to suck lazily. He took extreme pleasure in the way her body shifted, how those small sounds caught in her throat.

The lift of her hips convinced him to redirect, and he caressed his way down her body, over her ribs, the pronounced indent of her waist, the flare of her hip. He clasped her upper thigh, then rose up to see her face.

Head tipped back, eyes closed, she inhaled through parted lips. Seeing her like this…well, he wouldn't mind seeing her this way a lot. For weeks. Months.

But she hadn't promised anything close to that, so he'd make the most of the time they had.

"Open up for me." Ensuring she did, he urged her legs apart until her knee bent, leaving her exposed to his hungry gaze. He filled his lungs with needed oxygen. "Nice."

Balancing on his elbow, he looked at her mouth, then had to kiss it, first her full bottom lip, then the upper before sealing his mouth over hers. She grabbed for him, turning the kiss hungry, her tongue seeking his—still with her legs open.

Her mouth was hot and sweet, and somehow kissing her was so much more than it'd ever been with other women.

He didn't like that thought, especially since Vanity had a damned stopwatch ticking on their time together.

To regain himself, he rested his hand low on her belly. "You wet again, darlin'?"

Thick lashes lifted, and she stared at him. "You're naked, touching me. Of course I am."

Holding her gaze, he whispered, "Let me see." Using his palm, he rubbed over her until she again lifted to his touch. Little by little he curved his hand so that his fingers slid over her with each up and down rub.

"Ah…God," she breathed.

Damned if she didn't look close to coming again. He

wanted her to. A lot. With two fingers he slid over her slick lips. "Yeah," he growled. "Nice and wet."

"Stack," she said on a vibrating moan.

Using her own slick moisture, he moved up to her swollen clit.

Brows pinching in acute pleasure, she bit her lip, and her hips flexed up to meet his touch, to stroke in counterpoint to his.

"You wanna say *please* again, darlin'? I do like hearing it."

She lifted to him. "Ah… Stack!" Her breath caught, and she twisted. "Please, please, *please.*"

Yeah, he liked seeing that, too, the sinuous roll of her body as she reached for the orgasm he'd give her. Getting down to business, he gave up the visual of her and instead went back to her nipple, sucking more strongly now.

On a guttural groan, she gripped his hair and kept him locked to her. Knowing she'd like it, he shifted his hand so that two fingers pressed deep, easily because of her wetness. Making sure she wouldn't miss a beat, he brought his thumb up to her clitoris, softly circling—and she cried out.

Her whole body clenched, one of her thighs closing over his hand, new moisture bathing his fingers with each hot, rhythmic clasp of her body. At every inhalation, her heated scent filled his head.

Filled *him*.

Christ, she turned him inside out. As the tremors faded and she slowly sank away from him, Stack gave her breast one last, barely-there kiss, and again went to his elbow.

Her breasts were flushed. Pretty.

Sweat dampened her cheeks just beneath her eyes. Sweet.

And her hair… He took his time playing with it, re-arranging it around the pillow until finally she got her eyes open.

"Hey." He brushed his mouth over hers. "It's hot as hell the way you come."

That made her blink. She sucked in air, slowly blew it out, then did it again.

Stack smiled. He liked having Vanity Baker disoriented from pleasure. "You okay?"

She stared at him with wonder. "That was…"

"Yeah?"

"I don't have words."

Another grin. "I think *please* is the word you used most."

"Shush it, mister."

That made him laugh. Since when did he find sex this amusing? He'd wanted her for so long that he should have been driving deep already. Instead, he said helpfully, "Then how about stupendous? Awesome? Satisfying?"

She sighed dramatically, reached out and laid her palm to his chest, directly over his galloping heart. "All that." Suddenly her fingers tightened in his chest hair.

He flinched, but quickly stilled. "Ow, hey now."

Looking stern, she jokingly ordered, "No more playing, Hannigan." She lightly tugged. "Time to get down to business."

"Yeah, I think you're right." Catching her wrist so she couldn't render his chest bald, he leaned in.

Her lips parted. So did his.

The obnoxious, unique ringing from his cell made

them both jump. And since she still had her fingers caught in his chest hair, he gave a very real grimace.

"I'm sorry!" She turned him loose, only to let out an "oof" when he dropped his head to her breasts.

Catching on real quick, she asked, "What? You can ignore it, right? Tell me you can ignore it!"

He wished. "Sorry, no." Twisting away from her, he snatched up the phone, glanced at the caller ID out of habit—because he already knew he'd take the call—and swiped his thumb over the screen to answer. "Better be good, Armie, or I swear to God—"

"I'm sorry, dude. Really fucking sorry."

Yeah, he knew that already, too. Armie wouldn't have called him, not from the cell with that particular ringtone, without a damned good reason. "Let's hear it." The ensuing hesitation made Stack sit up a little straighter. *"Armie..."*

Finally, Armie said, "Your sis called."

Seriously? Because it'd been... Stack had to stop and think. But somewhere around six weeks or so had passed since last he'd talked to anyone in his whack-ass family. And that last time, well, it hadn't been good. He'd managed to alienate himself.

They'd all needed some time, so for the most part he'd been okay with that.

But if Tabitha had called, she had to have a reason. God knew she wouldn't be the first to break their silent war unless she'd had no choice. "Tell me."

"She said not to panic, but your mom is in the hospital. She collapsed or something. I tried to get the deets, but she was seriously having a meltdown."

That would have alarmed Stack more except that Tabby melted down over a broken nail. "I'll call her."

"Let me know if there's anything I can do."

"Thanks." Stack disconnected and then looked at his missed-calls log. Sure enough, Tabby had called him three times, all while he'd been in the shower with Vanity. And thinking of Vanity...

His hot gaze moved over her perfect form stretched out on the bed, buck-ass naked.

Everything in him protested, because he knew he'd have to go.

"What?" she asked without sitting up. "Everything okay?"

Her eyes, now more alert but still simmering with need, searched over his face.

"Sorry." Stack stood and turned his back on temptation. "I need to book."

He heard the rustle of sheets and the rush of air behind him. Vanity's arms came around him from behind, her breasts to his back.

"No." She squeezed him more tightly. *"Noooooooooo."*

Smiling at her forlorn wail, he brought her around in front of him. "If I had any other choice, no way would I budge."

"Then why?"

"Something's come up, and I'm needed elsewhere."

Now more subdued, Vanity hugged him as if trying to offer comfort.

But, yeah, being naked with her sort of obliterated any chance of him feeling soothed.

"That was Armie?"

"Yeah, and he sends his apologies." With that he stepped away to find his pants.

Which meant he'd have to hit up the hospital in a freaking tux. Shit.

From behind him, he heard Vanity moving around the room. "If it's that important, then I guess it's a good thing you didn't ignore it."

He turned in time to see her headed to a drawer. She lifted out silky little panties and stepped into them. Wanting to groan in frustration, Stack sat on the side of the bed and pulled on his socks. "Believe me, I would have if it hadn't been the signal."

"The signal?"

"Yeah. You know we all help out in the community, right? Well, we each carry two cell phones, and when something's up, we use the cell that we've set with a special ringtone to alert the others. That was from the emergency cell."

"With a special ringtone." Excited, she grinned as she hooked on a matching bra, then slid it around and adjusted her breasts in the cups.

Mind boggling.

While pulling on a shirt, she said, "So it's like a bat signal."

"What?" Watching Vanity dress was a huge distraction, slowing his own progress.

"You know. Like on *Batman*. Do-do, do-do, do-do, do-do, Baaatman."

"No," he told her flatly, a little insulted, a little turned on, a lot in a hurry. "Not like a bat signal."

"Sure it is." She stepped into skinny jeans, then jumped a few times—God save him—to get them up.

He had no idea why she was getting dressed, but the way the girl bounced was enough to keep him hard.

Lowering her voice comically, Vanity spoke like an announcer. "The town needs you, the signal goes out, and you guys…" Dropping the theatrics, she asked,

"What? Congregate and plot out formation or something?"

"You're poking fun."

Letting her finger and thumb almost touch, she said, "Just a little bit."

"I wanted to fuck you so bad."

Instead of being insulted, she propped her hands on her hips and gave him a look. "Instead, you kept messing around."

"Giving you screaming orgasms."

She softened. Harking back to the idiotic joke about him being a wolf and how ladies reacted, she said, "At least I didn't howl, right?"

Mocking her, he said, "Little bit."

She laughed. "Well, I wouldn't want to ruin your rep." Now decently covered, she sat on the bed beside him and pulled on socks. "So what's happening? A street light go out? Lady's cat stuck in a tree? Somebody have a flat tire?"

"No, smart-ass." Is that really what she thought they did? If so, he wouldn't correct her. Soon enough she'd find out that, with Cannon's leadership, they'd become watchdogs for the neighborhood. Together they'd run off drug dealers, stopped extortion, helped family-run businesses stay open, and secured the safety of the young and the elderly. Being honest, Stack told her, "But if that happened, we'd help if we could."

"Of course you would." She looked beneath the bed, found ankle boots and, sitting on the floor, pulled them on. "So what's going on then?"

He eyed the boots with curiosity. *Why the hell was she getting dressed?* "My mom collapsed."

Her face fell. "Oh, God, Stack." Scrambling back to her feet, she said, "I'm so sorry!"

She looked sincerely, deeply sorry. Huh. They hadn't yet slept together, she'd never met his mom, but she cared all the same. "My sister called while we were in the shower. When she couldn't reach me, she called Armie."

"She knows him?"

"They've met. In case of an emergency she has his number along with a few others."

Her small hand covered her mouth. "So this is an emergency?"

"Hard to say." He stood and buttoned up his tux shirt, leaving it untucked. "Tabby's all into drama, so if Mom stubbed her toe, she'd be as likely to call it life and death."

Gasping, Vanity whispered, "Life and death? That was her message?"

He had to grin at her horrified expression. "No, she just told Armie that Mom collapsed. I'll call her on my way out to find out the details."

Nodding, Vanity rushed to her closet and withdrew a dark poncho. She snagged his hand and started out of the room. "Come on."

When Stack didn't budge, she pulled up short.

They stared at each other.

"Why are you waiting? You need to make that call!"

Stack nodded. "Where do you think you're going?"

"With you."

She said that so matter-of-factly that he frowned in suspicion. "Why would you—"

Exasperated, she hooked her arm through his and tried to get him moving. "You haven't yet met your obligations. Until you do, I'm not giving you a chance to back out."

"Believe me, I'll be back as soon as possible." He allowed her to drag him to the front door. This time, knowing sex wasn't on the agenda, he looked around with more interest.

"I'm going with you."

"Not to a hospital to meet my family."

"Yes."

Giving up his perusal of her interesting artwork, he turned to her. The innocence in her face amped up his suspicions even more. "That makes zero sense, darlin', and you know it."

She huffed an impatient breath. "Look at it this way. All the wedding gifts are still in the trunk of your car."

"Like I said, I'll be back to finish this."

Her hands twisted in his dress shirt. "You might need me."

Yeah, he needed her all right. Naked and willing. And she would be. Soon. "Vanity—"

"What if things are worse than you're thinking?"

"I told you, my sister is a master of hysteria." He'd learned a long time ago not to get too bent out of shape when Tabby screamed gloom and destruction.

Staring up at him, Vanity bit her lip, waffled, then moved in for full-body contact, snaking her arms around his neck, aligning her mouth with his, kissing him until he damn near got another boner.

When she finally let up, she whispered, "Please?" Her hands were now in his hair, her lips wet and her eyes dark. "You promised me a day together after the wedding, and it's barely been an hour."

He'd promised her good sex, and, as he recalled,

she'd insisted it be brief. But whatever. Maybe this was his opportunity to turn it into more. Did he dare expose her to the craziness?

Would his mom latch on to her? Probably.

Would his sister try to make a big deal of it? He snorted. Yes.

"What?" Her gaze searched his. "What was that rude sound for?"

Warning her, Stack said, "My family is whack." He opened the door and led her outside. "Don't bitch to me later when you wish you'd stayed home."

"I never bitch." Now that she'd gotten her way she happily trotted alongside him to keep up with his long-legged gait. And she smiled.

Proof positive—women were impossible to understand.

DAMP EARLY-MORNING AIR cut through her excitement, making her shiver. Quickly, Vanity slipped the poncho over her head before getting back into Stack's car.

Rather than hurry around to his side, he leaned in, one hand overhead on the frame, the other on the open door. He looked bemused. And still very interested.

Of course, he hadn't yet gotten his. No, the wonderful man had put aside his own pleasure to give her two bone-melting orgasms.

When he reached out two fingers to stroke her hair away from her face, she stilled. The same rough fingers slid over her cheek, down beneath her chin, and tipped up her face so he could plant a soft, damp kiss on her lips.

Was he regretting her intrusion? Even she had to admit that she'd shoved her way in with the subtlety of a typhoon. Not to herself, much less to him, would she confess how fearful she was of him walking away—and considering the job done.

God, not that sex with her should be a job, but she wanted time enough to work on him, to show him they had more in common than lust. If a family illness kept him away all day, or even all week, would he still have any interest in finishing what they'd started?

Trying to sound blasé instead of uneasy, she said, "I know I'm a mess. But you're in a tux, so—"

He shook his head. "How is it you look this good? I watched you get ready in under two minutes. Your makeup is gone. You didn't even comb your hair, much less do all that other stuff women do. You're wearing jeans and this—" he lifted the edge of her big poncho "—blanket thing. And still you look like a centerfold model."

"Wow." The laugh hopefully covered her embarrassment. "Just what I was aiming for—something from a spank mag."

"You succeeded." Ignoring her sarcasm, he kissed her again. "Buckle up."

She watched him circle the car and get behind the wheel. He backed out of the driveway and onto the road. Using a button on his steering wheel, he brought up his hands-free calling. A second later a phone rang from the car speaker and was immediately answered by a shrill female voice.

"Where have you been?"

In contrast, Stack sounded like calm personified when he replied, "What hospital? I'm on my way."

"Finally!" And then, with annoyance, she named the local county hospital.

Not far away at all, Vanity realized. So, did that mean Stack's family all lived nearby? If so, how come she'd never seen any of them?

Keeping to the speed limit, Stack drove from the quiet back streets and headed for the main drag. "How's Mom?"

"I don't know!" his sister wailed. "The doctors haven't told us anything yet."

Knuckles going white on the wheel, Stack went from relaxed to tightly wound. "Us, meaning fucking Phil is there?"

Fucking Phil? Vanity had no idea who that might be, but clearly Stack didn't like him.

"Of course he's here—*with his wife.*"

"Guess there's a first time for everything."

Whoa. Vanity didn't need to be psychic to pick up on all the bad feelings. She made no pretense of not listening in, and even put her hand on Stack's shoulder.

When he frowned at her, she smiled.

Blowing out a breath, he returned his attention to his sister. "So, what happened?"

"I don't know. She just collapsed. I got home and…" The voice faded, then picked up anew. "When Mom fell, she hit her head. There was blood everywhere. I freaked."

"Listen to me, Tabby. Head wounds bleed a lot. You should know that. Was she hurt bad or was it just a cut?"

Silence, then a choked sob. "I don't know!"

Good God. If Stack didn't still look so calm, Vanity would have been scared to death for his mother.

"Let me talk to Phil."

"Why?"

With a hoarse laugh, Stack said, "I can't hurt him through the phone, sis, so just put him on."

"He went to the snack area to get a Coke."

Stack's chest expanded on a frustrated inhale. "He should be right back, then."

"No, probably not. He was going to get some air, too."

"Yeah, good thing he's there with his wife, offering so much moral support."

"Go to hell, Stack!"

As if that didn't faze him at all, he said, "I'm on my way."

Overcome with relief, she said faintly, "Thank God. Hurry, please."

"Try to keep it together until then, okay, sis?"

"I...I will. Stack? I'm scared. I don't want to be here alone."

Alone? Vanity glanced at Stack. So, as he'd said, the man who must be his sister's husband was of no use at all.

Stack said softly, "I know. Just hang in there. It'll only take me ten minutes, tops."

"Love you."

"Ditto." Stack disconnected and, like a bubble waiting to burst, silence filled the car.

Vanity tried to be patient, but when Stack said nothing, she gave up with a mental shrug. "Who's Phil?"

Irritation bunched his shoulders. "Fucking Phil." He flashed her a warning glare. "Stay away from him, okay?"

"Sure. But who is he?"

"My sister's asshole husband."

Oooookay. "That much I got from the conversation."

Running a hand over his head, Stack cursed low. "He's trouble. That's all you need to know. And seriously, steer clear of him." Again his gaze came her way, dipping over her with what felt like territorial privilege. "If he so much as looks at you funny, I want to know."

"I can take care of myself."

Just as the car fire had earlier, he seemed to explode. "This is why you should have kept your sweet ass at home! You don't even know Phil, so how the hell can you know—"

"You're yelling at me? Seriously?" Unlike him, she spoke low. And mean. Like...really mean. "My apologies for barging in. I shouldn't have. Soon as we reach the hospital I'll call a cab. I can wait in the lobby until it arrives."

"Fuck." Pressing the heel of his hand to his forehead, Stack muttered again, with more feeling, *"Fuck."*

Vanity folded her arms and stared out the passenger window. But she knew she wasn't being fair, so after six or seven minutes had passed, she took a breath and again faced him.

More moderately, without the sharp bite of anger, she said, "I overstepped when I promised you that I wouldn't. For that I really am sorry. This was supposed to be simple sex as friends, not a home invasion. My only excuse is that things have gotten off track in a big way. First that awful wreck, and now this..." A deep breath helped her regroup. "I just wanted you, that's all. And here I am bringing as much drama as your sister, and that just might...might run you off before I even get all the goods." She made a face. "Best laid plans, right?"

After her rambling explanation, his quiet, "I'm sorry," meant more just by the simplicity of it.

"You're sorry?"

"My family has the unique ability to make me lose my cool." He pulled into the hospital parking lot, chose a spot and stopped the car. Turning in the seat, he faced her. "We need to clear this up."

Disappointment weighed heavy on her. "I know."

He half grinned. "Short of aiming an Uzi at me, I'm not sure you could chase me off at this point."

Oh. Well, now, that sounded nice. She started to smile, but then Stack's gaze went past her, looking through the side window, and his eyes narrowed.

"Stay put a sec." Jaw locked, he opened his door and got out.

Vanity twisted to watch as he walked toward two men standing just outside the glare of security lights. Heads down, standing close together, they made an exchange.

Fucking Phil? She assumed so.

Yes, she would stay put as Stack had ordered, but he said nothing about leaving her window up, and in the dark quiet of pre-dawn, she was able to hear his every footfall.

So did the two men. One looked up, then faded farther into the shadows until he disappeared.

Stack didn't seem to care about him. No, he'd zeroed in on the other guy, the one with the shaggy brown hair, smarmy smile and dark eyes. He was tall, but not as tall as Stack. Leanly built. His posture slouched.

Steps long and sure, Stack made short work of closing the distance.

As if seeking escape, the man glanced around himself but then must have decided against trying to run. Instead, he quickly stuffed something into his pocket and, with terrible acting skills, attempted a jovial greeting.

"Stack. Whassup, man. Haven't seen you in a long—gak!"

The nervous chatter ended when Stack caught the man by the front of his shirt and stepped him up against a lamppost.

Vanity soaked it all in—mostly just impressed with Stack's imposing presence, his straight posture while lifting a full-grown man to his tiptoes, and the contained way he muttered a dire threat.

"Get rid of it before you come in the hospital. And I don't mean to hide it in the car with my sister."

"Hey, hey," Phil said, his tone conciliatory. "We drove separate, dude. Chill out."

"Drove separate, how?"

"Tabby came in your mom's car."

Stack released him with a light shove that made Phil's head ping against the metal pole. A finger pointed in his face kept him there. "You're on notice. Bring that shit anywhere near my family, and I'll take you apart." Turning his back on him, Stack strode away.

"You don't gotta be like that," Phil called after him. "It's just a little weed, man, that's all."

Stack didn't acknowledge him, and Phil, making a stupid face, flipped the bird at his back.

Then he saw Vanity watching. And Stack opening her door. He realized they were together, and he positively blanched.

Lacking any sympathy for the doofus, Vanity ignored him as rudely as Stack had. Together, with Stack's arm around her, they walked past Phil and into the ER entrance of the hospital.

Stack's sister was there, waiting for him, her face ravaged from crying—and yet Stack still didn't seem overly concerned.

He released Vanity just in time because the sister launched herself at him, her sobs out of control. With a long-suffering sigh, Stack caught her to him.

He looked at Vanity over his sister's head and said, "Vanity, this is my sister, Tabitha. Tabby, meet Vanity."

Hysterical cries died as if someone clicked off a movie. Silence, a stiffening of shoulders, and a second later her head left Stack's chest and instead jerked around to stab Vanity with ripe curiosity.

"You share similar features," Vanity said as if she hadn't just witnessed pure lunacy. "Though of course you're far more feminine."

Tabitha dropped back to her own feet. She swiped her cheeks, blindly sought a tissue from her pocket, blew her nose, and…beamed at Vanity.

Unsure what to make of that, Vanity tried a smile that didn't quite appear.

Sly, Tabby cast a look at Stack, then back to Vanity. "Well, well, well. Things just got very interesting."

CHAPTER FOUR

WALKING PNEUMONIA. NO WONDER his mother felt so bad.
She hadn't collapsed as Tabby had claimed, but she'd
been coughing, lost her breath, stumbled and fell. She'd
hit her head pretty hard, but luckily didn't have a concussion.

Still, she'd gotten a few stitches, a lot of bruises and,
according to the doctor, a bad attitude.

Sounded like his mom. She didn't take well to illness or injury. Like a petite steamroller, she always
plowed on.

Overall, she wasn't badly hurt. But she would need
a lot more rest, meds, and her head would no doubt
ache for a while.

Since she had her eyes closed, Stack took a moment
just to look at her. Thanks to her frequent salon visits,
her hair was a little lighter than his and Tabby's. She
usually had it styled. Tonight dried blood left it stiffened, darker around one side of her face.

A few new smile lines—his dad's description—
showed around her eyes and mouth. In better circumstances, she'd probably have downplayed them with
makeup. Being here like this, with the loss of dignity,
would make her nuts. She always tried to make the best
appearance.

Not that his dad had ever cared. Through good times

and bad, sickness and health, he'd loved her openly. Just as his mother had loved his dad.

Memories wrought a sad smile as Stack recalled the way his dad had always chased his mom, the outrageous compliments, the risqué teasing. Every day, for as long as Stack could remember, his dad had made it clear that he desired her, that he wanted her. That she was it for him. Always.

Stack and Tabby had grown so used to it, it hadn't embarrassed them. Much.

Always flustered his mom, though. She'd blush and smack at his dad and whisper for him to behave. But she'd also smile with love shining in her eyes.

There were times she'd been sick, times she'd been sad over the loss of a relative or friend, times she'd been stressed or worried, and his dad would pamper her into near insanity, to the point she could feel little except happiness.

They'd been deeply, demonstratively in love…until his dad died six years ago.

"I hope you're not mentally making funeral arrangements, because I'm not gone yet." Lynn Hannigan hadn't bothered to open her eyes to make that outrageous statement. "Do I look too awful to get a kiss? After all, it's been a while."

"You never look awful." Stack came in, carefully seated himself on the side of the bed, and took her hand.

When she gave him a one-eyed glare, he dutifully bent and kissed her cheek.

She closed that eye again. "Better. But if I'm not dying, why were you hanging over there, being all pensive and morbid?"

He huffed a small laugh. "Actually, I was thinking of Dad."

"Oh, Lord. If the man was still alive, he'd be fretting over me, pampering me and—"

"Loving you."

"Especially that." Her eyes tightened.

Stack considered her pained expression. "Headache?"

"It's like a herd of angry elephants are having a brawl."

The sentiment made him smile despite his concern. "I've missed you."

"Missed you more."

"All you had to do was call. You know that."

That same eye peeked open again. "And say what? That Tabby was the same, that Phil was still around, that nothing much had changed?"

He didn't reply. Yeah, he'd made those stipulations, told them all that until they got their shit together— which namely involved kicking Phil to the curb—he wouldn't be around to witness the lunacy.

Yet here he was.

"Tell you what." He concentrated on the nastiest of bruises just under her stitches. "Here on out, you and I can meet for lunch or something. At least once a week. More if you want."

She sighed. Of course she couldn't. Cleaning up Tabby's messes was a full-time job.

Stack gently patted her hand. "We'll make it work."

"I'd like that." Another peek. "Because I love you."

"Ditto."

The sniffling alerted them both, and a second later, Tabby peeked past the curtains. "Mom?"

"She's okay." Stack stood and made room for his weepy and worried sister to slip in. "No concussion. But she has walking pneumonia. And exhaustion. She needs some downtime, Tabby." He crossed his arms. "The doc tells me she was trying to take care of your dogs when she started coughing and fell."

Tabby glared at him. As if their mother was deaf, she hissed in a loud whisper, "What do you expect me to do? I have to work, and my landlord said I couldn't leave the dogs there unattended anymore."

Stack popped his neck and swallowed down his ire. No way would he get into this with her. Not again, definitely not here. Showing his teeth in a "we'll discuss it later" smile, he said, "I'll let the two of you visit."

"You don't have to run off. Your girlfriend seems to be enjoying herself."

Alarm raced up his spine.

Oblivious, Tabby said, "Mom, did you know Stack brought a woman with him?"

That got both of his mother's eyes open. She even lifted to one elbow. "What? Who?" She looked around. "Where is she?"

"In the waiting room with Phil. You should see her. She's beautiful, built and really nice, too."

"Stack," his mother said, getting her first good look at him. "Are you in a tux?"

"Be right back."

"I want to meet her!"

Stack didn't reply. For a woman who only moments before had been incapacitated with a headache, his mother still knew how to issue orders. Urgency made his stride long and hurried as he went down the hall, past friendly nurses and a few worried visitors, all the way to the waiting room.

Vanity had her nose in a magazine.

And Phil, *fucking Phil*, was seated too close beside her, talking nonstop, fake laughing, schmoozing, doing his utmost to get her attention.

Vanity ignored him—just as she sometimes ignored Stack.

But this time, as she felt his stare and looked up, she immediately put the magazine aside. Smiling, she came to him, walking right into his arms. "Hey." She squeezed him with comforting concern. "How's your mom?"

In that moment, Stack felt a lot of things. Too many things, damn it. At either side of her head he threaded his fingers into her long hair, anchoring her for his kiss.

Out of deference for the hospital atmosphere, he kept it brief. "She's okay. How are you holding up?"

"Me?" She laughed, looking not just gorgeous, but precious, too. Her hand rubbed his biceps. "I'm not the one who was hurt."

That earned her another kiss before he lifted her arm and feathered his fingertips over the soft skin above the bandage. "It's been one hell of a day. You haven't had any sleep."

"Neither have you." That sweet, teasing smile twitched into place. In the barest of whispers, she said, "But at least I had two orgasms, so all in all, for me, it's been a pretty good twenty-four hours."

Urges rushed through Stack. The urge to hold her. To laugh with her. To use her to chase away the endless frustration he worked so hard to hide. To maybe confide in her about how badly he wanted to demolish Phil—and why.

To somehow claim her...for more than a quick taste.

In that moment it all became clear to him. Vanity tried to control things. But he needed that control, and once he had it he'd sway her to his way of thinking.

Namely, that one day together would never be enough to get his fill. Hell, a week together might not do it.

She constantly took him by surprise, so maybe it was time for him to start surprising her. He'd start right now.

Because they lingered, Phil cautiously edged toward them. Stack stopped him with a dead stare meant to convey his utter disdain. Must've worked, too.

Raising his hands, Phil slunk away.

"Tsk. That wasn't very nice," Vanity chided. "You should save that wolf's glare for the cage."

"You don't need to concern yourself with him. Ever." Assuming she'd take heed of his warning, Stack drifted his hand down her arm until his fingers twined with hers. "Come on." He brought her along as he retraced his steps back to his mother's bed.

Bemused, she asked, "Where are we going?"

"I need to talk to my mom. And then to my sister." And maybe to fucking Phil. "But I want you with me."

"Aww." She leaned her head on his shoulder. "That's sweet."

Stack popped his neck again. "It's not *sweet*, and it doesn't mean anything." Even though he'd never before willingly introduced a woman to his family.

And if it wasn't for Phil...yeah, he'd probably still feel compelled to keep her close. He'd blame that on blue balls. She might have gotten hers, twice as she'd pointed out, but his was still very much on the "to do" list.

"Right. It means nothing." She came along, her attitude buoyant, happy. "I won't make anything of it. I mean, if I hadn't forced my way along in the first place, I wouldn't even be here now, able to accompany you—"

He stopped dead in his tracks.

Tilting her head, Vanity asked, "Stack?"

How could she be happy after the day they'd had? After performing as Yvette's maid of honor, partying for hours, then dealing with a wreck...and stalled sex. She had to be functioning on lost reserves.

But she didn't show it.

The only other person he knew with that much energy was Armie. God willing, that'd be the only thing Vanity had in common with him, because Armie was the most outrageous person he knew.

Forcing the words out, Stack explained, "It's just that I don't want you out there with Phil." He started walking again.

"Got it." They'd almost reached his mother before she added, "But you should know he's harmless, at least to me."

"Harmless, huh?" Not a description he'd apply to the scumbag user his sister adored.

"Next to you," Vanity said, "he's almost invisible. And how can an invisible man be a problem?"

This time his feet kept moving, but damned if everything else didn't stop. His heart. His thoughts.

Even his tempered anger receded.

Pausing outside the curtained-off room, Stack struggled to sort his thoughts.

Tucking closer to him, Vanity whispered, "She's really okay?"

Just as low, he replied, "Sick, injured, but she has a backbone of steel."

Through the curtain they heard, "A boot of steel, too, if you don't get in here, young man."

Despite the coming arguments, Stack had to grin. "Brace yourself," he told Vanity, and then he swept aside the curtain.

WITH THE EXCEPTION of f'ing Phil, Vanity really liked Stack's family. Both his mom and his sister were unique, and she appreciated that. Unique was good. It beat run-of-the-mill any day.

She socialized easily with just about everyone. But she'd always gravitated to people who stood out, who didn't just follow the pack. The ladies in Stack's life were as far from the pack as they could get.

Tabitha was indeed a drama queen, but in a very likable way. She overly emoted about everything. Her mother's illness and fall, the weather, her brother…

And Vanity.

She didn't just say, "Nice to meet you." No, she took the simple greeting to new heights, saying to her mother, "Isn't she *gorgeous*? And look at that hair! Ohmigod, her *hair*. Vanity, your *hair*! Ugh, it's amazing. And if you weren't so damned nice, I'd *hate* you for that body. Mom, can't you just hate her for that? I mean, look at her. Vanity, *look* at you."

Feeling a little self-conscious, Vanity had laughed and given the requisite, "Thank you."

Stack wore the smallest, most indulgent smile, and amusement had brightened his eyes.

The senior Hannigan, Lynn, just rolled with the punches, saying "Yes, Tabby, she's just plain lovely."

Then she'd narrowed her eyes at Stack and added, "You brought me a woman."

"No." Stack had stiffened, his mood switching from humor to defensive alarm. "I didn't bring her to you, Mom. She's not a gift."

Tabitha had elbowed him. "Because you damn sure plan to take her with you when you leave, huh?"

"You have the sharpest damned elbow!"

"Maybe I should compete, like you do."

"You'd defeat more guys with your big mouth than—"

And Lynn had ordered, "Both of you, desist. Tabby, keep your elbows to yourself. Stack, stop insulting your sister. Chairs. Sit. Quiet."

And they had.

That had left Vanity standing—until Stack had snagged her waist and drew her onto his lap.

Both Lynn and Tabitha had grinned over that.

Now, fifteen minutes after she'd arrived in the room, Vanity wasn't sure how to proceed. They were waiting for the doctor to sign Lynn out of the hospital and give them the discharge instructions. In that time, she'd run out of inane conversation, yet Tabitha and Lynn continued to watch her, almost as they would an oddity. Did they expect her to do tricks?

Into the silence, Tabitha sat forward and blurted, "How is it that Stack's in a tux and you're in jeans?"

Stack zeroed in on her, maybe thinking she'd spill the beans about their special arrangement. Not likely. She could only imagine how his mother and sister would react to that.

Though he tried to look relaxed, the thighs beneath her bottom were taut, and as she repeatedly traced his shoulder blades and pronounced muscles of his back, she felt the tension coiling.

"He drove me home," Vanity explained, sticking to partial truths. "I changed out of my dress to help unload all the wedding gifts from his trunk, but then we got the call that your mother was hurt."

"Hmm." His mother, a truly attractive woman despite the physical evidence of her recent mishap, took her shrewd gaze from Stack to Vanity and back again. "So you'd gone to the wedding together?"

"Yes." Vanity lightly patted his back, letting him know to trust her. "I had to beg and plead because, well, you do realize that Stack is date-phobic."

"Date-phobic?" Tabitha asked.

"You didn't know?"

His tone a clear warning, Stack said, "Vanity."

She ignored him but leaned in to share, sotto voce, "He doesn't want any woman getting ideas. So while he doesn't lack female company, he mostly just hooks up at Rowdy's bar or sometimes with the different women who frequent the rec center."

Both ladies were wide-eyed as she divulged those illicit details.

"Vanity," Stack said, "is best friends with Cannon's wife. They knew each other in California, and since Yvette moved here, Vanity recently did, too." He gave her a wicked smile. "Now she's one of those women who frequent the rec center."

"True enough," Vanity said with a shrug. Just to keep him on his toes, she tweaked him with some observations. "There is, of course, serious man-candy inhabiting the rec center. Hot fighters with hotter bodies." She bobbed her eyebrows. "But still, Stack stands out."

Stack gave a long-suffering sigh.

Fascinated, Lynn asked, "You like the looks of Stack, is that it?"

"Well, I'm not dead. Of course I appreciate how sexy he is."

Tabitha snickered.

"But," Lynn continued, "you think all the other men at the gym are also attractive?"

"Well, sure." Vanity tipped her head. "Have you met his fighter friends?"

"Many of them, yes."

"Then you know what I mean." Clearly Lynn hoped to get a lead on her feelings for Stack, but until Vanity made it clear to Stack herself, she figured it'd be best to keep her secrets.

Changing the subject, Tabitha leaned toward her brother. "Did she really beg and plead with you?"

Stack turned those smoky blue eyes on Vanity, and she gulped, barely able to keep her carefree smile in place. The corners of his sexy mouth lifted just enough to suggest she might regret taunting him.

Because, yes, she'd begged—but not for a date.

Only while they were in bed, when Stack had her on the cusp of release, had she pleaded with him.

"No," Vanity said suddenly, tearing her gaze from Stack's. "No, I didn't really plead. I wouldn't." Her laugh sounded ridiculous and far too phony. "But Stack is reasonable, so when I asked him to accompany me, as friends so I wouldn't have to go alone, he agreed."

From behind her, a male voice said, "No way would you have to go anywhere alone."

Stack went rigid, then deliberately remote.

Interesting. So he didn't want to upset his mother by giving his dislike of Phil free rein?

Seeming oblivious—or maybe secure in the fact that Stack wouldn't cause a scene in the hospital—f'ing Phil strode toward his wife.

Leaving Stack's lap, Vanity took a strategic stance between the two men.

Phil smiled at her, and the idiot's gaze dipped over her body.

Silently seething, Stack rose to his feet, all six feet of bad attitude and honed ability.

Would he cause a scene here? God, she hoped not.

Luckily, a nurse stepped through the curtain. "Mrs. Hannigan, are you ready to go home?"

"Yes," Tabitha said with feeling, as if she'd been the one stitched and bandaged.

Lynn only smiled. "If you're ready to sign me out, I just need to get dressed."

The nurse looked at Tabitha. "Would you like to help her while I take care of the remaining paperwork and go over her instructions?"

"Sounds like a plan." Stack maneuvered himself behind f'ing Phil, nudging him forward. "The ladies can stay here, and we guys can wait in the hall."

Startled, Phil looked to his wife for assistance, but she'd already moved to the folded pile of her mother's clothes.

Was Vanity the only one to see the concern on Lynn's face? She didn't know how she could help—but she knew how to hinder.

Hugging Stack's arm, she smiled at him. "Since I'm not a relative, I'll go with you guys."

Undeterred, Stack shrugged. "Suit yourself." Then he

proceeded to prod Phil forward, and since Vanity had latched on to Stack's arm, she had to take part in that.

They'd barely cleared the room before Stack gently shook her off, then locked a hand around the back of Phil's neck. Without a word, he propelled his brother-in-law forward. Where they were going, Vanity didn't know, but she hustled to keep up.

A few people gave them funny looks, maybe because Phil resisted—to no avail—or maybe because of the killing look on Stack's face.

Trying to soften the impression, Vanity smiled at everyone.

At Stack's silent instruction they entered an empty waiting room littered with half-empty foam cups of coffee. After shouldering the door shut, Stack released Phil.

He staggered forward but quickly turned as if he didn't trust Stack at his back. One hand rubbing his neck, he frowned. "What the hell, man?"

Stack pointed. "I told you I didn't want to see you."

"I have a right to visit my wife."

"And I have the right to beat the shit out of you."

"Uh…" Looking left and right, Phil sought escape.

"You're not going anywhere," Stack told him.

"Jesus!" As if he couldn't take it anymore, f'ing Phil shoved his fingers through his hair. "It's been three months, man."

"Shut up."

"Three fucking months. And you didn't even care about her! If you had, you would have—"

Before Vanity could get her mind around the fact that a woman had started the animosity, Stack grabbed Phil and slammed him into a wall.

"Whoa." She slipped up to Stack's side. "Okay, I get the idea that he probably deserves to be demolished."

Phil looked at her like a lifeline. He opened his mouth, and Vanity said, "Seriously, you need to shut it before he kills you."

Phil clamped his lips together.

Vanity watched him a moment more, decided he'd be quiet, and switched her attention to Stack.

He was smiling. At her.

Well…that was good. Unsettling, but good. "You're okay now?"

"I was never not okay." His gaze cut back to Phil. "But, no, I'm not done if that's what you're asking."

"Oh." Seeing that Stack did, indeed, have control of his temper, she stepped aside. "Carry on, then."

Keeping Phil pinned to the wall, Stack dropped his head and laughed.

"Uh…" Phil tried to wiggle free but didn't make any headway, especially when Stack tightened his hold.

Lifting his head again, Stack said to Vanity, "I don't need your permission, darlin'."

"Naturally not, since we're only friends."

His eyes narrowed but not with anger. Maybe with… heated insistence? "Friends with benefits," he reminded her.

She put her hands on her hips. "Now did f'ing Phil need to know that?"

"F'ing Phil?" he asked.

Examining a nail, she explained, "Unlike you, I try not to curse unnecessarily."

"When is it ever necessary?"

Jaw locking, she growled, "There are times." Like

right now, maybe. She tipped her head at Phil. "How long is this going to take?"

"Don't suppose you'd step out and let me handle this privately?"

Wrinkling her nose, she said, "I'd rather not."

He sighed. "Got yourself all curious now, don't you?"

About a woman who'd meant enough to Stack that he now hated his brother-in-law? She winced. "Yes?"

As if that somehow pleased him, Stack gave her a lingering look filled with heat—then turned his attention to Phil.

"C'mon, man." Phil turned his face to the side, trying to dodge the brunt of Stack's deadly glare. "You know she didn't matter to you."

"Not much, you're right about that. But how I felt about her doesn't excuse what you did. And the fact you're married to my sister does matter because I care about her, a lot."

"Tabby loves me."

"Tabby is delusional, but she's also an adult, so her decisions are her own. Fact remains, if you ever hurt her, I'll take you apart and enjoy doing it."

"I wouldn't!"

"You're a liar, a pothead and a cheat. You hurt her just by existing."

Ouch, Vanity thought. That was brutal.

"I haven't cheated," Phil said, not bothering to deny the rest. "And everyone smokes—"

Bouncing his skull against the wall effectively cut off Phil's confession. Stack crowded in. "I don't believe a damn thing you say, so save it. If you're smart, if you want me to keep ignoring you, I suggest you find a job, give up the dope that you fucking well can't afford, and

start giving my sister a little help. And that," he emphasized, "is the last warning I'm giving you."

"I've tried! Jobs are scarce, man. I'm not a hotshot
fighter like you. I—"

"Take off," Stack told him. "I don't want to see you
again today. And, trust me, you don't want to see me
either."

"But Tabby—"

Anxious to end the contretemps, Vanity said, "I'll
tell her you had to go. No worries!"

Leaving Phil to slump against the wall, Stack held
out a hand to Vanity. Why the gesture felt so signifi-
cant, she couldn't say, but she hustled to accept, to lace
her fingers through his. His hand engulfed hers. Gently. Securely.

For a double heartbeat, Stack just stared down at her.
Then, taking her by surprise, he brushed his mouth to
hers. "C'mon, troublemaker."

He said it affectionately, but still, she had to protest.
"You're accusing *me*?"

Stack snorted. "It's too late to act all innocent now."

Okay, so, yes, she'd deliberately provoked him in
front of his mother and sister. And she had teased—
with the truth!—about the hunks at the rec center. She
considered debating it when, as they exited the room,
Phil muttered low behind them, "Asshole."

Vanity's eyes flared, and she held her breath, but
other than Stack smirking, nothing happened.

Relieved that he didn't turn back around and annihi-
late the man, Vanity again leaned on his shoulder. She
adored all of Stack, but, wow, his shoulders were especially nice. Perfect, in fact. He was so big and strong
and tall, she knew leaning on him would never be a

problem. It was a wonderful feeling, and she hugged herself to his biceps.

Still walking, Stack slanted his gaze down at her. "You are the oddest woman."

"Hey." That wasn't even close to a compliment.

"It's true." He kissed her forehead. "I expected that whole scene to upset you."

"Naw. Clearly you had it under control. And clearly f'ing Phil is a problem."

He snorted. "That's it, huh? All you're going to say or do?"

"Well, what should I be doing? Crying? Fretting? You're not, so why would I?"

"Cry, no." He gave her a look. "But you know you're dying to pry."

"Mmm…maybe." She couldn't wait to get him back out of the damned dress shirt and pants. She wanted to glide her hands over all that sleek skin taut over pronounced muscles, to feel the roughness of his body hair on her palms, to touch him and kiss him everywhere. "I figured I'd wait for a moment of weakness. Better odds of getting the truth from you that way."

Gently, he warned, "I don't lie, Vanity."

The way he said that gave her pause. Inching into unknown territory, she asked mildly, "The truth is important to you?"

His gaze sharpened. "Very important. I don't tolerate lies."

Had he been the victim of untruths before? Seemed likely, which meant her methods might enrage him, even possibly alienate him. With uncertainty denting her confidence, she chose to watch her feet instead of his face. "What about lies of omission?"

Though she didn't look at him, his attention consumed her, and finally, unable to help herself, she glanced up and got caught.

He kept his tone soft, which somehow made it more unyielding. "What have you omitted?"

She wouldn't compound things by saying, *Nothing.* That'd just be another lie. "Given the nature of our... liaison, there are many things you don't yet know about me."

He narrowed his eyes. "Like the fact you don't cry?"

"Right." Then she amended, "At least not without really good reason." A fresh breath helped get her back on track. "Mostly I was worried about you telling me to butt out."

"If I did, would you?"

Well, shoot. Time to be serious. Stepping in front of him, she got him to stop. "I know I can be pushy. I'm upfront about that. But I try really hard not to pry, and I promise I'm not a gossipy woman. I hope I'm not too nosy, just...interested. And I am a good listener, so if you ever want to talk..." She let that hang out there.

"That's a hell of a list of accolades. No flaws at all, huh?"

She blushed.

He touched the wild pulse beating in her throat. "No need to sell yourself. Remember, I already bought in."

How did he make that sound so sexy? "Good. So you'll explain your conflict with Phil?"

"Forget Phil." Stack leaned down and brushed his nose over her cheek, teasing a path to her ear. Once there, he whispered, "I want to *fuck*, not talk."

Oh. Well... *Yes to that.* She cleared her throat, but it

didn't help loosen the sudden restriction of carnal need. "I want that, too, of course."

"Of course." He smiled lazily, and that smile further distracted her to the point she couldn't think beyond the image of Stack naked and over her.

To help her along, he prompted, "You have something to add?"

Right, she did. But what was it? To give her brain cells a chance to regroup, she avoided Stack's consuming gaze and instead stared at his chest. He'd left the snowy white dress shirt open enough that she could see his collarbone, and a hint of chest hair.

He tipped up her face. "Exhaustion is catching up to you."

"No." She released a tight breath. "I'm not tired." Far from it.

"You keep losing your thoughts."

Her mouth twitched. "Not really." Going for total honesty, she admitted, "It's just that I'm having a hard time thinking of anything other than you naked."

"Ahem."

They both turned to see Tabitha standing there, her grin enormous.

"I can't believe I just heard that. And, oh, God, no, no." She lightly pummeled her own forehead. "That image needs to go away right now."

Stack laughed. "Did you want something, Tabby? Other than to cause a scene?"

True, passersby were giving her very odd looks, as if she might be a psych patient who escaped her confines.

Tabby glared at the curious people, but when she faced Vanity again, her cheek-splitting grin was back in place. "Not to break up this fascinating love-fest, but Mom is ready to go."

"Right." Stack swung an arm around Vanity, edging her back to his side. "Sorry about that. We got distracted."

"Ha! You, brother dearest, stopped thinking with your head and started thinking with your—"

Planting a palm in her face, Stack quieted her.

Tabitha laughed and stepped out of reach. "Where's Phil?"

"Gone," Vanity said, trying to recover from being caught in the hospital hallway seducing Tabitha's brother while his injured mother waited on them. Oh, Lord, that was bad. *Bad*-bad.

What kind of impression would she make on them? "I told him I'd let you know."

Tabitha started back to her mother, assuming they'd follow. "That's weird. Where was he going?"

Oh, crap. Vanity had no idea what to say to that. "Uh…"

Stack filled in. "He left because I told him to, and you know it."

"Yeah." Tabitha glared at Stack over her shoulder. "You're always so mean to him."

"He's lucky I don't—"

"I know, I know. You want to tear him limb from limb." Tabitha waved off the possibility of such a dire consequence. "One of these days you two will get along."

"No," Stack assured her. "We won't. But hopefully you'll wise up and dump his sorry—"

"La, la-la, la," Tabitha said, her fingers in her ears as she kept walking.

Stack grinned at her back.

Huh. Vanity looked from one to the other, and a warm, peaceful sort of contentment settled over her. The siblings understood each other and cared enough to tease their way through major disagreements. That was nice.

"Now what?" Stack asked her. "You're getting melancholy."

She huffed. "I'm not tired, not melancholy, not weak."

He tugged on a lock of her hair. "God forbid you be human."

"I was just thinking it would have been nice to have a brother or sister."

Tabitha glanced at her. "You're an only child? Oh, how *tragic.*"

Stack gave his sister a light shove. "Not everyone is saddled with a lunatic for a sibling. Nothing tragic in that."

No, Vanity thought, not tragic. But there'd been so many times she would have given anything for a sibling. "Yes," she answered Tabitha. "I was the only one."

Which explained why she inherited everything from everyone in her family. If only they hadn't all left her the same year. Not that they'd ever really been there anyway.

When they were, there'd been no teasing, no laughter.

And sadly, never enough love.

CHAPTER FIVE

"No." THE HEAVY DARKNESS filling the near-empty parking lot carried sound over the damp pavement. From necessity, Stack kept his voice low so it wouldn't resonate to where his mother sat in her car with Vanity helping her to get comfortable.

Odd, how they'd bonded so quickly. He'd never seen that before, not that he'd brought many women around to meet his mom, but the few times he had—usually when a family affair required a date—she'd been politely distant and quietly critical.

Not so with Vanity.

In fact, Vanity had stepped seamlessly and effortlessly into the spot of doting daughter, a spot Tabby left unfulfilled.

"What do you expect me to do?" Tabby didn't bother keeping her voice low. Stack wasn't sure she knew how to whisper, or when it'd be a good idea.

Like now.

In his best *I'm-not-giving-on-this* voice, Stack growled, "She can't go home alone, Tabby. Forget it. If she can't stay with you, she can come to my place."

"You're never there," she reminded him, throwing her arms up in another melodramatic display. "Just how do you think that's going to help?"

"I'll work it out." How, he didn't yet know. But he wasn't about to let her—

"And who's going to watch my dogs?"

Slowly, he swung his incredulous gaze around to stare at her. Seriously? That was Tabby's top concern? "Keep. Your. Voice. Down."

"Those dogs love her, and she loves them."

Feeling red-eyed and mean, Stack frowned at her. The growl went deeper, and meaner, when he reiterated, "Mom is sick and hurt. She can't be your damned dog sitter."

"Then *who*? Because I have to work, and if I leave them alone in the apartment, they bark, and the landlord has already told me that if it happens again, I'm out. I can't lose my home. It's close enough for me to walk to work—"

"You have a car." He knew because he'd bought it for her.

Her face pinched. "I've been letting Phil use it."

Oh, fuck, no. Phil had said they'd ridden in separately, but he hadn't thought that much about it, not at the time.

Sawing his teeth together, Stack counted to three, and then to five, and finally to ten before he thought he could speak reasonably.

Letting the issue of the car go for now, he concentrated on the most pressing issue. "Why can't fucking Phil watch the dogs?"

Gasping as if he'd struck her, Tabitha withdrew. For only a second her bottom lip trembled, then she stiffened her mouth and her spine. "Phil helps a friend at a bar—"

"Helps how? By drinking?"

"—and he looks for work, you know that, but he—"

"Jesus, Tabby." Exhaustion suddenly hit him like a ton of bricks. Emotionally, physically. Vanity might be superhuman, but apparently he had some weaknesses. "Stop, okay? Just stop. We both know Phil isn't trying to find a job."

"Is too!"

He swept out an arm. "Everywhere I look, there are help-wanted signs!"

Another gasp. "You can't expect him to work at a convenience store or gas station."

Stepping into her space, enunciating clearly, Stack asked, "Why the hell not?" Phil wasn't qualified for anything else.

"I'll watch the dogs," Vanity said, drawing their attention.

Stack and Tabitha both pivoted to see that his mother was back out of the car, a frown of pain on her face, one hand at her temple. Vanity supported her, all worried and caring and so damned appealing that Stack almost couldn't stand it.

"I'll watch them," she insisted again. "Problem solved. So how about you get your mother home?"

Shit. Guilt slammed into the wall of tiredness. "Mom." In a few long strides, Stack reached his mother and helped her get seated again. "Vanity's right. You need to get home." He hadn't meant for the debate with his sister to get out of hand, but that's how it usually went with Tabby. "I'm sorry."

"Me, too," Tabby said, now wringing her hands with exaggerated worry.

"You kids are stealing my line." Moving slowly, their mother pulled her coat around herself more securely.

"I'm the one who's sorry. And really, I'm more than capable of seeing to the dogs. They're content when I'm there. Other than feeding them and taking them out a few times—"

"Not happening."

She treated Stack to a weak smile. "We can't ask your new girlfriend to do it. Maggie and Norwood are like overgrown puppies. Very frisky."

Which was another good reason why his mother shouldn't—*couldn't*—handle them right now. But with Tabby looking so pathetic and needy, he didn't say that aloud. "She's not my girlfriend, and I'll be the one watching the dogs, not her."

As she'd done from the time he was a toddler, his mother smoothed his hair. "I like her, Stack. I want her to be your girlfriend."

Beside him, Vanity said, "Thank you, Lynn! You're so sweet."

That had his mom frowning. "Sweet?"

"She thinks everyone is sweet." Stack sighed. "I'll watch the dogs, okay? It'll be fine. I don't want you to worry about it."

She struggled with her seat belt. "But you're in an apartment, too."

Stack hooked the belt for her. "I'll work it out."

"I have a house," Vanity interjected, gaining everyone's attention. "And I love pets. They'll be fine with me, I promise. My backyard is even fenced."

Before Stack could again reject that idea, Tabby nearly jumped Vanity with her enthusiastic acceptance.

"You'll really watch them?" Bubbling with gratitude, Tabby said, "Thank you, thank you, *thank you*! They're my babies and I love them, but good Lord, they've got-

ten big and they're rowdy and playful. They only bark
when they're alone, I promise. They hate being cooped
up inside. You'll have to pick up some food. I was going
to do that on my way home from work today, then Mom
fell and—"

"No." Stack's head almost exploded off his shoulders.
His quiet voice drew more attention than his growls had.
"Vanity is not watching your dogs."

"Not Mom, not Vanity… *What do you expect me
to do?*"

"Make Phil get off his lazy ass. Or hire someone. Or
I'll take them, but—"

At his side in a heartbeat, Vanity stroked his back.
"Stack, really, your mother needs to be in bed, and
clearly your sister can't deal with two dogs right now."
She turned to Tabby. "Your mother will go home with
you?"

"Of course. I work in the morning, but I'm only a five
minute walk away, so I can still check on her as often
as necessary. And Phil will be in and out."

"God help us," Stack muttered.

Protesting, Lynn said, "I don't need anyone checking on me."

"Now, Lynn, you know your kids will feel better
knowing you're okay." After directing his mother, Vanity did more stroking along his spine. "I'm glad you're
nearby, Tabby. It sounds like the perfect solution."

Stack couldn't believe how Vanity took over. Then
again, he supposed someone should.

Her hand slipped down to the small of his back, and
she asked his sister, "When would you like for me to
pick up the dogs?"

Tabby fretted. "They're at my mother's still." She

took one pace away and muttered, "Probably destroyed her house by now, too." Then she slapped on another smile. "I'll give you her key and you can get them from there. But again, the food—"

"I'll take care of it," Vanity assured her.

Stack wanted to groan. "This is nuts."

Hugging him, likely placating him, too, Vanity said, "You and I can discuss it in more detail later, after Tabitha has gotten your mother home."

Tabby dug out the key and thrust it toward him. "Here you go."

When Vanity took it, Tabby hugged her so tightly that Vanity looked to be strangling. "Thank you so, so, *so* much. *Seriously*. You're a lifesaver! A complete *lifesaver*. I don't know what I would have done—"

To shut her up and get her going, Stack pulled her away and steered her to the car. Vanity followed. "Drive carefully, and let me know if you need anything." He thought to add, "For Mom." Because Tabitha always, endlessly, needed something.

Leaving the women to say goodbye, he crouched down at the passenger's side of the car to talk privately to his mother.

Through the signs of discomfort, she smiled. "Thank you for doing this, Stack. I swear, I'm more attached to those dogs now than Tabby is."

He hadn't known that, but now that he did, he was glad Vanity had offered. "We'll take good care of them, I promise." He held her hands in his. "I'll call you mid-afternoon to see how you're doing."

"I'll keep my cell on me."

"If you need anything, anything at all, I want you to call me. I mean it."

"I will."

He knew she wouldn't. Damn. As needy and clinging as Tabby proved to be, his mother was the exact opposite. Independent to the point of being a martyr. He hated leaving her in his sister's ditzy hands. Tabby could barely take care of herself, much less deal with Phil, two dogs and their mother. But she hadn't lied; he was rarely home. At least at Tabby's, their mom wouldn't be alone.

He glanced at Tabby, but she stood just outside the driver's door, gushing to Vanity while alternately giving her directions on caring for the dogs.

"It's all right, son. Stop worrying. I'll be as good as new in no time."

Since she was one of the strongest women he knew, he believed her. "You need to rest to get well. Don't let Tabby work you."

"She won't. She loves me, too, you know."

"Yeah, I know. But she's…" Irresponsible. Sometimes blind. Occasionally self-centered. "Disorganized."

"She does her best."

Done beating around the bush, Stack said, "I don't trust Phil."

"Fucking Phil," his mother teased. "I know." She put a hand to his bristly jaw. "Your sister loves him, Stack. You have reason to distrust him, and more reason to dislike him, but I hope for Tabby's sake you'll continue being kind."

The car started, and he realized Tabby had finally gotten behind the wheel. With a last kiss to his mother's feverish cheek and a few more instructions to his lunatic sister, Stack closed the door, stood back and watched them drive away.

Vanity's hand slipped into his. "I hate to admit a weakness, but I'm close to suffering frostbite here."

Drawn from a dozen different worries, he forced his gaze to her face. The chill wind had painted her nose and cheeks bright pink. Her hand in his felt like ice. Their breaths frosted between them.

And all he could think about was kissing her, losing himself in the taste of her, the soft texture of her mouth, her incredible body.

"Come on." He led her to the car and opened her door, then left her to seat herself so he could get around to the driver's side and get the car started. The sooner the heater got going, the sooner she'd be warm.

While chafing her hands together, she said, "Your family is interesting."

Interesting. Was that her attempt at diplomacy?

"In case that sounded less than complimentary, I should add that I like them."

"Great." Looking over his shoulder, Stack backed out of his parking space, then drove from the lot. Antagonism had a stranglehold on his usually calm demeanor. "Seems they fell hard for you." And, yeah, even he heard the sarcasm.

Vanity always had something to say, so as he got onto the main roads again, the sudden silence bothered him.

A quick glance showed her watching him, her bottom lip caught in her teeth. "What?"

"You're annoyed with me."

True enough. But, hell, he was annoyed with everything at the moment. Maybe that's why he couldn't rein it in. "You butted in where you shouldn't have."

"I know."

"You know?" Disbelieving that innocent reply, he threw another look her way.

Her shoulder lifted. "I'm not dense. I know that was a family matter."

Yet it hadn't slowed her down at all.

"In my defense, I could tell that seeing the two of you spat upset your mother."

Jesus. "I don't *spat*." He was a professional MMA fighter with rapidly growing popularity, razor-sharp elbows, a solid ground game, and a record filled with knockouts and submissions. Spat. How dumb.

Half turning in the seat to face him, Vanity drew up her knees and got as cozy as the seat belt allowed. "I'm guessing you and your sister have a history of blowups."

Spot on.

"You're both alike, but also very, very different."

Curious about her perceptions, he said, "You're dying to tell me, so let's hear it."

Instead of pretending she didn't understand, she rested the side of her face on the seat back and smiled. "You're both headstrong, confident in your mother's love and comfortably affectionate with each other. Neither of you lets disagreements cause a rift."

"Close," he admitted. "But we did have a rift that lasted over six weeks."

Thoughtful, she said, "So your mom getting hurt is what ended it?"

"Yes." Only…was it ended? Fucking Phil was still in the picture. How did anyone expect him to tolerate that?

"And the rift?" she pressed. "That was because of something Phil did?"

"He's a prick." New annoyance surfaced, tightening

the muscles in the back of his neck, roiling in his guts. "You should have stayed away from him like I told you."

"That's not fair. In the waiting room there wasn't any way to avoid him completely. But I did ignore him."

"And you listened in. On everything." Meaning she'd just seen him at his worst.

Hell, he *had* spat with Tabby. He felt ten again, needling his sixteen-year-old sister.

"Should I have put my fingers in my ears?"

Without thinking it through, he reacted to her joking with uncensored candor. "You should have stayed behind like I asked."

The second the words left his mouth, he regretted them. Tiredness dragged at him. The insurmountable issue of his sister married to a lying creep while infringing on his mother wormed through his brain.

But he didn't usually lie to himself—as he just had.

Having Vanity along had been a balm against the rest of the night. She'd handled his sister, tended his mother, ignored fucking Phil, and all he'd done was bitch.

The seat squeaked with Vanity's movement. She retreated, straightening to look forward through the windshield, arms folded around herself.

"Shit." Drawing a breath, Stack reached for her hand. "I'm sorry. Again."

Without acknowledging his outstretched hand, she shook her head. Her long blond hair half hid her face from him, but by her voice alone he could imagine her dejected expression. "No need. I'm the one who needs to apologize."

"No, you don't."

She ducked her face even more. "We had an agreement, and I keep overstepping it."

"Screw the agreement, okay?" He caught her fore-arm, then gently tugged until she loosened her grip and freed her arm, allowing him to slide his fingers down to lace with hers. He moved her hand to his thigh and kept it there. "I'm glad you're here."

"Because I'll watch the dogs?"

Laughing, he squeezed her hand. "I'll watch them, and, no, it has nothing to do with that. But thank you for offering."

"We're going there first, right? To get them?"

The groan struggled to be free, but he manfully re-pressed it. "Guess so." If he didn't, the two German Shepherds would feel abandoned. They were soft-hearted beasts, overly protective, and deserved better than his sister gave them.

Not that she was bad to them. But she didn't have enough time for two energetic dogs, and he wouldn't trust Phil with a snake, much less a dog.

"By the time we pick up food and get them settled, it's going to be morning."

"Yeah."

"Are you going into the rec center?"

Sensing questions she didn't ask, Stack shrugged. "Sure. Havoc and Simon are coming in to work with us. I'm not going to miss that." Cannon, his friend and the owner of the rec center, had recently made a big name for himself. Gage and Denver were fast becoming fan favorites, and Stack was right on their heels.

But Havoc and Simon were legends in the world of MMA competition. It was a real honor to have them offer some advice, but to get to spar with them, yeah, he wasn't missing that.

Havoc had only recently talked Armie into signing

on with the SBC, which was the most popular, recognized and best-paying venue for MMA fighters. Now he and Simon hung around more often. If the rec center got any busier, they'd have to expand.

"You're going to Denver's next fight?"

"Yeah." He glanced at her. "You?"

"Probably."

Did she want to go together? He wouldn't mind that, except that he left early, and other than the after-party, he might not see her that much. "I'll be in back with Denver before he comes out."

She smiled. "With Cannon and Armie, too. I know. It's great how you guys support each other."

"We're a team." But that reminded him of something else. "Do you really check out the guys?"

She fought off a laugh. "Stack. I'm not blind."

So she did. Damn.

"Like you don't eye all the women! I've been there when some very pretty ladies came in, and you sure didn't hide your eyes."

Guilty. But then, a quick look never hurt anyone. "I don't check them out with any interest."

Her rude snort nettled him.

"It's just habit." Even he had to struggle not to laugh over that one. "Doesn't mean anything."

"You forget that I know you, Stack Hannigan. I've seen you holding court at Rowdy's bar, sometimes with three different women at your table."

Shaking his head at her wording—he didn't *hold court*—he pulled into an all-night grocery. "Okay, let's focus on one thing, and only one thing."

"Sex?"

Did she have to look so anxious when she said that?

"Me wanting *you*. So much so that, since we struck our deal, I haven't looked at other women, much less slept with them."

Finally she turned those big vivid-blue eyes on him. Surprise replaced every other emotion. "You've been celibate?"

She said that with a lot of skepticism. "If it sounds unbelievable from your view, you should try it from mine. I can tell you, it sucks." He brushed his thumb over her knuckles, then released her hand to park the car beneath a security lamp.

"Celibate," she breathed. "Wow."

He had to admit, it was pretty shocking to him, too. "I need this, Vanity. I need *you*. Don't make me wait any longer."

"That's…well, an awesome admission."

"And the verdict?"

"Was that ever in doubt?" she asked with a laugh. "This was my idea, remember? And now, after all the buildup, I think I need you more than you could ever need me. So many nights, I—" She hesitated, then bit her lip.

Lust shot through his bloodstream. He shifted closer. "What?"

Thick lashes lowered to hide her eyes. "I had to see to myself."

That visual sucked all the air out of him, leaving his chest tight and his heart thumping. "You have no idea how willing I would have been."

"Thank you."

Thank you?

She shook off the shyness like an annoying fly, then met his gaze squarely. "But we do have an agreement."

"Had," he corrected. "We had an agreement. D-day is now."

"Right. Now works for me. But the reasons for waiting were valid. Now they're not. And now I need to get my fill of you."

Her fill? Did she think she could?

Could she?

He hoped not, because he knew one night wouldn't cut it for him, especially now with all these interruptions.

Damn it, he wasn't in the habit of chasing women. He sure as shit didn't play these games. He'd never had to. But no way in hell would he chance another disagreement with her.

He hadn't lied. His need was so consuming, he thought he might self-detonate if he didn't get her under him.

After a quick glimpse of the car's clock, he said, "Let's go. We'll grab the food, grab the dogs, and hopefully that'll be the end of the interruptions."

Twenty minutes later, when he got to his mother's house, he knew the rest of his plans had just been shredded.

CHAPTER SIX

A DOZEN TIMES, Vanity checked the clock, counting the minutes until Stack would be back. Torture. How had things gone so haywire? At the onset, it had seemed like such a simple plan.

The tap at her front door woke Maggie and Norwood with a start. The young mutts looked mostly German Shepherd, maybe with a little Collie thrown in. Sounding like the hounds of hell, they charged the front door. Vanity couldn't hear herself over the ruckus, so it was no wonder the dogs didn't hear her when she tried to calm them.

Their wagging butts knocked her this way and that, but she finally managed to get leashes attached to their collars. Wrapping the leashes securely around her hand, she dared to open the door.

Big mistake.

The dogs shot out—and took her with them.

Luckily it was Armie who'd knocked, and he caught her before her face hit the porch.

"Hey now." He got her upright, then took the leashes from her. Though it was getting colder by the day, the November weather didn't seem to bother Armie. He wore a loose flannel shirt over a T-shirt that read I'm Irresistible, and then in smaller print beneath, You've Been Warned.

A recent shower had left his bleached hair spiky. Dark lashes cast long shadows over his chocolate-brown eyes.

He was a good friend to everyone, so she shouldn't have been surprised to see him.

"You know them?" she asked Armie, seeing how the dogs were beside themselves with joy at a visitor.

"Nope." Laughing, he sat on the stoop. "But they're obviously good judges of character."

The dogs were all over him, landing sloppy tongue kisses across his face, trying to wiggle into his lap, all in all being so funny that Vanity had to laugh, too.

She stepped back inside to grab her coat, then sat beside Armie on the cold concrete step.

It took a good five minutes for the dogs to start to quiet, and once they did, they wandered to the yard, going as far as the leashes allowed, then plopped down beneath the shifting rays of sunshine.

"They had a rough night," Vanity explained.

"Yeah, Stack told me all about it."

Her face went hot. Just how much had Stack shared? Surely he wouldn't—

Shoulder-nudging her, Armie laughed. "Now, Vee, you know Stack doesn't kiss and tell."

He was the only one to call her that ridiculous name. Around a yawn, she explained, "It was a crazy night."

"Sounds like. He said his mom's house was trashed?"

"The dogs had taken it apart. The garbage was chewed up everywhere. One curtain and some blinds pulled down from where they'd tried looking out the window, all the couch cushions kicked off, a few chairs overturned." The house had looked like a disaster zone, but Stack, being the awesomely wonderful man he was, had been more concerned with the dogs than the mess. "They'd had two accidents." She wrinkled her nose. "Luckily, on the tile and not the carpet."

"And you helped clean?"

She scooted closer to steal some of Armie's warmth. The afternoon was a lot warmer than the night had been, but winter was upon them. "Stack was already worried about his mom and stuff. Of course I helped."

He continued to look down at her. "And you insisted on keeping the dogs?"

"Look at them! They were already confused over being left alone all day. They knew Lynn had been hurt, so they were scared for her. And then they saw Tabitha just long enough for her to freak out and start crying and stuff."

As if they understood, the dogs shifted their eyebrows, and their eyes looked all big and innocent.

Armie laughed. "You're a pushover."

Maybe. "I like them. They're boisterous, but very sweet." Half under her breath, she added, "As long as I don't forget to take them out. Often."

"That's why I'm here. Stack was worrying about you, so after I finished up my training, he asked me to swing by."

"Well, thank you, but we're fine."

"We?"

"The dogs and I."

Armie pushed to his feet, and that prompted the dogs to leap up, too. "Come on, beasts. Let's go check out the backyard."

Feeling more sluggish than she wanted to admit, Vanity started to stand. Before she'd even gotten her tush half an inch off the step, Armie caught her arm and hauled her upright.

Once they were all inside, he bent to look into her face, then huffed in annoyance. "You're about to fall on your face. Have you slept at all since before the wedding?"

"I'm fine," she insisted—even though complete and utter lethargy tried to drag her down. Given half a chance, she could crash for a solid eight hours.

Right at sunrise Stack had left her with a short but stirring kiss, admonishing her to "regain your energy" before he returned. Knowing that as soon as his obligations ended, he'd be back, more than ready to live up to the promise of that kiss, she'd done her best to nap. But each and every time she'd started to doze off, the dogs wanted or needed something. They were more demanding than toddlers, and just as cute.

"Why don't you go to bed?" Armie watched her with critical concern. "I'll look after the dogs for a while."

"Don't be silly." Armie surely had better things to do than babysit dogs he didn't know. "I can handle things."

Cocking a brow, Armie grinned at her. "Know what I think?"

"No doubt something nasty and sexual that I shouldn't hear."

He laughed. "I think you're trying to keep up with fighters who are in prime condition. A lost effort, hon. Go, crash. You've earned it."

That last comment made her wonder. "Earned it how?"

"Stack told me about the car wreck, his mom, his sis and fucking Phil."

Rolling her eyes over that continued awful nickname

for Stack's brother-in-law, she copped an attitude-ridden pose. "So, is Stack crashing?"

Armie repeated, "Prime-condition fighter." He knuckled her chin. "There's no comparison."

"Okay, yes, I'm tired." Why not admit it? "But I'm not a wimp, so I'm not going to shirk my duty."

"Caring for his sis's dogs is now your duty?"

"I offered, so, yes." And whenever she offered, she took it seriously.

Armie was about to say more when another knock sounded on the door. They both looked, Armie frowned, then almost got jerked off his feet when the dogs went manic all over again.

Vanity stepped around them and opened the door.

Leese, Brand and Miles stood there.

"Wow," she said, eyeing each of them in turn. "Was there a casting call for certified studs that I somehow missed?"

The men all grinned at her.

Ducking his face, Leese ran a hand over his unruly black hair. Sunshine reflected off the inky depths and also highlighted a few dark bruises that contrasted with the paleness of his striking blue eyes.

Vanity knew him better than most of the others; as she'd told Stack, Leese was her wingman, aiding and abetting when she needed to dodge interested men.

Brand elbowed Miles, asking in a stage whisper, "Is she saying we're studs?"

Rubbing his ribs and scowling, Miles said, "If she is, I'll add it to my résumé. Endorsed by Vanity Baker. That has to carry some clout, right?"

"Studs," she repeated. "And also insane." Unlike Leese and Armie, who were light heavyweights, Miles and Brand were thicker heavyweights, each with dark brown hair. The difference, at least to Vanity, was in their eyes. Miles had vivid green eyes, and Brand's were the darkest she'd ever seen.

Because she liked all of them, she held the door open. "Come on in."

As they entered, they saw Armie holding back the dogs.

There was a moment of surprise before Armie said, "What are you guys doing here?" and the guys said almost in unison, "We thought she was alone."

Scowling, Armie turned the dogs loose, and the guys got slathered in wet doggy tongues and unrestrained love.

Laughing, Vanity separated herself from the chaos, going to the couch to sit with a deep sigh. It felt good to be off her feet, but now a steady throbbing started in her temples.

Around the raucous noise, she asked, "Did Stack send you guys, too?"

Studying her with concern, Leese came to stand over her. "I came to check on you." Two fingers beneath her chin lifted her face, then turned it side to side. "Mutt and Jeff just decided to trail along."

Miles settled the matter of jumping dogs by lifting Norwood into his arms. The dog looked momentarily shocked, then joyous as he rolled to his back to be cradled like a baby.

Laughing, Miles strode over and took a seat beside her. "We're all heading to Brand's to watch the game."

"Game?"

They gave her appalled stares. "Football," Armie finally explained.

Copying Miles, Brand lifted Maggie and joined them. "Bengals are playing the Steelers."

"So?"

Again they all stared at her.

Vanity shook her head and, around a yawn, muttered, "Never mind. I don't even care."

Leese crossed his arms. "You need to get some sleep."

"Exactly what I was telling her." Now that Armie didn't have to hold on to the dogs, he sat down and propped up his feet on the coffee table.

Brand shoved him. "Idiot. She decorates. You can't do that here."

Muffling a laugh, Vanity said, "It's okay." Yes, she had some decorative items on her coffee table, but she wanted visitors to be comfortable.

Too late, because Armie had already removed them and was now sitting straighter. To the men, he said, "Stack wanted me to look over her backyard, make sure the dogs couldn't get out. She needs some shut-eye before he gets here."

They all grinned, and ribald comments circulated the room.

"She won't get any after he's here, that's for sure."

"Oh, she'll get some, all right."

"Rested women are better than the comatose kind any day."

Feeling like an official member of the pack, Vanity smiled at each of them. Being Yvette's best friend, she'd already been accepted by them. But now, because they knew she and Stack had hooked up, they'd decided she was part of the inner circle.

And damned if that didn't get her teary-eyed, a sure sign of her true exhaustion.

For the longest time she'd wanted a family. A real family who was there for you when you needed it, who dropped in unexpectedly, who teased and supported and...included.

Here, in Warfield, Ohio, well away from her beloved California beaches, it felt like home.

When she sniffled, the men froze into awkward, helpless lumps of muscle. They watched her as if expecting her to crack, or maybe sob. Wariness kept them wide-eyed and poised to act.

She laughed around her tears. "You guys are pretty terrific, you know that, right?"

Armie was the first to relax. Shoulders dropping, he said to Leese, "Happy tears," in this nauseating, indulgent man-to-man tone that conveyed she was a little woman and fragile, and expressing her happiness in such a way was to be expected.

Leese said only, "Ah, right."

Cautiously staring at her, Miles asked, "You're okay now?"

Okay, happy, content.

Touched by their concern.

But telling them all that would probably turn them mute again. Smothering another yawn, she nodded. "I'm fine."

"Know what?" Brand nodded at her TV. "We could watch the game here."

Before she could weigh in on that one way or the other, the guys did.

"Yeah," Armie said. "The dogs are attached to Mutt and Jeff."

Brand said, "Ha ha," and cuddled a happy Maggie closer. She licked his chin, making Armie fake-gag.

Miles tried to put Norwood down, but the dog wasn't having it. "I'm covered in fur," he complained to Norwood. But without a single sign of remorse, the dog stuck his nose in Miles's neck and sighed.

"You're turning them into lapdogs."

"They turned long before we got here," Brand insisted. Then to Maggie, his voice high-pitched, he said, "Didn't you, baby? Yes, you did. Yes, that's a good girl," making the dog's tail go nuts.

Leese pulled Vanity from her seat. "Go to bed. We'll visit with the dogs."

Keys in hand, Armie said, "I'll go grab some snacks." He tipped his chin at Vanity. "Anything you need while I'm out?"

Laughter got the best of her. And once she started, she couldn't stop. They were all so intrusive and hilarious and...wonderful. She fell against Leese, leaving him no choice but to hold her up.

"She's hysterical," Brand accused.

Armie joined Leese, and together they walked her down the hall, peeking into each room until they finally found her bed.

Leese pried her loose. "Go," he told her. "Sleep."

"We'll try to keep it down," Armie promised.

With one last chuckle, she hugged Leese and even kissed his cheek. Armie had his brows up over that until she grabbed him next. He hugged her off her feet in return.

"This is so nice of you guys."

"Sleep well," Leese said.

"And Vee?" Armie winked at her. "We promise to clear out once Stack gets here."

She winked back. "Appreciate that. Thanks."

They were both speechless as she closed the door. Had they expected her to be subtle about her attraction for Stack? Not likely. She cared for Stack too much, and was far too exhausted to be subtle.

In one long stride she reached the bed, collapsed facedown across it, and immediately fell asleep.

With a smile on her face.

STACK FINISHED SPARRING with Denver, but as he stepped toward the end of the mats, Havoc called him over.

"You okay for a few more minutes?"

He was bone tired and covered in sweat. But that was nothing new. To be a top contender in the sport, he had to be able to deal with it—and he could. Depending on where you fought, the altitude or heat could factor in. Minor injuries often sidelined men who didn't have enough stamina and heart to push through.

Stack knew he could deal with just about anything, and had. But raging lust was a new one for him. Knowing Vanity was at home, waiting for him, that when he got there he'd finally be able to strip her down, kiss her all over, then sink into her... Yeah, a big distraction.

He wasn't about to tell Havoc any of that.

Normally they'd all have taken off the Sunday after a wedding, especially given it was Cannon's wedding and they'd been out late, some of them drinking.

But Havoc spent the week at his own camp, and Sunday afternoon was one of the few times the rec center was open only to established fighters. During the week they had classes for grade school kids, college grads and every age in between. The fighters also took turns teaching self-defense to women.

So he pushed aside all discomforts, including the

discomfort of wanting a specific woman more than his next breath, and said, "I'm good."

"Great. I wanted to work on some boxing moves with Denver."

Denver was one hell of a well-rounded fighter, excelling in his stand-up and his ground game—but no one turned down instruction from a seasoned pro like Havoc. The fact that Simon Evans, another icon in the sport, was also on-site made it a day of invaluable input.

"You good with that?" Havoc asked Denver.

Denver set aside the water bottle and grinned. "Hell, yeah."

"Just instruction," Havoc said. "You're too close to a fight to risk an injury."

And so for the next half hour Dean "Havoc" Connor went through moves on Stack, demonstrating for Denver, then had Denver go through the moves with Stack so he could watch.

Just when he thought they were done, Simon joined them with a few pointers of his own.

When he finally got a break, Stack went to the side to chug down some water. Of course his thoughts were already on Vanity. Had Armie secured the yard? Were the dogs letting her get any rest?

Harper, Gage's wife and the most frequent volunteer receptionist for the rec center, strolled over to Gage and Justice.

Stack was involved in lurid visions of Vanity naked in bed, hopefully dreaming of him, when he picked up on the words "party" and "football" in Harper's conversation. Justice declined, but Gage nodded agreement and headed to the shower.

Harper glanced his way. "What about you?"

Without asking for details, he shook his head. "Not this time, but thanks."

Looking impish and up to no good, Harper shook back her brown hair and propped a hand on her hip. "Got plans of your own, huh?"

He had no idea why her blue eyes were so bright and mischievous, but he knew Harper well enough to know it meant something. Probably she'd heard about his aborted rendezvous with Vanity. Women, he'd learned from Denver, liked to gossip. Of course, Cherry had been gossiping about Denver's size, and given the man was hung like a horse, he supposed he couldn't blame her.

"I do," Stack said, then he pointed at her. "Stay out of trouble."

Her laughter livened up the gym, making several guys pause to look. Luckily, Gage, a massive heavyweight, wasn't the jealous sort. He knew that most at the rec center considered Harper a kid sister.

She shook her head, saying, "You poor, poor man," and walked away from him.

He was wondering about that when Denver joined him.

"Thanks for hanging around. I know you had better shit to be doing."

"I won't tell her you said that."

Denver paused comically. "I didn't mean that the way it sounded."

Because they both knew he could be doing Vanity right now. Stack grinned. "You won't see me passing up instruction with veterans."

"Yeah, that's how I figured it. Still—the timing sucked."

Denver swiped a towel over his face. "Armie, the ass, should have stayed, too."

"He's still getting used to the idea of being in the SBC. He'll come around, though."

"Why he has to get used it—that's what I'd like to know."

True. It confounded Stack, as well.

Cannon, as Armie's best friend, was the only one to understand Armie's reservations over signing on to the elite SBC. He'd already taken apart the competition in local venues. Upping the ante was all he had left if he wanted to continue in the sport.

Not being the modest sort, Stack knew he was good. Denver, too. Hell, all of them were good. But Armie had something the rest didn't. Some insane drive, a remarkable fluidity of movement. He countered strikes and submission attempts as if he knew things his opponent didn't. As if it was a sixth sense. Because of that, he walked through the best with ease.

Yet he hadn't fought at the higher-level shows. Stack didn't doubt that Armie would win once the SBC got him on a card, but everything would be different—the size of the crowd, the fanfare, the rules. The pay. Most jumped at the opportunity.

But for far too long Armie had dodged it. Havoc had to literally run him to ground and corner him to make it happen.

One of these days, they'd all know why.

"You heading to the showers?" Denver asked.

Stack shook his head. "I'll shower at Vanity's." Like most of the fighters, he kept a change of clothes in his gym bag, so he didn't need to run to his apartment first.

With every second that passed, some anomalous urgency burned in his blood. He'd anticipated sex with other women. He'd been caught up in the moment.

This was as different as night to day.

He knew Vanity was dealing okay with the dogs; Armie would have called him otherwise. But for a woman who'd only wanted a sexual experience, she'd taken on a lot of shit that wasn't hers to deal with.

On the drive over, Stack called his mom again to check on her. He'd spoken to her once already, and she'd insisted she was fine, claiming Tabby had set her up in the family room on a big soft couch with pillows, a blanket, the TV remote and her meds close at hand.

This time she answered on the first ring. "Why aren't you at home getting some sleep of your own?"

"Mom." Her chiding tone made him smile. "It was a special day at the rec center. I didn't want to miss it."

"Well, then, tell me you're heading to bed now."

Yeah, he was. But not alone and sure as hell not to sleep. "How are you?"

"The same as I was this morning when you called—perfectly fine."

He checked the clock, then cursed low when he realized it was after four. "Have you eaten?"

"Why do you and Tabby keep acting like I'm teetering on the edge? Of course I ate."

He knew his mother well. Usually when she got defensive, it was because she knew she was wrong.

Like the time she loaned money to Tabby, knowing fucking Phil had blown their budget on gambling. Or the time she'd paid Phil's outstanding tickets because Tabby was crying over it. And still they'd lost that car. Like an idiot, Stack had replaced the transportation for his sister—only to find out last night that Tabby let Phil drive it.

In the past, whenever he thought of the twisted relationship his sister had with a dick like Phil, it enraged him. Now, on his way to Vanity, it only pissed him off a little.

"'S that right?" Stack said, wondering if she'd outright lied about eating. "So what'd you have?"

"Your sister brought me soup on her break."

Huh. So Tabby had done something right. "Is that it?"

She huffed in exasperation—and ended up coughing.

"I'm swinging by," Stack told her when she caught her breath. He'd make sure—

"No," she protested. "Stack, honey, you know I love you. But right now I just want to close my eyes and sleep. I promise I'm eating enough."

Given he was so anxious to see Vanity, he caved easily. "I'm coming by tomorrow, then."

"That would be very nice."

New suspicions gnawed on him, and damn it, he couldn't let it go. "No fibbing, Mom."

"I don't—"

"Is Phil there?"

Silence.

Right eye flinching, Stack asked, "What's he doing?"

"It's his home, Stack."

Right. A cheap apartment in a shit part of town— that was the best fucking Phil could do. But if he had to bet, he'd say Phil didn't even contribute on that. Most of the bills fell to Tabby to cover. "Mom."

She coughed, got a drink, and finally said, "He has a poker game going on."

Son-of-a-bitch.

More times than Stack could remember, his mother had bailed Phil out of trouble, and he repaid her by having a party while she was ill?

In a rush, she added, "They're in the kitchen and I'm in the family room. I can barely hear them..." Sensing that explanation wouldn't cut it, she lost the pleading tone and adopted the *this-is-your-mother* attitude instead. "Stack Hannigan, you will not come charging over here, do you understand me? We're nearing the holidays, and I don't want a lot of strife in the family. I'm *fine*, and Phil, even with his shortcomings, is the one your sister wants."

"She can do better," Stack said, for about the millionth time.

Understanding took the edge out of his mom's voice. "You know it, and I know it."

Wow. First time she'd admitted that.

"Eventually Tabby will see it, too. But you know how she is, sweetie. The more we press her, the more she's going to dig in."

"You mean the more I press her." He'd been the only one protesting. His mother, curse her patience, kept her nose out of her children's lives as much as possible.

"She's determined to prove you wrong. Leave Phil be. I promise you, he'll screw up enough all on his own that eventually Tabby will wipe her hands of him. Just you wait and see."

Stack had never looked at it that way before, and now that he did, he had to admit to the possibility. "I'll try."

"Thank you." Letting out a weary breath, she said, "Now I really do want to nap."

"All right." Still worried, he said, "Love you."

"I love you, too, son."

For the remainder of the drive Stack's thoughts bounced between his mother's illness, his sister's a-hole husband, and Vanity. Sweet, hot, irresistible Vanity.

Waiting on him. Anxious for him.

Would she be ready the moment he walked in the door? He wouldn't mind showering with her again. He'd love teasing her body more. He couldn't wait to take her completely...

That thought died an immediate and painful death the moment he saw her driveway filled with cars.

What the hell?

He parked on the street, slammed the car door and stalked up the walk with bad intentions.

As if she'd been watching for him, Harper opened the door.

That drew him up short.

"You get the joke now, don't you?" Hooking her arm through his, Harper drew him in. "It *is* funny, Stack. Surely you'll see that, right?"

CHAPTER SEVEN

No. STACK DIDN'T SEE a damn thing funny about all his hot plans turning into a puff of smoke. Usually football parties were boisterous. Not so this time. Someone made a touchdown, and everyone cheered in near silence.

Lounging in various positions on the couch were Armie, Leese and Gage. No feet on tables, no misplaced pillows. Miles shared a chair with Norwood, and as Brand came out of the kitchen, Maggie followed him. Stack understood why when Brand slipped her a bite of cheese.

Stack looked at the beers and Cokes sitting on coasters, and the big bowl full of nachos—without a single crumb on the coffee table. It was like stepping into the land of Oz or something. "What the fuck is going on?"

"Keep it down," Armie told him. "Vee's still in bed."

Brand offered him a beer. "She hadn't slept."

"Not a wink," Leese said. "And it showed."

"Dogs wouldn't let her," Miles chimed in.

"So we stayed." Armie pushed away from the couch, and Brand immediately took his seat. Maggie crawled into his lap.

Stack's mouth tightened, and though he had a lot to say, he couldn't get a single word out. Gently but firmly, he pried Harper off his arm, walked her over and "gave" her to Gage. Without taking his gaze off the TV, Gage pulled her into his lap and nuzzled her neck.

Armie nudged Stack toward the kitchen. "Let's talk."

"Yeah. Let's talk about all of you getting out."

Fighting a grin, Armie soothed, "Now, Stack," while still corralling him from the room. "You know no one is budging, at least not until halftime. And Vee's dead-out anyway."

His eyes flared. "How the hell do you know that?" If Armie had peeked in on her, he'd—

"She hasn't come out of her room. The girl is a born hostess, so if she was awake, she'd have been out here, right? Especially with the dogs here. She did seem to feel personally responsible for them."

Damn.

"Took us a bit to talk her into resting. And seriously, dude, if we'd left, the dogs would have been on her. The poor things are starved for attention."

Another failing of his sister's. *Why the hell had she let Phil talk her into getting dogs anyway?* He knew Tabby tried, and he didn't doubt she loved the animals, but she worked fifty-hour weeks or more, so she didn't have a lot of free time.

And she damn well should have known Phil wouldn't step up.

Unaware of the path Stack's thoughts had taken, Armie continued. "She needed to sleep, so why not let her catch up? In the end, I'm guessing that'll work out better for you. You know, having her frisky instead of wiped out."

"Shut up." They got to the kitchen and Stack groaned, dropping his head against the fridge.

Behind him, Armie snickered. "Looks like you could

use a few zees, as well. You don't want to disappoint her. I have a feeling her expectations are pretty high."

He'd rather have Vanity over sleep any day.

Taking pity on him, Armie clasped Stack's shoulder. "I promise to get everyone moving soon as we hit halftime. I'll bribe them all with pizza to ensure they go. How's that?"

His eyes felt gritty, his limbs heavy, and a dull throbbing reverberated through his brain. Yeah, he was pretty damned exhausted, so Vanity had to have felt the same.

That made him wonder, so he turned and straightened away from the fridge. "Did she tell you she was tired?"

Armie snorted—and scooted him aside so he could get a bottle of water. "No. She was all about manning up. It was cute."

If Vanity heard Armie say that, she'd find some nice, sweet way to eviscerate him. No doubt she'd smile the entire time.

That was another thing Stack liked about her. Her quick wit, always delivered with deceptive good humor. "I'm going to take a shower."

"Here?" Armie asked.

"Yeah, here. What of it?"

Holding up his hands in surrender, Armie said, "Just didn't realize you guys had gotten to the stage where you made yourself at home."

His shoulders bunched. "But you guys are okay moving in?"

Armie grinned. "Dude, I get it. Jealousy is a bitch. But you know the guys better than that."

"I know *all* of you." And that was part of the prob-

lem. Other than Gage, who was fully committed to
Harper, they were all players.

And Vanity had admired each of them.

"You wanna back up that particular train wreck?"

Yeah, maybe he did. Scrubbing a hand over his face,
Stack said, "Fuck you," by way of apology.

And Armie took it as such. "Guys in love are so pathetic."

Love? Whoa. Rallying real anger and a heaving
heapin' of frustration, Stack took a stance and opened
his mouth—

"Checked the fence," Armie said, cutting him off. "I
fixed a few spots, and now it's secure. I even did you a
solid by taking the mutts out a few times so they could
get used to things. Give them a few chews—which I
picked up for you when I made a snack run—and they
should give you an uninterrupted hour. Anything beyond that, though, is dicey."

Damn, but friends were nice. "I owe you."

"I won't let you forget," Armie promised him. "Now
go take your shower. Make it cold enough to freeze out
the stupidity."

Yeah, he'd shower, and hopefully that would revive
him, too. "Keep it down. And seriously, the second
halftime hits, I want everyone gone."

"Got it covered."

Yeah, he'd owe Armie. Big time. But right now, all
he could think about was what he owed Vanity.

It was a debt he couldn't wait to pay.

WHEN THE BACKGROUND noise faded, Vanity stirred
awake. A little disoriented, she lifted her head and

glanced at the clock on her nightstand. Wow, for sure she'd slept long enough.

Levering up on to her forearms, she realized she hadn't moved. She'd literally crashed to the mattress face-first, and that's where she'd stayed. A touch to her cheek confirmed a few creases caused by the comforter. Yawning, she rolled to her back and indulged in some luxurious stretching.

Now, finally, she'd get things underway with Stack. Smiling widely, she bounced out of the bed.

Taking two minutes in the bathroom, she splashed her face, brushed the tangles from her hair, and quickly cleaned her teeth. Makeup was out. She just plain didn't care enough. But she could at least change out of her wrinkled clothes.

Still feeling ebullient, she rummaged in a drawer and found one of her favorite T-shirts representing the SBC. It had special meaning to her for many reasons.

After she'd followed Yvette from California to Ohio, Cannon had given it to her. He'd told her it made her an official part of his family now that he and Yvette were reunited. Such a great guy. She couldn't be happier for them.

Lacking any close family, Yvette had become like a much-loved sister to her, and now she had a brother in Cannon, as well.

She'd also seen Stack eyeing her in the shirt whenever she wore it. It was big and boxy—clearly a man's shirt—from a limited-edition collection the SBC had done. Did Stack wonder if a fighter had given it to her?

Let him. It couldn't hurt her cause to keep him guessing.

But another reason she liked it was that it represented his beloved sport. Stack was a fighter through and through, and she liked supporting him while wearing the shirt.

Skipping a bra, she pulled on the shirt, pairing it with her most comfortably worn skinny jeans.

Barefoot, she emerged from her bedroom feeling like a new woman ready to take on the world—or one very sexy light heavyweight fighter.

Following the faint sounds of movement, she entered her kitchen and found Leese putting empty paper plates and napkins in the trash. As he bent over the can his T-shirt stretched tight over his shoulders, and his jeans hugged his backside.

One thing about having fighters for friends—the view was amazing.

The second she walked in, he looked up, then straightened. "Hey."

He spoke softly, and his smile looked wicked enough to seduce a hundred women. Just not her. "Hi. Everyone else is gone?"

"Pretty much. Armie used pizza to bribe them away to his place during halftime." Leese went to the sink and washed his hands, speaking to her over his shoulder. "Feeling better?"

"Much, thank you." The day had totally gotten away from her. Had Stack decided against coming to see her? God, she hoped not. She could barely wait a minute more; waiting another day was out of the question.

Drying his hands, Leese grinned at her. "You are so transparent."

"Really?" Not that it'd take a mind reader for Leese to know where her thoughts had gone. More than the others, he knew of her interest in Stack. She confided in her girlfriends—to a point. And she got along great with all the guys. But Leese had become a very dear friend, and whether he liked it or not, a confidante.

After putting aside the dish towel, he tweaked a long hank of her hair. "He's passed out on the couch."

"Stack?"

That made him laugh. "I sure didn't mean the pope."

Turning in a rush, Vanity headed to her living room but slowed at the sight of Stack's long, leanly muscled body slumped in the corner of the couch, legs stretched out and feet crossed on the coffee table. Maggie lay in his lap, and Norwood sprawled on his back with his head tucked up against Stack's side.

Her heart turned over. It was the oddest feeling, sweet but disturbing, life-altering.

Denial had only worked for so long. After seeing him rescue people without concern for his own safety, watching him interact with his sister and care for his mother…well, she couldn't deny the truth any longer. *She loved him. So, so much.*

It looked as though his light brown hair had dried without being combed, and he'd recently shaved.

"You've got it bad," Leese said beside her, then he looked at Stack and grinned. "Lucky bastard."

"Shhh!"

But it was already too late. With a deep rumbling, Stack stretched out his arms and tucked in his chin, flexing all those gloriously hot muscles on his gloriously hot body, making her pulse quicken in a delicious way.

She spun to Leese and said, "Thanks for everything. Appreciate it. You can go now."

His quirking smile turned to a grin, and that led to

a bark of laughter. His gaze went from her face to the couch, and he said, "She's throwing me out."

Vanity pivoted to Stack and wanted to sigh with greed.

Now relaxed, his eyes heavy but open, Stack stared at Vanity while saying, "Good idea. Later, Leese."

One-armed, Leese drew her in for a hug. "If you need anything else with the dogs, give a holler."

She nodded and walked him to the door. She watched as he got in his truck and backed out of the driveway before closing the door. She turned and almost ran into a solid wall of muscle. Eye level with Stack's chest, she said, "Good grief. You move like a ninja."

Both dogs sat beside him, expressions anxious to see what would happen. Reaching past her, Stack locked the door.

"Oh." Her heartbeat started tripping. She gazed at his mouth. Man, she loved his mouth. Looking at it made *her* mouth tingle, and she started to go on tiptoe to reach him.

"Hold that thought." After brushing his knuckles along her cheek, Stack headed for the back of the house. "You guys want to go out?"

Barking enthusiasm shattered the quiet. The dogs took off in a zigzagging run, occasionally turning circles, leaping.

Vanity rushed behind them. "Aren't we going to—"

"Damn straight." He opened the back door, and the dogs shot out without a care.

Huh. That morning she'd had one heck of a time getting them out. They'd only wanted to go if she also went, and whenever she tried to come back in, they followed.

Hands on her hips, she watched Maggie and Norwood chase after a bird, then bark at a squirrel. Together they ran the perimeter of the yard, then tussled like happy children.

"Remarkable."

"Armie said he worked with them a little while you napped."

"Armie, too, is remarkable."

That made him frown—and almost made her grin.

"Armie also bought them some treats. I should have thought of that myself—" he sent her a scalding look "—but I was too busy trying to get you naked."

Wondering how soon they could get to it, Vanity bit her bottom lip and nodded.

Standing in the open doorway to the yard, Stack slowly looked her over. "Speaking of naked, you aren't wearing a bra."

"No."

"Where'd you get the shirt?"

So he *had* been wondering. Nervous, anxious fingers twisted in the hem. "Cannon gave it to me."

That seemed to appease him. "Looks good on you." Turning, he whistled to the dogs, and once he had their attention, he knelt down and offered the big chew toys.

Norwood got his first. Eyes big with gluttony, he carried it over to a tree and hunkered down to enjoy it.

Maggie sniffed hers excitedly, then with delicate care, closed her teeth around it and joined Norwood.

"That ought to keep them busy."

Yes, she wanted uninterrupted time with Stack, but she refused to put the dogs at risk. "Is it safe?"

"Armie said he checked your fence. It's all good. And trust me, if they want back in, they'll let us know."

Ridiculous shyness came over her. "We're finally going to do this?"

Stepping in and quietly closing the door, Stack watched her. "You tell me."

"What?" He didn't sound all that anxious.

Snagging her hand, he pulled her in close and feathered a kiss over the bridge of her nose, the top of her cheek, her jaw. "It feels like I've been waiting forever." One hand opened over her back, urging her closer. "But if you think you need more time, I'll deal with it."

Such a remarkable offer. "You are the sweetest man."

Squeezing her in close, he put a tickling, growling bite to that sensitive spot where her neck met her shoulder.

Vanity wanted to both melt and giggle. *"Stack."*

"I'm not sweet, I'm horny." He cupped her face. "So what's the verdict?"

"It sure isn't waiting." She pushed out of his arms, grabbed his hand and practically hauled him down the hallway. Laughing behind her, Stack allowed himself to be led.

Right before they reached her bedroom, he took the lead, drew her into the room and closed the door with her up against it. Pressing his body to hers, he took her mouth, all soft and gentle—for about three seconds. Angling his head for a better fit, he licked her bottom lip, then stroked his way inside, playing with her tongue, exploring, getting her hotter by the second.

She clung to his shoulders and felt the rising tension in him as the kiss went deeper, wetter, more possessive. He needed this worse than she did—and that was saying a lot, given how badly she wanted him. But where he'd ensured her pleasure, *twice*, he'd forgone his own.

He could deny it all he wanted, but he was about the sweetest man on the face of the earth.

Snaking a hand down his shoulder, Vanity reveled in his strength, how her touch caused him to skip a beat in the middle of the devouring kiss—then to ramp it up tenfold with a deep groan of encouragement.

His abs were a thing of beauty, and when she slipped her hand up under his shirt to touch his hot, taut skin, he freed his mouth. His forehead to hers, he breathed heavily—and waited.

"I love your body," Vanity whispered, touching him all over, reaching around to his back, to the granite muscles there, the hot, sleek skin. Gliding her palm back to his chest, she dragged her fingers through the chest hair there, then followed the happy trail down to the front of his jeans.

Using only one finger, she traced his erection beneath the denim. His breathing stilled; his cock did not. She felt him pulsing, flexing as she wrapped her fingers around him as much as she could, stroking through the stiff material.

In a sudden rush he brushed her hand away, opened the snap of his jeans, lowered the zipper and shoved the jeans halfway down his hips, freeing himself. He lifted her hand and, looking into her eyes, kissed her palm, then wrapped her hand around him again, this time flesh to flesh.

His hand over hers kept her grip snug.

"Fuck," he whispered, his eyes closed and his jaw clenching. Now that she understood how he wanted it, he flattened both palms on the wall at either side of her head.

She loved watching his face, the contraction of small

muscles that signaled nearly painful pleasure. His posture gave her easy access to kiss his throat and jaw. She nibbled, licked, sucked on his hot skin—all the while working him firmly with her hand.

Cheekbones flushed, he turned his face against her, rubbing his nose over her hair, growling softly, trembling a little.

She brought her thumb up over the head—and his breath caught. "That's enough." Quickly he freed himself.

The sudden halt surprised her. "But—"

"Sorry, darlin'. I can't take any more."

She tried a pout, but that only made him smile with heated wickedness.

"Arms up," he said, seconds before he whisked her shirt up and over her head. Now in a rush, he gathered her close and kissed her breasts, drew on her nipples. Wherever his mouth wasn't, his hands were. She realized he'd opened her jeans when he easily slid both hands, fingers spread, into the back, covering her tush.

She automatically arched into him.

"Yeah," he murmured in approval. "Damn, you have a sweet ass."

She wiggled, loving the sensation of moving against his body.

"Nice." He shoved the jeans and panties down to her knees, then scooped her up and took the two long strides necessary to reach her rumpled bed.

He laid her down, then whisked away her jeans and panties. Keeping his gaze on her body, he shed his own jeans before putting two condoms on the nightstand.

Vanity realized in that moment that she wanted this to be different. For her and for him. What better way to make it more memorable than to give him something she hadn't given to anyone else?

He came down over her, kissing her hotly, all that bare flesh accessible to her hands, her thighs, her belly. She arched against him to feel more, lifted her thigh along his hip, and he pressed her legs open.

Knowing what he would do, she whimpered softly, and *oh, God*, when his fingers moved hotly over her, and then in her, it was even more electrifying than she remembered.

"I'm sorry," he whispered against her cheek, "but I can't go slow. Not this time." He started to move away, to get a condom, she knew.

"Stack, wait."

Breathing heavily, moving his hand to her breast, he admitted, "Not sure I can."

She nodded to acknowledge that. "Do you trust me?" *Please, say yes.*

Instead he said, "Maybe." Then kissed her again. "About what?"

An idea that felt so right in her mind, also felt very daring to say aloud. She moved a hand up his arm, over his thick shoulder. Mustering her courage, she met his gaze. "Going bareback."

He stilled, groaned, squeezed his eyes shut. "Good as that sounds, darlin', I never leave anything to chance."

"You wouldn't be," she rushed to assure him. "Because neither do I. I know you're healthy as a horse. And I promise I'm covered."

"Covered?"

"I won't get pregnant. I get the shot every three months like clockwork, I promise. I'm every bit as healthy as you are. And I *sooo* want to feel you and only you—I've been torturing myself about that since I first propositioned you."

His thumb moved over her nipple. "Yeah."

What he did, how absorbed he looked doing it, made it hard for her to focus. "You've been tortured, too?"

"You have no idea." He lightly rolled her nipple. "But the reality of you is far better than anything I could have dreamed up."

Now, see, how could she *not* love him?

"Stack." Holding his gaze, she drew him back to her, opening her legs so he could naturally settle between them. Locking her arms around his neck, she whispered, "Please, Stack."

He wanted to, she could tell, yet he fought it.

"Never, before right now with you, have I asked any man to skip the rubber. I swear it. You'd be the first—"

His mouth took the rest of her words, voracious and demanding. Without breaking the kiss he reached between their bodies. His fingers briefly explored her, petting, teasing, opening her…and she felt the head of his erection nudging against her.

She squeezed him tighter.

Lifting his head, his gaze fixed on her every small reaction, Stack eased in.

Moaning softly, she wrapped her legs around him, spurred him with her heels—and he broke, taking her in one powerful thrust.

Vanity cried out at the sensation of being filled, then cried out again as he began the slow, heavy rhythm that they'd both been anticipating for so long.

Keeping her crushed to him, Stack scooped an arm beneath her hips, angling her just right so that every thrust of his now slick cock stroked against her swollen clit. The feeling was so acute she tried to wiggle back, but Stack kept her locked in place.

"Shh…" he whispered, and then, with his mouth against her jaw, he added low, "So wet and hot."

"Ah…" Sweet pleasure sparked, then caught flame. *"God."*

He took her mouth, stealing her breath, heating her skin, driving her to the edge with the steady way he moved over her, in her. She felt every part of him, inside her, against her breasts and the insides of her thighs, her belly… The man knew how to kiss, and how to utilize a whole body caress.

Vanity tangled her fingers in his hair, locked her ankles at the small of his back, and let herself go. Less than a minute later an orgasm crashed over her.

Trembling, clenching around his erection, she freed her mouth and cried brokenly as burning pleasure escalated, peaked, then gradually receded in throbbing waves, leaving her quiet, boneless and replete.

Lazily opening her eyes, she found Stack watching her, blue eyes like live flames as he continued to gently ride her.

"Me waiting," he explained low, "until you finished. Now *that* was sweet."

She started to laugh, but he increased the tempo, rocking the bed with his urgency, and when he put his head back, shoulders straining, she watched him and concentrated on not speaking.

I love you.

The words burned in her brain, begging to be free. But more quickly than anything else could, they would drive him away when she didn't even know yet if she'd have more than the moment.

As his big body stopped shaking and he gradually slumped down against her, she stroked his now damp back, relishing the total connection.

Total for her—because she really had no idea what Stack felt. For him, it could be no more than any other hookup. Satisfying, but never enough to really hook him.

Sonorous breathing filled the room—hers and his.

Content with his weight over her, his rich scent enveloping her, Vanity hugged him. Minutes passed.

When he lifted his head to look at her, his crooked smile and mussed hair charmed her.

Tracing the line of his jaw, she asked, "What?"

"You." He nudged against her, making her aware of the creamy wetness between her legs. "This."

"What about me," she asked, then rolled her hips. "What about this?"

His eyes darkened. "That happened too fast." Taking her bottom lip in his teeth, he lightly tugged, licked and ended with a kiss. "I need more."

Her heart rejoiced, and tears tried to sting her eyes.

She blinked them away and joked, "I blame you," then watched his eyebrow arch at the accusation. "If you weren't so freaking sexy, I could have held out longer."

The corners of his mouth tipped up. "If that's how we're calling it, then I need to point out this body of yours." He kissed her shoulder. "And your face." His firm lips teased over her cheek. "And yeah—that smile right there." He licked her mouth, then sank in for a toe-curling kiss. "I'm only human, you know."

Vanity couldn't have rid herself of the silly smile if her life depended on it. "Oh, really?"

He nodded, all slow and serious. "Smokin' hot, darlin'." Then, without even a hint of a smile, he whispered, "You breathe, and I want you. Laid out naked under me, making those mewling little sounds—"

"Hey!" She went to swat him, but he caught her wrists.

"—and holding on to me so tight…" He lifted her hands to his shoulders. "Yeah. I didn't stand a chance."

Obligingly, she curled her arms around his neck. "I don't make weak sounds."

"You make honest, real sounds, and I get off on it." His hand went down to her hip. "How do you want to do this?"

"This?"

"I loved feeling you and only you."

Love. Hearing that particular word from him sucked all the oxygen from her lungs, making her mute.

"But now we need to tidy up before I talk you into round two."

Yes, yes, yes. Expression composed, she asked casually, "Round two, huh?"

His slow nod made her shiver. "Might turn into round three, or even round four." He stroked down her side, over her hip, to her thigh. "What do you say?"

"I like the way you think."

"No convincing?"

"Hey, you're still naked. I'm one hundred percent convinced." She kissed his chin. "Let me up, and I'll take care of things, then be right back."

"I have a better idea." He eased away, and as he separated from her he drifted a hand down her thigh, then rolled from the bed. "Stay put." Gaze shuttered, he looked her over, and his voice went husky. "Just like that works. I'll see to you, then check on the dogs, then I'll see if I can get you mewling again."

Dodging the pillow she threw at him, he laughed as he headed into the bathroom. Enjoying the view as muscles played over his back and his taut tush, Vanity dropped back to the bed with a happy sigh. Life, at the moment, was almost too wonderful for words.

CHAPTER EIGHT

AN HOUR OR so later, with Vanity tucked close to his side, Stack contemplated his next move. It was late. The dogs, brought in earlier, were now snuffling at the closed bedroom door. He was starved, so Vanity had to be, too.

But this was nice. Vanity close, her arm across him, her lips occasionally brushing his ribs. The thought of driving home to his own bed didn't appeal, so he hesitated to disturb the moment.

When her slender thigh moved over his, he lifted his head enough to look down at her.

Her eyes, still sated, a little dazed, stared into his. With uncharacteristic shyness, she said softly, "You need to make the first move."

"We're here, now, because you already did."

She lowered her gaze and hugged him more tightly, a direct contrast to her whispered, "And I'm glad I was so brazen."

"Me, too."

"But I meant you have to make a move…to leave."

There it was. The thing he didn't want to hear. He trailed his fingertips over her hip to her waist. "You want me to go?"

"No."

No? Turning slightly to face her, he waited.

"I want to keep on looking at you and touching you and smelling you—"

Teasing her, he asked, "You're saying I smell?"

She had gotten him sweaty. Got her a little sweaty, too. He liked it. When Vanity said, "Mmm," with her nose to his chest, he knew she liked it, as well.

Nuzzling against him, she deeply inhaled. "You smell so indescribably good that it's revving my motor all over again."

Idly, he cupped her firm breast. She wasn't overly endowed, but neither would he call her small. So often the word that best described her was *perfect*. "That's supposed to convince me to go?"

"That's to make you understand that in this, I won't be the strong one." Slowly she lifted her face until her gaze melted into his. "And if you stay, I might get stuck on you."

Though the statement made his heart kick and he automatically snuggled her closer, Stack wasn't at all sure how he felt about that. No, he wasn't ready to call it quits. But neither was he ready to commit just because he'd had the best sex of his life.

Control, he reminded himself. He would be the one deciding things, and they'd both enjoy themselves because of it.

He'd just about decided on what to say, but she beat him to the punch.

Eyes big and soft, she whispered, "Or you could get stuck on me. Either is possible."

The truth of that narrowed his eyes.

Hugging him, her voice wistful, Vanity said, "So be strong, Stack. Go now before I give into temptation, climb on board and steal all your options."

Climb on board? He breathed faster, his cock twitched, and damned if he didn't get hard again. "I'll go—after you give in." He helped her over him to sit on his abs. "After you climb on board." Hands on her hips, he lifted her so she could settle on to his already straining erection again. "That's the option I choose."

A FEW HOURS before sunrise, Stack awoke. He spooned Vanity, her petite, sweetly curved body fitting perfectly against his. He had one arm under her head, the other wrapped over her waist, then bent so he could hold her breast.

He surrounded her and liked it.

No surprise that he had morning wood. Throughout the night, she'd gotten him there again and again.

Over and over he'd taken her bareback, nothing between them, and damn, it felt like heaven. They'd taken a short break to care for the dogs, then another to grab sandwiches since neither of them had eaten.

Then they'd gone back to bed. He should have been satisfied, and instead every fiber of his being was only more sensitized to the sight of her smile, the sound of her quickened breathing, the heated scent of her sweet body.

The dogs, both snoring on the floor at the side of the bed, continued to sleep. But now, with his dick twitching against her perfect ass, Vanity wiggled and sighed her way awake.

"Stack?" she asked in a sleep rough voice that made him want to cuddle her, kiss her—and fuck her breathless.

He settled on caressing her breast. "Did you think

maybe I traded places with some other dude during the night?"

"Mmm." Her hand stroked his forearm. "Just thought I might be dreaming."

He wanted her again. But he also had a boatload of shit to get done before he headed to the rec center. One thought tumbled after another, and at the risk of spooking her, he asked, "You free later today?"

To his disappointment, she shook her head. "Sadly, no."

Far as brush-offs went, it wasn't the worst. But damn, he needed more time. "I could try to convince you."

She freed herself from his embrace, sat up on a hip and put her arms up to stretch.

Long, tangled blond hair hung down her narrow back, the tips just kissing the top of her sexy ass. Sleek muscles shifted in her shoulders and thighs. She was toned, not bulky, with a surfer's body. The remainder of a light tan seemed more pronounced against the paler skin of her breasts and heart-shaped bottom.

That stirred him, too. Seeing parts of Vanity Baker that even the sun hadn't seen.

Her movements woke Maggie and Norwood, and after they did their own stretching, they whined to go out.

"I'll get them." In a unique form of torture, she walked around her bedroom beautifully naked, collecting mocha-colored sheer lace panties, a shirt...and nothing else.

Before she left the room, she turned back to him. "I can put on coffee."

"That'd be nice." He usually didn't indulge, but it'd give him a few minutes to talk her into extending their time together. With only a corner of the sheet covering him, he folded his arms behind his head. "Thanks."

One hand resting on Maggie's head, she studied him. A little more breathless, she asked, "You drink it? I wasn't sure."

Hmm. Maybe he should have kicked the sheet aside completely. She did seem to enjoy his body. "I will today."

Her gaze jumped to his. "Will what?"

Smiling, he scratched his stomach, and saw her gaze track his hand in fascination. "Drink a cup of coffee with you."

"Oh. Right." Face flushed, she said, "Come on, Norwood. Let's go." In a rush, she fled the room.

Grinning, Stack took his time getting out of the bed. The pale yellow sheets were soft, and the pillow he lifted to his face smelled like Vanity, the scent rich and stirring.

And that, he knew, wasn't going to help him get the ol' John Henry to behave.

He made use of the connected bathroom and her mouthwash but didn't worry about shaving. He'd have to head home to shower and change before he went to the rec center anyway. He pulled on his boxers and went to look for her.

The hall bathroom door was closed as he passed it, so he went on to the kitchen. The dogs were still out, sniffing every blade of grass and running reconnaissance around the yard. The coffeemaker had just finished spitting and hissing when Vanity reappeared. She paused uncertainly in the doorway.

Her face looked dewy from a quick wash. She'd

taken the time to braid her long hair, and it hung over her shoulder alongside her right breast.

Against the cold tile floor, her toes curled.

Abs tightening at the sight of her, Stack accepted the truth—walking away would be tough.

Going back to treating her like one of the gang would be worse.

Like…maybe impossible.

He held out a hand, and she hurriedly stepped forward to take it. Drawing her in, he wrapped his other arm around her waist and kissed her good morning. "Even now, you look sexy."

"That's what I was going to say to you." Her fingers edged over the waistband of his boxers. "You can't expect me to be coherent if this is all you wear."

"Look who's talking." He dropped his hand to her sexy butt and gently squeezed.

She bit her bottom lip, stared up at him, and suddenly hugged him tight.

Not sure what had brought that on, Stack kissed her temple. "You okay?"

"I wish I wasn't busy all today." She straightened her arms, pushing back to see his face. "Were you going to ask to see me again? Or… Oh, God. Were you just making conversation?"

Insecurity didn't fit her well. "What do you think?"

She took the question seriously, then relaxed. "I think we were so good together that you want a repeat."

"Right in one." He turned to the cabinets. "Where are your mugs?"

Stepping around him, she went on tiptoe and got down two.

His gaze on her long legs and bottom, Stack smiled. "For a show like this, I'd drink coffee every morning."

She flashed him a smile. "Cream or sugar?"

"Black is good." Caffeine wasn't really in his menu plan. No reason to really blow it.

"Me, too."

Another surprise. He'd figured her for a cream-and-sugar type. Ms. Baker was one revelation after another. The one last night, though, wanting sex without a condom...that had been a biggie. Even now, he could feel the heat of her, how she'd clasped his cock, the sweet wetness as her excitement escalated.

"Damn."

While filling the mugs, she peeked at him over her shoulder. "What?"

"Sex stuff." He nodded at her body. "Just remembering."

She sighed. "Me, too."

He waited until they were both seated before he verbally circled back around to seeing her again. "What are you doing later?"

She wrinkled her nose. "Mostly working."

That didn't sound like too much of a barrier. He knew she helped out Yvette by working some hours at the resale shop, especially now, with Yvette a newlywed. "When do you finish up?"

"I'm taking Yvette's shift from eight to two. Then I have an hour to grab food and run some errands before I have to...be at my other job."

Other job? And why did she look away before saying that? She appeared...well, not guilty so much as evasive. "Two jobs?"

She swallowed her coffee, fidgeted and murmured something low.

"What's that?"

Huffing, she set her coffee aside. "Three jobs. Officially, that is. But I usually only work about twenty hours for Yvette. The other jobs…" She shrugged. "They vary."

"Three." Once again she'd taken him by surprise. Hadn't she claimed to be rich? Why would a woman her age, with supposed unlimited means, bog herself down like that? "Want to tell me why?"

"I like helping Yvette. She's my best friend. Like a sister, even."

While thinking it through, he nodded, accepting that. "She and Cannon deserve a week off."

"You and some of the others are filling in for Cannon?"

"Where we can."

"That's so—"

To keep her from calling him *sweet* again, he interrupted. "And the other jobs? What are they, anyway?"

Heat warmed her cheeks. Just then the dogs demanded to be let back in, so she was off the hook—temporarily—while they refilled the water and food dishes and took a few minutes to show the dogs some love.

It was nice, how easily Vanity accepted them, including wet paws, shedding fur and sloppy dog kisses. She took genuine pleasure in them, and it showed. In return, the dogs adored her.

When they went off to nap in the rays of the rising sun, he pulled Vanity into his lap. She started to kiss him, but he forestalled that by saying, "Jobs."

"It's boring stuff." She rubbed the backs of her knuckles over his bristly jaw, creating a rasp in the quiet morning. "I like you all macho like this."

"Beard shadow is macho?"

"Mmm." She traced his lips with one fingertip. "*You're* macho. And sexy. And—"

"And you're dodging," he interrupted before he caved, laid her on the table and took those boner-inspiring panties off her. "I have to wonder why."

Pretending to crumple in frustration, she fell back and left Stack to catch her. Which he laughingly did.

Then, to secure his hold, he rearranged her so that she straddled his lap. Nice. Enjoying the sight of her slender thighs opened around him, cushioned by his hairier legs, he almost got sidetracked.

"I'm trying to seduce you, and you want to talk about my work."

That brought him back around. "Tell me about the jobs, and then you can seduce me."

She perked up. "Seriously? Do we have time?"

A glance at the wall clock showed he'd be cutting it close. "For a quickie, maybe. But only if you quit stalling."

That must've been incentive enough because she blew out a breath and said, "Fine. But it's not a big deal, so don't make it into one, okay?"

"I'm not committing until I know what we're talking about."

Her mouth twisted to the side. Still hesitant, she admitted, "I model."

Yeah, he hadn't seen that coming, but given her looks and style, he should have. "You model." Why did she look so grave about it?

Nodding, she defended herself, saying, "It's harder than you think."

"Never said it wasn't." Though he really had no clue. He had a hundred questions but started with, "Where?" If she'd be flying off and leaving him, he wanted to know.

No, wait. He didn't like how that concern sounded, even to himself. They weren't an item, so she wouldn't be leaving *him*. Just...leaving.

Shit. *He hated that thought.*

"Just local stuff."

Stack released a tense breath. "Local, huh?"

She slid off his lap and went to her kitchen counter-top, then returned with a few mailers for stores at the mall. "This one is for fragrance."

The shot showed Vanity's shoulder and face in pro-file with lots of shadows, and she had this secret little smile. A dude was behind her, his nose in her hair. Well, fuck. Who would even see the small perfume bottle on the dresser in the background?

"This is for ice cream."

The brighter, more colorful photo showed her sitting cross-legged on the floor wearing an oversize football jersey and nothing else. She leaned back, her face tipped up to another dude on the couch who held a spoonful of ice cream to her mouth.

Again, who the hell was going to notice the name of the stuff with Vanity looking so hot in the ad?

The last was a lingerie catalogue, and even before she opened it, possessive, jealous heat churned inside him.

Then he saw the image—and relaxed. Or at least relaxed enough that he didn't want to chew the bark off a tree.

Dressed in loose flannel pajamas, the oversize top slipping off one shoulder, her hair in braids, Vanity appeared to innocently enjoy a lollipop.

Well, hell. It was better than slinky lingerie, but the fantasies would be rampant. He met her anxious gaze. "Suggestive much?"

"What does that mean?"

"You know exactly what it means." He nodded at the ad. "You're dressed like a tease, and I can see your tongue!"

"My tongue?" She looked at the image again as if she'd never seen it. "That's what you noticed?"

"It's designed for me to notice. Men will immediately think of blow jobs, guaranteed."

Laughing, she pointed out, "It's to sell pajamas to women, silly, not men."

He'd be willing to bet plenty of men would see it, too—and he knew exactly where their thoughts would go. "If you say so."

She frowned at the ad. "It's ridiculous, isn't it? I knew it. I felt so dumb doing it. But sometimes it's fun, so I agreed. It's the truth, I get easily bored. And until you, until now, I mean, maybe this one time, only now you're saying I could possibly seduce you again…" She shook her head. "Anyway, I usually have too much free time." She blinked at him, waiting.

Stack didn't know if she'd run out of breath or if she just wanted to see his reaction so far.

His attention went back to the ad. "You look like a wet dream."

Instead of being insulted, she smiled. "Really?"

"Yes, really." But damn it, he had no right to com-

plain or to tell her how badly he wanted to punch any
guy who saw her in the ads.

"I'm glad you think so."

Did she think any guy would be capable of thinking differently? "Third job?" Or maybe he didn't even
want to know.

Hands on her hips, she went back to talking at mach
speed. "I also paint. And yes, sometimes I sell my paintings. The proceeds go to different local charities, so no
way can I stop doing them. I have a few more to finish
before the next Furry Paws Ball and Auction. That's
where they're sometimes sold to help fund the no-kill
animal shelter."

"You're an artist?"

She narrowly pinched the air with her finger and
thumb. "Little bit."

An angel with a sinner's body who was wealthy
but worked at a resale shop to help a friend, modeled
out of boredom and painted for charity. And out of all
the interested guys in the world, she'd wanted him—
hopefully *still* wanted him.

His brain throbbed, as well as other body parts. "I'd
love to see your work."

Her mouth did that cute, twitching thing that eventually turned into a smile. "It sounds so official when
you say it like that."

"Say what?"

Making air quotes with her fingers, she said, "My
work." She shrugged. "I have some paintings I can show
you. Nothing serious. Just…whimsy." Snagging his
hand, she pulled him from the chair and started for the
living room. "I'll give you one minute to look, then you

have promises to keep. Or maybe I have promises since I did say I'd seduce you, not the other way around."

He went along, loving how her backside looked in nothing more than those sexy little panties that showed as much as they hid. When she stopped and gestured at the wall, his eyes refocused on the artwork he'd noticed before, and then widened.

No way. "You did these?"

"Yup."

He dragged his attention away from the artwork to better scrutinize Vanity. She had her fingers laced together, her eyes downcast. Modesty?

She had no reason for it. Putting his arm around her, he pulled her into his side and went back to the paintings. "These are amazing."

"Really?"

He nodded at the cottage. "It's personal to you?"

Her face lit up. "That you realize that is a huge compliment."

"I can see it in the way you've painted it. It looks like…" He searched for a word and settled on, "Home." Only that didn't make any sense. She claimed to be rich, and the cottage, while not exactly small, wasn't the home of the wealthy or elite.

Leaning her head on his shoulder, Vanity went silent. When she finally spoke, something in her voice told him this was important to her. "The house is where our gardener, Carl, used to stay before he died. I loved it. He always had something blooming. Even in the winter he'd grow bulbs indoors and in his small greenhouse."

She looked at the painting; Stack looked at her. "You had a gardener?"

"We had a lot of staff, but Carl was my favorite."

The way she stared at the painting, with memories in her eyes, told him things she hadn't said.

She turned her face up to his. "Carl showed me how to plant gardens so that something would always be in bloom. We experimented around the cottage." Her smile flickered with a memory, then went sad. "When he died, my parents hired a landscaping company instead. They didn't live on the premises, so the house went empty."

Sad. "You kept planting flowers there?" In his gut, Stack already knew the answer.

"Yes." She eased away and plastered on a very phony smile that didn't fool him and didn't reach her eyes. "I moved into the cottage for a while. My rebellious stage, according to my mother. But it was such a nice little cabin, cozier and warmer than our house." She looked at the picture again, then moved on to the next. "These are hybrid roses he helped me to grow."

Stack watched her touch the painting of a trellis that should have been run-of-the-mill artwork, except that…it wasn't. Not being an art critic or authority, he couldn't pinpoint exactly what it was about the roses. But he liked the way she'd painted the sunlight behind the petals. The image looked as though it'd be warm and velvety to the touch.

Like Vanity.

On the other side of the cottage painting was another depiction of flowers, these a mix of wild colors and patterns.

"We planted these behind the cottage, where my parents wouldn't see. They always told me wildflowers were weeds, but Carl would say they were painted by God's hand."

She looked at Stack, and something twisted inside him when he saw the sheen in her eyes.

She didn't cry. Vanity wouldn't. She had this thing about proving her strength that was both endearing and provoking.

"He said that about the sunrise and sunset, too. And stormy skies or clear skies, fall leaves or the spring buds…" Her smile, a genuine one this time, made him smile, as well. "Carl loved nature, so he had the perfect job."

Stack touched her cheek. "And you loved Carl?"

She swallowed, searched his face, then gave one short nod.

"You have other paintings here?"

Gesturing to the side, she said, "A few. In the basement. But—"

Stack took her hand and got her moving back toward the kitchen. "I want to see."

She tried to protest, but he kept her going. For the first time, he felt he was actually starting to know what made Vanity tick, and damned if it didn't fascinate him.

She fascinated him, in bed and out. He wanted to know all the complicated, contrasting facets of her personality. And he wanted more time to explore her sexually. One way or another, he'd figure it out—and along the way he'd learn all her secrets.

ON THE ONE HAND, Vanity was over-the-moon complimented with how enthusiastic Stack had been about her paintings. She hadn't anticipated that. In her family, people were expected to have talents. They had plenty of time to find and cultivate those talents. And so she had. No big deal.

She could paint, and she was good enough that people recognized what she painted. Good enough to sell her work for charity.

But she wasn't a true artist. She wasn't one of those who suffered for her talent, putting her heart and soul into her work. Nope. No suffering for her. She painted *pretty* things. Everyday images, like flowers or birds or, her favorite, seashells. Sometimes she went for more eclectic images: a half-empty glass of milk that appealed to her eye because of the small bubbles, the sheen, the… Vanity sighed. No, she wasn't a true artist.

But the way Stack had acted, she might as well have been.

She'd impressed him, and it had nothing to do with her looks, which made it so, *so* much nicer.

But on the other hand, he'd taken so long looking at her work that they'd lost the opportunity for the promised quickie. He'd run off—ten minutes late—to head to the rec center, and she'd hurried to get to the resale shop. Much of the remainder of her afternoon had been nuts, as well.

She'd been assigned to a holiday ad for a department store. She and three other women, two kids, and a couple of men had posed in designer clothes, with electronics, at a decorated Thanksgiving table setting, and even with some Christmasy stuff. The kids were adorable, the women aloof, and the men had ogled her. Now she was tired but determined to check on Lynn.

She knew Stack's mother missed the dogs because she'd told Vanity so when she'd called earlier in the day.

Now, as she loaded the dogs into her car, she wondered when she'd get to see Stack again. She'd planned to work on the paintings tonight because two more of them had to be turned in before Wednesday in order to be catalogued before the ball. But she really wished she'd worked up the courage to invite him back over.

She couldn't think of a better reason for missing work.

Luckily, the drive to his sister's apartment didn't take too long, because the dogs didn't do well in the car. Despite the nippy weather, she had to leave a window slightly open to keep Maggie from gagging. Norwood, bless his heart, just foamed at the mouth. A lot.

She and the dogs were all thrilled when she finally stopped across the street from the address Lynn had given her.

It made her a little nervous, looking around in the growing darkness of early evening. Tabby did not live in the best of neighborhoods. Leashing both dogs before letting them out, Vanity held tight, Maggie in one hand, Norwood in the other. She hit the button on her key ring to lock her car.

Good thing Tabby's apartment was only on the second floor. The dogs fought her every step, trying to bound this way, then that way, putting her in a virtual tug of war. Using her elbow, she pushed the doorbell.

Her luck ran out when f'ing Phil opened up. Shirtless, jeans hanging low, he let his gaze crawl all over her. Propping a shoulder on the door frame, he smiled. "Hey, Vanity. What are you doing here?"

Seriously, did he not see the dogs? "I brought Maggie and Norwood to visit with Lynn and Tabby."

"Lynn's napping, and Tabby isn't home yet." He leered, then reached for her face. Though she tried to lean out of reach, he followed and lightly brushed aside a curl that had half fallen over her eye. In a suggestive tone, he said, "Looks like it'll just be the two of us."

Norwood gave a low growl, and Vanity hurried to quiet him. She didn't trust Phil with the dogs.

Maybe she should talk to Lynn or Tabby about that? Or maybe, she decided, she should just mind her own business.

Maggie joined Norwood in the complaints, but Phil ignored them. Holding out his hand, he said to Vanity, "Come on in."

When she didn't take his hand, he clasped her wrist, tugging.

She strained away, ready to tell him to dream on. But with the dogs' leashes in her hands, she couldn't smack him as she wanted to.

Then the entry door to the building slammed shut, and she looked down to the foyer to see…Stack looking up.

His gaze narrowed on her, then shifted to Phil—specifically to Phil's hand on her wrist.

Wisely, Phil withdrew with alacrity, then backed into the apartment. "I think I hear Lynn. I'll tell her you're here."

Hoping to forestall the fireworks, Vanity smiled. "Stack! I was just missing you. How fun that we're both here."

As he climbed the steps, he didn't look amused.

In fact, he looked to be considering murder.

CHAPTER NINE

IN THE KITCHEN, away from his mother and Vanity, Stack stewed while getting drinks together. Phil, the creep, had wisely taken off.

When he'd seen him touching Vanity, he'd wanted to rip him apart.

But then, as his mother often pointed out, he didn't need another reason to despise Phil. Case in point, the barren kitchen. His sister put in a lot of hours, but most of her pay went for the monthly bills like rent, electric, insurance…

Clearly it hadn't gone for food in a while. The cupboards were all but empty. The fridge held beer for Phil, condiments and the remainder of the soup Tabby had made for their mom.

Okay, so he exaggerated. There was some bologna, iced tea, a bag of carrots. But not much more than that.

When he heard Vanity laugh, he leaned around the wall and saw both Norwood and Maggie trying to sit on his mother. She smiled and coughed and looked to love it.

Carrying two glasses of iced tea, Stack came in and told the dogs, "Down."

His mother was saying, "They don't know commands—" but the dogs had already left her to sit on the floor, staring at him as if awaiting further orders.

He handed a tea to Vanity, then one to his mother before praising the dogs with pets and ear rubs.

"He's a wizard," Vanity whispered loud enough for him to hear. "Probably put a spell or something on those sweet dogs."

"And you?" Stack asked while scratching Norwood's chin. "Did I put a spell on you?"

His mother watched with interest.

Vanity just laughed again. "No need." Then to Lynn, "Look at him! Like he needs a spell. *Pfft.*"

It was then that Stack saw his mother conniving. Her shrewd gaze bounced from Vanity to him and back again.

Oh, shit. That was never good, at least not for him. "Mom—"

"I know it's still weeks away, but would you join us for Thanksgiving?"

Vanity did a double take. As if she thought his mother was talking to him, she watched Stack and waited.

Stack sighed. "Mom, you know I don't want to be around—" he censored his language for his mother "—Phil."

"You can pull it together long enough for the holiday." She smiled at Vanity. "So, will you?"

Confusion lifted Vanity's brows. "Er...will I what?"

"Join us."

"Oh." Vanity straightened and glanced at Stack for help, but when he shrugged, she turned back to his mother. "I..."

Pensive, his mom asked, "Or do you fly home for the holidays?"

Damn. Stack hadn't even thought of that. But now that he did, he again hated the thought of her leaving.

He might not be ready to get too involved. But he sure as hell wasn't ready to say goodbye, either.

"No, I'll be here," Vanity said.

Relief clashed with concern. Because there were other things she didn't say, Stack asked, "You don't visit your family for Thanksgiving?"

Busying herself with a drip of condensation rolling down the glass, she shook her head. Silence made the seconds seem like minutes until she said, "I don't have any family left."

Lynn covered her mouth with a hand. "No family at all?"

Her smile small and wistful, Vanity shook her head. "It's just me now."

Well, hell. How come he didn't know that already? "Aunts or uncles?" Stack saw the banked melancholy in her eyes. "Cousins?"

Scooting off the couch to the floor, Vanity let Maggie crawl into her lap. She hugged the dog. "Mom had two sisters who never married and never had kids. Dad was an only child, as was I. They were all together in a private plane when it…crashed."

Drawn to her, Stack took the seat she'd vacated and pulled her back to lean against his legs.

It struck him that it was the same pose as the ad she'd done, minus the ice cream. "I'm sorry."

She slowly licked her lips, then glanced up at him. "Mom lived for a little while, but she never came out of her coma. The rest died instantly." She lifted her shoulders. "That's how I inherited so much. From all of them." She blew out a breath. "I'm the only one left."

Though she sat there looking strong and stoic, such a tragedy had to have been devastating beyond words.

She'd lost her whole family in one fell swoop. Fuck, he wanted to hold her. When he glanced at his mom he saw the same sentiment in her eyes.

So often, far too often, he took for granted that his mom and Tabby would always be there. Sure, they butted heads. Probably always would. Tabby was a perpetual victim, and his mom a constant enabler. The opposite of Tabby, he was independent enough that he'd never really needed their support. Yet if push came to shove, he knew they'd have his back.

Maybe it was time for him to rethink his attitude… especially with Vanity.

Nose scrunched, she turned back to his mother. "I don't know if Stack told you, but I'm financially set."

"I'm sorry," his mother said, then she blanched. "Oh, I don't mean I'm sorry that you have means. No, that's a blessing. I meant, for you to have gone through something like that…"

"Yes." She sighed. "My parents were very comfortable. I'd have eventually inherited from them, but I assumed it'd be much later in life, not at twenty-one. I'd never thought about it, not really. They had always ensured I had everything I needed."

And yet, Stack thought, that somehow didn't ring true.

"With everyone's estates coming to me, it was overwhelming. So many people, bankers and accountants and financial advisers, all wanted to meet with me." She swallowed. "And I just wanted to grieve."

Stack smoothed her hair, brushed her cheek with his thumb. "So you'll join us for Thanksgiving." Now that he was mending fences, he'd definitely be there, and he wanted her with him.

He almost choked, but he lied, "It'll be fun."

Vanity twisted again to see him, then laughed at his face. "Liar. I bet until this moment, you weren't even planning on going."

His mother did him in. "That would be my fault. I've showed far too much favoritism to Tabby. Stack was younger, but easier, and Tabby's always needed more attention. It was so unfair of me."

Odd that his mom would bring that up now, in front of Vanity. "That had nothing to do with it."

Expression pained, she said, "But you don't deny I've been unfair."

Gently, he said, "I'm a grown man, Mom. Not a kid."

"But you weren't always, and I'm sorry." She didn't wait for him to respond before saying to Vanity, "Until all that hoopla at the hospital, Stack had vowed never to set eyes on Phil again."

"I didn't *vow*," Stack protested. She made him sound as dramatic as Tabby. But he didn't want to be distracted with Phil's stupidity right now. He stroked his fingers through Vanity's hair and said, "I'm going to Thanksgiving dinner with my mom and sister, and you've been invited. I'd like for you to go with me. So, what do you say?"

Encouraging her, his mom added, "It'll be at my house. I like to cook the meal. It'll just be Stack, Tabby and Phil, maybe my brother and his wife. Not sure about that yet." She toyed with the edge of the throw blanket covering her legs. "We lost my husband six years ago, but he did love Thanksgiving."

"I'm so sorry." Vanity glanced at Stack, then back to Lynn. "I didn't realize. I'm sure you miss him very much."

Lynn smiled. "Yes. Tabby and I might even shed a few tears."

"They definitely will. It happens every holiday." But somehow Stack knew Vanity would understand.

"Those we've lost," Lynn said, "are especially missed at every holiday."

Vanity looked away. "It's…difficult to plan that far ahead."

Stack wondered if she preferred to be alone with her memories. Or maybe she was unsure of where their relationship would go. They were still measuring it in days, not weeks.

Lynn sat forward. "No one should spend those special times alone." Looking insanely hopeful, as if Stack had somehow deprived her up to that point, she tacked on, "Join us. Please."

Worried, Vanity glanced at Stack. "It's a family event, and I don't want to impose." Lower, like she thought Hawkeye, aka his mother, wouldn't notice, she added, "That wasn't our agreement and I'm not sure we…"

He wanted to say *Fuck the agreement*, but just then a key sounded in the apartment door, drawing everyone's attention as it swung open.

With twisted glee showing plain in his demeanor, Phil stepped in—and the dumbass had Whitney with him.

His mother gave a quiet gasp.

Too stunned to be mad, Stack stared at Whitney as he slowly stood, aware of Vanity scrambling out of his way.

Whitney looked exactly the same, like a brunette bombshell. Thick, dark hair hung past her shoulders and around her hefty rack. Blue eyes, as cold as her heart, zeroed in on him, and she gave a tremulous smile.

Smirking, Phil put a hand to her lower back, ushering her in. "Look who I found coming to visit you, Lynn. It's Whitney."

Whitney looked thrilled to be interrupting—until she spotted Vanity. Then she drew upon absurd indignation and suspicion, scowling as if Stack had somehow betrayed her.

Standing, Vanity took it all in, slipped her hand into Stack's, and said to his mother, "I'd love to join you for Thanksgiving. Thank you for inviting me."

IT TOOK LESS than two seconds for Vanity to know that Whitney, the voluptuous beauty standing poised before her, was pure trouble. Some women were like that, she knew. They enjoyed causing drama and conflict. No doubt, Whitney was the source of negativity between Phil and Stack.

And yet f'ing stupid Phil had dragged her in here, now, when Stack was only just reuniting with his family.

She turned to Stack—seeing six feet, 185 pounds of badass ability. But in that moment, she wanted to defend him.

Not her place. Not yet anyway.

Would she let that stop her? Nope.

Only after she'd hugged up to Stack's arm did she extend a hand toward the other woman. Putting on her airiest blonde bombshell attitude, she said, "Hi, Whitney. How are you? I'm Vanity." *And yeah, Stack is* mine. *So eat that.*

Eyes narrowed, Whitney took her hand. It'd be best

if Whitney had no clue of her backbone, so Vanity kept the shake deliberately limp.

That earned her a strange look from Stack.

"Vanity?" Whitney asked with a mocking surprise. "Odd name."

"Yes." Another demonstrative squeeze to Stack—and another "WTF" look from him. "It's funny how I got the name. See, my mama says I was a beautiful baby with curly blond hair and big blue eyes, smiling at everyone. She and my aunts decided that I was so cute, vanity would be my vice, so I might as well be named that."

Unimpressed, Whitney gave a malicious smile. "And are you?"

"Cute? I like to think so." She tipped her head back against Stack. "He certainly thinks so."

Playing along, Stack kissed her forehead and said, "Cute doesn't begin to cover it."

Vanity beamed at him. "I'm proud," she continued to Whitney. "But not narcissistic. Overall my worst fault is that I'm possessive. Very, *very* possessive."

Lynn choked but turned it into a cough that turned into a laugh.

Using it as an opportunity, Stack freed his arm from Vanity's grip and snagged up his mother's tea glass. "I'll refill your drink."

Vanity watched him stride to the kitchen. *You can run, but you can't hide.* She was onto him now. No, she didn't know the details. Had Whitney cheated on him with Phil? Betrayed Stack in some other way?

She wouldn't pry. When he was ready, he'd tell her. She hoped.

In the meantime, she'd do her best to behave.

"Where's Tabby?" Lynn asked. "Shouldn't she have been home by now?"

Very disinterested, Phil rolled one shoulder. "She's working overtime and then hitting up the grocery store. Past due, by the way. There's nothing here to eat."

Vanity tipped her head at him. "You don't grocery shop?"

The direct challenge—given nicely—threw him. "Tabby likes to do it."

"After working overtime. Wow, she's like super-woman. I bet that's intimidating at times, being with someone so strong." She smiled after delivering that barb.

It took Phil a bit to come up with a reply, and then, sounding like a petulant boy, he snapped, "Tabby knows I'm strong, too. She always says we're a good match."

Ignoring that was the worst insult she could give, so that's what Vanity did. Eyeing the other woman, who still hovered near the door, she said, "Whitney, did you want to come in?"

Lynn smiled at Vanity. "You're a very good hostess. I don't know where my manners have gone."

"You've always been a *wonderful* hostess," Whitney gushed, while casting a mean look Vanity's way.

As Whitney stepped farther into the room, the dogs moved to greet her. "No, go. *Git.*" Whitney swatted at them on her way to sit by Lynn.

"I'll close them in the bathroom," Phil offered.

"No," Vanity said, not bothering to hide her temper. "You won't." She held out a hand, and the dogs returned to plop down by her feet. "It's all right, babies," she told them. "Not everyone likes dogs." *Because not everyone has a heart.*

Phil stood there glaring at her—and again Vanity ignored him while listening to Whitney coo and gush—oh-so-falsely—over Lynn. Had Stack been in love with that vile woman? Did he love her still? She couldn't see it; it took little time in Whitney's presence to know she wasn't a nice person.

Yet Phil had brought her here for a reason, that much was plain. Did he expect Stack to weaken in Whitney's presence?

Vanity figured she should probably come up with a plan. She was good at plans, at creating them and following through. It's what she'd done when Carl passed, when she'd lost her family, and when her best friend left California and moved to Ohio.

What she'd done when she decided she wanted Stack.

If you thought things through, there was usually a way to make your goals happen. Plan. Carry through. *Voilà*—success.

She glanced toward the kitchen and saw Stack, his back to the room, his cell phone to his ear. The conversation was low, so she didn't know who he'd called, but she did know not to intrude.

Whitney, apparently, didn't.

Standing, she told Lynn, "I'll just go see what's keeping Stack." Then to Vanity, "Stay put. I'll take care of it."

"Really?" Vanity said, all sarcastic sugar. "Thank you. I'll treasure this moment of respite."

Confusion had Whitney searching the room for an ally, but Phil was nowhere around, and Lynn just smiled at her. Without another word, Whitney hustled away. Vanity watched as the woman approached Stack, as her hand went to his back—as Stack stepped out of her reach.

Whispering, Lynn said, "Ignore her. Stack is smarter than that."

Vanity nodded. She hoped so, but when it came to easy conquests, men could be ridiculous.

Lynn patted the seat beside her, so Vanity joined her on the sofa. So did the dogs. And unlike Whitney, she and Lynn enjoyed their company.

"Is there anything I can get you?" Vanity asked, then clarified, "Other than a drink, because no way am I walking into that kitchen."

"Pride," Lynn said with a grin. "I love it. And I like you. A lot. You say you're wealthy…?"

"Yes." It still embarrassed her a little to explain how easily, and how awfully, the money had come to her. She hadn't earned it. And she had no one special to share it with.

"You don't act like someone who is rich."

Her dislike of stereotypes made it impossible for Vanity to keep the protests to herself. "Have you known many wealthy people?"

Lynn shrugged. "No. But I listen to the news, and I see how they're portrayed in movies."

"It's mostly bunk. People are people, good and bad. Some poor and some privileged. But I've known really good people at every income level. My parents were… distant. My aunts, too. But I had friends who came from very close families. And some of my parents' associates were major philanthropists. Very involved, not just by donating money but their time also."

Looking more pleased by the moment, Lynn said gently, "I stand corrected."

"I hope you don't think I'm lecturing—"

"Not at all." She took Vanity's hand and gave it a squeeze. "But I'm starting to think you're one of those philanthropists."

Heat rushed into her face. "I wasn't trying to brag, either."

"I know that." With a final squeeze, Lynn released her. "I'm just tickled pink that you're joining us for the holidays."

PHIL STOOD JUST around the corner, out of sight but within hearing range. And he'd heard plenty, enough that his mind churned with ideas.

So Stack's new squeeze was rolling in dough? Fucking awesome. There had to be a way for him to use that to his advantage. Maybe with Whitney's help— although that stupid bitch had already allowed herself to be done in.

Maybe it had been a mistake to use her to irk Stack. Maybe all he needed was to get on Vanity's good side. She was so clueless, it shouldn't be too tough.

Clueless, but incredibly hot.

He'd find out where she lived, pay her a visit and see what he could work out. Very, very soon.

WHEN SHE HEARD Whitney laugh in the kitchen, Vanity made up her mind. She was a pragmatist but not a masochist.

Time for her to go.

Hoping to make a strategic exit, she whispered to Lynn, "If you need anything, anything at all, please, let me know. And again, thank you for the invitation to Thanksgiving. I'm honored to be included."

Then it struck her. The invite could be rescinded if Stack reunited with Whitney!

Just as quickly, she shook her head.

Stack wouldn't. As Lynn said, he was smart. Whatever reasons he'd had for breaking things off with the woman, they would have been valid. He was not a weak man, not in any way.

He wouldn't be easily fooled by Whitney's nonsense.

Watching her, Lynn laughed and patted her arm. With a nod toward the kitchen, she said, "You have nothing to worry about from that one. Stack isn't Tabby. He knows how to take care of himself."

Maybe. But Vanity sensed that Phil was up to something, and she didn't like it.

"Thank you." Vanity started to rise, but Lynn pulled her in for a hug. And it felt so good, so motherly, that Vanity soaked it up, lingering a second or two longer than she should have.

Deciding she'd imposed long enough, she thanked Lynn again, gathered the dogs and, being as quiet as she could with two unruly midsize animals, snuck away.

"HOLD UP." OUTSIDE the apartment, Stack saw Vanity continue across the street. He knew she'd heard him. Just as clearly she planned to ignore him. Rather than chase her down, he stopped, whistled, and the dogs, which he liked more by the minute, nearly pulled her off her feet when they turned back to him.

Vanity didn't face him, but he saw her shoulders slump in acceptance of the inevitable. *Got you now.*

The things she did, and the reasons she did them, often eluded him. She'd staked a claim in front of Whitney—a claim she'd probably deny—and then had hightailed it out the door the minute Whitney tried to get clingy with him.

As Stack strode across the street toward her, the wind picked up her long hair and made it dance to the side. She didn't shiver. She didn't move at all except for when the dogs tugged at their leashes, making her stumble. She just stood there, her back to him, waiting.

He'd have walked her out, damn it, but she'd waited until Whitney trapped him alone in the kitchen and then snuck off like a thief. Somehow she'd even kept the dogs quiet.

If it hadn't been for his mother alerting him, he'd have returned to the room to find her gone.

Thinking of Whitney's hands on him, how she'd stared suggestively at his mouth, then his crotch, made him want to shower.

Or maybe just rub himself all over Vanity's naked body; replace the bad with the good.

Yeah, that idea appealed more.

When he reached her, he stepped right up to her slender back, slipped his arms around her, and kissed the back of her neck that the wind had nicely exposed.

Now she shivered. "Wanna tell me why you ran out on me?"

One shoulder lifted in a halfhearted shrug. "I didn't run."

"No, you tiptoed."

She didn't deny that. "I just had to go, that's all."

He could read nothing in her tone, but her posture said a lot. "Come on." He relieved her of one of the leashes and led the way to her car. Many times now he'd admired her new-model Mustang convertible. The car suited her—classy, beautiful and far from wimpy. "That's an awfully nice ride for dogs."

Totally missing his point, she said, "Thanks," as she unlocked the door and, with total disregard for the buttery soft leather seats, urged the dogs into the back.

After the dogs got situated, Stack took her upper arms and pulled her into his chest. "Kiss me."

She looked up in surprise. Street lamps added interesting shadows to her face; the cold turned her nose and cheeks pink. "Here?"

Meaning it, he said, "Anywhere you want."

And damned if her gaze didn't drop down his body.

The effect of her interest was far, far different from Whitney's.

Stifling a groan, Stack urged her closer. "Yeah, don't get me going if you can't follow through. I'm in a bad way already."

Pleased, she grinned up at him. "You're the one who wanted to talk so much this morning."

He could feel her warming, softening, and it spurred him on. "We talked about you. Fascinating topic. How could I resist?"

Her husky laugh sharpened the ache. "I was offering sex."

Against her lips, he whispered, "Offer it again."

She stared at his mouth, teasing busy fingers over the neckline of his shirt, occasionally stroking his skin. "I want to."

Kissing her seemed like a really good idea, so he did. Softly, barely there. Except that as he leaned away she followed, then licked his bottom lip in invitation.

Which he accepted.

Drawing her in, he turned his head and fit their

mouths together for a prelude-to-sex type kiss. The wet warmth of her mouth reminded him of wetter, warmer places. His dick remembered, too, and now the unruly bastard wanted to salute.

Stack tried to think of something other than Vanity's body, but her hands fisted in his open jacket, then moved to his shirt.

Then under his shirt—and he lost it.

Someone beeped, and Stack lifted his head to hear cheers from the passing carload of high school boys.

"Damn." He kissed her lips again, the corner of her mouth, her throat. "I need you, Vanity."

"You do? Still?"

"Hell, yeah. We could have had sex this morning and this afternoon, and I'd want you again." *And again and again and again.* He held her face so she couldn't look away. "Let's put the agreement aside."

Eyes widening, she breathed faster. "Meaning…?"

"I don't want a stopwatch ticking in my ear."

Fascinated, she again looked at his mouth, then back up to his eyes with yearning. "What do you want?"

A complex question—but he chose to answer it simply. "You. Tonight and tomorrow." After that, who knew?

Something shifted in her eyes, there and gone before he could decipher it. Her smile slipped into place, and she nodded. "Okay, sure, that works. But…Denver's fight is next weekend, and then Thanksgiving is after that. Neither of those were part of our agreement, and they go way beyond tomorrow, so I'm not sure—"

Warm and soft, Stack pressed another kiss to her parted lips. "Quit keeping score, okay? Let's just play

it by ear instead of sticking to rules that never made
sense in the first place."

"Hey." She playfully swatted at him. "My rules are
what got me a date to the wedding."

"No strings attached, I know. I was an ass."

Clutching her heart, she pretended to faint. "You
admitted it!"

Now it was his turn to swat her—and he did. Reaching around her, he landed a perfect smack to her ass.

Yelping, she bounced forward and against him.
"Hey! That stung."

Nowhere near contrite, he rubbed the lush spot with
his palm. "Mmm. Want me to kiss it to make it better?"

"I do." Before his gonads could celebrate, she sighed.
"But I have to paint tonight. If I don't, I won't get things
done by the deadline on Wednesday."

"Tomorrow?"

Her gaze searched his. "I plan to finish painting in
the morning, then I'm working at the resale shop a few
hours. I'll take the dogs with me—I think they'll like
that. But afterward I'll have to run them back home,
and then it's my night at the rec center."

From what he knew of her, she never missed her
exercise. "How about I hang around after I finish my
workout, and I'll see you there?"

She visibly thought through several scenarios before
pulling his mouth down to hers. "Hang around, and you
could come home with me afterward."

Finally. He'd started to think she'd keep putting
him off with one commitment after another. He wasn't
insecure, and he didn't need her to put him above
other obligations—but he needed to know he wasn't in
this alone.

"Sounds like a plan." Her lips were so soft under his. God, he loved her mouth. *No more getting carried away on the street in front of his sister's apartment.* Wasn't easy, but Stack pulled back. "Okay if I stay the night?"

Happiness brightened her smile. "It'd be awesome if you did."

Now that was a reaction he could get into. "Awesome, huh? I promise to do my best."

Her arms went around his neck, and she hugged him tight. "Stack?"

"Yeah?"

"Whitney is the reason you despise Phil, isn't she?"

Well, hell. What a way to blindside a guy. First she got him thinking about tomorrow and sex, and then she threw out the tricky questions about the ex.

Taking a step back from her, physically and emotionally, Stack gave her a partial truth. "Phil is a lazy, unemployed, self-centered pothead who would use his own mother to keep from doing an honest day's work or having to face his own responsibilities."

Vanity nodded. "It's your mother he takes advantage of, using her love for Tabby against her. I get that."

Stack couldn't hide his surprise at her perception, or her unfettered leap into his family's private business.

Not bothering to temper his tone, he gave a cynical smile and said, "So on top of being sexy, you're observant as hell. A nice combo."

She ignored his sarcasm. "I'm observant enough to see that something happened between Phil and Whitney. And, given how she tried to sex you up in the kitchen, I assume she's—"

"Sex me up?" Stack didn't mean to, but he grinned.

She cocked a brow. "If we weren't being watched, I'd slug you for laughing at me."

If we weren't being watched. Reality hit like ice water, and he turned his head to see Whitney at the glass entry doors to the apartment building, staring at them both.

No doubt plotting a way to get him back in her bed.

The ice water settled into his veins. "Ignore her."

"Oh, my God." Flattening her mouth, Vanity accused, "You're still hung up on her."

Lacking any humor, he laughed. "No." He'd never been hung up on Whitney, but she had dented his pride. What he found most unforgiveable? How she'd fooled him. How he'd ended up feeling like an ass.

She let out a tense breath. "Well...good."

Stack chucked her under her chin. "That reminds me. I appreciated your show of clinging worship. But if your intent was to scare her off, it didn't work. In fact, I think she feels challenged."

Vanity's eyes turned watchful. "Not that it will do her any good."

"No good at all," he assured her. And still, Vanity studied him so long, he considered kissing her again to break her concentration.

"Okay." She finally accepted that with a nod. "So maybe you aren't still in love with her, but—"

"I was never in love with her." To keep her from digging further, he partially explained. "Whitney and I were seeing each other until I dropped in on her one day and found Phil there. They both claimed he was only selling her pot. Doesn't matter to me if she was buying from him or fucking him, neither is acceptable. She lied to me. End of story."

Vanity bit her lip, looked away, but then squared her shoulders and faced him again. "That's when you started hating Phil?"

"I disliked and distrusted the prick long before that. My sister could do better, if not for herself, then at least so she could stop dragging my mom down all the time."

Vanity tipped her head. "What else happened?"

Stack looked up at the dark sky. "It's getting late and you said you had work to do. There's no reason to keep rehashing old news."

Without argument she let him off the hook. "Okay."

That shouldn't have surprised Stack; she'd said from the start that she wouldn't pry. He glanced at the dogs. "You're okay with them still?"

"They're awesome."

Great. So he and the dogs now ranked the same.

Without admitting she was cold, Vanity stepped in closer to steal his heat. After a few seconds, she said, "I know you don't like lies."

New alertness surged into his veins. "No, I don't." Wondering what she was up to now, he put his arms around her and rested his chin on top of her head. "Did you lie to me, darlin'?"

"You don't have to use that silky voice on me."

Silky voice? The things she said… "I didn't—"

"I did lie," she blurted, making him go rigid.

He tipped up her chin. "About?"

"Lynn said I could return the dogs to her." She snuggled back in, her face to his neck. "I hope you don't mind, but I told her that you insisted she have at least a week to get rested up."

That was it? "I do insist."

He felt her smile against his throat. "Good, then I didn't fib after all."

It was ridiculous to keep her standing there in the brisk night air. But he wasn't ready to let her go.

"Stack?"

"Hmm?"

She leaned away to make eye contact. "I won't pry. I promise."

"Thanks."

"But…"

There were always buts. He waited.

"If you're lingering so you can talk to Whitney again, you can just tell me to go. Since we don't have any type of agreement—"

"Wrong." Damn, how did she so easily get him twisted up? "The original agreement is gone. Now we have a new agreement."

"A new one?"

Damn right. And soon as he figured it out, he'd explain it to her.

Eyes wider, she said, "But—"

Stack put his mouth over hers, kissed her quiet and then softly admitted, "I'm lingering because I wasn't ready to let you go."

She didn't look spooked by his possessive admission. Actually, she looked really pleased.

A good time to state his intentions. "New agreement—when you have free time, you save it for me."

Her eyes widened. "I wasn't seeing anyone else right now anyway. Were you?"

"No." With Vanity around, how could he even think of another woman? "You're it."

She looked startled by that bold statement. *You're it.* True enough for him, but would it scare her off?

Showing uncertainty, she licked her lips and spent far too long thinking about it. "Sooo…neither of us will mix it up?"

"Right." Truthfully, he couldn't bear the thought of any other man touching her.

It irked that she tacked on, "For as long as it lasts?"

He'd make it last as long as he needed. "Fine."

Vanity gave it quick consideration. "Fine."

He started to exhale in relief.

"But I have a stipulation."

Damn. "Let's hear it."

"A onetime thing would be no big deal. Anything more could get awkward if we let it. So promise me now, when it ends, it ends. No blame and no hard feelings."

So she already expected it to end? Until she said it, he had, too. With his career on the fast track, he didn't want to complicate things with a time-sucking committed relationship. But all the same, he didn't like having it spelled out. "You do seem to have a thing for stating the rules up-front."

She gave him a stern look. "I relocated all the way from California. Your friends are, for the most part, my only friends, too. I don't want there to be a falling-out."

Like a knockout blow, it hit him. Vanity had lost her entire family, then followed her best friend to Ohio. She and Yvette were close, he and Cannon were close. Vanity didn't want to risk losing anyone else, not for any reason.

Definitely not for a fling with him.

With a lot to think about, Stack opened her car door and waited for her to get in. Once she'd fastened her seat belt, he leaned down, cupped her face and took one more taste to last him through the night. "No awkwardness, I promise." How the hell he'd keep that promise, he didn't know. But he knew he wouldn't let her be hurt, so if it came to that, he'd work it out. Somehow. "If you need help with the dogs, let me know."

"I won't."

Always unexpected confusion from Vanity. "Won't need help, or won't let me know?"

She smiled. "Either." She started up her car, looked him over again, and said with ripe anticipation, "Tomorrow."

He nodded. "Tomorrow." He closed her door, stepped back, and watched her pull away.

Before Vanity had even reached the next block, Whitney started toward him. Cold inside and out, Stack took in her leggy, swingy stride—then turned his back on her and went to his own car.

"Stack!"

He wouldn't reply. She had nothing to say that he wanted to hear.

"Stack, *please*. Talk to me. Let me explain."

For a single heartbeat he hesitated, curious as to what excuse she'd give for showing up here, now. He had a feeling Phil had manipulated things. He wondered why. But he wasn't an idiot.

Vanity might act cool about him "carrying on," as she'd once put it. But he knew women better than that.

They'd clicked, and for right now, he didn't want to do anything to rock the boat. What he wanted was Vanity. Again. Repeatedly. And he wanted to hear more about her work, the loss of family members.

He wanted to discover all the different facets to her

personality, because so far what he'd seen had been pretty impressive.

Whitney had almost reached his car when he pulled away—leaving her without a backward glance.

He thought only about tomorrow. About Vanity.

About the fact that she was slowly reeling him in, and she didn't appear to be trying. More unsettling than that—he enjoyed her efforts.

CHAPTER TEN

THE LIGHT TAP sounded on her door just as she poured her third cup of coffee. Blowing over the top to cool it, she padded barefoot to the front room, peeked out the window, and saw Stack wearing a big sweatshirt, jogging pants and running shoes.

The chilly morning fogged his every breath, and he had this small, sexy, maybe anticipatory smile on his mouth.

The accelerating of her heartbeat made it tough to keep it cool, but she opened the door with a casual, "Hey, Stack. I wasn't expecting you."

He pressed in without an invitation, closed the door, took her mug from her, and then took her mouth.

Yup, anticipation. Had he missed her? She hoped so, because she'd sure missed him. Long into the night she'd thought about him, about him with Whitney, about his reaction if he ever learned of her machinations.

The lingering kiss swept away her worries.

God, he was better than the coffee, delivering a stronger jolt than caffeine ever could.

With small nibbling kisses, he eased away. "I needed that."

Eyes still closed, she nodded. "Mmm. Me, too."

The smile sounded in his tone when he whispered, "Hi."

She struggled to ground herself. "Okay. I could get used to that."

"To unexpected visitors?"

Her eyes felt heavy as she got them open. "To morning kisses."

Bringing his brows together, he said, "You want to clarify that as per our understanding last night?"

Lifting a brow, she showed her confusion.

"Morning kisses from…?"

"Oh." She leaned in and hugged him. "I could get used to hot morning kissing from a hotter fighter—"

He reached as if to smack her butt again.

Laughing, her bottom now covered with both of her hands, she blurted, "A hot fighter named Stack Hannigan!"

He grinned with her. "There you go." Then he pointed to his mouth. "One more?"

"With pleasure." She slipped her arms around his neck and teased, catching his bottom lip in her teeth, then licking his upper lip, and lastly angling her head to taste him deeply.

He growled, held her with one arm, and took over.

She was about to drag him to the floor when he said, "Much more of that and I'll spill your coffee."

Oh, yeah, she'd forgotten all about it.

He looked her over and smiled. "Cute."

"What?"

"The messy hair, flannel pants, naked toes and paint on your cheek." Between his fingers, he rubbed a hank of hair that had fallen from her hasty updo. "It'll wash out?"

"Hmm?" She pulled the thick lock of hair out to see it, and grimaced at the blue paint with flecks of yellow and amber. Quickly she tucked it behind her ear. "It will, yes."

"Toes aren't cold?"

"A little. I was downstairs painting but left my slippers at the bottom of the stairs."

"Got paint on them, too, huh?"

His grin charmed her. "Maybe." When she painted, she tended to get it everywhere. Luckily she also had a shower in the basement, and a utility tub for cleaning her brushes.

"I especially like this camisole." Bold as you please, Stack traced one finger around her nipple, sending a shiver all the way to her core.

Returning to reality, she inhaled sharply and stepped out of reach. "Did you come by just to warm me up, or for another reason?"

"Since you said you'd be working, I figured I'd take the dogs for a jog." Wearing a curious frown, he glanced beyond her. "Where are they?"

Uh-oh. Heat flashed to her face, making her warmer still. "Um…" Somehow she just knew he would end up irked. "See, I was painting and they were great, except that they kept wanting in and out, so when Leese called—"

With no inflection whatsoever—which sort of made it worse—he restated, "Leese called you."

Fascinating how his eyes darkened to gray-blue. She nodded. "Remember, he and I are *friends*."

He started around her for the kitchen—looking for Leese?

Vanity hurried after him. "He had the same idea as you! They're all out jogging."

Stopping abruptly, Stack kept his back to her. The set of his shoulders, his spine, showed his displeasure.

And still Vanity soaked up the sight of him.

Bright morning sunshine poured through the window, showing the blond highlights in his brown hair, caressing the breadth of those amazing shoulders.

She paused right behind him. "I'm not interested in Leese. Not that way."

"What way is that?"

She stepped closer to his back, slid her hands under his loose sweatshirt, up his bare sides, then crisscrossed them over his chest. She rested her cheek against him. "The way I'm interested in you."

His head tipped back. "Sexually."

"That, yes." She trailed one hand down, over those lust-inspiring abs that tightened even more with her touch, then lower still.

"Vanity," he warned in a voice turned to gravel.

But he made no attempt to stop her.

Through the soft material of his jogging pants, she cupped his testicles, felt him stiffen—pretty much all over—and lightly fondled him. "I have no interest in Leese other than as a friend. But with you... I hope it doesn't scare you off, but everything about you interests me."

After drawing three quick breaths, he retrieved her hand from his pants and turned to face her. He kept his gaze steady, his expression impassive.

She couldn't read his mood, and that worried her.

"If you needed help with the dogs, you should have called me. Not another man, Vanity. *Me*."

Tricky. She licked her lips as she considered how to explain without irritating him more. "The thing is, I didn't call Leese, he called me."

His jaw worked, his right eye ticked. "He shouldn't have."

Indignation chased off her concern. Much as she loved Stack, much as she hoped for a forever kind of relationship with him, there were certain things she wouldn't allow. "I want you, Stack. A lot."

He didn't book, and he didn't look alarmed by that declaration. In fact, the slight easing at the corners of his mouth encouraged her.

Best that she get things cleared up right now.

"But—"

His gaze went to the ceiling. "Always a 'but.'"

"—you won't dictate my friends to me." She didn't take friends lightly, ever. Leese, with his platonic caring and no-pressure support, was her second best friend, right behind Yvette.

Gaze clashing back to hers, Stack put his fists to his hips. "You can't expect me to—"

"Trust me? Yes, I do. Just as I trust you." Though he didn't look receptive, she pressed closer and knotted her hands in his sweatshirt. "You and me, like you said last night. I agreed to that, remember?"

His hands clasped her wrists. "What I'm remembering is that you threatened to ask Leese to be your date to the wedding if I said no."

Frustration twisted her mouth. "Again? We've been over this." Going to tiptoe, she enunciated sharply, "I do not want to have sex with Leese."

A cough sounded behind them.

Vanity froze, then dropped her head to Stack's chest. "It's Leese, isn't it?"

Stack rubbed between her shoulder blades. She heard

his amusement and his satisfaction when he confirmed it. "None other."

Vanity twirled around with a strangled welcome. "Leese, hi." He was now sweaty and undeniably sexy. Wind had tousled his dark hair, and his cold-chafed cheeks made the pale blue of his eyes more pronounced. Like Stack, Leese's cut body did amazing things for sweatshirts and running pants. "The dogs behaved?"

"They have more energy than I do." He laid the leashes on the counter and helped himself to a glass of water.

Stack tracked his every step with sharpened animosity.

Vanity nudged him, and when his gaze shifted down to her, she shook her head—an indication that he should knock it off.

He didn't.

"Why'd you call her?"

Leese finished the water, his throat working as he drank it all. When the glass was empty, he put it in the dishwasher.

Stack didn't miss how comfortable Leese was in her kitchen.

To Vanity, Leese said, "I let them into the backyard since they weren't ready to chill yet, and I thought you were still painting." He rested back against the counter, folded his arms, and finally addressed Stack. "I knew she had a lot to get done today. Just checked to see if she needed anything."

Match, meet fuse.

"That's exactly why I'm here." Stack took a step toward Leese. "They're my sister's dogs. If Vanity needs help with them, I'll help."

Not even a little intimidated, Leese advanced a step, as well. "If it was Armie who'd helped, would you be staging a pissing contest, or is that just reserved for me?"

"You tell me. Is there a reason you're different?"

Vanity threw up her hands. "Know what? You're *both* asses, and I don't have time for it. Let yourselves out. I've got work to do."

Ready to make a grand exit, she headed for the basement stairs, but Stack snagged the rear of her pajama pants and hauled her back. Wrapping her up in his arms, this time with her back to his front, he said to Leese, "See you at the rec center."

With his gaze going over Stack's firm hold on her, Leese nodded. "Right. Later." On his way past, he winked at Vanity, which made Stack growl.

Ready to throttle him, Vanity strained away. "Let go."

No reply. Stack held her, occasionally pressing a kiss to her cheek or temple, until he heard the front door close. Then, as the anger uncoiled, he nuzzled her neck. "I'm sorry."

Un-freaking-believable. "Oh, *now* you're sorry." Everywhere his mouth touched, her skin tingled—but she fought it. "You owed the apology to Leese."

"He and I will talk." His clever mouth drifted to her ear, making her toes curl. Using his breath as a tease, he whispered, "Not for you to worry about."

She started to relax against his big, hot body—then it hit her, and she strained away again, twisting to face him. "Oh, my God. You moved the pissing contest to the rec center."

Giving up, Stack released her. "He and I will talk, that's all."

Crossing her arms and tapping one foot, Vanity demanded, "About *what*?"

"You." The dogs hit her back door, and Stack moved around her to let them in. Euphoric at finding Stack there, they began a frantic yapping. Stack knelt down, and Norwood climbed into his lap with his entire body jiggling.

Maggie piddled on the floor.

Sighing, Vanity gathered up paper towels and cleaner. While reassuring Maggie that she was forgiven, Vanity swabbed up the mess.

Stack just watched her. "You're good with the dogs."

"But not so good with friends?" She threw the paper towels in the trash with more force than necessary.

Slowly Stack stood again. "You're under the misguided perception that straight men can actually be friends with women that look like you."

Looks! Few things could set her off as easily as that.

"Oh?" She swung around to face him. "So you aren't Merissa's friend? Yvette's? Cherry's? They're all attractive, so are you lusting after them?"

He rubbed the back of his neck. "No?"

Eyes widening, she gaped at him. "Oh. My. God. You *do!* You lust after all of them!"

Making a face, he said, "I don't go around *lusting* after anyone." Then he verbally backtracked, "Well, you, now. But only because you've pushed me—"

"Oh, poor Stack. Have I driven you to distraction?"

Curious, he leaned a hip against the counter and studied her. After what felt like an eternity, he said, "Let me start this over."

Gesturing grandly, Vanity said, "Go."

"All men have sexual thoughts about all attractive women who aren't related."

Her jaw loosened at such an outrageous outpouring of nonsense. She concentrated on her umbrage, rather than her heartache, because it seriously broke her heart to think of Stack wanting every other woman…meaning she wasn't special to him at all. "So you *have*—"

"Considered it? Yes. Ever thought to act on it? No." He didn't approach her. When the dogs tried to regain his attention, he pulled two chew treats from his pocket.

The dogs went nuts.

After a long look at her face, Stack tended to the dogs. "C'mon Maggie, Norwood. You guys want treats? Good dogs, let's go." He led the leaping, woofing dogs to the living room.

So now he'd just walk away without a word. Throat tight and heart heavy, Vanity turned away to face the window over the sink and concentrated on hiding her hurt.

Then, big warm hands settled on her shoulders, and Stack leaned around to see her face.

She ducked, avoiding eye contact.

"Vanity." His arms came around her for a hug. He propped his chin atop her head and for the longest time just held her.

Refusing to be the first to talk, Vanity stood there, loving his touch, wondering what it meant, and knowing she had to get it together.

Stack gave her another squeeze. "I'm going to try total honesty here, and I hope I don't dig myself in deeper."

She said nothing.

"I am friends with the ladies. Harper most of all because she's around the rec center so often. Friends only, because they're a part of our group. Have I noticed them as smoking hot women? I'm not blind, so, yeah. Have I ever given it thought? Yes. I'm a man."

She felt him shrug, and her eyes narrowed. She had to pinch her mouth tight to keep silent.

"But would I have ever made a move on them? No."

Bully for him. So while he imagined sex with all of them, he kept his hands to himself. Big whooping deal.

When she said nothing, he continued.

"For a long time we all knew Gage had a thing for Harper. Maybe even before Gage knew it."

Yes, one only had to see Gage and Harper together to know they were meant to be.

"For the most part, we've always treated her as a relative. Now that they're married, that's what she is to us. Family."

His hands went to her shoulders, gently massaging while he talked.

"The day Cherry showed up, everyone noticed, believe me. Cherry's stacked, and she's cute and likes to party. But Denver made it clear he wanted her. End of story. We all respected that, and none of us would ruin a friendship over a woman."

No, they wouldn't. They were loyal to each other, and Vanity admired that a lot.

Stack's tone went quieter, heavier. "We all remembered when Yvette left. She was still young. We knew what happened to her, what she'd gone through. And of course we knew Cannon had been there when it all went down."

Yvette, a sister of her heart. Vanity turned in Stack's arms, silently asking for comfort from the memories.

He gave it, gathering her close.

Yvette had been hunted by a madman, almost raped, threatened with being burned alive... Vanity shivered, and Stack's arms tightened around her.

She relaxed enough to share with him. "Yvette had told me about Cannon. She made him sound like Superman. Larger than life and very heroic."

"That about covers it."

"I knew he was special to her."

One of his hands dipped down to the small of her back. "None of us realized she was the one for Cannon, not until she came back to town. Then it clicked. During the years she was away, Cannon dated plenty. But he never settled on anyone. When he saw Yvette again, it was pretty clear. He wasn't himself anymore. He was... I don't know. Part of her, too." He dipped to see her face. "Does that make sense?"

"Yes. They're a couple." Together, they were whole.

"Part and parcel with each other." Stack's hand smoothed up and down her back, then settled lower near her hip. "Merissa is Cannon's little sis. That alone makes her off-limits. But the fact that Cannon knows us all so well, knows how we think—"

Indignation dug back in. "Meaning *what*?"

Fighting off a smile, Stack said, "Meaning we pretty much focus some part of our brains on sex 24/7. *All* guys. But it's just random thoughts. Not intent."

Having finally regained her aplomb, Vanity patted his chest. "I understand."

"You do?"

"Sure." She almost smiled over her deviousness, but

she managed to keep it in check as she said, "Women are the same."

His relieved expression fell in a comical way. "What does that mean?"

"Oh, please. You think guys have a copyright on lust? *Pfft*."

Brows gathering together, Stack levered her back the length of his long arms. "So you *have* been lusting after Leese?"

Swallowing her laugh, she managed a credible shrug. "I'm saying I've noticed his gorgeous blue eyes, that his body is different from yours but just as shredded. Heck, all the guys at the rec center are drop-dead sexy—in their own unique ways."

His hands fell away from her. "Un-fucking-believable."

"Oh, poor Stack. You were so honest, I wanted to be honest with you, too. I didn't realize you thought women had only pure thoughts. Were you under the assumption that we sit around thinking about knitting or shopping or doing our nails?" Vanity poked him in the chest. "You think we wear virtual blinders and only notice a guy's shoulders, abs or butt when we fall in love?"

"Butts?" Disbelief lightened his scowl. "You're telling me you moon over guy's *asses*?"

The laugh bubbled out. When she saw the flare of outrage in his eyes, she slapped a hand over her mouth, but it didn't help. "Muscled glutes." She could barely get it said around her giggles. "Mmm."

His eyes narrowed. "Now you're fucking with me."

Pinching the air, she confirmed, "Little bit."

Relief had him taking a deep breath. "Brat."

"You are too funny, Stack." She drew him down for a kiss, then hugged him tight and said, "But we really do."

Again he stiffened. Luckily her hold was tight, so he couldn't get away.

"You really do what? And, no, don't you dare start snickering again!"

She gave him another squeeze for good measure. "Women notice all the same things men notice, including a well-shaped butt."

"Hell."

"Yours is really nice. All the ladies think so."

He groaned.

"But for now—" she moved both hands down to clasp his sexy backside "—this ass is *mine*."

He grinned with her. "I have no problem with that."

"No, you just have a problem with me having friends." Before he could get his anger going again, she moved away and then pointed at him. "We're the same. We both appreciate good eye candy."

His lip curled. "Men are not eye candy."

"That is the dumbest, most sexist thing I've ever heard. Men are *totally* eye candy—especially when we're talking buff fighters. But my point is that, like you, I can admire without crossing a boundary. And so can Leese."

"Not the same thing at all. Leese would be in your pants in a heartbeat if you gave him any encouragement."

"I…" She closed her mouth, because that one stymied her. Would Leese be amenable to that? Sure, she admired him physically. But he wasn't for her, not that way.

Stack crossed his arms, waiting.

Rolling her finger in the air, she said, "Rewind. Do you think Leese is honorable?"

His jaw worked before he gave a grudging confirmation. "Yes."

"And an honorable man wouldn't overstep, especially among friends. Right?"

A pulse in his temple throbbed. "Depends on how well he understands the circumstances."

"Well, there you go!" She threw up her hands. "I'd already told Leese we were hooking up after the wedding."

Cold disbelief washed over his expression. His whispered *"What?"* sounded worse than a shout.

But given her own annoyance, Vanity didn't care. "And this morning I told him that we'd extended things. Believe me, Leese understands because I explained it to him." And he'd been happy for her.

Stack's eyes burned. "You gossiped about us to Leese?"

Retrenching a little, Vanity turned her tone reasonable instead of defensive. "Talked, not gossiped. He's a friend. Friends share things."

"What exactly did you tell him about us?"

A knock sounded on her front door, followed by the manic barking of the dogs.

Expression lethal, Stack stepped aside, giving her a path to the living room.

Glad for the reprieve, Vanity hurried her step, nudged the dogs aside, peeked out, and then wanted to groan. She rubbed her face, mentally braced herself, and opened the door to Armie and Justice.

"Hey, doll." Catching Maggie's collar so she couldn't get out, Armie bent to put a kiss to Vanity's cheek and stepped in uninvited.

Restraining Norwood, Justice followed him. "Vanity. How goes it?"

She knew Justice, but not as well as the others. She had to tilt her head back to meet his gaze. A veritable behemoth at six feet five inches tall, his dark hair hacked into a mohawk, his goatee untrimmed, Justice might intimidate most people. But Vanity knew he was friends with the others, and that told her he was one of the good guys.

"It goes well." She closed the door behind them. "What's up?"

"On our way to the rec center," Armie said, while giving the dogs a few pets. "Figured we might as well swing by to see if you need anything."

Justice held up a pack of colas. "And I needed to replace these since I helped myself during the football game."

Reminding the dogs of their fresh chews, she said, "Maggie, Norwood. Look what I have." Enthused all over again, the dogs gave up their adoration of the guests and went back to snacking.

With that accomplished, Vanity said to Justice, "I wanted you to make yourself at home." She prided herself on being a good and generous hostess.

"And I want to repay." He turned to head to the kitchen and tripped over his own feet. "Stack. Whassup, man?"

Armie glanced that way, too, then did a double take. "What the hell, man. Someone steal your favorite toy or kick your puppy or something?"

Stack's narrowed gaze transferred to her.

Oh, great. So he wanted her to explain? Fine, she would explain. "We were discussing life and relationships and the differences between men and women. Some of my insights have left him less than pleased." She pushed past everyone and headed through the kitchen for the basement door. "I'm touched by all this sudden concern, and the revolving door visits have been fun, but now I really do need to get to work."

Again, Stack caught her as she passed, pulling her in for a kiss she assumed would be quick and...wasn't.

Holy smokes, it wasn't.

When he finally let her up for air, he brushed her cheek with his thumb and smiled. "I'll see you tonight at the rec center."

A reminder, or did he need confirmation that she wouldn't back out?

Like she'd let a little disagreement throw off her big plans. Not likely.

"I'll be there." She forced one foot in front of the other, each step taking her farther away from what she really wanted, which was more of that heated kissing.

More of Stack.

The dogs rushed to join her and almost trampled her on the way down the stairs.

Her painting waited. She needed to finish it. She really did.

But without another thought she set it aside and replaced it with a smaller blank canvas. As she mixed a bit of acrylic paint, she smiled.

Yes, she and Stack had hit a few roadblocks. But like her, he didn't hold a grudge. Tonight she'd have him all to herself again.

Little by little, she'd win him over—as planned.

STACK TOOK THE colas from Justice, put them in the fridge, then pointed to the front door.

Wearing jackass grins, both Armie and Justice retreated.

"Care to share the details of your and Vanity's little chat?" Armie asked.

"No." He opened the door, and after they'd all stepped out, he locked it and pulled it shut. "How about you tell me what happened after the wedding instead?"

Brows up, Justice bounced his gaze from Stack to Armie. "Something happened after Saint's wedding?"

Playing it cool, Armie shrugged. "Don't know what you're talking about."

Right. Well, Stack was glad to enlighten him. "Last I saw you, Merissa was leading you away."

A sort of blindsided panic fell over Armie. "The fuck you say."

"Oh ho," Justice crowed. "You booked with Rissy and don't remember it?"

Armie rounded on him. "You don't say her name!"

Justice rolled in his lips, but his big body shook with silent laughter.

"And you." Armie bunched his shoulders toward Stack. "Don't start fucking rumors about Cannon's baby sis."

Ah. So now she was "Cannon's baby sis" when usually they referred to her as Rissy—a pet name Cannon had given her. Was it Armie's way of reminding himself of her relationship to a friend? "The way I heard it, Cannon's the one who told her to see that you got home."

"Bullshit. I don't need anyone to see any damn thing, especially not Rissy."

Especially not Rissy, because Stack knew Armie had it for her bad. But there was that baby-sis issue, and few men would dare go there.

Then again, he knew Merissa well enough to know it'd take Cannon's equal for her to be truly interested. Her brother cast a big shadow, and few could ever step out from under it.

Armie, however, had always been the exception.

The problem, beyond her connection to Cannon, was that Armie had an outrageous, totally warranted reputation. He was a sexual glutton who broke through boundaries with gusto.

Given his preferences for sexual variance, Armie had an almost fanatical avoidance of "nice" girls.

And Merissa was nicer than most.

"Saint," Justice said, again referring to Cannon's fight name, "knew you were smashed. He probably wanted her to play your babysitter."

Armie popped his neck. "I wasn't so drunk that I don't remember, you ass. I'm just saying, Rissy hailed me a cab, and I said thanks and goodbye at the curb. End of story."

Stack nodded toward Armie's truck. "She left her MO on the back window."

They all turned, and there, written in the dust on the window it said, "Rissy was here."

Armie stared at it. Justice grinned.

Rissy often left that particular message to let others know if she missed them in a visit or a call. Apparently she had missed Armie recently—or maybe she'd driven his truck home for him. Who knew?

Now that he'd effectively deflected their interest, Stack got them moving again. "I'm guessing the next wedding will be for Denver and Cherry."

Armie nudged Justice. "Sounds like the Wolf has marriage on his mind, huh?"

Grinning, Justice threw a massive arm around Stack, almost knocking him over. "That so, Wolf?"

"What's with the fight names today?"

"Avoidance?" Armie accused Stack. "Okay, got it. Well, I can help you with that. See, we can talk instead about how Justice prefers his fight moniker to what he got saddled with at birth."

Stack grinned. "Let's hear it."

Justice tried to protest, but Armie announced, "Eugene Wallington," with proper gravity for such a weighty name.

Balled up like a gigantic bulldog, Justice said, "That's right, boys. Laugh it up. But if I hear either of you repeating it, you'll pay for it in the cage."

Stack and Armie shared a look, then both burst out laughing. Justice was good, but he'd dropped down from heavyweight to light heavyweight because he'd hit an obstacle to the belt. Unlucky for him that Stack, Cannon and soon Armie would create even more obstacles to a LHW belt.

"Assholes," Justice muttered.

"Ah, Eugene," Armie said. "I didn't mean to hurt your tender feelings."

Relieved that they were no longer poking around in his business, Stack bade them goodbye with a wave and headed toward his car. He'd be getting to the park late now, and his good morning mood was blown to hell.

And still he'd enjoyed seeing Vanity. Even arguing with her was somehow satisfying.

He was in it up to his neck, and he knew it. Now he just needed to make sure everyone else knew it.

Vanity could have all the friends she wanted, as long as those friends understood she was off-limits—to everyone but him. He'd make that clear once he hit the rec center.

Then tonight, he'd have her again.

It'd be a long day and a slow burn. Good thing he had plenty to keep him busy.

CHAPTER ELEVEN

MIDWAY THROUGH THE DAY, Stack went to his sister's place. He brought a grilled chicken sandwich for his mother from her favorite fast-food restaurant, but also unloaded some groceries into the cabinet. Tabby's preferred cereal, pasta, jarred spaghetti sauce…lots of stuff that'd keep, as well as some fresh foods.

Tabby wasn't on a healthy diet like him. Sometimes he envied her the freedom of junk food and the abundance of sugary treats. He knew her sweet tooth well and loaded the pantry with packaged brownies, donuts, cookies and cakes.

"You didn't need to do this."

He glanced up at his mom. "Should you be up and about?"

Snorting, she pulled out a kitchen chair and sat down with her sandwich and drink. "I'm not an invalid." She nodded at the lunch meat he put in the drawer of the fridge. "Tabby picked up some groceries yesterday."

"I know." Just as he knew she was stretched thin and had to buy discriminately, or impose on their mom. Fucking Phil never contributed, but the bastard ate. "I wanted to." Luckily, Phil was nowhere around, so Stack didn't have to deal with him. "Tell her I did it for you if you want to."

"All right." She nodded at the chair. "Sit with me for a little while."

Stack glanced at the kitchen clock. He could spare ten minutes. Barely. He turned a chair and straddled it. "No fibbing. How do you feel?"

"Only a slight headache and a little congestion left." She ate a fry, then said, "Tell me more about Vanity."

He didn't know much more than she did, and what he did know he couldn't share. Like how Vanity had that sweet spot behind her ear that made her breath catch. And how her breasts filled his hands. How pretty and pink her nipples were.

The sexy sounds she made when he—

"I'm going to blush," his mom warned, snapping him out of the memories. She circled her finger in front of his face. "It's all there. Plain as day."

"Sorry." He grinned, unrepentant. "Let's just say she keeps me on my toes."

"So I saw. I like that about her."

Stack liked it, too. "I never know what to expect."

"Perfect!"

Never before had his mother gushed over a woman. Usually the opposite. But then, she always knew he wasn't in it for the long haul. Whitney had been his one and only foray into an actual relationship, and that had turned into a Grade-A disaster.

"You're a handful," Lynn said. "Maybe because you mostly raised yourself."

She did seem mighty hung up on that lately. "You did fine, Mom."

"So many times you told me Tabby needed tough love, not more coddling. Hindsight is a terrible thing, but now…"

Now she agreed? "It's never too late."

Her smile was fleeting.

Stack understood. Tabby had dug herself into such a deep hole, there really weren't many options for climbing out.

But neither did he want her to just sit in there.

"You're so competent and clear on what you want in life, it makes you a little difficult."

"And here I thought I was laid-back."

"I imagine it's tough for a woman to get a read on you."

Vanity seemed to read him just fine. "If you say so."

"It'd take a strong woman to win you over."

"No one is 'winning me over.' I make my own rules." Except that Vanity had led him by the nose through the craziest rules he'd ever heard of.

"Maybe," she said, "you need a little tough love, too."

When the knock sounded on the door, he frowned at his mom. "You expecting anyone?"

"No." She turned in her seat to watch as Stack went to the door.

Before he reached it, he heard the dogs, and he knew. He jerked the door open, and there stood Vanity, arms overflowing, the dogs' leashes held tight in one hand.

Over the top of her load, he saw her eyes widen.

"Stack! What are you doing here?"

He took a large box from her and an enormous tote bag with something big inside. "That's my question to you."

The scent of spicy chili rose from the box.

"Don't tip it!" She hurried in, closed the door and unleashed the dogs, who made a beeline for his mother. "Kitchen, please," she told Stack.

Lynn smiled at her while petting Norwood and Maggie. "Vanity. What a nice surprise."

"Am I intruding?" Pulling back the hood of a snowy-white zip-up, Vanity explained, "I won't stay." She pulled off mittens and dragged down the zipper. "I just wanted to drop off a pot of chili I made for you. I figured with as late as Tabby works, you might like it for dinner."

Stack set the box on the counter, then lifted the heavy tote bag to the seat of a chair. He started to open it to see what was inside.

Vanity slapped it shut again, then barred the tote with her body. "That's not for you." She kept her hands behind her, sealing the tote.

Interesting. Especially with the way her breasts pressed against the front of her turquoise top.

Holding her gaze, he asked, "Why are you cooking for my family?"

"It seemed the considerate thing to do."

That made little sense. Maybe his best course would be to confuse her. Given his own confusion, it seemed fair. "Chili, you said?"

Suspicious, she studied him askance. "Yes. And fresh cheesy bread. I figured that'd be easy to reheat." She leaned to see around him, saying to his mom, "I hope you like it."

"*Love* it," she said. "If I hadn't just finished the lunch Stack brought me, I'd get a bowlful right now."

Vanity beamed at him. "You brought your mother lunch?"

"Yeah." He had no idea why that pleased her so much. "Don't make a big deal of it. She's my mother, she's sick, and—"

"And," Lynn interjected, "he also brought groceries. The cabinets are now full." Goading him, she finished with a mushy smile. "I have such a considerate son."

"Awww." Taking the bait, Vanity stroked a hand over his pec. "That is so sweet."

Stack rolled his eyes. She did seem obsessed with thinking that of him—and with his mother helping her along in that misconception, he saw no point in trying to deny it. "You told me you had to paint."

"I did." Her cheeks warmed. "It went well this morning."

She was hedging about something. Stack reached around her, took the tote and held the chair for her to sit.

She stared at it, then him.

Lifting a brow, he waited.

She conceded with ill grace. "Fine." Abandoning her protection of the tote bag, she dropped into the seat.

Stack leaned the cumbersome tote against the counter, giving her a minute to regroup. "The chili smells good." He lifted out the big pot and set it on the stove, then removed the carefully wrapped loaf of bread.

"There's more for us at home. That is…" She darted an embarrassed glance toward his mother. "I mean…"

Unconcerned, Stack said, "I'm a big boy, Vanity. My mother won't faint if she knows we're spending the night together."

"Stack!" Vanity looked like *she* might faint.

Lynn laughed, then took pity on her and changed the subject. "So on top of your other many talents, you can cook?"

"I can read a recipe as well as the next person." She glanced again at the tote bag. "But I'm not really talented. Just…well…"

It was a unique thing, to see Vanity showing so much uncertainty. In the time he'd known her, and especially since she'd propositioned him, she'd been balls-to-the-wall on everything. She said what she thought without holding back, went after what she wanted, full steam ahead.

But now, she appeared anxious about the outcome of her visit. Did she seek out his mother because she missed her own? Sure, his mom was great, but he'd never had a date work to befriend her before.

That is, until Whitney had tried to worm her way back into his life by kissing up to his mom with fake concern. Back when they had been a couple, her interest in his family had been nonexistent, with the obvious exception of fucking Phil. But Stack wasn't stupid, and neither was his mom. They'd both seen through her ploy.

Whitney was as transparent as glass, but as usual, he didn't understand Vanity's motives, and that made him wary. Being near her always made him hot. And seeing her like this, so eager to please, left his heart full.

One way or another, Vanity kept him in emotional turmoil.

Her cheeks colored, and she looked again at the tote bag. "I, ah…"

"You brought my mother a gift?" Stack asked gently.

As if the suspense had been killing her, she went limp. "Yes." Then in a rush to his mother, "It's just a little thing. Well, I mean, the gesture is little. Clearly the gift is not." She gestured at the oversize tote. "Not too big either, at least, I hope not. I hadn't planned it, but then I was inspired, so I just went with it. I don't expect you to hang it or anything. And if you don't like it, that's okay. Seriously. But I thought—"

"Wow." Stack couldn't believe it when he peeked into the tote.

Vanity went quiet.

Lifting out the painting, Stack took in the impression of Norwood and Maggie. He had no words. The exact way Norwood's tongue hung out of his mouth, the way Maggie let one ear droop, the glimmer in their dark eyes, the barely suppressed energy and happiness— she'd captured it all.

Slowly, he turned it so his mother could see.

She stared while Vanity chewed her bottom lip.

Amazingly, tears stung his mother's eyes.

Well, what do you know? It took a lot to make his mother well up, and Vanity had done it…with consideration.

"It's beautiful." Hand to her heart, Lynn sighed. "Oh, my, just beautiful."

"Really?" Vanity laughed as she blew out a relieved breath. "I'm so glad you like it."

"I love it, and I know exactly where to hang it."

Vanity glanced at him, and there wasn't a damn thing he could do about his wide smile.

"I know the dogs aren't really yours," she explained. "But it's clear you love them and they love you—"

"If Tabby would give them to me," Lynn swore, "I'd keep them." She stared at the painting. "This is the next best thing."

Stack had no idea how Vanity had completed the painting so quickly, but he liked his mother's reaction. When she left her seat and went to Vanity, taking her hands and drawing her up, Vanity freely accepted her embrace.

"Thank you, Vanity. Thank you so much."

Vanity squeezed her back. "You're very, very welcome."

Stack met his mother's gaze and saw happiness along with the same emotional uproar he often felt.

Vanity had that effect on people.

Feeling the need to remove himself from the disturbing overload, Stack set the painting aside. "I need to get going."

His announcement separated the women, but they both continued to smile.

Looking happier than he'd ever seen her, Vanity said, "This was fun. I'm so glad I stopped by."

His mother laughed. Stack had the same reaction. How could Vanity consider so much imposition on her life fun? She not only babysat his sister's dogs, dragging them around with her nearly everywhere she went, but now she was cooking for them, and bearing gifts, as well.

"I want to go home now, just so I can get the painting hung on the wall."

"Not yet," Stack cautioned. "You promised to stay put a few more days." He carried the painting to the room his mother used. When he returned, Vanity was bundled back up in her hoodie.

"I need to get scooting, too." She picked up the leashes and called the dogs to her.

"You're coming to the rec center?" Stack asked her. After her impromptu visit, he wanted her more than ever.

"Yes, but I have to get Norwood and Maggie back to my place first." She hooked the leashes to each dog's collar, then allowed them to go to his mother for goodbyes.

When his mother stood, Stack took the leashes from Vanity. "We can walk out together."

Lynn stopped them with a hand to Vanity's arm. "Will you visit again?"

"I'd love to." As if they were old friends, Vanity said, "I'll call you tomorrow to see what works."

"Thank you." His mother shot him a look. "Since Stack won't let me go home and Tabby works all the time, I'll enjoy the company."

Holding up his arms, Stack asked, "What am I? Chopped liver?"

"You're wonderful, that's what you are. Now come here." She hugged him close, then made him bend down so she could kiss his cheek. Being sly while trying to act innocent, she said, "Maybe the two of you could visit together next time?"

Vanity busied herself unnecessarily with the dogs.

Shaking his head, Stack told Vanity, "Subtlety is not her strong suit."

"No," Lynn agreed. "It's not. So, what do you say?"

He turned to Vanity. "You free?"

She looked surprised, then more than willing.

Now if he could just keep her in that frame of mind.

"I'd love to visit again, thank you. My schedule is a little nuts tomorrow, so how about Stack and I see what we can work out, then one of us will let you know."

Just like an official couple, Stack thought. "Well, Mom? Does that work for you?"

"It's perfect."

It took them a few more minutes to finally get out the door. Each day the weather got more bitter, and now a strong wind whistled through the barren trees.

Stack watched her walk, enjoying her long stride and

the sway of her hips. "How is it a California surfer girl isn't shivering in this weather?"

She glanced at him with bright eyes and a wide smile. "I love it. It's so different from what I'm used to." Hands in her hoodie pockets, she watched as he let the dogs sniff a tree; Norwood chose to piddle on it.

"My parents were well traveled. We used to go everywhere. By high school, though, I usually chose to stay behind. It got too disruptive trying to keep up with my studies from abroad."

"How is that even possible?"

Whenever she discussed money, she wrinkled her nose—as she did now. "Dad hired private tutors. That was never a problem."

Stack was eternally grateful that she hadn't been with them when the private plane had crashed. It made his stomach feel like lead to even consider it.

They reached her car and she opened the back door. When the dogs immediately jumped in, she praised them. "Such good puppies."

"They're learning."

"They do really well with consistent instruction." She closed the door, then leaned back on it. "I used to love the travel, but I hated missing my friends."

Stack tucked aside a long tendril of silky hair that kept blowing past her face. "I bet you made friends everywhere you went."

"I was shier when I was young."

He gave her a "yeah, right" look.

Laughing, she ducked her head. "Okay, so I've never really been shy. Maybe stuck-up was a better word."

"I'm not buying that either." He kept his fingers at

her cheek, enjoying the smoothness of her skin, how she leaned into his touch.

"My parents insulated me from a lot."

"They were protective?" He hoped so. Vanity deserved to be well loved, and guarded.

"With some things. Like, I'd meet their business associates' kids, but they were different from me. The people I wanted to hang with, the guys I thought were interesting, they barred from getting anywhere near me."

"What type of guys?"

A grin teased over her mouth, twitching her lips as she tried to suppress it, then finally breaking free. Laughing, she admitted, "Musicians. Artists. A few athletes." She looked at his mouth, then moved against him. "Those guys were nothing like you. If my parents were alive, they'd like you."

He slid his hand inside her hood, cupping the back of her head. "What about you, Vanity? You like me?"

As he drew her closer, she tipped her face up to his, meeting him halfway. "I like you a lot."

"Good to know." He kissed her, but kept it light.

Patting his chest, Vanity said, "I have to go." One more kiss. "I'll see you soon."

Right. At the rec center, with all the men she admired around her.

But after that, she'd be all his. He drew a breath and nodded. "Drive carefully."

Stepping back, he watched her buckle up and then drive away. Thinking about all the different things he'd do with her tonight, he headed for his own car. He opened the door and was about to get in, but something—some unknown, anomalous threat—stirred the hairs on the back of his neck. He looked around, seeing all the long shadows and feeling a shift in the air.

Given the clouds, it had gotten dark early.

Eyes narrowed, Stack searched the surrounding area. He was still trying to decide if he should forget it and get in the car or go with his gut, when he heard the rushing footsteps behind him.

He turned—and dodged a fist aimed at his face.

Reacting on autopilot, he threw his own punch and connected solidly with a muscled gut. The big bruiser back-stepped but didn't go down.

Instincts prickling, Stack turned again and blocked a small wooden bat with his forearm.

Two of them! *Son of a bitch.*

Seething, he looked around fast but didn't spot anyone else. No words were spoken. Hoping his mother would remain oblivious, he didn't call out.

The men glared at him, their intent obvious. He smiled back with eagerness.

He didn't think this was a robbery. They didn't want his wallet or his car.

They wanted to physically attack. Why?

He ignored the pain in his arm where he'd blocked the bat, grateful that the blow hadn't landed on his temple, where it had been aimed.

Grateful, too, that Vanity had left before they showed up.

He took stock, rolled his shoulder, decided his arm was fine, and nodded. "Let's go, boys. I don't have all night."

The big guy charged in first. Stack kicked him in the face. The jeans were restrictive, but he wore his cowboy boots, and the shit-kickers were perfect for removing a few teeth and destroying a nose.

The bastard stumbled back, a hand to his face as he teetered and fell, splaying blood everywhere.

Stack regained his stance in time to brace for the full-body impact of the other man. They went down hard to the cold pavement, Stack on his back. But he had a slick ground game and knew how to land, how to roll into a submission, and in no time he'd locked up the other fucker so tight the dude couldn't move. Arm around his attacker's throat in a rear choke, deep under his chin, Stack squeezed while hooking the other man's legs with his own. He stretched him out, heard him gurgle, and then felt him go limp.

Knowing he wouldn't stay out long, Stack shoved the body aside, did a quick frisk checking for weapons, then regained his feet. The first man was trying to slink away, his zigzagging walk leaving a bloody trail behind him on the dark street. Several of his teeth remained on the ground.

"Not another step," Stack said, already advancing on him in case he was packing. It'd be a hell of a lot easier to disarm him at close range than be a sitting duck yards away.

The man panicked and tried to run, but it took a mere jog for Stack to catch him and trip him up.

Sprawled on the ground, the man tried to curse around his injuries. Stack divided his attention between both of the men. "Why?"

The dude shook his head. "Don't know."

"What the fuck does that mean?"

Half sitting, the guy dug a meaty fist into his front pocket and pulled out cash. He flung it on the ground.

"Fifty bucks to bust you up a little. Thought it would be easy."

Well, hell. "No, not easy at all."

"No," the bloodied man agreed.

"Who paid you?"

Glaring, he repeated, "Don't know."

Stack quickly weighed his options, then withdrew his second phone. He couldn't call Cannon. Hell, Cannon was probably still in bed with Yvette, round the clock if he had to guess, celebrating love and marriage in the best way—physically, sexually.

He dialed Armie instead.

In the middle of the chaos, he smiled, imagining Vanity's reaction if she knew he'd used, as she called it, the bat signal.

Before the first ring finished going through, Armie answered with, "What's up?"

Flexing his shoulders, trying to relieve the strain, Stack explained. He and Armie agreed on how to handle things. Armie was busy—apparently doing his own physical celebration with a couple of groupies—and once Stack assured him he didn't need to personally show up, he promised to send backup ASAP.

Finishing the call, Stack returned the phone to his pocket.

The guy on the ground propped his elbows on his knees and let his head drop forward. "Cops?"

"Naw. Worse."

His head lifted. "Worse?"

The second guy finally came to. He lumbered to his feet, took one look at Stack with the other man, then turned tail and ran.

"Why's he allowed to get away and I'm not?"

Smirking, Stack looked back at his quarry. "He won't get far."

The man's eyes narrowed, and given the blood on his face and swollen lips and jaw, he looked pretty hideous. "You just became my snitch, bitch." Registering the shock gave Stack little satisfaction, but it was better than no satisfaction at all. "You're going to tell me who your chickenshit friend is, and you're going to help me find the asshole who hired you."

"I told you I don't know."

"But you'll find out." Stack crouched down before him. "Because if you don't, if you disappoint me, I'll find you. You can trust me on this—you don't want that to happen."

It took only five minutes more before Denver and Justice showed up. Justice, the ass, stepped out of the car cracking his knuckles. Denver just looked his usual imposing self. As heavyweights, they were both massive, layered in muscle, and could easily inspire a healthy dose of fear in any man.

The man he'd already softened up was duly impressed.

Stack left it in their capable hands. He didn't mention his arm, which now hurt like a son of a bitch. He didn't think it was serious, but he'd figure it out at the rec center.

It'd take a hell of a lot more than a sneak attack by an unknown assailant or an injured arm to keep him away. Vanity would be there, and that was all the incentive he needed to prioritize.

Sex with Vanity, yup. Top priority all the way.

CHAPTER TWELVE

VANITY HAD THE DOGS settled in the main part of the house, toys and chews available. To keep them from destroying too much, she'd closed the doors to the bedrooms, basement and hall bath.

That left a lot of destruction possible, but she'd done all she could.

She stepped out of the house, closed and locked her front door—and became instantly aware that she wasn't alone.

Startled, her hand automatically grabbing for the mace in her purse, she turned and came face-to-face with f'ing Phil.

"Hey there." He smiled, nonthreatening, not too close. He kept his hands shoved deep into his coat pockets, a knit hat pulled low over his head.

"Phil." Vanity didn't move. "What are you doing here?" She looked beyond him but didn't see Lynn or Tabby. Odd. She didn't feel exactly threatened, but neither was she comfortably at ease. Few had her address, and no one who did would have shared it. Did that mean Phil had followed her?

"Sorry to drop in like this." He nodded at the keys in her hand. "You're on your way out?"

"Heading to the rec center to meet Stack." Just in

case Phil had any unruly thoughts, she added, "He's expecting me."

Nodding to acknowledge that, Phil said, "I won't keep you. I just… I was hoping I could impose on you."

Keeping her expression carefully blank, Vanity asked, "Impose how?"

"A small loan?" As if shamed, he winced. "I hate to ask, and God knows Stack would lose his shit if he knew I asked you."

Most definitely, Stack would be enraged. He pretty much stayed enraged at Phil anyway, but this…it was over the top, so much so that Stack just might take him apart if he knew.

Not that she planned to start keeping secrets from Stack. But she could be judicious in how and when she shared this particular exchange. And if she could influence things that made Stack's life easier, that improved his relationship with his family, she'd jump on it.

Heading to her car, she asked, "A loan for what?"

"I'm trying to find a job. You know that, right?"

It felt very unnerving to have Phil at her back, so she turned and walked backward to keep him in her sights. "I had heard that, yes."

"Well, there's this one possibility at a drywall plant. Decent starting pay and bennies. But I need some stuff. Steel-toed boots, overalls, a hard hat."

"The plant doesn't supply the equipment?" She'd never heard of such a thing, but, granted, she'd never worked at a factory job either.

He shook his head—and maybe, though Vanity couldn't be sure, his gaze went to her breasts, lingering longer than was proper.

She zipped up her hoodie. "How much would you need?"

"Five hundred?"

For boots and a hard hat? She gave him a look. "Phil, really, do I look stupid?"

"No! No, not at all." His gaze darted over her again, and he licked his slack lips.

Vanity had to fight off a shudder. What was wrong with him? She wore her workout clothes of leggings with thick socks and athletic shoes, a cami under a thicker shirt and her hoodie. Not exactly sexy garb. No reason for him to keep gawking.

"The boots are expensive," he explained. "And I'll need to buy some stuff to pack for my lunch, and gas for the car..."

How had he gotten himself so broke? He was a healthy, able-bodied man who should have had no problem holding down a job. If not the ideal job, then *any* job until he found the right one.

Vanity scrutinized him. It annoyed him, she could tell, but he kept his mouth shut. Motivated to make life easier for Stack, trying—just once—to give Phil the benefit of the doubt, Vanity said, "I'll give you three hundred." She opened her purse and pulled out her wallet.

Phil focused on her wording. "Give?"

So easy to see exactly why Stack disliked him. "Give," she confirmed. "If you're just starting a job, it wouldn't be easy to pay me back. Consider it a gift, with my best wishes that things work out for you." She opened her wallet, thumbed through her money, and separated the decided amount.

When she looked at Phil, his gaze was no longer on her person.

No, his slack-jawed look rested solely on her cash. What a cretin.

Deciding to push him, Vanity kept the money in her hand. "I trust you won't be smoking this?"

"Smoking it?"

"You enjoy getting high. I've seen it in your eyes."

He shook his head hard and took a step closer. "The place does random drug testing. Gotta stay clean."

She had her doubts, but it'd be worth the cost either way. If Phil actually got a job, if he started to contribute to his marriage, he'd make Tabby and Lynn happy, and ultimately Stack, too. And if he didn't, then she'd have a good reason to never help him again.

Vanity held out the money.

"This is just between us?"

She nodded. "Between us." For now at least.

He took the money, folded it and stuck it in his pocket. His wide grin looked less appreciative and more predatory. "Thanks, hon."

"Let's eschew the endearments, okay?"

One eye tightened. "Huh?"

"I barely know you. We're not friends, and I'm definitely not your hon." Firm, and very clear, she explained things to him. "Understand that I'm giving you the money for Tabby, because I know it would relieve her burden for you to have a job."

"Right, right. Yeah. It'll be a big help." He hooked his thumbs in his pockets and struck a leisurely stance. Sleazy to the core, he angled toward her. "Whatever I can do to repay the favor…"

"Not necessary." Seriously, Phil absolutely had noth-

ing she wanted. She got in the car. "Good luck with
the job. I hope it all works out for you." Done with the
small talk, anxious to see Stack, she put the car in gear
and drove away.

A glance in her side-view mirror showed Phil still
standing on the curb, now looking at her house.

She had a very bad feeling about this. About him.

Being the proactive sort, Vanity made up her mind
about what to do.

On her way to the rec center, she made a few calls.

WITH HIS FOREARM wrapped in ice, Stack stood before
the heavy bag practicing kicks. Sweat soaked the front
and back of his shirt, the waistband of his sweatpants,
his neck and temples. He'd worked on kicks, and now
concentrated on a reverse roundhouse kick.

Between the jog in the morning, the visit to his
mother, and now his extended workout, he'd gone
through a whole laundry load of clothes.

When the bell on the door pinged, he immediately
looked up. Cannon and Yvette strolled in. They were
immediately mobbed, ribbed, hugged and all around
congratulated. Again.

Cannon pulled off his knit hat, ran a hand through
his hair, then tugged it on again. Glowing like a woman
who'd just rolled off an orgasm, Yvette smiled dream-
ily at him.

Stack hoped like hell they weren't here because of
him.

Stepping away from the heavy bag, he mopped off
the sweat and waited for Cannon to wade through his
always present fan club. After about five minutes, he
made his way to Stack.

"You should be at home," Stack told him.

"In bed, I know." Cannon grinned. "We went out for groceries and decided to drop in for a bit."

"Shit. Denver told you, didn't he?"

Without a word, Cannon reached for Stack's arm and removed the taped-on ice pack.

"It's not broke."

"Damn." Cannon checked it over, turned his wrist, manipulated his elbow. No, he wasn't a doctor, but he was the most experienced of the bunch and recognized a lot from his own injuries. "How's it feel?"

"Before or after you decided to work it over?"

Cannon flashed him a grin. "So you'll live. Any idea why you were jumped?"

"Not yet. Word is out." He explained what he knew and what had been done. "The jerk knows how to contact me once he finds out anything."

"Think he will?"

"I checked his ID so I know where he lives. And I didn't turn him in to the cops." Stack upended a water bottle, quenching his thirst, then wiping his mouth. "I made it clear it was in his best interest to be helpful, then Denver and Justice reinforced the message."

"I almost feel sorry for the dumbass." Brow raised, he glanced at Stack's arm. "Or maybe not."

Without asking, Cannon knew no one had used unnecessary force against the thug. It'd be a bitch move for Stack to walk away, only to have two other hulks step in and pulverize an already beat-up guy. But he also knew they would have impressed upon the goon how important it was to do as told, along with cluing him in on what they considered good intel, and how and where to share it.

Denver joined them, then Leese. They talked a little longer, coordinating plans. They looked out for each other, and while Stack knew he could take care of himself, if fighters were suddenly targets, everyone needed to be on guard.

When the door chimed again, he looked up and met Vanity's gaze. Nice that she'd immediately sought him out with her eyes.

"Here." He handed the water bottle to Leese and, being sure to draw everyone's attention first, strode over to her.

"Stack." Her smile flickered with uncertainty. "What's—"

Dipping in for a thorough kiss, he stole her gasp, nudged her lips apart, and eased his tongue in to tease. Because he was sweaty, he kept his body from touching hers. But that didn't mean he had to make the kiss quick, or easy.

She tasted so good, he almost forgot the purpose of this display: making it clear to one and all that she was his, and only his.

When she reached for him, her small, cool hands coming to his hot, damp shoulders, he ended things.

Her eyes, unfocused, stared at him as she licked her lips.

Such an invitation. "Hey."

Took her a second, and she nodded. "Hey." She glanced around, and a sly smile replaced some of the dazed lust. "Was that for the spectators?"

No reason to lie about it. "The male spectators, yeah."

"Wow." She pushed back her hoodie, her mouth still playing with a smile. "I'm flattered."

Flattered? "Come again?"

Her eyes went heavy, her smile sly. "Oh, I will. To-night." She went on tiptoe to peck his mouth. "With you."

Damn. Way to turn the tables on him.

"So." As she shed the hoodie, she eyed his arm. "What happened?"

"Long, boring story." The last thing he wanted was her involved. "It's fine."

"You're sure?"

She brushed her fingertips over his forearm in a butterfly caress…that he felt in his dick. "Yeah."

"It's awfully colorful."

"Just bruising. No big deal." He expected her to fuss, but he should have known better. So far Vanity had never done the expected.

"I'm glad." She checked the big clock on the wall. "Thanks for the wonderful greeting, but now I need to get my gear stored and get to it." She patted his chest and walked off.

Stack stood there, admiring the departing shot of her ass in the leggings—until he realized a lot of other people were watching, too. He mean-mugged some new guys, then Brand and Miles, and lastly Leese.

Leese just grinned, the dick.

An hour later, Vanity was finishing up on the elliptical when she got a call. She turned off the machine and stepped off before retrieving her cell from a wrist strap.

One-handed, she fetched a towel and patted her face while listening to whoever had called. When her brows pulled together, and she separated from the crowd, moving to a corner on the other side of the registration desk, he called it quits on his own workout and joined her.

She didn't appear bothered that he'd invaded her space or that he was listening in.

Smiling at him, she spoke into the cell, saying, "Could I think about it, please?...Tomorrow? That soon...All right. I'll call you back in the morning... Yes, thank you... Okay, you, too." She disconnected and put the phone back in the wrist holder. "You all done?"

Curiosity gnawed on him. "Yeah. I'm supposed to help teach the self-defense class, though." Mostly he'd volunteered since Vanity was taking the class.

"With that arm," she said, appearing concerned, "you should maybe sit it out."

"It's fine." He got her back on track. "Important call?"

"What? Oh, no. Not important. Just..." She bit her lip. "Another offer for modeling."

"Yeah?" It distracted him, seeing how good she looked sweaty. She'd braided her long hair, but loose wisps clung to her damp neck and temples. Every breath filled his head with her intensified scent. "Where at this time?"

She didn't meet his gaze. "Remember that pajama ad?"

"At the lingerie store." He didn't like where this was going. "Yeah?"

She cleared her throat. "Right. Same place."

A sort of edgy possessiveness crawled over him. "More pajamas?" He hoped.

"Not this time, no." Somewhat defiantly, she met his gaze. "This would be tasteful underthings."

"Underthings?"

Hand in the air, she gestured. "Yeah, you know. Bras and panties."

Stack just stared at her.

"It's a new line of animal prints. Really pretty."

There were no words. Vanity in slinky little panties in a magazine where everyone could see her? He shook his head but stayed silent, unsure what he should or could say.

She slipped in closer, and now that they were both sweaty, he didn't mind. "Do you think I should—"

"No."

"No?"

Damn it, he didn't want to admit how much it mattered to him. "Do you want to?"

"I'm not sure. I enjoy modeling. It's fun." She scrunched up her nose. "But I have to admit, I'm a little squeamish about everyone seeing me in a bra and panties. I mean, it'd cover as much as a bikini, and being from California, I wore a lot of bikinis. But still…"

He nodded, agreed. "Still."

Looking beyond him at the crowded rec center, she said, "You think the guys here—"

"Yes." And then he added, "Definitely."

"You didn't let me finish."

"Didn't need to." The dam burst, and somehow, he couldn't get himself to shut up. "No, you shouldn't model lingerie even though—maybe especially because—you'll look amazing in it, and, yes, every dude here would know, would have a copy of the mag, and would probably keep it under his fucking pillow so he could—"

She smashed a hand over his mouth, red-faced but laughing.

Stack bit her finger, making her jump. Holding her face, he leaned down, his forehead to hers. "You're about the hottest woman I've ever known."

"Looks shouldn't matter so much."

"They don't." Not entirely, anyway. "When it comes to you, I like the whole package."

Pleased, she smiled up at him.

"But that doesn't change the fact that you're gorgeous." He pressed his mouth to hers for a firm kiss. "I don't mean to overstep, but damn, darlin', I don't want every guy here ogling you."

"Honestly, I don't really want that either."

Thank God. "So you'll skip the panty pics?"

Laughing, she nodded. "Yes, I'll skip them. I wasn't all that enthusiastic about it anyway."

Stack gave quick thought to leaving the rec center early. He wanted her. Right now. He was considering ways to convince her when the front door opened.

Standing in the doorway, holding it open and letting in a gust of cold air, Armie spoke to two women. They were both cute, one with short, spiky red hair, the other a blonde with purple streaks. "Go on now," Armie told the ladies. "I have work to do."

"You promise you'll show up?"

"Yeah, yeah." He started to ease the door shut on them. "I'll be there."

"Tomorrow, eight o'clock."

He tapped his temple. "Locked away the details. I won't forget." The door was almost closed.

"She's going to love it! Thank you!"

"My pleasure." The door finally shut.

Through the glass, both women blew him kisses. Laughing, Armie turned, and realized Stack and Vanity had been listening in.

"Hey, Stack, Vee. What's up?"

Surprised, Vanity said, "You changed your hair!"

Until she mentioned it, Stack hadn't noticed. But yeah, Armie's usually bleached hair was closer to a real color now. Sort of a light brown.

Armie ran a hand over his head. "Yeah, I was due a change." He bounced his gaze between them. "Everything okay?" He looked at Stack's arm. "You're slipping, man. Why'd you let him hit you?"

Before Stack could warn Armie to shut it, it was already out there, and Vanity slowly pivoted to face him.

Stalling, Stack said, "Those girls follow you home like stray puppies?"

"Something like that." He grinned. "I tried to shake them off, but they were determined."

"To invite you to an orgy?"

Armie laughed. "Nah." Grin sheepish, he rubbed the back of his neck. "Their friend is getting married, so they're throwing her a bridal shower. I'll be the entertainment."

Stack wanted to praise him for that outrageous announcement because it reclaimed Vanity's attention.

Eyes wide, she pivoted back to Armie. "You're serious?"

"Yeah, apparently I'm going to offer lap dances, maybe strip or something. Not sure what all the plans are." Shaking his head, he laughed again. "But whatever. Sounded fun."

"You're nuts." Stack knew Armie was up for just about anything, so he shouldn't have been surprised. But that was over the top even for him.

Armie glanced at Vanity. "You sticking around?"

"I'm taking the self-defense class."

"Great, then let me borrow Stack a minute, 'kay? You can catch up with him when the class starts."

Not fooled, Vanity pointed at Stack. "You'll explain later." Then she headed down the hallway, taking advantage of the five minutes remaining before the class.

Soon as she was out of hearing range, Stack said, "Big mouth."

"How was I to know it's a secret? You're standing there all purple and swollen, and it's not like the girl is blind." He frowned at Stack's arm, grimacing for him. "Why are you dodging the truth, anyway?"

Stack shook his head, unsure how to answer. "I just didn't want her involved."

"Oh, really? You look plenty involved to me."

He shrugged. "Getting there. Maybe." Stack didn't even know what he wanted, so he sure as hell couldn't be sure of Vanity's intent. A fling? Convenience? Or more? "She has a way of plowing in full-steam ahead. It's bad enough when it's my family, but I don't want her mixed up in this."

"Did you tell that to Leese?"

"No, why would I?"

Armie tipped his chin toward the room. "Because they're friends—and he's chatting her up right now."

Trying for the tone of casual conversation, Vanity asked offhand, "So how did Stack hurt his arm?"

Leese barely smiled while collecting his equipment and stuffing it into his gym bag. "Did you try asking Stack?"

Okay, so Leese wasn't fooled. "I have a feeling he won't tell me."

"So you want me to be a snitch?"

She lightly punched his arm. "You're my wingman. You're supposed to back me up."

He finished with the bag and straightened, looking down at her with his pale blue eyes. "Not this time. Case you're unaware, Stack is staring daggers at us both."

She stiffened but didn't turn to see. Lowering her voice, even though she knew he couldn't hear, she asked, "Is he coming this way?"

"Nope. Just staring."

Her shoulders relaxed. "I'm glad he has enough sense not to cause a scene."

"And why would he cause a scene about me?" Leese studied her. "What did you tell him after I left this morning?"

Flapping a hand and struggling against the urge to glance guiltily at Stack, Vanity said, "We agreed that you were an honorable man. He knows there's nothing between us."

Dryly, Leese laughed. "Let me clue you in about men. He might know we're not involved, but he won't like it all the same."

Her heart plummeted. "Does that mean you're going to stop being my friend?"

"Never that. Anytime you need me, I'll be around." He tugged at her braid. "But it does mean you might want to consider making Stack your wingman, at least whenever you can."

Probably very good advice. "Thank you."

As Leese walked away, he lifted a hand, letting her know he accepted her gratitude.

Now Vanity turned to see Stack. He stood alone, his expression dark and contemplative. About what?

With the class ready to start, she blew Stack a kiss and got in line. And though she did her best to listen as instructions were given, part of her mind stayed focused on Stack.

She'd played an uncertain game to win him over. Did his possessiveness mean it was working—or would she drive him away by being herself?

CHAPTER THIRTEEN

AS STACK DIRECTED the class of women, he tried to ensure he didn't pay more attention to Vanity than anyone else. She helped by not really looking at him, even the few times he spoke directly to her.

Was she so focused on the defense class that she could relegate him to the back burner?

He didn't like that idea at all. Especially when thoughts of her stayed crowded into the front of his mind.

Some of the women were younger, not really into the class. They were more about flirting. Stack easily looked past them, but Armie made up for it by flirting right back, teasing each and every one.

Only Cherry, Denver's fiancée, and Vanity were off-limits to Armie's interest. Cherry stayed at Vanity's side, and occasionally the two of them would whisper or laugh about something.

Likely they were amused by the attention he and Armie got from the women who were supposed to be learning how to defend themselves from attackers.

"I need a volunteer." Armie glanced over the class, bypassed the raised hands, and said, "C'mon, Vee. You'll do."

Stack swung around. What the hell was Armie doing?

Vanity lifted her hand and Cherry gave her a high

five. Without an ounce of hesitation, Vanity stepped up front.

Feeling like an extra in a bad play, Stack stood there as Armie arranged her in front of him so they were both in profile to the rest of the ladies.

"If someone jumps you," Armie said, "it's go time. You can't be timid and you can't be polite. So where are the best places to aim?"

Vanity took a stance. "A woman my size against a man your size would do best aiming for the eyes, nose, or ears." With each part she listed, she went through a practiced move.

"Right. But if you're going for my nose, then you use the heel of your hand, and you really bring it. A tap is just going to piss me off."

She grinned. "Can't have that." In slow motion she went through the strike again, this time with the heel of her hand aimed at the base of Armie's nose.

"Better." He held up his palm. "Pretend that's my nose. Go for it."

She struck, smacking Armie's palm with precision, the sound of the impact loud and sharp.

"Nice." He stood over her, then clasped her forearms. "Now what?"

She brought up her knee, fast and hard, stopping just shy of nutting Armie.

He lurched, ducking his hips back, and she laughed.

So did the rest of the ladies.

"Brat." Armie put her in a headlock, knuckled the top of her head, then turned her loose. She snickered as she smoothed her hair back into place.

And Stack stood there behind them, taking it in, a little annoyed and absurdly proud of her.

He turned her to face him. "You saw how Armie moved? Your groin strike would have missed. Whenever possible, you always want to aim for the body parts where you can do the most damage. Whether the guy is big or small, trained or a dolt, the eyes are always vulnerable."

Vanity nodded, then curled her small hands into claws. "Raking, scratching, gouging and poking."

Stack and Armie took turns engaging her in different examples for the class. She hung in there, showing that she knew the moves but wasn't comfortable in actually implementing them.

"We need to do some real drills," Stack said to Armie, who agreed.

"Next time," Armie announced to the class, "what do you think about putting on protective gear and actually sparring?"

Vanity's elbow landed in Stack's ribs, and she spoke to the class. "Oh, seriously, Armie. I'm sure no one here wants to get locked up close and personal with any of you guys." Her eyebrows bobbed suggestively. "What do you say, ladies?"

The women cheered.

Armie covered his crotch and warned, "I'll be wearing my cup, so don't anyone get any ideas."

"Too late," someone yelled, leading to more laughter and a lot of agreement.

Stack's pride expanded. Vanity was comfortable and confident in any situation.

A few of the women had questions, so with the class over, he stepped to the side to answer. He tried to concentrate, but damn. He couldn't keep his gaze off Vanity.

Now that he'd slept with her, he looked at everything she did or said differently, more personally.

Arms over her head, she stretched. Her workout clothes clung to her body in all the right places. She'd long since removed the over-shirt and now wore only the camisole-type sports top that pretty much squished her boobs. It wasn't that different from what many of the other women wore. It covered her so that nothing showed through, but Vanity looked far better than most.

Using a soft white towel, she patted her face, her upper chest, then lifted her braid to dry the back of her neck.

The rest of the class finished up and wandered off, most bundling up and heading for the door. Denver and Cannon started putting supplies away. Leese rolled out the mop bucket. They had a cleaning crew come in once a week for a really thorough job, but in between that they took turns mopping the mats with a special sanitizer.

Holding her hair off her neck with one hand, fanning her face with the other, Cherry came back over by Vanity. Yvette, who hadn't taken the class but had worked out while at the rec center, also joined them.

When Vanity caught Stack staring toward them, she smiled. "I really think you guys should let us use the locker room. I'm perspiring. Cherry's perspiring."

Cherry went still, then looked down at herself and blushed. Sweat dampened the front of her tank top, especially between and beneath her big boobs.

Denver scowled, giving Stack a shove. Which in turn knocked him into Armie. None of them spoke.

Cannon took up the torch. "It's only set up for men."

"We don't need the urinals," Vanity said. "Just the showers."

Yvette plucked at her top. "I really could—"

Cannon put his hand over her mouth. "We don't have a door on the locker room, and sure, we'd all know not to step in, but there are other people here, other *guys*, and—"

Vanity said, "So put someone there to keep watch for us."

Stack opened his mouth, but at first nothing came out. He cleared his throat. "Sounds carry down there." He gestured. "There not being a door and all."

Grinning, Armie said, "Meaning whoever keeps guard—"

"Watch," Vanity corrected.

"—will hear every little detail. Like clothes dropping. And water running. Even slick, soapy hands—"

This time, Stack shoved him without Denver's help.

"I'll do it," Cannon offered, and he sounded like he'd just thrown himself on the sacrificial altar.

"Fuck that." Denver took a step forward. "I don't want you listening to Cherry shower."

Cherry's face got hotter. "Denver!"

Folding his arms, Cannon stared at him. "You think I'd let *you* listen to Yvette?"

"Cannon!" Yvette joined the brigade of embarrassed women.

Only Vanity remained unflustered. "Let Armie do it."

Mutually appalled, Stack, Denver and Cannon all stared at her.

Going along, Armie nodded and rubbed his hands together. "Yeah, let *me* do it."

"Hell, no."

"In his dreams."

"Not in this lifetime."

Armie laughed. "You guys know I won't be thinking anything you wouldn't be thinking."

"Maybe," Denver said. "But we wouldn't go blabbing it everywhere."

Crossing his heart dramatically, Armie swore, "It'll be between me and my pillow."

Denver took a step toward him, but Vanity put herself in his way. "We're showering. For the future, you might want to think about creating a space for women."

"Tried," Cannon argued. "We're out of room here. I wanted to expand, but the guy who owns the lot next to us doesn't want to sell."

"Hmm…" Vanity got a thoughtful look on her face. "Well then, I suggest you find a desk to put down there and then, perhaps, we could plan this around when Harper is here doing the scheduling. She could be our lookout."

"I could call her—" Cannon tried to offer.

But Stack noticed that Vanity already had both her arms wrapped around one of Armie's.

And damn him, Armie just let her, smiling in a way that just might lose him a few teeth.

Leese looked at each of the men and started snickering.

"They're pathetic, right?" Armie said.

"They're something," Leese agreed. "Not sure what."

"You two losers are just jealous," Cannon accused.

"Yeah," Armie said, patting at Vanity's arm. "So jealous."

Denver growled when Cherry cozied up to the other

side of Armie, and even Yvette smiled as she followed along, all of them heading to the locker room.

The men stared until the group was out of sight.

"I'm going to have to punch him," Denver said. "At least once."

"Get in line," Cannon told him. Then he pointed at Leese. "Not a word out of you!"

Trying to bite back his grin, Leese got started mopping.

Damn, Stack wondered, did Vanity enjoy making him nuts? And unlike Cannon and Denver, he couldn't protest as much as he wanted because, though he'd thrown out some signals, he and Vanity weren't official.

Fuck.

The door chimed, and they all turned to see Merissa breezing in, her long dark hair blowing out behind her. She had a stack of yellow papers held securely in her arms.

Cannon all but pounced on her. "Do me a favor, honey, will you?"

Suspicious, she reared back to look at him, then at Stack and Denver. "What's going on?"

"The ladies insisted on a shower, and Armie, the ass, is down there playing watchdog."

"And listening," Denver added, which got Leese snickering again.

Hip cocked out, Merissa glared at the men. "So, what do you expect me to do?"

With evil delight, Cannon said, "He's watching the door, so I want you to watch him."

"Um…"

"Tell him I sent you. Tell him he's to stay put in case

any guys wander down that way. He wouldn't want you to deal with that any more than I do."

"So…"

Hands on his sister's shoulders, Cannon said, "But you can deal with him, right?"

Looking very unsure, Merissa shrugged. "Sure." Her gaze scanned each of them. "I only stopped by to drop off the new forms Harper wanted me to copy."

"Great. Thanks." Cannon took the stack of papers from her. "Since you're here, why not stick around and keep Armie company so he won't get an opportunity to eavesdrop on anyone?"

Merissa looked toward the hallway that led to the lockers. She looked at her brother's smiling face. She took in Stack and Denver's expectant expressions. With a quick inhale and great determination, she hiked her purse strap higher on her shoulder and nodded. "Consider it done." Her smile long gone, she marched away.

Stack whistled. Talk about payback… He almost felt sorry for Armie.

When Cannon turned back to them, Denver grinned. "That was mean."

Cannon clapped him on the shoulder. "I love Armie like a brother, you know that."

Cannon never hesitated to talk about love. He was the most comfortable guy Stack had ever known. And his ease with emotions put others at ease, as well.

Stack and Denver nodded.

Satisfied, Cannon told them both, "I wouldn't do anything that wasn't for his own good." And with that, Cannon headed toward the reception area with the papers.

Scratching at his scruffy chin, Denver asked Stack, "What the hell was that about?"

Stack shrugged. "No idea." But as long as Armie wasn't listening to Vanity while she showered, he wouldn't spend too much time stewing on it.

He had better things to think about—like getting Vanity alone again tonight. Getting her naked.

Getting her under him.

He hoped she showered quickly. He was so far off the deep end, he didn't think he could wait much longer.

SMIRKING, ARMIE STOOD with arms folded, his shoulders against the outside wall on the other side of the locker room entrance. He could hear the women talking about their respective men.

Funny shit.

Only Vanity seemed unfazed, but then Stack was dragging his feet about stating the obvious. After tonight, he expected Stack would remedy that.

The women—all of them as nice as nice girls could be—were pretty awesome. He was happy for his friends. Not that he wanted the same for himself. Hell no.

Not in the cards. Not for someone like him.

His future had been molded a long time ago, and rather than fight it, he'd just rolled with the punches. And the kicks.

And the devastation.

Fuck 'em all. What had been stolen from him, he didn't need. Or so he told himself. Often. Until recently he'd made it so, and he'd been happy with his life.

Okay, maybe "happy" was a stretch, but he'd been content. He'd made it work. He lived by his own rules and ignored the restrictions.

Until the SBC had insisted on signing him on, meaning more exposure…to everyone.

His past would get dredged up in a big way. Cannon

claimed it was time. He knew Cannon would stand beside him. All the guys would. But needing them for this, for anything, made him feel pathetic, and he'd done his utmost to leave that shit behind.

When a sudden burst of laughter came from the showers, Armie realized he hadn't been listening to the ladies after all. He'd gotten lost in thought, and damn it, he'd missed the joke.

"You changed your hair."

Startled by the husky timbre of that familiar voice, he slowly turned his head. Backlit by the fluorescent lights of the main room, Merissa Colter stood there in the long hallway. Silky ebony hair trailed over her shoulders all the way to her tiny waist. His attention went to her cleavage. She usually wore crew neck tops, but now, tonight, her sweater dipped low enough to make his mouth go dry.

"Yeah." Who knew a small change with his hair would get so much attention?

"Why?"

He shrugged. Just because he felt like he had to control something, even something as dumb as his outward appearance…no reason to share that with her.

He focused on her cleavage instead of his warped issues. Her tan top fell to mid hip, leading his gaze to her endlessly long legs hugged in skinny jeans that showed off every subtle curve. His nostrils flared with a breath.

Her height almost equaled her brother's, so she seldom wore heels. But her boots tonight lifted her an inch, maybe two, meaning their mouths would be perfectly aligned…

"Armie?" She shifted, arms crossing under her

breasts and one hip jutting out. "You're making me feel naked."

Shit. "Don't put ideas in my head, Stretch." He had enough of them in there already—and they always made him feel guilty. Pushing off the wall, he took one step toward her. "So, what's up?"

She and Cannon shared the same light blue eyes, but on Cannon they were just there. On Merissa... Jesus. The impact of those eyes staring into his made his balls tighten.

"For one second," she said, "you managed to treat me like other women. Should have known it wouldn't last." She brushed past him, put her back to the wall, and slid down to her curvy little ass.

Confused by her presence but craving it all the same, Armie stood over her; it was safer than joining her on the floor. "You know me. Why in God's name would you want me to treat you the way I treat other women?"

From the showers, Vanity yelled, "I like how you treat me."

Rolling his eyes, Armie yelled back, "Concentrate on your shower, Vee."

A giggle, and then Cherry added, "That overhearing thing goes both ways, just so you know."

Merissa put her face in her hands.

"Busybodies!" Taking the wall across from her, Armie joined her on the floor. She looked so bleak, he stretched out his legs, letting his feet go on either side of hers. Keeping his voice lower, he asked, "What's the matter?"

She dropped her hands and, looking mean, narrowed her gaze at him. "Not a thing. I'm here to babysit you. *Again*."

"The night of the wedding was bullshit. I was fine and everyone knows it." Mostly fine, anyway. "You sent me home in a cab?"

Her thick lashes half lowered. "No. I drove you and your truck home, then I called a cab for me."

He rubbed the back of his neck. "I saw your message on my window."

She shrugged. "I wasn't sure you'd remember any of it."

Nudging her foot with his, he said, "I didn't do anything to offend you, did I?"

"You mostly ignored me."

Well…good. "So, what's the reason you're here now?"

"Apparently the men don't trust the nefarious Armie Jacobson near their girlfriends."

"Then that's bullshit, too. They trust me. They just know their own minds would be rolling 'round in the gutter, and they figure you'd be a distraction to keep mine from doing the same."

Interest sparked in her eyes. "And am I?"

"A distraction?" Always. Even when she wasn't around. Most especially at night when he tried to sleep, when substitute women didn't measure up, when… Shit. "We're jawing, aren't we?"

For too long, maybe drawing wrong conclusions, she studied him. "If Cannon hadn't sent me, would you be thinking…things? I mean, about them naked and—"

"There you go again," he answered softly, mesmerized by her curiosity as always. "Putting thoughts in my head."

This time her foot nudged his. "I'm serious."

Should he tell her the truth? That instead of thinking about a gaggle of gorgeous women naked in the shower, he'd taken a melancholy stroll down memory lane? Fuck that.

"I was just thinking." He let his head drop back against the concrete block wall. "But not about them."

She nodded. "Good." Drawing back, she stammered, "I mean, the guys would be glad to hear that."

Don't do it, don't do it— "And you?" *Shut up, Armie.* But for some reason, he couldn't. Maybe because he'd be entering the SBC instead of smaller local venues. Maybe because, as Cannon had insisted, it was time. Past time.

Maybe because he was tired of being a fraud.

He let his foot rest against hers, watched her eyes flare over the simple touch, and couldn't help wondering about touching her in better, hotter ways. "What would you say if I told you I was thinking about them?"

Focused on their feet, she didn't answer.

That amused him. Sweet, innocent Rissy. His best friend's baby sis.

His kinkiest fantasy—and that said a lot, because if there was one thing Armie knew, it was kink.

She also starred in other fantasies, those that were less sexual and more…emotional. Heavier. Sweeter.

More real.

Heart beating harder, he prompted her again. "Rissy?"

Her gaze shot up to lock on his. A deep inhale drew his attention to her breasts. Her lips parted. "I—"

Clustered together in a gossipy group, the ladies stepped into the hall. Vanity, who'd been looking at Cherry as she spoke, tripped over Armie's outstretched legs before he could withdraw them.

Yelping, on her way to meeting the floor, Vee threw

out her arms. Acting on instinct, Armie rolled under her and managed to break her fall.

She landed awkwardly against his chest, her boobs in his face, one of his hands on her ass.

Yvette and Cherry fell into each other laughing.

Straightening, Vanity joined them.

Armie readjusted his hold, and when she remained sitting on his thighs, he squeezed her. "Brat. My hands were in forbidden territory. Stack's going to murder me."

"My fault," Vanity said around her continued hilarity. "Stack will be glad I didn't break my nose."

"It was my fault for occupying the hallway." He looked to Merissa—and realized she'd left. He swiveled his head in time to see her backside turn the corner and disappear.

Well, damn.

Vanity cupped his cheek. "You're getting smarter, Armie. Don't disillusion me, okay?"

He didn't like the way she said that. "Meaning what?"

"Meaning I consider you kind as well as sexual." Her pat to his cheek was a little harder than necessary. "You deserve it all."

Leaving him confused and a little antagonistic, she scrambled back to her feet, but then bent low to add, "You made some strides tonight. Keep it up."

He was still lying there, his frown so fierce it made his temples throb, when all three ladies walked off, their heads together as they whispered.

About him.

Vee had it wrong. Merissa was the one who deserved it all.

Unfortunately, he probably wouldn't be the one to give it to her.

NEVER BEFORE HAD the locker room smelled of flowers, but after the women left it, the scents of feminine lotion and perfume had lingered.

And exacerbated Stack's lust.

By the time he reached Vanity's house, anticipation had him semi-erect. With winter rolling in, the evening air had a definite nip to it, but it didn't help cool him down. Nothing would, except sex with Vanity.

Tonight she had plenty of outside lights on, and she'd parked her car in the garage.

He went up the walkway, each step ramping up his urgency.

Twice he reminded himself that he couldn't just rush her off to bed. She deserved better than that.

She deserved more than her original bargain, and so did he.

He'd been at the rec center longer than her, but she'd remained there with him right through dinnertime. He should have offered to take her to dinner. Soon, he would. But not tonight.

The dogs would want to visit. Desperate as he was to have Vanity again, he couldn't disregard Maggie and Norwood.

His forearm provided a nonstop ache. He should ice it again, and he would, later. Until then, he wouldn't let it slow him down.

Was Vanity tired after her workout and then the self-defense class? If so, she'd done a good job hiding it. While some women finished up their workouts looking exhausted, Vanity had emerged from the showers all smiles and laughter, and so damned beautiful.

Her energy level astounded him and turned him on.

But then she could do nothing at all, and he wanted her. Especially now that he'd gotten a small taste of her.

And thinking of tasting her... Damn. There was a lot he wanted to do, all of it making the restriction in his jeans more noticeable.

He reached the front door, raised his hand to knock— and a shadow shifted in the side yard.

No fucking way would he get caught off guard twice. Senses sharpened, he silently stepped to the side of her porch. He heard movement, and then saw a deer bolt off. The white tail disappeared into the darkness. With a sense of unease still prickling the back of his neck, he continued to search the area.

Behind him the front door opened. "Stack?"

He turned back to Vanity and mentally reeled.

Her pale hair reflected the glow of the porch light. A pink, long-sleeved tee fit snug to her breasts, the hem not quite reaching the waistband of the soft flannel pants hanging low on her narrow hips. He saw a tantalizing strip of belly in between, and it made him burn.

In her eyes, he saw the same urgency he felt.

Breathing fast, her gaze devouring him, she held out a hand.

Stack made himself stand still. "Where are the dogs?"

"Waiting to say hi."

"I don't want to rush you."

"How about you let me do the rushing?"

That did it. He could fight himself, but he couldn't fight them both. He took her hand, used it to drag her out to the porch, then backed her up to the wall and kissed her. The door fell shut behind her.

Everything he'd just told himself faded away. Vanity

clutched at him, squeezing him tighter to her, hooking one calf around his.

Scooping his hand under her bottom, he aligned their bodies so that his straining erection nestled against the warm junction of her thighs.

Her faint gasp spurred him on.

Cold air whispered around them, but he barely felt it. Her lips softened, opened; he turned his head, licked in, stroked deep. Devoured.

Their breaths labored, fogging the air around them. She moved against him, needy, ready. He felt explosive.

When the dogs scratched at the door, Stack forced himself to come up for air. "Damn, I need you," he growled.

"Need you more," she whispered, her hands knotted in his shirt. She nipped his chin, his jaw, made her way to his throat and opened her mouth against his skin.

Fuck. His guts tightened, his muscles clenching. Hand still on her ass, he lifted and rocked her against him.

A gust of icy wind drifted her hair against his forearm.

Hadn't he just thought about how cold it was now? And here he had her out on the porch wearing only socks, flannel pants and a long-sleeved tee. "I'm sorry."

Brushing her nose over his throat, she asked, "For?"

He rubbed his hands up and down her arms. "It's cold out here."

Meeting his gaze, she took his hand and pressed it low to her belly. "It's hot enough inside that it doesn't matter."

He had to kiss her again and did. But this time he

kept enough sense not to get carried away. Tucking her hair back, he asked, "You hungry?"

She purred. "Starving."

That made him smile. "For food, darlin'."

Her hand repeatedly smoothed over his shoulder. "Maybe just a little."

"Then how about we get some food together and give the dogs a chance to calm down." He brushed his knuckles over her cheek. "Then you're mine for the rest of the night."

Another purr and a murmured, "Love that plan." Again she took his hand, turned and led him inside.

Even while kneeling down to greet the dogs, he watched her sexy walk as she headed to the kitchen. Didn't matter what she fixed. He planned to inhale it.

Then he planned to have her for dessert.

HUNKERED IN THE SHADOWS, heart still tripping, Phil waited until he was dead-sure they were inside, and that they'd stay there.

If that damned deer hadn't startled him, he wouldn't have made a noise. But once he did, he'd known—*just known*—that Stack was going to kill him. And it wouldn't be a quick death. No, Stack would probably enjoy pulverizing him one punch or kick at a time.

He still couldn't believe the thugs had been so easily stopped. Not that it mattered. They didn't know who he was. And they had served their purpose—to keep Stack occupied so he could approach Vanity alone.

That hadn't gone quite as well as he'd hoped. She might be hot as hell, but she wasn't a pushover. Not completely, anyway. Still, he'd scored some cash. It was a start.

Getting to her now would be trickier. But not impossible. Sucked that he had to sneak around, but the payoff would be worth it.

Sticking to the shadows, in a half-crouching run, Phil got as far from the danger as he could. The pills he'd taken earlier were wearing off. He was no longer as mellow as he needed to be.

Yeah, when Stack had heard the noise, Phil's damned heart had punched into his throat, obliterating his calm. But he'd liked seeing how quick Vanity turned on. She'd all but melted on Stack the minute the bastard touched her. Tabby used to melt for him like that.

Stack was the one who ruined everything, so he owed him. Since his new lady was rolling in it, she could even Stack's debt—with cold, hard cash.

CHAPTER FOURTEEN

VANITY WANTED TO rush through the meal, but Stack wouldn't.

She wanted to tidy up the dishes herself, but he insisted on helping.

Obstinate. Considerate.

Wonderful.

"You look good in boots."

His hands, covered in soapsuds, paused while cleaning the frying pan. In slo-mo, he turned his head to stare at her. "Come again?"

She nodded in the general direction of his backside, which she'd been watching while wiping off the table. "You," she said. "In those worn jeans and cowboy boots. It's a good look."

He snorted and went back to cleaning the pan. "You don't have to butter me up. Believe me, I'm ready."

He didn't act ready. He acted like patience personified. "I'm serious." She strode up to him, reached her arms around his waist, and dropped the dishrag back into the sink. And now that she was flattened up against him, she hugged him tight.

He went still, his hands again suspended in soapy water.

From the corner of the kitchen, Norwood opened one

eye to look at them, then let out a doggy huff and went back to sleep curled up by Maggie.

"I'll be done in two minutes."

"Mmm." She slipped her hands up under his flannel and T-shirt. "I'll just entertain myself until then."

"You're distracting me, and I wanted to talk."

Right. He was going to explain about his arm. She slid away from him, took the pan and turned off the water. After setting the pan in the dish drainer, she took his hand in one of hers, then gently touched his forearm.

"Vanity?"

"Hmm?"

"What are you doing?"

She looked up at him. It was something of a thrill that he stood so tall. And she hadn't lied about his wardrobe preferences. She liked his laid-back cowboy vibe, minus a hat. His long muscular legs looked great in jeans and boots. His narrow hips and flat abs made everything look good. And his chest, his shoulders—

A finger under her chin lifted her face. "Vanity?"

"I wanted to check your boo-boo."

Incredulous, he lifted a brow and said deadpan, "My boo-boo?"

"This." She brushed her cheek against his forearm, exposed by his rolled-up sleeves. The bruises had already darkened, looking ugly and painful. "Does it hurt?"

"No."

She knew he had to be fibbing. "You were going to tell me what happened."

"No, I was going to ask you why you always insist looks don't matter."

She opened her mouth but then closed it without saying anything.

Stack just watched her, waiting, making her sigh.

"Fine, but you first."

Lifting one shoulder, he said, "I got jumped. Now you."

No freaking way! "What do you mean you got jumped?"

He cracked his head to one side, then the other, and visibly held on to his patience. "It was nothing. Two goons jumped me in front of my sister's apartment. I beat the snot out of them both, end of story."

"If you beat the…the *snot* out of them, then what's this?" She put her hand protectively over the worst of the bruises.

"One lucky strike with a small wooden bat. It's superficial. In a few days it'll be back to normal."

"Did you call the police?" she demanded.

"No."

"No?"

Amused, he half smiled. "It was just an altercation, and they learned the error of their ways. No reason to drag the cops into it."

"But…why not?"

He sighed as if harassed. "I don't need to be mothered, okay? Got a mother, a pushy one. You've met her. Got an older sister, too, who likes to butt into my life. That's enough female concern, believe me."

Not wanting to chase him off, Vanity reluctantly let it drop. "Fine."

Her attitude didn't put him off. "Now you." He turned his hand over to effectively displace her touch, then laced his fingers in hers. "Why do you have a hang-up about being gorgeous?"

Her face heated. "I'm not."

Enunciating clearly, he said again, "Gorgeous. And for some reason, you're bothered by it."

Shaking her head to deny it, she lied, "That's not true."

"Vanity."

"It's not a hang-up." It was *totally* a hang-up. A dumb one to boot. But still… "It's reality. Looks fade, beauty is only skin deep, all that. If you find me attractive, I'm glad."

"I find you very attractive. Anyone with eyes and a brain cell will agree. Especially anyone male."

Okay, so she knew she wasn't a hag. She'd been shopping in the mall when a local talent scout begged for her info. If his office hadn't been there in the mall, she would have kept walking. But it had intrigued her.

So, not a hag. Better than just average. She appreciated that nature had been kind to her. Sighing, she gave a dramatic, *"But…"*

"But?" he prompted.

Flattening her mouth and staring him in the eyes, she stated the truth. "I don't want looks to be the only thing you see."

For the longest time he scrutinized her; contemplative, understanding. Curious. "There's more to it, something more personal."

She gave up. "Yes, personal." To help her get through the uncomfortable confession, she toyed with the front of his shirt…and sneakily opened a button on his flannel. "My mother was beautiful."

"She looked like you?"

"More...refined." How to explain that? "Higher cheekbones, a narrower nose. I have my mother's coloring, but I favor my father."

"Then both your parents were attractive." His eyes searched hers. "You explained about your mother's family, and I know you said your dad was an only child. But didn't he have any relatives?"

"He had uncles and aunts, and a few cousins. They weren't close, and we don't stay in touch. Some of them live in England, a few in the Bahamas."

Stack's fingertips did this interesting, stirring thing where he lightly touched her, tracing her jawline, up and around her ear. She inhaled and tried to focus enough to get through the explanation. "Dad had a mistress."

Oh, wow, she hadn't meant to just blurt that out.

His mouth went crooked with a reluctant smile. Definitely not the reaction she'd expected.

Scowling, she poked his chest. "What's funny about that?"

He quickly sobered. "Sorry, your word choice... You're saying he cheated?"

Somehow "had a mistress" sounded less awful than "cheated." Her mother had developed the practice of prettying up reality with loftier word choices. Denial in its finest form.

Perhaps, Vanity decided, she shouldn't do the same. "Yes." Her throat tightened, but she forced out the words. "He cheated."

"They were divorced?"

It shamed her to admit the truth. "Mom felt the only thing worse than Dad leaving her for a younger woman would be to go through the disgrace of a divorce."

Stack whistled. "Old school."

Her heart cracked a little at that attitude. "Marriage should be forever."

Taking her words seriously, Stack slid a hand around her neck. "Love should be forever. Without it, it's not a marriage anyway."

So true. Sadly, her mother had never realized that. "I'm sure you're right. But she stayed with him anyway, and he stayed with her, and after they died, his mistress expected to inherit."

"But she didn't."

"Not a dime." Vanity had almost felt sorry for her. *Almost.*

Stack moved his fingers in a light caress. "My mom and dad were devoted, to each other and to Tabby and me." Some fond memory curled his mouth, then brought a short laugh. "Dad was outrageous. Until the day he died he chased after Mom like they were still teenagers. I remember one day we were waiting on dinner, and Mom bent to take a roast out of the oven. Dad smacked her on the butt, and when she protested, hitting him with the oven mitt, he pulled her onto his lap and kissed her until they were both laughing. Tabby and I pretended to be grossed out, but it wasn't gross. It was just…nice. Normal. At least for us."

"Other than a peck on the cheek, I don't think I ever saw my dad kiss my mother."

"You'd have been shocked around my house. They didn't make out in front of us or anything like that. But Dad was always pretty demonstrative. I was twenty when a massive heart attack took him, and a week before that, he'd hugged me. A big bear hug. He was touchy-feely with the ones he loved, and that included my mom big-time."

"That must have been so nice. My parents weren't touchers." She gave that quick thought. "Not around me anyway. But I don't know how Dad was with his young, pretty mistress."

"So you, and your mother, assumed he cheated because this other woman was younger and prettier?"

Vanity wasn't sure. "My mother often said that love lasted only as long as looks did." Feeling sick about it, she looked away. "She said having me had ruined her body, although it seemed to me that she worked out all the time."

Stack frowned. "Is that why you work out?"

Snorting, Vanity shook her head. "I've always enjoyed being active. If I could swim or surf, that's what I'd be doing. But there aren't any oceans nearby."

He grinned. "Not in Ohio, no. But we could hit up some waterparks if you want."

"Really?"

He touched her face. "I'd enjoy it."

Emotion burned her eyes. "Me, too."

Easing the moment, Stack said, "I can't imagine anyone prettier than you."

A reluctant smile warmed her. "You're sweet. Thank you."

"Sweet." He shook his head, then both his hands cupped gently around her neck, forcing her to make eye contact. "I think you're beautiful." Then, surprising her, he added, "Just as Cannon thinks Yvette is beautiful and Denver thinks Cherry is."

What did that comparison mean?

Feeling very unsure, she said nothing.

"When a man is involved," Stack continued, "married or not, but especially when he has a family, he should never cheat. It's not just a betrayal of the person you promised to love, honor and cherish. It betrays the family unit, too."

So many times she'd felt betrayed by her father.

Sometimes…by her mother, as well. Together they'd created a cold and uncomfortable atmosphere, the antithesis of family.

"No disrespect to your parents, but when someone cheats, it's a reflection on the cheater, only. Your dad was willing to do that, so I don't think it would've mattered what your mom looked like."

Vanity admitted the truth. "I've thought that sometimes, too. Mom made it about looks, but I think maybe it was about a whole lot more."

"Your father shouldn't have done that. Your mother shouldn't have accepted it." Stack put a quick kiss on her mouth. "You sure as hell shouldn't, and I damn straight wouldn't."

No, she couldn't see Stack sneaking around. He was too up-front, and far too honorable.

As if he'd read her thoughts, he said, "I wouldn't marry unless I could have what my parents had. And you can believe me, Dad always thought Mom was hot." He grinned as he said it. "Didn't matter if she was dressed up or wearing sweats while she cleaned the house." Stack shrugged. "He loved her."

Hearing him talk so earnestly about his family thrilled her. Practically overnight they'd advanced from one-time hookup to saving free time for each other… however long it lasted.

Stack tipped his head. "Understand?"

"Yes," Vanity assured him. She got another button

open, then tried to lead him back to his earlier statement. "You mentioned the other couples…?"

He didn't deny that they were a couple, too. "You're all attractive."

"All?"

He ignored the question. "I think you're by far the hottest. But I'm willing to bet Cannon and Denver would disagree. Armie, too, given he's hung up on Merissa."

"I know."

His mouth quirked. "Everyone seems to know except the two of them."

Another button gave way. "Are you saying you're hung up on me?"

He lightly kissed her, and teased, "Little bit."

Her heart took leaps around her chest. "Really?"

His gaze turned smoky. "You like that, huh?"

Throwing her arms around him, she pressed her face to his throat. "Yes." His scent, dark and masculine and delicious, filled her head. "I like it a lot."

"Understand, darlin', I like everything about you. Whether you're spattered in paint or wearing sweats at the gym or—" he nipped her neck "—buck-ass, which I'm pretty sure will always be my preference."

"Then maybe I should get *buck-ass* right now."

"Now you're talking." As if she weighed nothing, he scooped an arm under her legs and lifted her. Norwood and Maggie both perked up, but she said, "Stay," and with twitching ears, they both remained in the kitchen as Stack carried her away.

She loved him. More so every minute.

Pretty soon she'd have to come clean and admit that she'd seduced him under false pretenses.

He'd thought to get uncomplicated sex.

But all along, she'd been going for happily-ever-after.

STACK GOT HER in the bedroom, closed the door, then lowered her to the bed. He stretched out beside her, one leg pinning her down while he kissed her senseless. Covering her breast with one hand, he groaned. Her nipple was already puckered tight, and he tormented them both by playing with her while getting his fill of her soft mouth.

Each time she adjusted, he did, too, until he got lost in the ravenous kiss, her taste and heat and the fragrant air around her.

Dragging his mouth away, he shoved up the shirt until it bunched around her upper chest. Her breasts trembled with her ragged breathing. In a fog of need, he held her in his hand, licked the ripe nipple, then sucked her hard and sweet.

Her back arched, and he felt the sting of her nails on his shoulders, quickly replaced with a deliberately easier hold.

He wanted to tell her that he didn't mind if she got carried away; he loved turning her on. But he wasn't about to give up suckling her to say anything. Not when she showed so much amazing reaction.

Squirming, she lifted her body against his leg. Every breath sounded like a faint gasp that turned into a soft moan and then a sharper groan. Jesus, would she come just from this?

The idea of that nearly put him over the edge. Before he lost it completely he sat up and wrestled the shirt off over her head. The second her hands were free she reached for him.

"Not yet, darlin'." He bent to kiss her midriff, then her cute belly. The scent of her skin drew him back again and again until he was nuzzling against her with soft love bites.

Groaning, he slid off the bed to stand at the side, then grabbed her waistband and dragged down the flannel pants.

She'd gone commando, and he hadn't realized it. Breathing hard, he lightly touched her with his fingertips.

"My socks..." she whispered.

"They're cute." Who the hell cared about socks? He opened the remaining buttons on his shirt. "Next time, tell me if you want my shirt off. I'm happy to oblige."

"Note—I always want your shirt off." She came up to her knees in front of him and opened both hands on his chest. "Your body is amazing."

Throwing her concerns back at her, he asked, "Is that what you like most about me?"

"I like everything about you."

"Yeah?" He opened his jeans and eased the zipper past his erection. "This?"

Her hand slid around him, and she murmured huskily, "Yes, this."

For a minute or two he let her play. Not like he had the willpower to stop her, not when it felt so damned good. When her thumb teased over the head, slicking pre-cum in lazy circles guaranteed to make him explode, he caught her wrist.

It wasn't his preference, but since a gentleman always asked, he said, "Condom?"

Her eyes, dazed and dark, stared into his. "Just you and just me."

"Perfect." Better than perfect. He'd like a week with just the two of them. Maybe a month.

Maybe longer.

He stepped back from her. "Lie down. Let me look at you."

"You'll finish stripping?"

"Hell yeah."

She smiled and reclined, one arm over her head, the other resting on her stomach. She bent a knee, and all the lust and need inside him coiled tight.

Lifting first his right foot, then his left, he tugged off his boots—and all the while his gaze strayed over her body, investigating and appreciating every curve and hollow and swell. Her skin had that peachy residual glow from the sun, except for her whiter breasts, tipped by tight pink nipples.

And the neat triangle around her sex.

He could see exactly where her little bikini had covered, and now, naked, the paler skin highlighted the most sexual parts of her.

Parts he needed to touch, and kiss. And lick.

Still looking at her, he pushed down his jeans and boxers.

She inhaled, shifted, clutched her hands in the bedding.

Stepping up to her, Stack rested a hand on each of her knees—and parted her legs.

"Stack," she whispered.

He came down over her, balanced on one forearm, and kissed her other breast. "I've thought nonstop about this. About you." He circled a nipple with his tongue, caught her in his teeth and lightly tugged.

Her back arched on a vibrating groan.

He did the same to the other breast, then kissed her ribs. Down her waist to her belly.

"Stack?"

The high, breathless way she said his name told him she knew what was coming and wanted it. Not as badly as he did, but maybe enough.

Leaving warm, damp, open-mouth love bites all over her softly fragrant skin, he inched his way down. She put the back of her hand against her mouth, her eyes closed and her breathing labored.

"Damn, you're hot." And quick to respond.

She whispered, "With you."

Only him? He'd like to think this was special for her, because it sure as hell was special for him. In so many small, indefinable ways, making love with Vanity was a revelation. Hotter. Sweeter.

More.

He lifted her legs over his shoulders. She made a small, anxious sound and bit her lip.

Adjusting her to his liking, he kissed the inside of each thigh, nuzzling, breathing in her musky scent and going so taut it seemed she could break him.

He liked seeing her like this. Open to him and what he wanted to do to her and with her. *His.*

Instead of alarming him, that thought settled in comfortably. He wanted her, every part of her, like this and in other ways. *All* ways.

Her energy level astounded him. Her disregard of wealth intrigued him. The warm way she accepted his family, how she quickly aligned with them, touched him in immeasurable ways.

And her sexuality, the perfect way they matched up, burned him to the core.

Sliding an arm under her hips, he lifted her up. "So pretty." He hadn't yet touched her here, but already her lips were glistening from her excitement, her clit swollen. With one fingertip he explored, dipping slightly between her lips, relishing her moan, the rush of new wetness. He traced her, teasing up and over that ultra-sensitive bud, enjoying how she tensed and moved, the sounds she made.

Without warning, he added a second finger, moved back and forth along her entrance—and sank deep.

Her body bowed, then quickly resettled, as if she feared discouraging him.

Not likely.

Blowing softly on her, easing closer, he kept his fingers in her, curling them slightly to find just the right spot. With his other hand, he used his fingers to part her, then opened his mouth over her.

This time they both groaned.

Now it was his tongue exploring, teasing. Her taste was indescribable. The heat of her, her sweetness intoxicated him, making him want more. He licked and sucked, aware of her growing tension, the way she stiffened and the quickening of her breath.

"Stack," she moaned.

He felt ready to come just from hearing her, tasting her.

More urgently, she cried, "Stack!"

He held her closer, concentrating on suckling in just the right spot, at the same time using his tongue to rasp—and she broke, her body lifting on a high cry, her legs tightening, her tender inner thighs closing on his jaws.

Damn, he loved it.

He loved having her like this.

He loved her response, and the way she made him feel.

Refusing to let his brain travel beyond that, he kept pace with her, wringing as much pleasure from her as he could. When her body sank back to the mattress, when her fingers tunneled into his hair and she whimpered, he eased away, kissed a hot path back up her body until he took her mouth.

She remained limp, not really participating but not rejecting him either. He smiled against her mouth. "Stay with me, darlin'."

"I'm here," she said drowsily, her voice rough.

"Like this, okay?" He hooked each of her legs into the crook of his elbows, then raised them high.

That got her eyes open. "Oh, um…"

Not giving her time to think about it, he sank in.

Creamy wet, hot and wide-open to him, he entered easily.

Heaven.

The way she gripped him made him want to explode. He paused, his chest billowing, eyes squeezed tight, concentration flagging. He needed it to last more than a minute.

He wouldn't mind if it lasted forever.

Idly, Vanity's hand touched his chest, then flattened over his galloping heart. "You are so deep," she whispered. She inhaled, her inner muscles gripping him, and she softly moaned his name.

He lost it. Taking her mouth in a tongue-twining kiss, he pounded into her, loving how she reacted and tightened over each strong thrust.

Her arms curled around his neck. Clutching at him, she freed her mouth on a wild cry, releasing once more.

Opening his mouth on her neck to muffle his own shout, Stack let himself go. The draining pleasure seemed to go on and on until Vanity started stroking his back and making shushing noises in his ear.

Still struggling for breath, Stack released her legs carefully, waited for her to adjust, then eased on to her. He loved how her full breasts cushioned his chest, the way her face tucked against his neck, how she curled one leg over his, giving him a full body hug. She continued petting him, every so often kissing his shoulder.

Hell, he'd spent more time thinking on all the things he loved about her than about the mind-blowing sex they had.

She whispered, "You are such a stud," making him grin tiredly. He'd never had a woman offer so many compliments, sometimes on the oddest things—like his ass—while disregarding the compliments he gave her.

He smoothed a hand down her side to her hip. And yeah, he loved that, too, the warmth of her silky skin, how she luxuriated like a cat every time he stroked her. Everything.

Damn it, he loved everything about her. Drawing her closer, he asked, "You're okay?"

"Mmm. Still pulsing all over, sticky from you and me—" she lightly bit his throat "—and pretty much blown away."

"Sounds good to me." He turned to his back but brought her along so she rested atop him. Using both hands to hold her bottom, he kept her close so that they stayed connected. "I like this."

She pressed in her hips, emphasizing that he was still inside her. "You and me, together?"

"Yeah." He drifted his thumbs over those sweet dimples at the top of her behind. Maybe it was the satisfaction glowing from her beautiful blue eyes, or maybe it was the satisfaction inside him, leaving him utterly sated in a way he hadn't felt before. But whatever the cause, it seemed the right time to ask. He kissed her shoulder, her cheek, her temple. "What do you think of that?"

Quizzical, she shook her head. "What?"

"You and me, exclusive. Not for convenience, not just for sex, but because I want you, only you. And I think you want me?"

Eyes widening, she nodded quick confirmation.

Nice that she didn't make him wait and wonder. Vanity was always so honest; he loved that about her. "Then it's official." *You with me and only me, now and into the near future.* "I want everyone to know you're mine."

A breathtaking smile brightened her flushed, damp face. Putting her pointy elbows on his chest, she pushed back her hair. "You're sure?"

She looked far from disturbed by the idea. "Very sure." Her hair was wild, everywhere, and he helped her in smoothing it. Making sure she understood, he cupped her face. "I don't want to share you with anyone. I get that you're friends with the guys. I'm okay with that as long as they know you're off-limits." After losing her family, those friendships were especially important to her. To him, it was just as important that she have backup if or when she ever needed it. He wouldn't always be available. Fighters traveled, sometimes out of the country.

By staking a claim, he also ensured she had a new family, one well equipped to ensure her safety, to offer support when she needed it, whenever he wasn't around.

Her lips trembled, alarming him before she managed to turn the show of emotion into a shaky smile. "Okay." She nodded hard. "As long as everyone understands that you're off-limits as well, then, yes, I'd like that."

He wanted her to love it, but for now he'd take what he could get.

Again he rolled, putting her on her back, then reluctantly leaving her. "Let me check on the dogs, then what do you think about a soak in the tub?"

Her gaze went immediately to his arm. "It's hurting?"

Like a mother. "Just a dull ache." He couldn't think of a better way to ease it than relaxing in a hot tub with Vanity naked, wet, soapy, leaning back on him. *His.* "What do you say?"

Interest darkened her eyes yet again. "Go check the dogs," she told him with a slow smile. "I'll get the tub ready."

CHAPTER FIFTEEN

SOME DISTANT NOISE roused Stack, and as he went to stretch awake, his bruised arm protested. Disgusted with himself for getting caught, he opened his eyes and winced at the bright light sneaking through a part in the curtain.

He turned his head, found the other side of the bed empty, and rose to an elbow.

Eight-thirty.

What the hell? He hadn't slept past five in forever. His routine included rising early, often starting his day with a jog. Sure, he and Vanity had extended the night with sex, but he was pretty sure they'd both passed out by midnight.

He threw back the covers, put his legs over the side of the bed, and listened to yet another unfamiliar sound. Barking, as if the dogs were outside playing, but in the front instead of the back.

The silence of the house made him more than curious, maybe even a little worried. He made a quick trip to the john, then pulled on jeans and his flannel shirt. Coffee awaited him in the kitchen. Through the window over the sink he saw a sea of white in the backyard.

Snow. Not just a sprinkling, either. The backyard glistened, unmarred by footprints, each tree branch layered in ice, tinkling with the breeze.

Carrying a mug of coffee, he went to the front room, lifted aside a curtain, and looked out.

Son of a bitch.

Bundled up like a sexy snow bunny, Vanity stood in the yard, her boots nearly covered. She wore a white puffy jacket, white fuzzy hat and white mittens. She held a shovel and the dogs bounded this way and that around her.

The walkway was shoveled clear and half the driveway…because Leese, with his own shovel, his back to the house and Vanity, was working on it.

A salt truck drove by—the odd sound that had awakened Stack. The winter storm had come early and unexpectedly. Not that Vanity seemed to mind.

Grinning, she set aside her shovel, then packed a snowball in her mittens. Drawing back, she sent it zinging toward Leese.

It hit him dead center between his shoulder blades, and he whipped around, incredulous, before dropping the shovel and bending to scoop up his own snow. Vanity squealed, lifting her shovel to use like a shield. When she peeked out, Leese lobbed the snowball at her face.

As she ducked, her laughter carried across the yard.

Stack opened the door and immediately drew their attention. He said nothing. Hell, he wasn't sure what to say.

Elated, Vanity came clumping through the snow toward him. Both dogs, woofing happily, followed her.

"It snowed!"

"So I see." He sipped the coffee and ignored the freezing air on his naked toes. "Having fun?"

"Yes. I *love* the snow. Isn't it beautiful?"

She'd tugged the hat down to her brows, and her long

blond hair tangled around her shoulders. A red nose and cheeks made her blue eyes appear brighter. "Very."

"Usually I only saw it when we traveled, and then only to ski, not to play in. It's amazing—*oof*." She bumped into Stack, then whipped around. "Hey!"

Leese had thrown another snowball, and this one got her right in the butt.

Laughing, she dusted off her backside. "You're fired!"

"Fine by me." Carrying the shovel, Leese started toward them. He glanced at Stack and smirked. "I know you said he needed to rest, but now that Stack's dragged his sorry ass out of the bed, he can take over."

"His arm is hurt," Vanity protested. "I'll finish up."

Before Stack could get the protest said, Leese slanted him a look—one that both quelled his objections and said there was more to the situation than he realized. "She did the walkway." Leese shrugged while maintaining eye contact. "Says she enjoys it."

"I do." Vanity patted Leese's shoulder. "You two go on in, and I'll be there as soon as I finish up. You've almost finished it already anyway."

Expecting them both to obey, to just leave her outside in frigid temps and a half foot of snow, Vanity headed to the driveway. Both dogs leaped happily after her.

"Get that evil glint out of your eyes," Leese said low while stomping his feet to shake off the snow. "I came to talk to you."

"Right. You wanted to see me, so instead you played in the snow with Vanity."

"I brought along a snow shovel and a canister of salt as an excuse to stop by since you haven't yet told her you got jumped." He propped the second shovel on the porch. "Then I was going to head back to my place to clean the walkway. The kids play outside, but the landlord is slow to do anything."

Ignoring most of that, Stack asked, "What makes you think I haven't?"

Leese grinned. "She asked me about it."

"Yeah?" Standing back, Stack held the door for Leese to enter. "What'd you tell her?"

"To ask you."

The perfect answer. "She did."

Leese paused. "So you gave her all the details?"

"No." Hell no. Stack looked at Vanity. "Not all."

Leese glanced back, too, then shook his head as Vanity dumped a heavy shovelful of snow to the side. "She's a workhorse. I gave her that shovel, and she acted like it was Christmas morning and I'd given the best gift."

Stack watched her work a moment, saw she wasn't overtaxed, and closed the door. "She's unusual."

"Unique," Leese corrected as he tugged off his boots. The second he finished, he headed to the kitchen and got a mug from the cabinet.

The way he made himself at home continued to irk Stack, but he kept it to himself. He and Vanity had a new, more concrete relationship, and he'd trust in it.

He'd trust in *her.*

"Why'd you want to see me?"

Instead of answering, Leese sipped his coffee while noting Stack's "just out of bed" rumpled appearance. "So, you two are an item now?"

Holding back his ire became more difficult. "She told you that, too?"

Leese shrugged. "Pretty much."

"Then you already have your answer."

Quietly, Leese contemplated him before he set his coffee mug aside and folded his arms. "I've never had reason to do the whole big-brother routine, but I feel compelled to give it a shot now."

"Going to threaten my kneecaps?"

"Something like that." He tipped his chin. "You know she doesn't deserve to be hurt."

"Agreed." Hurting Vanity was the last thing he wanted. "I care about her." How much, he couldn't yet say. Though he'd known her for months now, they'd only just gotten intimate. He knew he wanted more. A lot more.

But it was far too soon to say he wanted forever.

"You're making a go of it?"

Stack gave him a direct stare. "She's mine."

Appearing satisfied by that, Leese nodded. "Okay then." He strode to the chair opposite Stack and sat down. Arms crossed on the table, he said, "The guys who attacked you were hired by a small-time dealer."

Stack frowned. He had a dozen questions but started with, "Why? What's his beef with me?"

"Don't know that yet. But the fact you have people asking around about it means more people are talking. I heard it from a lady friend who claims to know the dope peddler."

"You keep friends in low places."

With a short laugh, Leese sat back. "Maybe I overstated things. We hooked up one night. I haven't seen her since."

"Ah. That type of lady friend."

"She knew I'm a fighter—probably the reason she approached me in the first place."

Stack well understood pushy groupies. Many fighters dealt with them, him included.

"Right after…well, *after*, she asked if I knew you. Said she'd heard you were a *wanted* man." Leese gave a small shake of his head. "I already shared all this with the others, but I figured you'd want to hear it directly from me."

"I do, thanks." It all seemed more than curious to Stack. Why would the chick hit on Leese and then ask about another man? Bad form, for sure. "What's her name?"

"I'm not sure." Leese tugged on his ear. "Honestly, we didn't do much talking. She came on strong, took me to her hotel room, wrung me out, and just as I was leaving a few hours later, she asked about you."

"What'd you tell her?"

"Not a damn thing."

Smart. "Appreciate that."

"Course." Leese sat forward again. "She asked if I knew you. I asked why she was asking." His brows angled down. "She said she was just curious because you'd pissed off some people, specifically this dealer, and that he was looking for you. When I tried to ask her more, she clammed up."

"Hotel room, huh?"

"Yeah, sorry. I went back to that room later, but she'd already checked out."

In too many ways, it all felt like a setup. "Can you describe her?"

"Medium height, big boobs, nice legs. She wore a shit-ton of makeup and had her hair in some tight little bun thing on top of her head." Leese shrugged. "I'd have paid closer attention if I'd known she was going to grill me on you. Gotta say, she took me by surprise with it, then practically shoved me out the door."

"Did you meet her at Rowdy's?" The once shady bar was now a favorite hangout since Rowdy had bought and renovated it. He kept the place clean but laid-back, offered decent food, drinks, dancing and billiards. All in all, a comfortable ambiance.

"Sorry, no. I hit up this place nearer to my apartment. I'd only been there a few minutes when she hit on me, so we weren't there long."

"Would the bartender know her?"

Leese shook his head. "Already asked around and no one did." Uncomfortable, he shifted. "It's not really the kind of place where you can grill people without causing some suspicion. I'd only been there a few times."

Curious, Stack asked, "Why'd you go there last night?"

Leese pinched the bridge of his nose, then sent a hand through his hair. "Personal shit, okay? Nothing important."

Stack understood that. Leese was newer to the group. He'd been a mediocre fighter when Denver invited him to the rec center. But since then, he'd shown real potential. He had a lot of natural talent that only needed to be challenged and refined. Soon, Stack thought, Leese could be a real contender.

The front door opened and closed, and the sound of dogs thundering toward the kitchen made Stack smile. He turned, saw Maggie hit the kitchen floor and slide on wet paws, and then Norwood did the same. Their snow-covered feet sent them skating across the tile. Stack jumped up, as did Leese, and they'd just about contained the dogs when Vanity stepped in. She'd removed her boots, so she didn't slip, and to Stack's surprise, she seemed unconcerned with the wet tracks the dogs left everywhere.

"I hope you guys left me some coffee." On her way to the pot she chafed her hands. "I think it's getting colder instead of warmer, and it started snowing again." She poured a mug of coffee with one hand and reached for paper towels with the other. Whipping off several, she handed them to Stack.

He shared a bemused look with Leese, then cleaned the dogs' paws before soaking up the melted snow mess. Somehow the more Vanity did, the more energy she had.

Leese cleared his throat. "Another thing before I go."

From his kneeling position on the floor, Stack asked, "Yeah?"

"Some reporter called the rec center looking for you." He glanced at Vanity. "He wants to interview you both about a car fire you helped with."

Stack barely restrained his groan. He had no interest in an interview, but until he knew Vanity's feeling on it, he kept his opinion to himself.

Done cleaning the dogs, he stood and threw away the paper towels, then refilled their food dishes. At least Norwood and Maggie looked tired from their snow play. They grabbed a few bites of chow before collapsing near a ray of sunshine coming through a window.

Smiling at the exhausted "huff" Norwood gave as he half rested on Maggie, Stack went to Vanity. She had hat hair, a red nose and a wary expression. "Coffee helping?"

"Yes." Both hands curled around the mug, she sipped again.

"So, what do you think?"

"Shoveling snow is hard but fun. The cold is great, until it seeps into the bones. Overall, it's pretty cool."

Stack grinned at her. "You know that's not what I meant." He ruffled her hair, loosening it up from the smashed-hat look. "Your nose is as red as a cherry."

"Is it cute?"

He and Leese both said, "Yes," at the same time.

Stack resisted the urge to tell Leese to shut it.

Taking the coffee from her, Stack set it aside and pulled Vanity up against his chest. "You can steal some of my heat."

"Thank you." She burrowed in. "Is there a way to dodge reporters without being rude?"

Relieved, Stack hugged her. "Sure." Looking over her shoulder to Leese, he asked, "Mind giving him a statement for us?"

Zipping up his jacket in preparation to go, Leese said, "No problem."

"Just say we're glad we were there to help out. Neither of us was injured, and we're thrilled the others weren't either. If the reporter has more specific questions, tell him I can give him a call—from the rec center number. Just find out what day and time is convenient for him."

"Sounds like a plan."

Vanity pulled away to give Leese a quick hug. "Thanks for the snow shovel. I'd never even thought about it, but today it was the perfect gift."

Leese returned her hug one-armed, keeping it as casual as a man could. "My pleasure." He jeered at Stack, "Next time, kick him out of bed earlier so he can help."

Stack didn't mind the ribbing, especially since Vanity was already back in his arms.

They walked Leese to the door, cautioned him to drive carefully, and then, finally, they were alone again.

Breathing in her now-familiar scent, made crisper by her play outdoors, Stack asked, "What do you have planned today?"

"In a couple of hours I need to get the paintings to the shelter, and then I'm getting my hair and nails done." Vanity smiled up at him. "How soon do you have to go?"

He should have been out the door hours ago, but in his head he'd already been rearranging his schedule. "Depends. What'd you have in mind?"

"Sex."

Enjoying how freely she threw that out there, he grinned. "Love the way you think."

She flattened a hand on his chest, stepped into him until that hand had slid up and around his neck. "You're here, looking like you look and being so sweet with the dogs, and last night you told me we were officially an item. How could I think about anything other than getting you naked and back in bed?"

Definitely, he loved her honesty, the direct way she spoke her mind. With Vanity he didn't have to worry about her misunderstanding or, thankfully, lying to him. She was the most up-front woman he'd ever known.

Stack gathered her closer, his heart already punching hard—and her phone rang.

She touched a finger to his lips and said softly, "Hold that thought." Then she darted away to the kitchen to answer her landline.

Joining her in the kitchen, Stack refreshed both their mugs of coffee just to give himself something to do.

After her initial greeting, she said, "Oh, I'd forgotten all about it." She laughed. "Yes, good thing you called!" She listened, nodded. "I know. I was shoveling snow, too...No, it's not a problem at all. That will actually be better for me. Thank you again."

After she'd replaced the phone in the cradle, she turned to Stack with twinkling eyes and a twitchy smile. "You see what you do to me?"

He pulled her against him, ready to get back to business. "I make you forget things?"

"Everything except you." She went on tiptoe to plant a quick kiss on his mouth.

"You had another appointment?" Hopefully not more modeling of the risqué variety.

"Security installers were due here shortly. Good thing the weather threw them off. Otherwise we might have been—" she gave him a heated look "—occupied, when they knocked. They said they're behind schedule because of the snow."

Stack's brain reeled. "Security installers?"

"Afraid so." She wrinkled her nose. "This means I need to get the paintings to the shelter soon, so I can be back before they get here."

Stack shook his head. "Why are you meeting security installers?"

"I figured it was a good idea to get my house wired. You know, alarms for the doors and windows. One of those setups where the police are called if anyone breaks in." She slipped a hand up under his shirt, her palm on his bare skin. "What do you think about a quickie? I'm game if you are."

Stack ignored that, just as he ignored her provoking touch. "What's going on here? Why are you suddenly worried about a break-in?" He thought about the night before, when he'd heard something in the yard. A deer…or had it been?

"I'm not worried, exactly," she denied. "But as a woman alone, I figured I should be more cautious."

He agreed, but if anything had happened to spook her, he wanted to know. "You don't have to be alone."

"No?" She grinned—and hooked her fingers into the front waistband of his jeans. "Are you suggesting I move in some random guy?"

Hyperaware of her touch, he stared down at her. "When I can't stay with you, you can stay with me."

Her eyes rounded and her smile went slack. "You're not serious."

Shit. Yeah, he was appalled at himself, too. No way had he meant to say that. Not yet, not so soon. Floundering, he tried to retrench. "It'd be nice here and there."

She searched his face, maybe looking for the truth—a truth he hadn't yet acknowledged to himself. Rather than dig the hole deeper, Stack said nothing. He didn't trust himself.

She withdrew her hand but only to lock her arms around his neck. "When you're around I don't get much sleep, but you always make the tiredness worthwhile."

The vise on his nape loosened. Not only did Vanity skip past his invitation, she lightened the moment, letting him off the hook.

And that, too, made her special. "So you *do* get tired? And here I was beginning to think you had more stamina than a champion fighter."

"Mmm." Her fingers sank into his hair. "My stamina has improved with all our bedroom…exercise."

Before she totally distracted him with sex, Stack nodded to Maggie and Norwood. "The dogs could be considered protection." The reason fucking Phil first claimed to get them.

"No." Vanity scowled at him for making the suggestion. "I don't ever want them to be in a position of having to protect me. They could get hurt, and then I'd never forgive myself." She turned to the dogs with a fond smile. "Plus, they aren't mine. I know eventually your mother will want them back."

"They're Tabby's dogs, not Mom's."

The look she gave him spoke volumes. "F'ing Phil may have gotten them for Tabby, but they're your mother's dogs now."

True enough. "About that quickie…"

This time it was her cell that rang. Vanity laughed at his crestfallen expression, patted his chest and located her purse on the counter. She dug out the cell. The second she answered, she looked guilty and turned her back on him.

Stack worked his jaw, fighting the surge of jealousy. He had no reason, he reminded himself, so to give her privacy, he picked up his coffee and left the room.

VANITY ONLY HALF heard Tabby's invitation. She was too busy wondering if Stack's departure meant he trusted her, that he didn't care if she spoke to another man, or that she'd offended him when she turned her back.

Truthfully, despite the amazing progress they'd made and his request that they be exclusive, she still felt very unsure about things. This new facet to their relationship was tentative at best, and she didn't want him to read too much into his sister's call. If he wasn't feeling as full steam ahead as she was, he might get spooked by her rapidly growing relationship with his family.

"So, what do you say?" Tabby asked. "Want to see a movie with me tonight?"

"I can't. I have to get my hair and nails done, and then I'm seeing your brother again." Saying it aloud made it all the more real, and she couldn't keep the fat smile at bay.

She and the awesome Stack Hannigan were a couple. Her heart danced as she thought of it.

Bummed, Tabby said, "Oh. Okay. I understand."

Inspired, Vanity ventured forth an invite of her own. "Want to join me at the salon? We can get the works together. Mani, pedi, facial, all that."

Tabby heaved a long sigh. "Oh, God, that sounds *so* amazing. Like heaven. Absolute *heaven*. But I can't afford it. It was stretching the budget just to consider the movies." She laughed. "I should be buying laundry detergent, but I really wanted to see you, so…"

"It'll be my treat." Really getting into the idea, Vanity said, "Let me, please. You'd be doing me a favor, keeping me company during the whole thing. The salon can be so boring. Please? Will you join me?"

A moment of silence, and then: "Seriously? You'd do that for me?"

"I would love it, I promise."

"Are you sure you can get an appointment? What if they can't fit me in?"

"Trust me. They'll love the idea as much as I do." And if she had to promise triple in a tip, she would. "So, what do you say?"

Tabby screeched, making Vanity laugh as she held the phone away from her ear. "Yes! I say yes, yes, *yes*! Oh, *thank you*. It's been forever since I've gotten pampered. Oh, my God, I have goose bumps. *Goose bumps!*"

Gratified by that response, Vanity told her what time and where to meet her, then she ended the call and tapped in the number for the spa. Her stylist was more than happy to arrange things for Tabby, especially since another stylist had the opening.

With that done, Vanity went to look for Stack.

She found him in her bedroom, standing at the window and looking out at the yard.

Without a word Vanity skimmed off her jeans and socks, then her heavy sweatshirt, T-shirt and cami. To gain his attention, she closed the door with a click.

Stack turned, sucked in a breath at finding her naked, and stared heatedly. "Done with your call?"

"Yes." She could tell he was curious, but on a gut level she knew Stack would object to her picking up the tab on his sister's salon visit.

"Anyone important?"

Well, shoot. Apparently he wouldn't let it go without knowing. "It was Tabby."

His brows came together. "Why is she calling you?"

Here she stood, naked, and there he stood, on the other side of the room. Unacceptable. "She invited me to the movies with her. I would have loved to go but couldn't. Hopefully, we'll make it another evening." Leaving out part of the truth wasn't really a lie, she promised herself. He'd eventually find out, but then it'd be too late for him to spoil her fun or Tabby's excitement.

To shore up the arguments she'd just given herself, she grinned at him.

Suspicious, he crossed his arms.

And it was then she noticed his erection. *Nice.* So he wasn't unaffected, just being alpha.

"I hadn't realized you and Tabby were getting so cozy."

"Is that a problem?"

"No. It's just that you two are totally different."

Hmm. So he didn't mind that they were friendly. Perfect. "I'd love to have you expound on that—later. Right now I have other things on my mind." She gestured at her naked body. "I'm beginning to think I should redress."

"I much prefer you like this." While striding to her, he asked, "How much time do we have?"

"Thirty minutes, tops."

"Hmm." He stopped before her. "I can do a lot in thirty minutes."

"I was counting on that." She looked him over, then met his gaze. "Strip."

"First, let me see your arm."

Heaving a sigh, Vanity said, "I don't understand you."

"I know." Carefully, Stack opened the bandage and gently touched her skin. "Stay still while I rewrap it."

Until that moment she hadn't noticed the ointment and gauze wrapping he'd brought to her room and put on the nightstand.

"You're making me feel foolish."

He didn't look up from her arm, but he asked, "Why?"

"I have this teeny tiny burn that most wouldn't look

at twice, while your arm looks like it went through a five-round fight and lost."

The corners of his mouth tipped up. "Burns are serious. They can get infected. Bruises can't. And they'll fade quickly, I promise." He finished tending her, kissed her arm through the wrap, and said, "There. All done."

"Your arm doesn't hurt?"

"Not much."

She was still naked, and he wasn't, but she couldn't help asking, "Is that why Leese came by? Did he have news for you about the guys who jumped you?"

That startled him. He tried to hide it, but she saw it in his eyes.

"Stack, I keep telling you I'm not dumb." He and Leese were friendly but not really friends. For Leese to stop by, especially during a snowstorm, he had to have reason to talk to Stack.

"You also told me you wanted a quickie, and we don't have time for me to regale you with details of an insignificant incident *and* give you a screaming orgasm."

How he said that, the look in his eyes, made her stomach flutter. "Screaming?"

He stepped closer. "And groaning. Maybe even begging a little."

She inhaled, exhaled and nodded. "Okay, enough. Clothes off."

Saying nothing more, his smile smug, Stack reached back for a handful of his shirt and stripped it off over his head. His jeans were already open, so he dragged down the zipper, but he didn't take them off.

"Stack," she protested.

"Shh, trust me. Taking off my pants might encourage me to jump the gun, but I want to ensure you come all nice and hot for me first."

Vanity shivered. Hard to argue with that logic, so she again agreed. "Okay."

"Rest back on the wall. Yeah, like that." Taking her hands, he crisscrossed them over her chest so that she covered each breast. Looking into her eyes, he said huskily, "Hold these for me, okay?"

Beyond words, she nodded.

Smiling his approval, Stack gave her a small kiss. She wanted more, but he went to one knee in front her. "Open your legs."

Heartbeat frantic and breath rushing, Vanity braced her feet apart.

Stack looked up at her and whispered, "Wider."

He hadn't even touched her yet, and already she felt her body warming, softening. She bit her lip and widened her legs.

"Mmm. Perfect." He cupped his hands low on either side of her hips, his long fingers curling around to her bottom cheeks.

Keeping her eyes closed, she waited—and jumped when he opened her with his thumbs. She felt his breath and heard his smile when he said, "You are so pretty."

Knowing where he looked at her, her face went hot.

The first touch of his tongue made her lock her knees. Less than three minutes later she gave a soft moan.

Five minutes after that she wasn't sure she could continue standing. "Stack!"

His hands held her backside more securely, supporting her while his mouth continued to eat at her, licking and sucking until her muscles all clenched in a powerful orgasm. Crying out, she grabbed the doorknob with one hand, and tangled the other in his hair.

He maintained the rhythm, and when the last of the trembling sensation drained out of her, he shot to his feet, hooked one of her legs in his arm, and before she could even catch her breath, he was in her.

Against her cheek, while thrusting hard and fast, he whispered darkly, "You taste so fucking good."

Vanity held on to him. "I bet you'll taste good, too."

He went still for three heartbeats, then gathered her closer with a harsh groan, and she knew he was coming.

She coasted a hand down his damp back, solid with tensed muscled, all the way to that tight, sexy butt.

When he slumped against her, satisfaction kept her smiling. Satisfaction, and love. *So much love.*

She hugged him tight. "You are so good at this."

His ragged laugh shook them both.

"Careful," she said. "I'm barely keeping myself upright. If you drop, we're both going down."

He heaved a deep breath, levered back the length of one strong arm, and smiled so tenderly at her, she almost choked up.

He kissed her mouth, her cheek, her neck. "I would love to take you back to bed just to hold you awhile, but I'm already late."

"I know. It's okay."

"Have you ever driven in the snow? I want you to be extra careful today."

"As a matter of fact, I have, in other countries. And, yes, I will be."

"If anything happens, if you need me for any reason, call."

His concern had to count for something, and that

buoyed her hope. "I will." Pretending to pout, she added, "I'll just have to do a regular old call though. No bat signal for me."

"I was thinking about that." When Stack kissed her this time, it wasn't a kiss to excite, but rather a kiss of affection. "You should have emergency access, just in case. I'll pick up a phone for you, and we'll get that taken care of tonight."

Shocked, she said nothing as he gave her one last, quick kiss, gathered up his clothes, and prepared to go.

Vanity kept it together until she told him goodbye at the front door. Then she danced, twirling through the house and laughing with excitement. Maggie and Norwood joined her. The dogs liked her. Stack's mother and sister liked her. Soon, hopefully, Stack would more than like her.

She wanted his love. She wanted to be a part of his wonderful family.

And she wanted Stack Hannigan for forever.

CHAPTER SIXTEEN

TABBY NOW HAD golden highlights in her dark blond hair, which the stylist trimmed and shaped, making it fuller. Vanity loved the new look, and, given how Tabby continually shook her hair, touched it, smoothed it, she did, too.

"It *feels* better."

Vanity grinned. "I love their deep conditioning." Both women had fresh polish on their nails, and their feet were submerged in bubbling pools of warm water over polished pebbles.

Turning her head to face Vanity, tears in her eyes, Tabby smiled. "Thank you for this. It's been…well, amazing."

Gently, Vanity smiled at her. "I'm glad you're enjoying it. Having you here made it so fun. We should set up regular appointments."

That made Tabby laugh. "This place is awesome, but also high-end. I've never even been in here, and I definitely can't afford to visit. This is a onetime, very special day for me."

The nail techs returned to the room, so Vanity didn't say anything more. But if Tabby would agree, well, she'd love to have a regular salon day with her. Stack's sister emoted with flair, but she was also honest and enthusiastic, and despite the siblings' continued bickering, Vanity knew Tabby truly loved Stack, and vice versa. While their feet were buffed and massaged, and their toenails painted, she and Tabby indulged in idle chitchat.

"You and my brother are getting awfully cozy."

"I know." Vanity still wanted to hug herself. "Stack is just incredible."

Tabby laughed. "I can only speak about him as a brother, but, yeah, he's pretty terrific."

Vanity bit her lip, but she couldn't hold it in. "We're officially monogamous," she blurted.

"You weren't before?"

Oh. No, Vanity couldn't actually explain about her illicit proposition to Tabby's brother. So instead she said, "We'd sort of…tried it on for size. You know, to see if we'd suit."

Grinning, Tabby said, "And you do."

"We do!"

"I'm glad. Stack has dated some real wieners, but we like you."

"We?"

"Mom and me." Tabby looked away and shrugged. "Phil, too."

"I'm glad, because I like you and Lynn a lot, also." She preferred not to touch the subject of f'ing Phil.

Vanity had prepaid, including gratuity, so as soon as they were done, they headed to the front lobby.

That's when she got her first look at Tabby's winter coat.

Damn. She'd arrived at the spa before Tabby and had already been in a seat when a hostess showed her in. Until now she hadn't realized that Tabby wore a threadbare coat at least five years old. It didn't look all that warm either.

Vanity took a quick peek at the clock. Bummer. If she didn't leave now, she'd be late meeting with Stack. But surely he could wait an hour or two.

She couldn't, in good conscience, send Tabby out into the winter storm without first trying to get her something warmer.

"Are you in a rush?"

Seeming very distracted and maybe a little sad, Tabby glanced back at her. "No. Just heading home to check on Mom. She's feeling much better, even insisting that she wants to move back to her own place. I've liked having her there. She's good company in the evening."

Where was f'ing Phil in the evenings? "If Lynn doesn't need you, do you think we could hit up the mall for an hour or two?" Vanity took her hands. "Please, please, don't be offended. But I'm having so much fun, and you're such great company, I'd love to spend a little more time with you. Shopping with a friend is as much fun as the salon with a friend." She tried an engaging smile. "I know you're on a budget, so don't worry about that. This will still be my treat. A special day for the two of us. What do you say?" And to better her odds, Vanity added, "Pretty please?"

As Vanity watched, Tabby's face crumpled. Her eyes went red, her bottom lip trembled, and she pulled away to cover her face with her hands.

Oh, no! Crying? Vanity didn't hear any sobs, but the way Tabby's shoulders shook alarmed her.

"Tabby?" Vanity inched closer, dipping her head to try to see her friend's face. "I'm sorry. I didn't mean to upset you."

In the next second, Tabby had her clutched in a hug so tight, Vanity could barely breathe.

Uh… Unsure what to make of that, Vanity awkwardly patted her back. "Are you okay?"

Tabby nodded. "Yes. I'm sorry. It's just…" She held Vanity back, and to her relief, Tabby smiled. "You are the nicest, most considerate person I've ever known. And I…well, things have been so rough lately, and I guess I just…"

Vanity found her own smile, and this time she pulled Tabby in for the hug. "I know, I understand."

It was a few seconds more before the women separated.

Tabby said, "Just let me call Mom to make sure there's nothing she needs."

"Ohhh, great idea! Tell her we'd love to pick her out something, too."

Laughing, Tabby shook her head. "Mom will definitely refuse, but I'll try."

"While you do that, I'll give your brother a call." Still giddy about it, she explained, "We're getting together again tonight."

"He's lucky to have you."

"Thank you." Bubbling with happiness, Vanity stepped a few feet away and thumbed in Stack's number on her cell.

He answered with, "I've missed you."

Awww. Her heart melted. "Same here."

"Plan on going straight to bed, okay? I promise to feed you after."

Vanity laughed. "This is probably a bad time to tell you that I'm going to be a little late. Maybe an hour or two."

He groaned with great feeling.

Making sure Tabby wouldn't overhear, she murmured, "I promise to make it up to you."

"Talk like that and I'll get a boner."

Vanity imagined it, then issued her own groan.

With amusement in his tone, Stack said, "Soon, darlin'. Real soon." He blew out a breath. "You get things hammered out with those security installers?"

"Yes. They've already taken care of everything. Very efficient." She cleared her throat. "Guess I'll need to give you the code tonight. And I was thinking..." Taking the next step on the phone seemed easier than in person. "You should have a key."

Without missing a beat, Stack asked, "To your place?"

Very unsure of herself, she nodded. "Yes?"

"Great idea. I'll give you one to my apartment, too."

Her jaw loosened. He'd accepted that with no hesitation at all. "Um, okay, great."

"Did the shelter like your paintings?"

"They were really pleased. Remember the one of the mama dog and her puppies? They liked it enough that they want to hang it in the shelter lobby instead of including it in the auction. I told them I'd make a donation so they wouldn't have to sell it."

"I remember it. All the paintings are fantastic, though, so I'm sure the shelter will make a bundle."

She glowed with his praise. "Thank you." Belatedly, she realized Tabby was done with her call and waiting. "I guess I should go."

"Drive carefully."

"You, too." She wanted so badly to add that she loved him. It felt natural, like the perfect, appropriate thing to say to Stack. Instead she sighed. "See you soon."

"Not soon enough."

Okay, so his impatience was almost as good. Grinning, Vanity put away her phone, pulled on her mittens, and together she and Tabby went out to her car. "Want to just ride with me?"

"Since I took the bus, that'd be great."

"You didn't drive?" Vanity unlocked the doors, so they could both get inside.

"Phil has the car." Tabby smoothed a hand over the leather seat. "Usually walking to the bus stop isn't a big deal, but it was awfully icy outside today."

With each passing minute, Vanity disliked Phil more. "I'll drive you home after we're done." Luckily the snow had stopped, and without the wind, it didn't feel so miserably cold. After Vanity started the car it didn't take long for the heater to warm the interior, especially with the help of heated seats.

Tabby kept looking around. "I like your car."

"Thanks. I do, too." It wasn't a luxury car by any stretch, but she supposed any new car held appeal. Driving out of the lot, Vanity tried to find the right words. "Didn't Phil say something about finding a new job?"

Tabby looked away. "I don't think so."

"Oh. I thought maybe that's why he needed the car."

Tabby just shook her head.

Ooookay. A dead end there. Vanity wasn't sure how to tactfully ask her about the money she'd given Phil for work boots and such. So she didn't. Right now, it didn't matter. She just wanted Tabby to have fun.

The salon wasn't far from the mall. In true power-shopping mode, Vanity bought herself a few new, cozy sweaters and convinced Tabby to accept two new outfits, new boots, a coat, scarf and mittens.

Within an hour and a half, they were heading home. The roads were clear, the air crystal cold, the early evening a beautiful shade of blue-gray.

Looking somewhat dazed by it all, Tabby kept glancing at the bags in the backseat. "It feels like my birthday and Christmas all rolled together."

"I loved it," Vanity assured her. "This has been so much fun."

"I think you're nuts, but it's a terrific kind of nuts." Admiring her manicured nails, Tabby added, "I don't know how to thank you enough."

"I know how. Promise you'll wear one of the new outfits when we go to the movies."

Her head lifted. "You still want to?"

"Shoot, yes! You're terrific company. And you know what? You have to start going to the MMA competitions with me. You'll love my friend Yvette. She's married to Cannon Colter."

"Stack's friend."

"Right, do you know him?"

For the rest of the ride home they talked about the fighters, the competitions, and by the time Vanity pulled up to the curb, she'd gained Tabby's promise to go to some of the local SBC fights with her. Denver Lewis would fight in a week in Columbus, and even though Vanity offered to pay her way, Tabby said she couldn't yet afford the time off work.

Soon, though.

Parked at the curb, Vanity turned to face the passenger seat. "Did you need help carrying everything in?"

Tabby shook her head. She bit her lip, looked at the packages again—and drew in a shuddering breath. "I'm sorry!" Eyes wide, she fanned her face and tried to keep the sudden well of tears from falling. "I'm such a dope and an emotional mess and you're being so nice and understanding, and for some reason that only *makes it worse*."

Vanity stared in horror. The last few words had been a wail, and she wasn't sure what to do about it. She reached for Tabby's hand. "What am I making worse?"

"My stupid tears!" Tabby choked, the tears dropped, and frantically she pulled away to dig in her purse for a tissue. "Damn it!"

Vanity opened the glove box and pulled out several to hand to her. "Take a breath."

She did, then let it out with more garbled apologies.

Stack hadn't been kidding about his sister being dramatic. Never in her life, even after she'd lost everyone, had Vanity cried with so much...verve.

She sort of envied Tabby the ability. "I'd like to help, but I need to know the problem."

Tabby blew her nose, blindly reached out for more tissues—which Vanity supplied—then cleaned the tears off her cheeks. "It's not your problem to deal with."

"We're friends now. At least, I hope we are."

Even more dramatic, Tabby said, "I hope so, tooooo!"

Vanity almost smiled at the forlorn way Tabby said that. "Friends share."

Nodding, Tabby swallowed hard. Waffled, sobbed a little more, and finally confessed, "Oh, God, Vanity. I'm *pregnant*."

"You're...oh. Oh!" Her thoughts scrambled. "I think maybe that's wonderful...isn't it?"

"It would be. I mean, I love kids." Hand over her midsection, Tabby said more softly, "I especially love this kid. And Mom will go nuts." Her gaze sought Vanity's.

"I only just found out, and I'm not very far along. Only five weeks. But I want the baby. I swear I do."

"I believe you." Taking a leap, Vanity said, "You're upset because there are other things to consider?"

"Yes." Tabby looked down at her hands. "I was finally ready to admit that Stack was right."

"About?"

"Phil." Tabby blew her nose again. "I found out that he hasn't even been looking for a job. And he's back to smoking dope. And Mom said he brought that bitch, Whitney, to the apartment." Suddenly furious, Tabby looked up. "I put in all the overtime I can get, and Phil blows it on pot and partying with his buddies! That's bad enough. But he knows I love my brother, he knows things are strained between Stack and me, and he knew, damn him, he *knew* how Stack would react to Whitney."

"I'm so sorry." Vanity's thoughts scrambled. Clearly Tabby didn't wonder if Phil had cheated with Whitney. Stack had said he wasn't sure, but even if it did happen, maybe, for Tabby's sake, it'd be better if she didn't know.

Breathing hard, Tabby said, "You know Phil is a terrible person. *Everyone* knows. It's not like Stack makes a secret of it."

"Stack loves you, so he's biased. I'm not sure he'll be convinced anyone is good enough for you."

That took the steam out of Tabby's grief. "Really?"

Smiling, Vanity patted her hand. "You don't know how much your brother loves you?"

"Sure I do. Even though we argue almost constantly, we're still close. I meant the part about him not thinking anyone was good enough."

Vanity had only guessed on that. "Brothers are like

that, right?" Another guess, but from what she'd seen, most of Stack's ire stemmed from concern for his sister.

"Well, he'll be glad to know I'm finally leaving Phil."

"I don't think he'll be glad. But it hurts him to think Phil doesn't put as much into the relationship as he should. Your brother wants you to have an equal partner, not someone who takes advantage of you."

"I've made such a mess of things. Stack could tell you that my whole life is disorganized." Tabby did more dabbing of her eyes, and her voice went faint with worry. "Being alone scares me so much. Phil isn't much, but I can barely take care of me, so how am I going to take care of my baby?"

This time Vanity could speak with more confidence. "You're not alone. You have Stack and Lynn, and now we're friends, too, right? I promise you, it's all going to work out." Again, Vanity took her hand. "When will you tell Stack?"

"I don't know yet." She gave a watery laugh. "I have to work up my nerve, especially since he told me long ago to kick Phil out. Stack has it together in a way I never have. I... I know I've hogged the limelight, but damn it, it's so easy for him. He wants something, and he makes it happen. Me, I just screw up. Over and over."

"So," Vanity said gently, "now you're going to stop screwing up. Now you're going to make things right."

Tabby nodded, and more tears fell. "Oh, Vanity, why didn't I listen?"

"You gave your marriage a chance. There's nothing wrong with that. In fact, I think it's admirable. Just as it's admirable for you to make your own decision on whether or not to continue the marriage."

"I'm ending it," Tabby assured her. She gripped Vanity's hands. "Just…just not yet. Not while my mom is staying with me. Please don't say anything to Stack, okay?"

"I promise I won't." Vanity sighed. "A baby. It's funny, because we've only just met, but I'm excited."

Tabby sniffled, but her smile slipped into place, too. "You are?"

She nodded, in awe of one fact. "Stack is going to be an uncle."

"Yes." Tabby actually laughed. "The best uncle in the whole world."

IN A VERY short time, it seemed they fell into the perfect routine. For the past three days, he and Vanity went about their days doing whatever needed to be done, and then came together again at her house. Sex generally preceded dinner.

It also preceded breakfast more often than not.

Every night they slept together, and they stayed in touch throughout the day.

Stack had to admit, the security system at her house made him feel better about her being without him. And now that she also had the extra cell phone—the bat signal as she had them all calling it—he had little reason to worry.

Nothing had come from pressuring the guys who'd jumped him. Neither of the men had been approached for a repeat performance, and until they were, they wouldn't know anything new. They'd been hired and paid by a nameless thug. End of story.

He hoped.

With his arm now healed, Stack felt less inclined to keep chasing the problem. Leese hadn't seen the woman again, and nothing more had happened. They'd all keep an eye out, Vanity wasn't at risk, so what did it matter?

He had better things to concentrate on—like the woman sleeping beside him.

For once he'd awakened before her, so Stack rose to an elbow to look at her. He'd never tire of seeing Vanity like this, relaxed, at her ease with him.

Naked.

In public, Vanity was comfortable with her body, but still somewhat modest. She didn't dress for sex appeal as much as comfort.

In private, however, she reveled in a lack of inhibition.

For years, he'd wondered how a woman could ever fit into his life. Being a fighter brought its own challenges to a relationship. Women, in his experience, could be needy. For time, attention. And not overly understanding, not with the hours it took to train, and the travel involved in competing.

Vanity didn't fit any of those preconceived notions.

She might look high-maintenance, but she had no problem getting sweaty at the gym. She put her all into her workouts, and got along great with the other fighters.

He couldn't imagine a woman more delicate than her, but her independence rivaled his own. She wanted him, but she didn't need him. Somehow that felt more complimentary.

She had talent that she discounted. Money that she didn't flaunt.

And she was honest with him, about everything. No doubt about it, Vanity was one of the hottest women he'd ever seen, but it was her bold tendency to speak her mind that he found most appealing.

"Hey." Drowsily, she scooted closer, slipping an arm around his waist and hooking a leg over his. "Why didn't you wake me?"

"No reason to." His fingertips sought her silky skin, trailing over the arm she had around him. "It's early still."

"But you're awake," she said sleepily. "So I want to be awake with you."

Going to his back, Stack pulled her over him. They had sex every day, often twice a day, and still he didn't think he could ever get enough of her. "What do you have planned today?"

"Hmm…" Her murmur faded away to soft, warm breaths against his flesh.

It took so little for her to scald him with lust. He thought of her, and he strained with need.

Time ticked by. Stack assumed she'd fallen back asleep. He was okay with that. Much as he wanted her, holding her was equally nice. He kissed the top of her head over the crooked part in her hair.

As if that roused her, she whispered, "Well, first, there's this handsome fighter I need to debauch."

In a million different ways, she amused him. "Debauch, huh?" That sounded intriguing.

"Thoroughly." She squirmed against his erection, making his breath catch and his muscles tighten. "After we recover from that, I need to make my arrangements for Denver's fight."

Luckily, they didn't have to travel far, just to Columbus. Drivable distance. "You're staying the night?"

"Yes." Her hand traveled over his heated skin. "Will you have time to sneak to my room?"

"Count on it." Usually at a fight, either for himself or a friend, he stayed totally focused until the competition ended. With Vanity there, accessible, he knew that wouldn't be possible. "I'm sorry I can't ride up with you." The fighters would leave for Columbus a few days beforehand. Whenever possible, the organization liked to schedule local talent to greet the fans, autograph memorabilia, mug for pictures, all in all, talk up the sport. Stack wasn't competing, but before the actual night of the competition he'd take part in all the promo and a few interviews, as would Cannon, Gage and Armie.

Leese would stay behind to keep the rec center running; that was something they took turns doing. Not that Harper, Gage's wife, couldn't handle it in their absence. She could probably run Union Terminal without breaking a sweat. But since the rec center's inception, the guys had made a point of always having at least one of them around…just in case.

"It's okay," Vanity mumbled around a yawn. "Cherry and Merissa are going up together, so Yvette will ride with me. Besides, you'll probably be too busy to even think about me."

Never that. Hell, he missed her the second he stepped out the door. But admitting it didn't feel right. Their relationship was still too new, too tentative.

And in the back of his mind, resentment lingered over the way Whitney had burned him. Never again would he take a chance on getting duped like that.

Unaware of his thoughts, Vanity pressed a kiss to his ribs. "After I take care of that, I'm working for Yvette at the shop, and then doing a photo shoot for another department store. But I should be home early."

Home. He loved the sound of that. Her modest house felt like a real home, especially with Vanity in it. Already his clothes had a place in her closet and dresser. She'd designated a spot in the bathroom for his toothbrush and razor. They took turns cooking and cleaning, depending on who was available.

Without either of them confirming it aloud, they were now living together.

Vanity's fingertips moved over his chest. "Want me to cook dinner?"

"Or I could take you out for once."

"Mmm." She slowly scooted up to nuzzle his neck. "Maybe Rowdy's? We haven't been there in forever."

If less than a week was forever. But the bar was so popular, pretty much everyone enjoyed hanging out there. "Sounds good." Stack teased a finger along her spine, and lowered his voice suggestively. "Long as we don't stay too late."

"Right. Because I'm pretty sure I'll need to debauch you again tonight."

Damn, he loved her enthusiasm.

Knowing it'd be a touchy subject for her, he stroked her hair as he asked, "When are the dogs going back to Tabby?"

She rose up to look at him with sleep-heavy eyes. That impossibly long, fair hair fell around them, draping his shoulders, spilling over his chest. He smoothed it back and to one side, then couldn't help admiring her breasts, mostly squashed against his chest. He could feel her stiffened nipples.

No way to ignore that.

"The dogs will go to your mother's. You didn't know that?"

Yesterday his mother had insisted on returning to her own place. He'd stopped in to check on her, and of course he'd run into Vanity there. She'd infiltrated his family with ease, and as often as not, when he saw his mother and sister, they spent half their time talking about her.

His mother wouldn't stop singing Vanity's praises, claiming repeatedly that she was "a keeper." Tabby took a different tact, warning him not to screw up, telling him Vanity was so beautiful, she could have any man she wanted, but she'd chosen him and he should appreciate that.

Vanity was gorgeous, no denying that.

But as she'd often reminded him, looks weren't everything. What Vanity didn't seem to realize was that he found her even more beautiful inside than out.

"Stack?"

More and more around her, he had a hard time keeping on track. "Mom's retired. She shouldn't have to care for Tabby's dogs."

"Stack," she said again, this time with censure. Dipping down, she kissed him. "Lynn loves those dogs as much as I do. As much as *you* do." She rubbed her nose against his, then scooted to sit up beside him. "Plus, I think she's lonely. She misses your dad so much."

"I know." Stack deeply appreciated Vanity's empathy to others. She had a very big heart. "You think the dogs keep her company?"

"Yes. And they give her a focus." Going thoughtful, she pulled her hair over her shoulder and began braiding it. "You know I'm right, you're just set on being annoyed about it."

Stack put his hands behind his head and enjoyed the view of Vanity naked, doing something so infinitely feminine. "I'm not annoyed. But I would like to see Tabby accept her responsibilities. For *her*, as much as for my mom. I think she'll be happier if she does."

"I agree, and I know she's trying."

Stack smiled. "You know something? You treat Tabby like a kid sister, but she's eight years older than you."

Vanity shrugged, which did interesting things to her bare breasts. "I've had an easier life than she has."

It astounded him that she thought so. For most of her life Tabby had been spoiled by two loving parents, was *still* spoiled by their mother. Vanity came from a dysfunctional home, and now she had no one.

Stack immediately rethought that. She had him. She had his family. He wondered if she realized that.

Vanity eyed him. "Why are you looking at me like that?"

"Because you're very special." He lifted his chin. "Now come here and debauch me as promised."

Gaze smoldering, she released her hair and leaned toward him.

With incomparable timing, his cell phone rang.

Vanity bounced back. "The bat signal!"

"It's probably nothing." Many times, the extra cells were used to share info, not for anything urgent. Using the cell with the special ringtone ensured the call would be answered, rather than put on hold for other, possibly more corporal pursuits.

The lost moment frustrated Stack. Rolling to sit on

the side of the bed, he grabbed the cell, glanced at the caller ID and answered. "What's up, Leese?"

Crowding in close behind him, her breasts to his back, Vanity draped her arms over his shoulders and listened in. To let her know he didn't mind, Stack curled a hand over her forearm.

Leese said, "Sorry to call so early."

"No problem. Assume it's important."

"Yeah, remember how that chick said a drug dealer had hired the guys to jump you? Now she says he's been hired to kill you."

Whoa. Slowly Stack stood; he couldn't take the distraction of Vanity inciting his lust right now. "No shit?"

"That's what she said. I was heading out for a jog early this morning, and she was at the park. I swear, I think she was waiting for me. She didn't look like an early bird, and she wasn't dressed to jog. She called me over and told me to tell you to watch your ass because the dealer was hiring better guys to make a second run against you."

Stack whistled. Murder. Okay, so maybe he wouldn't let it go after all.

"She also said the dealer had nothing against you, that someone else had hired him to arrange the hit on you." Filled with disgust, Leese added, "From what I gathered, you were supposed to be beat near to death that first time."

"And that's the best they sent?"

With a shrug in his tone, Leese said, "Apparently the guy who paid the dealer was pissed that better men hadn't been sent. From what she said, he's out to correct that mistake this time."

Leese drew a breath. "For the record, I pressed for

her name, but she refused to share it. If you ask me, it's so fishy it reeks, but I wanted you to know."

Unbelievable. "I'll talk to Cannon." Until now, Stack hadn't considered the situation too important. But this news changed everything. "He has an in with the cops."

"Right. The detectives and lieutenant that were at his wedding. I remember." Leese was silent a moment, then said, "Not sure how factual any of this is, but you should stay on guard."

Stack heard the implication. "Go on."

"I think she knows you, dude. Sounded that way to me. She didn't really talk about you the way someone would a stranger."

Suspicions gelled. "Can you describe her again?"

"Even though it was still dark, I took a better look this time. Light blue eyes. Brown hair with a little bit of a reddish tint, at least that's how it looked under the street lamp. She had it down this time, a little past her shoulders. She's shapely, with a big rack."

Whitney. "Around twenty-five or so?"

"That'd be my guess."

"Thanks, Leese." A knock sounded on Vanity's front door. Stack held her back when she started to leave the bed. To Leese he said, "I owe you one."

"Or two, but who's keeping count? I hope the info helps. If there's anything you need…"

He left that open-ended, maybe because Stack had been so resistant to Leese's friendship with Vanity. Now, with the possibility of real danger, he'd as soon every fighter keep an eye on her.

"Thanks, man. If I do, I'll be in touch." Stack disconnected the call and pulled on his jeans, saying to Vanity, "I'll get the door while you get dressed."

"Okay, but be careful!"

She couldn't know the specifics of the conversation, but Vanity was good at picking up on cues. Another of her endearing qualities.

The minute he left the bedroom, Norwood and Maggie fell into step beside him. Extra cautious with Vanity nearby, Stack lifted a side curtain and saw his sister standing on the porch.

He jerked the door open. "Tabby?"

She looked surprised to see him.

Given the tear tracks marring her cheeks, he was more surprised. "What's wrong?"

"Stack!" She threw herself against him.

Automatically he gathered her close. Many times, in many ways, his sister made him nuts. But he loved her, and to this day he couldn't be immune to her tears, common as they might be. "Are you okay?"

"I thought you'd be gone already."

So she'd brought the drama to Vanity? Through long practice, he understood what it took to get the answers he needed. He held her back. "Mom's okay?"

"Yes."

"You're not physically hurt?"

"No." She hiccupped, absently patted the anxious dogs, then faced him with trumped-up bravado. "I want to talk to Vanity."

When he said nothing, the tears started flowing again.

From behind them, Vanity said, "What's going on? Tabby?"

To Stack's annoyance, Tabby abandoned him and ran to Vanity.

Worse, Vanity opened her arms and offered comfort. "Shh. It's okay now. I'm here."

Stack resisted the urge to growl.

"I need to…to…talk to you." She cast Stack a glance. "A…alone."

Vanity gazed at Stack with silent apology.

Amazing how fast a day could go to hell. "Come on." Stack pulled his sister away and got them all started for the kitchen. "First, no, I'm not leaving you here alone with Vanity."

Her face crumpled again.

Stack ignored it. "Take a seat. The dogs need to go out, and I need coffee."

"I'll get the coffee going," Vanity offered. She seemed anxious to have something to do. Not that he could blame her. Anything was preferable to being the recipient of Tabby's tears.

Stack pulled out a chair at the kitchen table and pressed his sister into it, then handed her two napkins so she could clean her face. Next he opened the back door and whistled for the dogs. As soon as Norwood and Maggie ran out to the yard, he went to Vanity, kissed her cheek and whispered, "Sorry."

She sent him a soft smile—as if she was proud of him for something. Had she expected him to close the door on his own sister? To deny her? No, he didn't like Tabby's theatrics, but she was his sister through the good and the bad.

Feeling as if he faced the gallows, Stack joined Tabby at the table. She looked marginally composed now—but also capable of letting loose again if he said the wrong thing. "Better?"

She sniffled. "Yes."

"Tell me what's going on."

She clutched the wadded napkins in her hands and looked to Vanity for support.

"Go on," Vanity urged her. "It'll be okay."

Tabby nodded, drew a breath and blurted, "I've left Phil."

CHAPTER SEVENTEEN

WELL, HELL. STACK SAT back in his seat, studied his sister's anxious face, then Vanity's expectant expression, and he shook his head. The irony of it almost made him laugh. "I really wish you hadn't done that."

Both women gawked at him.

Stack squeezed the bridge of his nose. He felt a headache coming on, and the day had barely begun. A day that, moments ago, had seemed so promising with sizzling sex on the breakfast menu.

"Stack." Scowling, Vanity touched his arm. "You know you're pleased that your sister has left Phil. It's what you wanted. Tell her so."

Un-freaking-believable. "Are you instructing me?"

She frowned at him, her gaze unflinching. "If I need to, yes."

The bold way she tried to stare him down made his mouth quirk. Damn, but he loved her. It struck him that he'd probably loved her for a while now.

Likely even before she'd made the offer of uncommitted sex.

The coffeepot finished sputtering, so he got up and poured three mugs. He knew how both Vanity and his sister drank theirs, so while he prepped the drinks, he shared his thoughts.

"You're serious, Tabby? You won't change your mind?"

"I won't." She swallowed hard again. "You were right about him all along. I know I've been an idiot."

Stack handed her the coffee with sugar and cream. Then he kissed her cheek. "I'm glad you're done with him."

"You are?"

"He was never good enough for you."

The women shared a knowing look.

Stack handed the second mug to Vanity. "You knew this was coming?"

"I knew she was thinking about it." She sipped her coffee, then murmured, "Perfect. Thank you."

Standing over her, Stack crossed his arms. For the moment he let Tabby stew and concentrated on Vanity. "So, you and my sister were keeping secrets from me?"

"Tabby asked me to keep her secret, so I did. You don't have to know everything, Stack Hannigan. Women are allowed to talk without updating you."

"This was more than usual girl talk."

Vanity jumped on that like a dog on a bone. "Girl talk? What, pray tell, is girl talk?" Shoving her seat back, she stood and squared off with him. "Is this more of your sexist nonsense where women only focus on nails and hair and—"

Stack kissed her to wind her down. It worked better than he expected, given she fisted a hand in his shirt and held on, making the kiss longer than he'd intended.

In fact, by the time *she* ended it, he'd forgotten what he wanted to say.

Vanity, however, went straight back to topic. "Sometimes," she told him gently, "a woman wants to talk to another woman, not her overprotective, macho brother."

"I'm not macho."

They both snorted. He turned to Tabby, saying, "Stow it."

Tears still clung to her lashes, but she smiled and pretended to zip her lips.

Vanity brought his face back around to her. "Tabby and I are friends. Friends talk."

Jumping in, Tabby said, "She's the best of friends." Smoothing her hand down her sweater, she added, "She bought me this, and my coat and boots. And she paid for me to get my hair done and—"

"Tabby," Vanity cut in, her face now flushed. "Weren't we just saying that he *doesn't* need a blow-by-blow report of how we've spent our time?"

Stack studied her. It didn't surprise him that Tabby would take advantage. And he even understood Vanity's need to help where she could. He didn't like it, but he got it.

What bothered him was that she'd never, not once, mentioned it.

Narrowing his eyes, he asked, "Are you *friends* with my mother, too?"

Guilty, she pinched the air and admitted, "Little bit."

Shit. "So you're funding my whole family?"

She took exception to that. "Not *funding* them. I've bought a few gifts because I enjoy gift-giving. There's no harm in that."

"If there's no harm, then why didn't you tell me?"

Lifting to her toes, her nose almost touching his, she said succinctly and with a lot of sass, "It wasn't your business."

He leaned into her anger. "My family isn't my business?"

"Your relationship with them is, of course. But not

my relationship with them." She dropped back to her heels and crossed her arms. "It's independent of whatever happens with us."

"What the hell does that mean?"

"Even when this—" she gestured between them "—ends, I hope they'll remain my friends."

"Nothing between us is ending."

She blinked at him, making him realize that he'd raised his voice. Stomping down the irritation, Stack gathered his control, lowered his tone and tried to sound more reasonable.

"You know how I feel about lies."

She gasped hard. "I didn't lie."

Distraught, Tabby rushed to agree. "Seriously, Stack, I begged her to keep my secrets." Fresh tears sprouted. "I couldn't talk to you, knowing how you hated Phil and how…how stupid I'd been." Her choked voice immediately brought Vanity to her side. This time it didn't calm Tabby. "I know I've screwed up *everything*. But this time, it's the worst!"

For once, Tabby's upset seemed sincere. Stack stared down at her, knowing there were things she hadn't yet told him.

Vanity glared at him as if he were the one who'd upset her.

"Whatever it is," he said over the noise Tabby made, "we'll figure it out."

"There, you see?" Vanity told her. "Didn't I tell you it'd be okay?"

Tabby nodded while wiping away her ruined makeup. "I'm so sorry, Stack. I know I've said that a million times, but I mean it. I'm sorry, and somehow I'm going to make it work."

Make *what* work?

Vanity rubbed her shoulder. "You have no reason to be sorry. Trust your brother."

Did Vanity trust him, then? He hoped so. "Tabby?"

She wouldn't look at him, but when she whispered, "I'm pregnant," he heard her loud and clear.

And still he repeated dumbly, "Pregnant?"

With another sob, she nodded.

"Phil's?"

Wailing, Tabby buried her face in her crossed arms on the table.

Stack nudged Vanity aside and went to his knees beside his sister. He smiled just a little. *A baby.* Wow. "Tabby?" He goosed her side. "Turn off the waterworks, okay? A baby is…well, not a bad thing. Not at all."

Her head jerked up. "You mean it?"

Never had he seen his sister look so miserable. "Of course I mean it." The smile widened. "Mom's going to flip."

Tabby cried, laughed, choked a little more. "That's what I told Vanity."

He twisted to see Vanity standing there, her face filled with uncertainty. "You knew about this, too?"

She nodded.

Damn, she was good at keeping a secret. He'd have to remember that.

He turned back to his sister. "I promise you, this isn't going to be the hardship you're imagining."

"She wants the baby," Vanity interjected.

"Of course she does." He glanced at her again. "I do know my sister, darlin'."

"Oh." Vanity rubbed her arms. "Yes, of course you do."

Reclaiming his attention, Tabby said with accusation, "You weren't happy to know I kicked Phil out."

"I misspoke and I'm sorry. Believe me, whatever
your reasons, I'm sure it was one hundred percent the
right thing to do." However it happened, no matter why
it happened, removing Phil from her life was a good
move. Especially now, with a kid involved.

But at least when Phil lived with Tabby, Stack knew
where to find him. Now, if the bastard went to ground,
it'd be tougher to corral him.

"You asked if the baby was his." Tabby waited for
his explanation on that.

"Only because you were so upset. I thought maybe
something else was going on." A thought occurred to
him, and he frowned. "Does Phil know?"

Tabby's eyes went liquid again. "I told him." She
shredded the napkins in her wringing hands. "He…he
said it wasn't his problem."

Pleased to know Phil wouldn't be in the picture,
mucking it up, Stack smiled at his sister. "How could a
baby be anyone's problem?"

"Even if Phil's the father?"

"You're the mother," Vanity said. "That's all that
matters."

"Exactly." Stack stood, pulled Tabby from her seat,
and wrapped her in his arms to admit the truth. "I'm
excited."

She laughed against his chest, using his shirt to dry
her eyes. "Because I'm leaving Phil," she teased, "or
because you'll be an uncle?"

Squeezing her, he said, "Both." He set her away from
him. "You two might want to sit down again."

Alarmed, Tabby said, "What are you going to do?"

Before he could get exasperated, Vanity stepped in. "Don't be silly, Tabby." She urged his sister into her seat. "Stack's not going to *do* anything. Nothing bad anyway. I think it's just that he has something important to tell us." Keeping one hand on Tabby's shoulder, Vanity tipped her head at him. "Something to do with that phone call?"

Always so astute. "Yes." He held Vanity's chair out for her, waited for her to take it, then seated himself. "You both know some yahoo jumped me."

"Two yahoos," Tabby said.

Vanity kept quiet.

"Two," he confirmed. "We've been keeping up with them, but so far that hadn't gotten us much. They claim they don't know who hired them, but if the guy made contact again, they were supposed to let us know."

Both women listened intently.

"Then this morning," Stack said, "I got a call from Leese." He explained about the woman, and with every word, Vanity looked more enraged. Interesting. He'd seen many emotions from her, but not that one. Tabby, for the most part, didn't seem to be getting it. Laying it out there, Stack said, "By the description, I think the woman is Whitney."

Tabby gasped. "That *bitch*. I never did like her!"

With a very different reaction, Vanity said, "But that would mean…" She glanced at Tabby, then shook her head and fell mum again.

Stack took his sister's cold, trembling hand. "Sis, you know Phil and Whitney have remained…friends."

Going blank, all expression wiped clean, Tabby watched him. "What are you saying?"

She'd already been through a lot today, but she

needed to hear it all. Stack collected her other hand, holding both. "If the woman is Whitney, then it's probable that the man she says is instigating all this is—"

"Phil?" Tabby gave a nervous laugh. "Don't be silly. Phil is too lazy to plan anything like that."

Stack refused to release her when she tried to pull away. "Whitney told Leese that the guys weren't just hired to rough me up."

Vanity wrapped her arms around her middle.

Eyes flaring wide, Tabby said, "Oh, my God. You're saying they were supposed to *kill* you?"

"That's what she said. No idea yet if it's true."

The laugh turned hysterical. "And you think Phil was behind it? That's insane!"

Typical of Tabby, anything inconvenient got denied. "I'm going to run down some leads today to see what I can find out." Stack gave her hands a gentle squeeze. "I'll also give Phil a call, and hopefully he'll make this easy. When I thought he was still with you, I planned to stop by and talk to him face-to-face. Now he might be able to dodge me."

Tabby groaned. "Don't hate me, okay?"

Softer, Stack said, "Never a possibility."

She winced. "I demolished Phil's phone."

Releasing her, Stack sat back. This just kept getting better and better.

Tabby rushed into frantic explanations. "I paid for that phone! It was under my name, my plan. I told him to get his own damn phone. I didn't know…didn't know that all of this was happening."

Shit. Stack blew out a frustrated breath. "You have any idea where he might have gone?"

She shook her head. "No. I'm sorry. He sometimes

claimed to help a friend at a bar, not that I ever saw any money from it, and I don't know what bar."

"Or what friend?"

Smothered in guilt, she flattened her mouth and fought off renewed weeping. "I'm sorry. Phil and I... our lives haven't been in sync for a while."

Because she'd been working and Phil had been loafing. Stack rubbed the back of his neck. He had to get it together. For his sister, for Vanity. "It's okay," he lied. It was far from okay. "I'll figure out something." What, he had no idea.

Vanity curled a hand around his biceps. "Shouldn't you talk to the police?"

"Yeah." His thoughts churned, then settled on a single course. Mind made up, he announced, "I'm going to talk with Whitney first." At least she should be easy to find. And maybe she could lead him to fucking Phil.

Vanity dropped back in her chair. "Are you sure that's a good idea?"

He looked into her beautiful eyes, saw a hint of jealousy—and something more. "You need to trust me on this."

Her gaze darted away. Stack didn't entirely understand that reaction, but he'd figure it out soon. Right now, he had more important things to cover. "I want you both to be really careful. And sis, no contact with Phil, okay? If he shows up, call me. Or the cops. But stay away from him."

"All right, but..." Desperate, she hugged herself. "I can't believe Phil had anything to do with this."

Stack wasn't sure how to convince her. He'd seen his sister in a variety of dramatic roles, but this was different. The last time she'd appeared this fragile had been at his father's funeral. In no way did he want to add to her grief.

"Everything was arranged through some small-time dope dealer. I don't suppose you happen to know where Phil bought his weed?"

"I didn't want to know." Her fist hit the table, making Vanity jump. "I'm useless!"

Now, that was more like the old Tabby. She said things that made him reassure and compliment her.

Smiling, Stack gave her what she needed. "Don't be ridiculous. You've taken a big first step, and I'm proud of you."

"I should have asked more questions. I should have seen things sooner. We'd argued about his habit so many times. I hated it because it was a waste of money we didn't have." She stared at Stack. "Phil was—*is*—a jerk. But how could he be involved in this? The only money he had, he got from me, and I'd put him on a very small allowance over a month ago. I didn't even give him cash for gas. I filled up the car myself."

Vanity made a small sound, and Stack squeezed her hand. "I have no idea how much it might've cost, or where he could have gotten the money, but in my gut I know he was involved."

Breathing fast, Tabby stood. Anger emanated from her, always preferable to the hurt. "Oh, God, if he did this, so help me—"

"Shh." Stack stood, too. "We don't know for sure yet, and until we do, you'll promise to stay away from him. Understood?"

Hand shaking, she tucked her hair back and nodded. "I took the day off work. I just... I couldn't face anyone there today. I'm going to talk to Mom next."

"Do me a favor and stay the day with her, okay? If Phil comes back to the apartment, I don't want you there alone."

Giving him a sad smile, she said, "I kind of wanted my mom today anyway."

Stack understood that. They were close, and whenever necessary, their folks had been there for them, always supportive, always the perfect backup.

He thought Tabby leaned on their mom far too often, but in this, he'd encourage it.

"You're okay." He cupped Tabby's face. "You know that, right?"

"Yes." She put a hand to her midsection, and the smile came unwillingly. "Yes, we're both okay."

Stack covered her hand with his own. "I'm going to be an awesome uncle."

"Vanity and I already said so." She gave him a hug, sniffled, hugged him more tightly, then stepped away. Shoulders back, she said, "I need to get going."

"Me, too." He was late enough now that he didn't have time to indulge himself with Vanity. Probably for the best. He needed to share this new info with Cannon and the others as soon as possible. "I'll walk you out, and then I need to get a move on."

Vanity hugged Tabby in the kitchen but didn't walk with them to the door. When Stack returned, she was at the table looking a little lost.

He lifted his half-empty coffee mug to finish it off. "You okay?"

One arm curled around her middle as if she might be getting sick. "Yes, I'm fine."

She didn't look fine. Far from it. "Are you ill?"

"No."

Stack put the back of his hand to her forehead. "You're not feverish."

"Of course not." Her smile didn't reach her eyes. "What will you do first?"

"Get to the rec center. Talk to the guys." He rolled a shoulder and said as casually as he could, "I'll give Whitney a call and arrange to see her after."

Though she tried to hide it, he could see that Vanity didn't like that idea. "You'll see her in person?"

"Best way to tell if she's being truthful when I ask her some pointed questions." He slid right by that, not wanting her to put too much importance on it. He wasn't, and never again would be, attracted to Whitney. "I'll try to locate Phil, too, but I'm guessing he'll be dodging me for a while."

Vanity fretted. "Promise me you'll be careful."

He set the coffee aside and pulled her from her seat. "That's my line to you, darlin'. I know how independent you are, but I want you to use extra care."

"I'm always careful." She put one hand to his chest and bit her lip. "Stack…"

Feeling indulgent, surprised to see her so shaken, Stack hugged her close. He'd gotten used to her being unshakeable, a rock impervious to cold or exhaustion or worry. But he supposed death threats from old girlfriends would make any woman antsy. "I'm sorry we got off track this morning. I was really looking forward to being debauched."

Nothing. No laughter, no jokes. She just tightened her hold on him.

"Hey." He tilted her back. The worry in her eyes squeezed his heart. "It's going to be fine."

She briefly closed her eyes, then squared her shoulders and nodded with new determination. "Yes. It will."

The sudden about-face sparked suspicions. "You've done enough, okay?"

Her eyes widened. "What?"

"Gifts for my sister?" he reminded her. He stroked back her hair, liking how it slid silkily through his fingers. "The urge is always to make her life easier. Believe me, I know. I did it for years myself. But it hasn't helped. She needs tough love, not coddling. At some point she has to start taking care of herself instead of making bad decisions that always compound her problems."

"She's getting rid of Phil," Vanity reminded him.

"Yeah, and I'm damned proud of her. It's a step in the right direction. But it's only the start. I want to encourage her, but I also want to let her get there on her own, at least as much as she can. It'll mean more to her, and I think it'll do a lot to restore her self-esteem."

"She's not you, Stack." Vanity's hand touched his chest, right over his heart. "You're more resolute than most. You see things very black and white. But Tabby needs a little more help."

"Mom has been running behind her for years. That's only made it easier for her to screw up because there've never been any real consequences." He needed Vanity to understand. "I love her. I want to see her get it together. Especially now that she's going to have a baby. I just don't think anyone can get it together for her. She has to want it enough for herself to make it happen."

Vanity watched him a moment longer, then she smiled, a real smile this time. "You are the most amazing man."

Thankful that she no longer looked so upset, he teased, "Not sweet, huh?"

"Amazing and very, very sweet." She stepped in closer. "You don't mind if I buy her the occasional gift?" Without giving him a chance to reply, she explained, "I like her. I promise I'm not just schmoozing you. Tabby and I enjoyed a day at the spa and shopping, and just because she doesn't have her own money to spend doesn't mean I should have to go alone. She's really grateful, and I have a lot of fun with her and—"

Stack quieted her with a finger to her lush lips. "It's your money, babe. I can't tell you how to spend it. I just ask that you use moderation."

She nodded.

He moved his hand only so he could kiss her. And that, he knew, was something he'd enjoy doing for the rest of his life.

Kissing Vanity was about the nicest thing he'd ever experienced.

"For the record, I know you would never use Tabby, or my mom, to get closer to me. You're more honest than that." He drifted his thumb over her downy cheek. "You're the most up-front, honest woman I've ever met."

Her mouth opened, but nothing came out.

With Tabby's announcement, everything had just changed in a very big way. A baby.

That thought, soft and sweet, made him think of other soft, sweet moments.

Moments with Vanity.

He was excited about being an uncle, but when he considered it, it was with Vanity at his side. He leaned down, kissed her bottom lip, her jaw, her temple. "I care about you, Vanity." That didn't feel adequate, so he added quietly, "A lot."

She went still, but it didn't worry him. One way or another, he'd ensure that Vanity felt the same. She was his, now and always, whether she realized it yet or not.

Blinking big eyes at him, she whispered, "You do?"

Stack nodded. "Tonight, after we get home from Rowdy's, I'm going to show you how much."

PHIL DIDN'T KNOW where to go or what to do, so he walked. Down the street, aimless, irate. A little scared.

Hands shoved in his pockets and shoulders hunched against the cold, he kept on plodding. He didn't have a car or a phone, and he only had forty-two bucks in his pocket. It shocked him that Tabby would end it like that.

Pregnant. Jesus, he didn't want a kid. Most of the time he hadn't really wanted Tabby. Not anymore. But now...

She'd kicked him out.

That stung. Who the fuck did she think she was? He'd said all the wrong things, he knew that now. He should have demanded time to get his shit together. His clothes, his stash in the dresser drawer.

His gun.

And if demands hadn't worked, he could have pleaded a little. She'd always been a sucker for his groveling. In the past, she'd forgiven him everything.

It was her asshole brother that had her being so unreasonable now. God, he hated Stack Hannigan and his holier-than-thou attitude. He wished he'd hired the guys to do more than slow Stack down. He wished he'd had them cut him a few times. Maybe that'd take the cockiness away.

But probably not. Everything was always so easy for Stack.

So what if Tabby funded Phil? They were married. That's what married couples did. Hadn't he stuck with her even though Stack despised him? And he hadn't said shit when she moved in her mom.

He'd gotten her dogs, damn it. Hell of a gift. Now she'd thrown it all back in his face, making him leave with only the clothes on his back and his coat...

It suddenly occurred to him that he had his wallet. He yanked it out and saw the bank card. Oh, hell yeah.

Did they have any cash in the account?

Tabby had always done the banking and bill paying, but he assumed she had enough there to cover the rent and utilities.

Whatever the amount, it'd help.

With a new purpose, he quickened his step, and two blocks down he found a trio of teens hanging out. "Any of you got a phone I can use?"

They laughed. The tallest one said, "Fuck off, dude."

Phil jutted his chin. "I'll give you five bucks. A two-minute local call, that's all I need."

The kid eyed him. "Who you gonna call?"

"A friend. I just need to wrangle a ride, that's all."

After some more thought, the boy said, "Give me the money first."

Phil pulled a five from his wallet and held it up. "Phone?"

The kid eyed him some more, and finally pulled a cell from his pocket.

As promised, Phil kept the call short and sweet. Soon as he finished the boy took his fin, and the group moseyed on. Twenty minutes after that, Whitney pulled up.

She grinned when she saw him huddled next to a tree, trying to avoid the wind. "Aw, poor baby. She kicked you out?"

Phil strode around the hood and got in. The heat of the car permeated his frozen limbs, and he took his first deep breath. During the time he'd waited, his anger had grown, and now he fairly pulsed with it.

He'd make Tabby sorry. The bitch would regret treating him like this. He'd see to it.

And there wasn't a fucking thing her brother could do about it.

CHAPTER EIGHTEEN

ALL DAY LONG, Vanity replayed the morning's events in her mind.

I care about you. Her heart clenched, recalling those precious words from Stack. Oh, God, she loved him so much, and now he cared for her, too.

But did he care enough? What would he do when she told him everything?

Phil might've taken out a hit on Stack. *She'd given Phil the money.* Doubts, guilt, worry kept circling her brain until she did indeed feel sick. At Yvette's shop she'd had too much time to think, and at the photo shoot she'd been distracted. Twice, the photographer had reminded her to smile.

Reluctantly, she decided she wouldn't tell Stack about giving Phil money. Not yet. It would only exacerbate the animosity between Stack and Phil.

Instead, she put in a few calls and arranged for a private investigator to locate Phil. Jack Woolridge came highly recommended. He'd find out the truth for Vanity, and if it turned out that Phil had tried to hurt Stack, she'd hire the very best lawyers to see to it that he was punished.

There were times that having money was a huge benefit.

In the meantime, Stack had promised to show her

how much he cared. Once he did, she could tell him how much she loved him. How she'd been in love with him for a while.

How she'd manipulated things to get his attention.

She'd confess everything, and hope he cared enough that it wouldn't matter.

She'd just finished changing clothes to go to Rowdy's when Stack called. Wanting to look her best tonight, she'd taken extra care with her outfit, hair and makeup.

She wanted to bowl Stack over.

"Hello, handsome."

She heard the smile in his voice when he said, "Hey, darlin'. You're back home?"

"Yes. Just about ready to walk out the door."

He sighed. "This is one of those times that I wish you weren't always so prompt."

Her heart stuttered. "Why? What's wrong?"

"Nothing. But I'm going to be a little late."

She didn't mean to say it, especially with so much snark, but the words just tumbled out. "Visiting Whitney?"

There was a moment of silence, and Stack laughed. "Is that jealousy I hear?"

Damn. Dropping to sit on the side of the bed, she glumly admitted, "Yes."

"Vanity," he chided. "You know there's no reason."

"Because you care about me, not her."

"Yes."

She believed him, she really did. But damn it, Whitney wanted him back. What woman wouldn't? "I just hope Whitney understands that."

"I promise I won't let her misunderstand."

Huffing a breath, Vanity gave up. "I'm sorry. I'm being clingy and a pain, and I'll stop right now." Maybe.

"No need to apologize. I'll prove that to you tonight, too."

Good thing she was sitting down. In a whisper, she said, "I can't wait."

"Afraid we'll both have to. I called Whitney all day, but she only answered a little while ago. I'll stop by her place to find out what I can about Phil, and then head to Rowdy's. Everyone's meeting us there." He lowered his voice. "I want you to relax and have fun."

"Soon as you get there," she promised, "I will."

After they hung up, she got hold of Yvette. The new bride agreed to meet with her at Rowdy's, as did Cherry and Merissa. Vanity also called and invited Tabby, but Lynn said she was napping. The dogs, whom Vanity had returned to Lynn earlier that day, were sleeping with Tabby.

She missed them.

She missed Stack.

Hopefully a drink or two with a few friends would get her out of her gloomy mood.

WHITNEY BEAMED WHEN she opened the door and found Stack standing there. She knew him well, and while he looked as good as ever, she saw bitterness in his stormy blue eyes, anger in the set of his jaw and flex of his shoulders.

He didn't want to be here, but things were working out in her favor.

Smiling, she said, "Stack. What a nice surprise."

If anything, her greeting hardened his mood more. "This isn't a social visit."

"Given the fumes coming out of your ears, I'd already picked up on that." In silent invitation, she opened the door wider, and Stack came in.

The urge to touch him, to stroke that finely honed body and feel all those tantalizing muscles, left her fingers tingling. She could still picture him naked, tensed over her, driving deep.

When she shivered, Stack's eyes narrowed, and he said, "Knock it off, Whit. I'm not in the mood."

"That's unusual. As I recall, you were always in the mood."

Expression bordering on cruel, he looked her over. "Not here, not with you."

That hurt, but she didn't let it show. After closing the door, she smiled and led the way to the kitchen. If Stack wanted to talk to her, he could follow.

And he did.

She poured herself a drink, and then him.

He ignored the glass. "You were with Phil at my sister's apartment. Have you seen him since then?"

"Yes." She said nothing more; why make it easy on him? Pulling out a stool at the bar in her kitchen, she took a seat, crossed her legs in a way that made her short skirt ride higher, and waited.

"You know Tabby kicked him out."

A statement, not a question. But it wasn't a problem. She'd thought about this for a long time, and she knew exactly how to work it to her advantage. "Yes, I know."

"Tell me where I can find him."

Ah, ah. Not that easy, Stack. She sipped her drink, taking her time—and testing his patience. When it looked as though he might turn around and walk out, she finally answered. "I honestly don't know. The last time I saw him, he was looking for a ride to the bank."

"Shit." Hands on his hips, Stack turned his face away. As much to himself as to her, he growled, "I'm betting Tabby didn't think to close out her accounts."

"Your sister is a ditz, so, no, I'm sure she didn't." And now it'd be far too late. For many, many things.

All of them for her benefit.

His gaze cut to her. "Here's a clue, Whit. You have zero rights to insult my family. Don't do it again."

Wow. She hadn't expected that reaction. Anyone who met Tabitha knew the woman was an utter airhead.

Much like Stack's new girlfriend.

To soften him back up, she made a peace offering. "I assume I'll hear from Phil again. Should I call you if I do?"

"I'd appreciate that."

"Your number is the same?"

"Yeah." He hesitated, then propped a shoulder on the wall and folded his arms over his chest. "Is any of it true?"

Confused, she slid off the stool and approached him. With his arms that way, his biceps were positively huge. She went liquid inside, wanting him bad and determined to have him. If not now, then soon. "I don't know what you mean."

"All those things you've been whispering in Leese's ear about a drug dealer sending out a hit on me."

She nearly dropped her drink. How in the world did he know it was her? She'd never, not once, given her name to the hunky fighter. Stunned, she took a step back. "I don't—"

His hand slashed the air. "Save the lies, Whitney. I know you too well. I see it on your face."

She surged forward again, her hand on his forearm, her eyes as earnest as she could make them. "Leese means nothing to me. He was just a diversion, a way to pass the time." She slid her hand higher, up to that rock-solid biceps. "I've been lonely since you broke things off."

Smirking, Stack removed her hand, dropping it away as if she repulsed him. "Screw anyone you want, Whitney. I have no problem with that."

"But—"

"I'm just trying to decide if you shared with Leese as part of a game, or if you were telling the truth."

Damn him, she had her pride. Lifting her chin, she said, "I was trying to protect you."

"Funny. Might've been easier if you'd just called me."

"As I remember it, you refused my calls."

That hit a note, given the softening of his expression. "All right. Then why not just come see me?"

She set her drink aside and, taking him by surprise, threw herself against him. Even though he didn't return the embrace, he felt good, so good, and as she inhaled his musky scent, memories assailed her.

Red-hot, smoldering memories.

It didn't matter that he went rigid, that he braced away from her. She opened one hand on the back of his neck and tunneled the other into his warm hair. "I saw you at your mother's, and you were nasty to me."

His hands clasped her upper arms as he attempted to free himself. "Stop coming on to me, and we can talk more civilly."

Instead of allowing him an escape, she clenched him tighter and kissed his jaw, his throat—even managed to reach his mouth for a heartbeat.

Without the gentleness she knew so well, Stack thrust her away. Because her fingers had been tangled in his hair, she was sure the move hurt him as much as, maybe more than, it frustrated her.

Staggering, so turned on she didn't care if he hated her, Whitney said, "I want you. Right now."

His eyes were cold as he scrubbed a hand over his mouth. "Not happening."

Breathing heavily, Whitney stared at him, trying to decide her next move.

He might have removed her lipstick from his lips, but not from his jaw or his neck, and the fact that she'd marked him gave her a small measure of satisfaction. "You'll come back to me."

He laughed.

Undeterred, she straightened. "You're in danger. I wish I had more facts to share, but right now I don't."

"I know you're still smoking. Who's your dealer? Where can I find him?"

Her dealer was Phil. But she wouldn't admit that. Shaking her head, she said, "I don't know. If I ask too many questions, it could put me in danger, too."

"If any of it is true."

She licked her lips, imagining his taste. "When I hear from Phil again, I'll let you know."

Eyes narrowed, he studied her, maybe trying to determine her honesty. Finally he nodded. "Anything you hear, anything at all, call me."

And this time, she knew, he'd take her calls.

It was a start. A lot more than she'd had yesterday.

Smiling, she watched him turn and walk away. The
front door opened and quietly closed.

Mmm. Despite his denials, she knew she'd have him
again.

But first, she needed to get hold of Phil. If he didn't
play his role right, everything could tumble back on
her. She needed Phil to be the scapegoat.

And she needed Stack to believe it all, one hundred
percent.

LEESE HAD JUST gotten to Rowdy's bar when the ladies
came in. Turning on his bar stool, he admired each of
them. Vanity led the group, and tonight she'd ramped
up the sex appeal in a low-cut black sweater that hugged
her rack and emphasized her tiny waist. The contrast to
her fair hair had every guy in the place taking a second,
more lingering, look. Worn jeans, fashionably threadbare in tantalizing spots, fit tight enough to her long
thighs to be leggings. The edgy heeled boots added an
extra couple of inches to her height. In every way imag-
inable, she was stunning.

Before Stack got so territorial, Leese had considered going after her. But she'd made it clear she wanted
Stack, not for the short term but in a happily-ever-
after way.

Not his thing. Hell, he was just starting to enjoy life
and all the perks of working with a Grade-A camp. By
the day he became a better fighter, and in the process
he redeemed past mistakes.

He wouldn't rock the boat by chasing a woman already taken—but he could indulge an occasional fantasy.

Speaking of fantasies, Cherry and Yvette trailed

Vanity, both of them very sweet on the eyes. He watched them laughing and chatting as they shed coats and hung purses on the backs of chairs at a round table situated in the corner.

Leese grinned. Hell, they were all worthy of fantasies; Cherry with her lush little body and Yvette with her tempered sex appeal. But he'd never admit it to anyone.

Merissa came in late and joined them at the table. She was taller than the others, and considering she was Cannon's little sis, as off-limits as a girl could get. There was also something going on between her and Armie, but damned if he could figure it out.

Just then Vanity looked up, and their gazes met. She waved him over.

Leese left the stool and ambled over to them. "Ladies."

Merissa kicked out a chair. "Join us."

He probably shouldn't. "Not sure I fit into this particular tea party." He glanced around but still didn't see Cannon, Denver, Armie or Stack.

Cherry made chicken noises. "Be brave, Leese. We're harmless, I promise."

"Right. And next you have a bridge to sell me?"

Yvette laughed. "You see, Cherry? He knows you too well."

Cherry threw a napkin at her friend.

Vanity gave him a long look. "Seriously. Sit and visit." She grinned. "We'll behave."

"And there's that bridge." But Leese figured, why not? He spun around the offered chair and straddled it. It wasn't easy, but he did his best not to stare at Vanity's cleavage. "Is this a celebration or just a ladies' night out?"

"The guys are joining us," Yvette explained. "But they're running late."

Okay, then. If only to needle the others, he'd hang around. Leese raised a hand, and a waitress started in their direction. "First round of drinks is on me," he told them all.

And for that, the ladies cheered him.

DISGUSTED THAT HIS trip to Whitney's had been a waste of time, Stack pushed through the doors of Rowdy's bar. As if they'd just arrived, Cannon and Armie stood off to the side with their jackets open but still on, talking to Denver, who nodded across the room with a scowl. When Stack got closer he followed the direction of their collective gazes—and realized they focused on the women all seated at a table with...Leese.

Staring, Stack watched Leese lean into the table to say something. He couldn't hear him, not with the noise from the crowded bar, but Vanity and the other ladies all laughed.

Having suffered a lousy day already, Stack bristled. "That's bullshit."

Looking like a thundercloud, Denver said, "I know, right?"

"The sly bastard," Armie agreed with menace.

Cannon laughed at all of them. "Relax. The ladies like him."

That earned a lot of grunts and grumbles.

Still grinning, Cannon said, "From what I can tell, Leese doesn't hit on any of them."

"Oh, he's hittin'," Stack said. "He's just slick about it."

Cannon slapped him on the back. "Breathing or being cordial doesn't count. Besides, I trust Leese." He eyed each of them. "And I trust Yvette."

Denver rubbed the back of his neck. "Yeah. Same with Cherry."

"Doesn't make it any easier," Stack added.

Armie kept mum. Stack understood. He'd only just given himself the right to be an idiot about Vanity; Armie was still trying to pretend he didn't have a thing for Merissa.

"Before you update us," Cannon said to Stack, "would you mind fetching Leese? He should be in on this since he was Whitney's initial contact."

Stack straightened. "Sure. Why not?" Leaving the others behind, he made his way across the bar. Spotting him before he reached her, Vanity left her seat to meet him halfway. Her silly, uncertain smile slipped into place, but she didn't touch him.

Stack didn't understand her sudden reserve, and he'd missed her enough to ignore it. He pulled her in and put his mouth to hers. Blocking out his frustration with Whitney and Phil and his sister's personal situation, blocking out the noise of the bar and his gawking friends, he lost himself in kissing Vanity.

An elbow clipped his ribs, and Rowdy, the bar owner, said, "There's a hotel down the block. Hell, I'll loan you the eighty bucks. But take it off the floor."

Easing up, Stack laughed. Vanity ducked her face against his chest and mumbled an apology.

Rowdy, a badass of the first order, grinned at her. "I blame him, honey, not you."

"Thank you."

After Rowdy walked on, Stack tipped up her chin. "I'm sorry, darlin'. I didn't mean to get carried away."

"It's okay. I got a little lost, myself." Face hot, she stared into his eyes. "Is everyone looking?"

"No," he lied. "And anyone who is, is just jealous." Arm around her, he led her back to her table. Leese was already standing, but as they got close, Yvette, Cherry and Merissa all stood, too. Then they applauded him.

Covering her face, snickering, Vanity slumped into her seat.

Grin crooked, Stack took a bow.

The women made some pretty ribald comments to each other. Cherry pretended to swoon. Merissa patted a hand over her heart. Yvette just smiled.

Ready to get back on track, Stack said, "If you ladies will excuse us, I need to steal Leese."

That got Vanity's attention. "Where are you going?"

"Nowhere. I have a few things to discuss with the guys, that's all. I won't be long."

The women teased her about being impatient, which worked for him because he was impatient as hell to get her alone. He'd promised her a night out, and instead he was stuck dealing with Phil's bullshit.

On their way to the others, Leese glanced at him, saw his black frown, and said, "I was trying not to look."

Drawing a blank, Stack said, "What?"

Leese lifted a brow, then coughed. "Never mind."

Stopping in the middle of the floor, Stack said darkly, "No. Tell me."

Leese eyed him, then shrugged. "Fine. You went from joking to glaring, so I figured it was over me being with the ladies. Just wanted you to know, even though Vanity dolled up extra fine tonight with—" he coughed again when Stack stiffened "—that low top, I wasn't looking."

Stack folded his arms. "You said you were *trying* not to look, not that you hadn't."

Unrepentant, Leese grinned. "Yeah, well, I'm not the only one, so sue me."

Stack twisted back to take another look. Huh. She had dolled up, and damn, she looked fine.

"You hadn't noticed." Leese shook his head. "Hard to believe."

"To me, no matter what, she always looks hot." The longer he knew her and the closer he got to her, the more beautiful she seemed to him. Stack turned to Leese. "And she's mine."

"She's as clear on that as you are."

Nice. That took some of the tension from Stack's shoulders. "Good to know you've been listening."

"To both of you." Leese looked around the room at all the available ladies vying for attention. "Besides, I'm enjoying my freedom, and Vanity's all about settling down."

That was news to Stack. When had Vanity discussed it with Leese? He wanted to ask more, and he would— when he talked to Vanity. If she was thinking along those lines, well…he liked it.

In fact, it filled him with a certain sort of peace. Sleeping with Vanity each night, waking with her every morning, keeping her with him when he traveled, when he took part in family gatherings…it enticed him.

Settle down with Vanity? In his heart and mind he already had.

They joined Cannon and the others, and Stack quickly updated them on what he knew. Leese offered to make his own visit to Whitney, to see if he could catch her with Phil, and if not, maybe she'd divulge more to him. Armie and Denver would keep tabs on the two men who had jumped Stack, possibly press them for more answers.

And now that they could share descriptions of Phil and Whitney, Cannon insisted on making the rounds with his contacts on the street. It was possible someone would recognize one of them.

"You should still be honeymooning," Denver told him.

With deep satisfaction, Cannon smiled. "We have a lifetime, and I'm pretty sure the honeymoon isn't ever going to end."

Good-natured jokes ensued, but nothing dented Cannon's satisfaction. Stack had to hand it to him; Cannon made marriage look pretty damned appealing.

His gaze sought Vanity, and of course, seeing her meant he wanted her. Now. Tomorrow.

Always.

With everyone up to speed, the group dispersed, each guy going after his lady. Leese headed back to the table to reclaim his drink, but by then, only Merissa remained.

Telling himself to be patient, to give Vanity the night out that she deserved, Stack followed her to the pool tables. He could take a few hours, but he wasn't sure he'd last any longer than that.

Tonight, as promised, he'd show her how much he cared. Given what he felt for her, it just might take all night.

LEESE KICKED BACK the rest of his drink, told Merissa to have fun, and headed for the john. He was in the hallway when he felt a hand touch his arm.

Turning, he realized Merissa had followed. She stood so close, he could see her individual eyelashes. Lifting a brow in query, he backed up a pace. "What's up?"

Her small pink tongue came out to slick over her lips. "You in a hurry?"

Confusion pulled at his brows, and, yeah, he'd noticed her tongue. "Not really." She blushed, and he got instantly wary. "Everything okay?"

With a lot of uncertainty, she stepped closer again.

Ah, hell. A dozen different thoughts scrambled. Here in the hallway it was quieter, cooler. More intimate.

"Rissy..." he started, trying to fight off the temptation. Not easy, because part of him wanted to take her hand and find a little privacy.

The better part, the more reasonable part, told him something more was going on. He'd spent plenty of time letting the other fighters know he understood the boundaries. With Denver and Cherry, he'd almost screwed up. But instead of hating him, they'd included him in the training. He was a better fighter for it.

Hopefully, too, a better man.

Being still new to the group, he didn't want to do even the smallest thing to lose their trust.

Getting busy with Merissa would be far from small. It'd be gigantic.

He leaned back on the wall and smiled at her. "What's going on, hon?"

For a single second she stared at him, then with a gigantic sigh she dropped against the wall beside him. Shoulders touching, she said, "You aren't interested, right?"

He nudged her gently. "It's the other way around."

Her head lifted, and she turned to him. "What?"

"If you were actually interested in me, I'd be on it in a New York minute."

Teasing, she said, "It?"

Leese's gaze dipped over her. He popped his neck, determined not to waver, but she looked so damned cute. Tall, with every inch slim but shapely. "You," he said, nodding at her face, then looking down. "Your body."

She glanced down at herself, too.

"Sex," he growled more deeply than he'd intended.

Her gaze shot back to his. "Really?"

Leese nodded. "But I'm not the guy you're into."

Her shoulders slumped. "The guy I'm into isn't into me."

"Just give him a little more time. I don't know him well enough to say for sure, but seems to me he's fighting too many battles right now." Leese nudged her again. "Besides, I like you, and I like having you as a friend. If we did the nasty, everything would change."

"The nasty," she repeated with a grin.

Unable to resist, Leese leaned in and, voice low and husky, said near her ear, "Nasty, nice and smoldering hot." He settled back a safe distance.

Rissy looked suitably impressed.

He nodded, fighting a grin. "Guaranteed." Chucking her chin, he said, "But not for gal pals."

After a big blink, she laughed and punched his shoulder. "You're dangerous."

"Got ya thinking, huh?" He winked, then made himself move away, to not take advantage. "You see any willing women even half as hot as you, spread the good word for me, okay?"

"Sure thing. And, Leese?"

"Yeah?"

She put her arms around his waist and hugged him tight. It was a unique thing, being hugged by a woman who matched his height. Leese gave in, indulging in one hug while breathing in her scent and thinking of what could be if he wasn't determined to be scrupulous.

She released him with a smile. "Thank you."

"Anytime." He turned to leave—and almost plowed into Armie.

CHAPTER NINETEEN

ARMIE STOOD THERE, his damned feet glued to the floor as Leese walked past and deliberately shouldered him. Under his breath, he muttered, "Make up your mind before it's too late."

What a joke. He could make up his mind a dozen times, but it wouldn't change anything.

Merissa looked as frozen as he felt, then she forced a smile. "Lurking in hallways, Armie? Tsk."

"I'm thinking lurking is better than whatever the fuck you had planned."

She puffed up like an imminent explosion. With her long legs, she reached him in one stride. Angled in, her nose almost touching his, she snarled, *"You don't have the right to—"*

Armie kissed her. Hell, he didn't mean to. Actually, he'd meant *not* to.

But she had her mouth right *there*, all soft and sweet and within reach.

He didn't stop at kissing her. No, once they touched, he all but lost it, backing her up to the wall and pressing his body to her body and dying just a little.

She was long and lithe, her thighs aligning with his, her breasts a soft cushion for his chest. She wiggled, and he went hard in a heartbeat.

From beside them, he heard, "What is it with you guys tonight? Is it a full moon or something?"

Shit. Armie took his tongue from her mouth, his hands from her body and, trying hard to regain his sanity, turned to face Rowdy. He would have shielded Rissy, but she was so tall there was no way to hide her.

One look at the amusement in Rowdy's eyes and Armie ran a hand over his face. "Jesus. Sorry, man. I..." What could he say? *She pushes all my buttons.* Or *I've wanted her too long to keep resisting.* Maybe *I need her so fucking bad I can't stop thinking about it.*

"I get it." Rowdy made a point of not looking at Rissy. Armie wasn't so lucky; he got the full force of Rowdy's no-nonsense stare. "I suggest you find someplace more private."

Wrong. That'd be the absolute worst thing Armie could do. But he nodded, and thankfully Rowdy left.

Keeping his back to Rissy, Armie tried to calm his galloping heart. Impossible. With his brain cells all focused on how she tasted, how it felt to finally feel the warmth of her body flush to his... Jesus.

"I liked that, Armie."

Her small, quiet voice nearly took out his knees. *She liked it.* He shored up his weak resistance, and, both dreading it and needing it, he turned to face her.

Ah, hell. Eyes soft and aroused, lips swollen, she watched him with unspoken invitation.

An invitation he couldn't accept. "Fuck me," he complained, one finger pointing at her. "Don't do that!"

She blinked.

Armie took a step back, ran into someone and muttered an apology.

Rissy touched his arm. "I wasn't—"

"You're giving me those 'I'm ready' looks, but no way in hell are you ready. Not even close."

She licked her lips and asked suggestively, "Ready for what?"

God. He tried not to, but his gaze went over her, and he breathed harder, imagining her naked, sweaty.

Under him.

"For any of the stuff I want to do to you."

He didn't miss her stiffened nipples pressing against her sweater. He wanted her in his mouth. He wanted to suck on her, maybe bite her lightly, make her squirm.

Make her come.

She whispered, "I can imagine what you're thinking."

"Don't," he warned.

She reached for him.

He quickly sidestepped. "I mean it, Rissy." His eyes burned. His cock strained. Physical and emotional need pulsed hotly inside him. "Don't imagine. Don't think about it. Don't fucking tempt me. Just...*don't.*"

She staged a visual standoff, but Armie held his ground. He had to. He'd lost enough of himself to know it sucked. He wouldn't take from her just so he could feel better.

Finally, her eyes getting glassy, she turned and hurried away through the bar.

Fucking felt like someone just pulled his heart from his chest. He wanted to punch the wall, but he had better control than that.

If he didn't, he'd be on her already.

Time for him to go.

Unfortunately, he hadn't quite made it to the door when Stack got a call—and all hell broke loose.

"I HAVE TO GO."

Armie looked ragged, but he quickly pulled it together. "What can I do?"

That was the thing with good friends; they knew when to ask questions, and when to quietly back you up. "Tell the others for me. Whitney just called to say Phil was heading to my sister's apartment. The prick is going to clean her out. He already took everything from the bank—"

"I get it, man. No worries."

On the way to the front door, he said, "You'll stick with Vanity for me?"

Armie gave a nod. "Like glue."

"I don't have time to explain to her, and who knows if I can trust anything Whitney says. This—"

"Could be a trap, I know."

Coat pulled on but not buttoned, Stack clapped Armie on the shoulder. "I appreciate this."

Armie pointed at him. "If it looks bad, if you need anything at all, let me know. Don't be an idiot."

Stack laughed. "Sure." All he really wanted was to get to the truth. He'd use as much caution as necessary, but he *would* make Phil talk.

Armie stepped outside with him, following him to the curb. "You might get company. You know how the guys are. But I'll make sure they know to come in quiet."

Lifting a hand in understanding, Stack jogged across the street to his car. He wouldn't be at all surprised if Cannon, Denver or both showed up at the apartment.

Armie stood there, impervious to the cold, watching until Stack drove away without incident. In his side-view mirror, Stack saw him head back inside.

In less than fifteen minutes Stack arrived at his sister's apartment. Was Phil already inside?

Whitney claimed Phil had just told her of his plans, so it was possible he hadn't gotten there yet.

She'd also begged him not to tell Phil that she'd ratted him out. Whitney worried, she said, about Phil turning on her, perhaps targeting her as she claimed he'd targeted Stack.

At this point, Stack wasn't sure who or what to believe. But he hadn't wanted Vanity involved, and knowing she was safe with a group of friends, Armie watching over her at the bar, made it easier to put her from his mind.

He scanned the street as he crossed it but didn't see Phil anywhere. Still, he used care as he entered the building. A few neighbors were just heading out; he'd seen them before during visits and knew they lived there.

When Stack reached it, he found the apartment door unlocked. Silently, he slipped inside, then paused to listen. Noises came from the bedroom, so, after a cautionary glance in the kitchen, that's where Stack headed. As he passed the bathroom, the guest bedroom, he peeked into those rooms, too. Empty.

So it'd just be him and Phil. *Perfect.*

At the bedroom door, Stack leaned in the door frame. Phil had his back to him while loading all of his clothes from a dresser onto a sheet spread across the bed. Beside the clothing pile rested a plastic freezer bag filled with pot. Stack had no idea of the street value, but he knew Phil didn't have that kind of cash on hand, so how had he gotten it?

Worse, Stack saw a small array of Tabby's jewelry laid

out on a T-shirt, some of it cheap, a few nicer pieces Stack had given her and a special necklace from their dad.

His jaw ticked, but Stack continued to wait, curious how long it would take the idiot to realize he wasn't alone.

When Phil clunked a gun to the top of the dresser, Stack's patience ended. Having no idea if it was loaded and not about to chance it, Stack used the element of surprise to stride in and snatch it up.

Phil was so startled he lunged back, tripped over his own feet, crashed into the nightstand and broke a lamp. He started to scramble up, no doubt to flee.

"Stop." Stack loomed over him. "Break anything else, and you'll be paying for it."

"What are you doing here?"

Smirking, Stack hefted the gun. "Yours?"

Phil nodded, his eyes a little wild.

"Planning to shoot someone?"

"No! I mean, I got it for protection."

What a joke. "Protection from what?"

Phil swallowed loudly. "You."

That made him laugh. Sure, he wanted to pulverize Phil, but he wasn't a thug. Only if physically provoked would he ever hit him.

Stack still held out hope that just such an occasion might arise.

He hefted the small black revolver. "A .38 Special, huh? My sister know you had this in her apartment?"

Phil glanced around, maybe hoping for a way to escape, but Stack had him cornered. Cautiously, he struggled back up to his feet. "I just got it."

From the same dope dealer Phil had paid to hire the attackers? Probably.

Playing along, Stack asked, "And the weed?"

"I bought it right before she told me to get out." Knotting his hands, Phil argued, "This is my shit! She has no right to keep it from me."

"The clothes, sure. I agree. You can even have the weed." He sure as hell didn't want it left behind in his sister's home. "But her jewelry? Is that how you managed it? You been selling Tabby's stuff for cash?" Was that how he'd paid the attackers?

"What? No." Phil breathed harder. "I had her jewelry there to get it out of my way."

Stack laughed. "You are such a pathetic liar."

"Keep the jewelry. I don't care!"

"Yeah, I'm keeping it." Stack frowned in thought. "How'd you get in, anyway?"

"Landlord let me in. He knows I live here."

Ah, yeah. That made sense. "Guess I need to get Tabby's name off the lease, then you're welcome to it."

"I can't afford this place! The lease isn't up for another six months."

Stack shrugged. "Either you get your name off it, today, or she will."

He slumped. "I'll do it."

"I thought so." Stack set the gun aside, well out of Phil's reach, then nodded to the pot. "How'd you buy that?"

Now that Stack didn't hold the gun, Phil regained some of his cockiness. "What do you care anyway? It's just weed."

"I don't care—if you weren't robbing my sister for it."

"I didn't rob anyone." Phil bunched his fists.

"Right. I guess your supplier just gave it to you? The same guy that Whitney uses?"

Again Phil's gaze darted around.

Interesting reaction to the mention of Whitney's name. Stack sighed. "You're busted, Phil. There aren't enough lies to get you out of it. Just make it easier on yourself and own up to the truth."

He took an aggressive step forward. "You want the truth? Fine. Your girlfriend gave me the money for the pot."

"Whitney isn't my girlfriend."

Phil shook his head. "I meant Vanity. I got the cash from her."

Like a sucker punch to the gut, the words knocked the air out of Stack. It took him a second to recover, and when he did his first reaction was denial. "Bullshit."

"It's true!" Cautiously, Phil inched closer to the pot, then lifted the bag. "I asked her for the money, she had the cash in her purse, and she gave it to me on the spot."

If that was true, then maybe Whitney hadn't lied. Maybe Phil was the one who'd paid for him to be jumped.

With Vanity's money?

Fuck. How much had she given him?

Sickness burned in Stack's stomach. He'd been played for a fool once before. Never again would he let that happen.

Drawing a deep breath, he stepped into Phil's space. "Know what I think? I think you're a fucking liar."

"No, dude, I swear." He backed up.

Stack let him retreat. He needed to clear his head, and he needed to stay focused. "The idiots who tried to jump me. You hired them?"

Like a cornered rat, Phil started to sweat.

Stack pushed him. "Now you want someone to kill me?"

"What?"

That reaction looked real enough, and it confounded Stack. "I was told you paid some dealer to arrange a hit."

Before he'd even finished, Phil started babbling. "No! That's nuts. Of course I didn't do that. I wouldn't. Yeah, we ain't friends, but I'm not a murderer, man."

"You paid guys to jump me."

"To slow you down, that's all. I swear! I wanted to hit up Vanity for the cash, and I knew if you were around, you'd nix it. That's all." Panicked, Phil stepped closer again. "She can afford it, man. I saw the wad of cash in her purse. She's rollin' in it. Not like she's going to miss a few hundred dollars."

Stack couldn't picture it in his mind. Vanity and Phil together. Money exchanging hands.

Vanity never, not once, telling him about it.

"She was nice to me," Phil continued. "Said I didn't even have to pay the money back. Told me it was a gift. She—"

"Shut up."

Phil fell instantly silent.

A pervading numbness set in. Just like Whitney, Vanity had pretended to despise Phil, only to get friendly with him behind Stack's back. At least this time he knew sex wasn't involved. Vanity kept too damn many secrets, more secrets than he could bear. But she wasn't the type to cheat.

To lie, though… Well, the evidence was right in front of him. For reasons he didn't understand, she'd aligned herself with Phil, enough to give him money.

Somehow he had to put that all aside, the hurt, the disappointment. The suspicion. Later, he could decide what to do about Vanity. Right now, he needed to know the name of Phil's dealer. He should—

A ruckus sounded, and a second later two men entered the bedroom. Bigger, brawnier and probably more capable than the previous two thugs, they eyed Stack, then nodded to Phil.

Phil looked more stunned than ever.

"Get your shit and go," the bigger of the two men said to Phil.

"Friends of yours?" Stack asked him.

"You, be quiet," the talker said, and then to Phil, "Get. Your shit. And *get out*."

Jolted by the menace in that tone, Phil hurried to tuck the pot inside his shirt, then closed the sheet around the haphazard pile of clothes. He glanced at the jewelry he'd laid out.

"I wouldn't," Stack warned him.

Showing a modicum of sense, Phil bolted over the bed and made a run for the front door.

At the same time, the biggest of the two men attacked. In the closed space, it wasn't going to be easy to maneuver. Stack had never been a street brawler. He didn't cause conflicts in bars. When he fought, it was in the cage with room to move.

But what the hell, he'd improvise.

Stack let the big man swing. He ducked his head just enough to avoid the blow and landed one of his own. He quickly followed that with a brutal knee to the nuts, wrenching a scream from the man. As the big dude started to drop, another knee caught him in the chin.

The guy fell with a thundering crash, his body awkwardly stuck between the bed and the dresser.

"You're going to regret that."

Stack turned and saw the other man grinning, showing a gold tooth.

"Who sent you?"

He didn't answer, saying instead, "When I finish with you, your girlfriend is next."

Furious over the thought of that, Stack kicked out. His aim was off, and instead of getting the man in the face, he caught him in the shoulder. It forced him to stumble back but didn't do any real damage.

Off balance, the guy floundered.

Even as Stack took advantage, launching himself at the man, he recalled how Vanity had suddenly decided to get her house wired. He remembered the shadows lurking around her porch, the noise he'd thought was a deer.

Jesus, he'd done it again.

Vanity had known something was going on. She'd known there was a threat, and she'd still handed money to Phil.

Not once had she clued him in.

Rage nearly consumed him as the second man landed a few blows. Stack took them—hell, taking a hit was a necessity for any fighter—and gave back his own. Instead of making this one quick and clean, as he'd done with the first guy, he let his fists work.

"Fuck you," the guy said when Stack hit his mouth.

"You won't touch her." Stack blocked the knee to his midsection, grabbed the man's leg and dropped him to his back. Following him down, he gained a dominant position and pounded on him some more. Face, body, face, body.

There wasn't much resistance left, and yet he couldn't seem to pull back.

"Stack, hey. Enough, man."

He heard the voice, saw the movement in his periphery, but it didn't register.

"He's had enough, Stack. Let up," said another voice.

A hand caught his upper arm, but he shrugged it off. It returned, clamping on more tightly. "Stack!"

By small degrees, he heard Cannon, and then Denver, both talking to him. In the distance he heard the sirens.

He hated himself, but he turned to his friends, one major concern on his mind. "Vanity?"

"She's at the bar with Armie."

Safe.

Deceptive, but safe.

Cannon pulled him to his feet, lifted one of Stack's hands, then cursed at his battered knuckles. "You're going to need more ice."

Stack pulled away, looked around and sucked in a breath. Fuck.

He'd ruined his sister's bedroom.

There were now two broken lamps, along with blood on the carpet, wall and bedspread. The jewelry he'd thought to protect had fallen to the floor.

"You okay?" Denver asked.

Scrubbing his hands over his face, Stack felt the bruise swelling near his eye. His forearm was still sore. His lip split. Compared to the two who'd attacked him, he couldn't complain.

Popping the tension from his neck, he narrowed his

gaze on the first man. "He's going to be singing in the choir."

"Nut shot?" Denver asked.

Nodding, Stack added, "Hard."

Cannon shrugged. "Probably doesn't need to be pro-creating anyway."

"And that one." Stack swallowed back his disgust at seeing the second man's distorted face. "He threatened Vanity."

"Then he deserved it," Denver said.

Cannon pulled off his stocking cap, ran fingers through his hair, then let his arm drop to his side. "I called Logan."

Great. The cops. "At least he knows us." Logan was one of Cannon's detective friends. He was also a good, fair man. With one last glance around, Stack picked up his sister's jewelry. Some of it had been stepped on, but the most important pieces were fine. He set them on the dresser and withdrew his phone. "I should call Tabby before the interrogation starts."

"Go ahead," Denver told him. "We'll keep an eye on your friends."

Stack went into the living room to give his sister the news. It was going to be a long night.

And the worst was yet to come.

ARMIE AND LEESE kept her company, but that just made Vanity feel worse, like an imposition. She knew they both had better things to do.

In Leese's case, he had any number of ladies trying to get his attention. He teased back, flirted, but he didn't leave her side.

Armie, for the most part, ignored other ladies. For

the first time that Vanity could ever remember, he seemed utterly disinterested in their come-ons. With her, he smiled and chatted, but it all felt very forced.

What had started as a festive, fun night out, now felt dark and depressed. The urge to call Stack gnawed on her peace of mind. Cannon had checked in with Yvette, Denver with Cherry.

But not one word from Stack.

Twenty minutes later, when he, Denver and Cannon finally came in through the front doors, Vanity's heart shot into overdrive. She wanted to race to him, but something held her back. Even from a distance, she felt the difference, saw it in the set of his shoulders and the remoteness in his eyes.

As Yvette went to Cannon, and Cherry ran to Denver, Vanity couldn't seem to move.

Since she didn't budge, neither did Leese or Armie. She tried to swallow, but emotion left a lump in her throat the size of a softball.

Something was wrong, but what? Stack hadn't even looked at her yet. The others started giving her worried looks and still she just stood there, uncertain, worried.

Finally, after speaking to the guys, Stack looked up, saw her and, mouth grim, headed her way.

He'd been fighting. She'd known that from what Cannon and Denver had relayed during their calls, but seeing the bruises on his face was very different from just hearing about it.

He stopped in front of her. No smile, no touch. It felt like a mile separated them. "You ready to go?"

Her heart plummeted. His cold eyes told her what he hadn't yet said.

"Vanity?"

Nodding, she whispered, "What's wrong?" As she reached out for him, he leaned away. Crushed, she retreated, then sought her pride as a defense. "I drove my own car."

"I'll follow you home."

Home. She'd begun to think that meant the same to him as it did to her, but something tonight had changed him. "Fine." Taking her coat from the back of her chair, she pulled it on and tugged her purse strap up to her shoulder.

Thinking to tell everyone goodbye, she looked up and realized she and Stack were now alone at the table.

She wasn't great at these group-type relationships. Did their absence mean a rejection of her, that they knew of a problem, or were they just giving her and Stack privacy?

She searched the room, but the only one to make eye contact was Leese. As soon as she looked at him, he started in her direction.

Bunching up with barely tempered animosity, Stack took a stance.

Oh, no. Vanity didn't want a private conflict to spill over to one of Stack's friends.

Moving in front of Stack, she hurriedly told Leese, "I just wanted to say goodbye. We're heading out now."

His hard gaze cut beyond her to Stack. When his eyes met hers again, he asked, "You okay?"

"Yes." She forced a tight smile. "Of course. Thank you."

He didn't look convinced.

She patted his shoulder. "I'll see you soon, okay?"

"If you need me, call."

Stepping up alongside her, Stack growled to Leese, *"Back off."*

"Sure thing." Tone cordial as if he didn't have a care, Leese said to Vanity, "I mean it, hon. Anytime, okay?"

Gratitude swelled, choking her more. "Thank you." Turning, not bothering to see if anyone else looked her way, she marched out. Her car was across the street, and as she blindly headed toward it, a horn blared.

Stack pulled her back. "What the hell?" He scowled down at her. "You almost got hit."

Stupid, stupid, stupid. She would not be a pathetic victim. She'd gone into this game with Stack knowing it could backfire.

Now that it probably had, she'd get it together and be a responsible, strong adult. "I'm sorry." For so many things. "I didn't see… I'll be more careful now." She freed her arm, glanced up and down the street, then all but ran to get in her car.

By the time she'd driven the first block, Stack was behind her, and he stayed close all the way to her house.

More than ever she wished Norwood and Maggie were waiting for her. Their unconditional love always filled her heart with contentment. It had been a very long time since she'd felt so alone.

In fact, the only time she ever remembered feeling so desolate was after she'd lost her entire family.

She pulled into the garage, thought about hurrying into the house to ensure whatever Stack had to say, he'd have to say inside. But that seemed cowardly, so she was still sitting behind the wheel when he opened her door.

When he remained silent, she decided he planned to come in anyway.

Dropping her keys into her purse, Vanity opened her seat belt and stepped out, shoulders back, spine straight. If she didn't feel confident, at least she could fake it.

Stack waited for her to precede him through the garage, pausing before going through the door to the house to hit the automatic garage door unit.

Once inside, Vanity immediately reset the code on the alarm system, then decided to be proactive.

Flipping on the kitchen lights to chase away the shadows, she faced Stack and shrugged out of her coat. "All right. What's happened?"

His gaze briefly dipped to her cleavage, making her regret her outfit choice for the night. Sure, when she'd first chosen the top, her intent had been to get his attention.

Now she just felt exposed and foolish.

Stack still had his keys in his hand, and while he dispassionately studied her body, he jangled them as if impatient to be on his way. "Phil broke into Tabby's apartment."

"I knew that much." She'd worried about Stack and about Tabby. In a very short time they'd become more like family than her own family had ever been. It scared her that now, out of the blue, she felt that relationship slipping through her fingers. "I hope you got there in time to keep him from taking anything valuable."

He nodded but moved on from that. "All those times you called him f'ing Phil, it was almost as if you understood that he's a creep."

"I do understand that. Phil is self-centered, lazy and lacks any sense of responsibility."

"Yeah, you know all that because I told you often enough, right?"

He sounded so bitter, Vanity felt a trap coming on. "Yes, you mentioned it. But I have eyes of my own. I didn't need you to tell me."

Stack smiled, but it wasn't a sign of pleasure or humor. "You saw everything so clearly that you decided to give him money? Money that he could have used to hire people to—"

"No!" Urgency brought Vanity forward until she stood against him. With him looking so grim, her heart tried to pound out of her chest. "He said he needed stuff for a job. Shoes and other equipment, gas for the car. That's all. You have to know I'd never give him money to hurt you."

Stack didn't push her away, but he didn't embrace her either, and that seemed worse. "You believed him about the shoes?"

Seeing the distrust in his eyes set her stomach roiling. She dropped her forehead to his chest, for only a moment borrowing the strength he'd so often given freely.

But no more.

Sensing it all crumbling down around her, Vanity stepped back. It was past time to tell Stack everything. It might be too late, but she'd try her best and hope it was good enough.

A deep breath helped to fortify her. "No, I didn't believe Phil." Chilled from the inside out, she clasped her hands together tightly. "I gave him the benefit of the doubt, hoping that maybe just this once, he really was looking for work. I hoped that if he got a job, it'd make your life easier, maybe ease the tension between you and Tabby."

"So it was all about helping me, huh?"

Fear and guilt made her eyes burn. She wasn't a crier, damn it, but never before had she been faced with a problem like this.

Never before had she been in love.

"Is that what happened?" She had to know. "Did Phil use that money to hire someone to come after you? It occurred to me that he might have."

"Huh. And still you never said a word."

Though she doubted it would help, Vanity told him of her plans. "I hired a private detective to find him, to see what he was up to. I wanted to protect you."

"A PI?"

"Jack Woolridge. He's supposed to be one of the best."

Laughing, Stack held out a hand, rubbing together two fingers and his thumb. "You've got plenty of cash to throw around, right? Why not spend it on that? Makes more sense than just telling me the truth."

Was that how he saw her efforts? As her throwing around her inheritance?

She shook her head in denial. "I wanted to tell you."

"No opportunity? That's right, after Tabby left, I was so busy declaring how much I cared, you couldn't get a word in edgewise."

Hurt sat like a lead weight on her chest. "I believed you, that you cared."

He stared at her, not a single sign of giving in his eyes. "You wanted to know what happened between Whitney and me?"

At one point she had very much wanted to know. But not now. "It doesn't matter."

"No?" He moved closer but still stopped with too much distance between them. "I want to tell you anyway."

That's when she saw the mark on his neck. All other

sensations faded beneath disbelief and red-hot jealousy. She stared at his neck. "Whitney kissed you?"

"What?" He touched his fingers to the spot, and they came away with lipstick. Stack at first looked disgusted, then he smirked. "Yeah, she did."

"You let her?" She couldn't imagine it, but his dislike felt palpable. If he'd been with another woman, how could she ever recover from that?

His eyes narrowed. "No."

The relief made her weak.

"Whitney made a fool of me."

I'm not Whitney—not that he saw the difference. Not anymore. "I'm sorry."

As if she hadn't spoken, Stack continued. "All along, she told me she didn't like Phil. She said she hated the way he treated my sister. So many times after I'd argued with Tabby about it, Whitney commiserated, telling me she understood."

"I'm sure she did. Phil didn't just use your sister, he used your mother, too."

"There, you see?" He narrowed his eyes. "You and Whitney say damn near the same things. It's fucking uncanny."

Vanity flinched, both at his language and the insulting comparison.

Not that Stack seemed to notice. "Remember I told you I walked in on them together?"

Vanity saw how that had affected him, the betrayal he'd felt. "Yes, I remember."

"They were talking about me."

She reached out but didn't quite touch him. "Whitney is a fool."

"That's exactly what she called me. She was so busy

telling Phil to ignore me, bragging that she could handle me, neither of them heard me come in. They were friends, laughing about me. Good friends. Maybe fucking, but like I said, it didn't matter." He locked his gaze with hers. "I detest liars."

"I didn't lie." But she knew she had. Lies of omission.

Stack gave another of those ugly smiles. "Haven't you?"

Giving up, deciding to come clean on everything, Vanity put up her chin. "All right, so I have. Because I love you."

He looked taken aback, then barked a laugh.

Vanity ignored his humor. "You want the truth? Fine, I'll tell you the truth. Every word of it." And hopefully, when she finished, he'd stop being mad…and start loving her back.

CHAPTER TWENTY

THOUGH THE CONFRONTATION in Tabby's apartment had ended hours ago, Stack still seethed with anger. He needed to hit up the rec center, to take his temper out on a heavy bag.

He'd been a dupe with Whitney, and that still stung.

But this…he felt so much more for Vanity that being played this time was far worse. He'd considered her different, up-front and ballsy and honest to a fault. He'd even started thinking long-term. Marriage, kids and pets and a house…the whole love story.

Now…now he didn't know how to deal with the crushing blow to his pride.

Before going to the bar, he'd considered just asking Armie or Cannon to see Vanity home. It would have been easier. No matter the deception, he didn't want to take his anger out on her.

But he couldn't do it. He'd needed to see her, hoping that somehow she'd be able to deny what he knew was true, that she'd have a logical explanation.

She didn't.

He'd also wanted to ensure she made it home safe and sound, that she had her alarms set.

And maybe, being a masochist, he'd wanted to torture himself a little more.

His mouth twisted. "I'm waiting."

That seemed to snap her out of the unfamiliar mood, and the old Vanity returned.

Posture confident, she glared at him. "You know what, Stack? You're being a jerk! Here are your miserable truths, and I hope you choke on them."

He was choking all right. On deception.

"I met you and fell hard. Almost from the day I met you, I knew I wanted you. Within a few weeks, I was in love. But you never paid any attention to me, so I decided to proposition you."

Every time she mentioned love his damned heartbeat galloped. He couldn't believe her, not now, not while feeling like the biggest chump alive. So he reacted with sarcasm. "When all else fails, use sex. Tried and true way to lure a guy in."

"Yes," she snapped, "it is. And like most men, you jumped all over it."

True. He'd been nauseatingly easy.

"I figured I had nothing to lose, right? I mean, if it stayed a one-night stand, I'd have gotten to sleep with the Wolf."

Heat burned his face. "That's a stupid fight name and you know it."

As if he hadn't spoken, she continued. "But if it turned into more, as I hoped, that'd be perfect."

New, angrier heat coursed through him. "So all those times you brought up that idiotic agreement, that was just to continue your lies?"

No longer fazed by his rage, she lifted her chin. "Lies, plot, whatever you want to call it." Mocking him, she sneered, "I hoped to reel you in."

Humiliation choked him. "And you did."

Breathing hard, she stared at him…and her scowl eased, her voice softened. "Did I?"

No way would he answer her.

"I only wanted you to see that things would be good between us."

After the taunts, he ignored the sincerity in her eyes. "The sex, sure. Or…wait. Was that also a lie?"

Confused, she searched his face, then shook her head.

Stack laughed, as much at himself as her. "All those sweet moans and easy climaxes. Were you pretendin', darlin'?" He put two fingers under her chin. "Stroking my ego to soften me up? Was that part of your plan? Let me think we burned up the sheets, maybe think that sex between us was somehow special?"

If so, her plan had worked because it had felt special, more special than anything he'd ever known.

She jerked away from him, her entire, sleek body trembling. "I wasn't pretending."

"So at least the sex was real? I'm relieved *something* was."

Movements rough with anger, she flipped back her hair and pushed up her sleeves. Stack saw the small pink reminder of her burn the night of the car fire. He'd been so impressed with her, her poise under pressure, her quick thinking and her bravery.

So many redeeming qualities, but he couldn't put aside the lies.

After two deep breaths, she reached out to him. "Stack…"

New humiliations occurred to him. "You and Leese are close. Does he know you've been faking it?"

She withdrew, her expression shuttered. "It's true, I

pretended not to love you. I figured if I told you up-front how much I care, you'd have run in the other direction."

"We'll never know now, will we?" But she was probably right. He hadn't wanted to get involved, not until Vanity blindsided him with that damned proposal for sex.

She kept saying it, over and over, that she loved him. Could that be true? At the moment, in his present state of mind, he didn't trust himself to decide. He needed to think over everything, to come to grips with what he wanted.

He needed to be clearheaded, and right now, he wasn't.

"I should go." He didn't want to. He wanted to go back to the morning when everything had seemed possible, instead of impossible.

For a lengthy stretch of silence, Vanity stared at him. He could see there were other things she wanted to say…but she held back. Finally, body stiff, she turned and led the way to the front door. Stack silently followed.

In profile, she looked defiant and a little wounded.

Not touching her was hard. In a million different ways, he wanted to comfort her, to tell her they'd work it out. But he was afraid if he gave in even a little, he'd end up rushing her to bed, and nothing would ever get settled. She needed to understand that lying wouldn't be tolerated, and he needed the rest of the night to sort through his disappointment.

Did she really love him?

Tomorrow, after he finished up at the gym, they'd get together and talk.

Accepting that plan as the most reasonable, Stack turned her to face him.

Still she said nothing.

"You should stay inside the rest of the night. Tomorrow, if you go out, be careful."

For an answer, Vanity opened the door. "Don't worry about me, Stack. I can take care of myself."

Didn't he know it? She was smart, resourceful, with an amazing inner strength and unrelenting energy. Add in her disposable cash, and she could certainly handle her own protection. Still, he needed her to know, so as he stepped out to her porch, he turned and said, "One of the guys who came after me at Tabby's apartment said you'd be next."

That perked her up. She didn't look fearful as much as curious. "It was someone I know?"

Stack shook his head. "He threatened me, and said my girlfriend would be next."

Expression flat, Vanity said, "Then he probably meant Whitney." And with that she closed the door in his face. Immediately Stack heard the lock click into place, then the dead bolt.

He knew Vanity would set the alarm system, too. He'd meant to ask her about that, if Phil's visit had inspired the extra security. Probably. The woman wasn't a dummy. Just the opposite, she was cagey enough to fool him.

And yet, damn it, he knew she was different from Whitney. As different as night from day.

Tomorrow they'd get everything worked out.

Tonight he needed to regroup. He wasn't willing to end things with her, so that meant he needed to come to grips with the fact that…what? She wasn't perfect?

He laughed at himself as he went down the walk-way into the cold, quiet night. Vanity Baker might look perfect, but she was as human and fallible as he was.

Maybe, despite everything, that made her absolutely perfect…for him.

AFTER A NIGHT spent painting, binge eating, and stu-pidly crying, Vanity canceled everything except her shift at Yvette's secondhand store. Wanting uninter-rupted time alone, she'd shut off her phone, and now, when she turned it back on, she saw a lot of messages.

All from Stack's friends.

New tears welled up. Throughout the long night, she'd wondered if losing Stack would also mean losing everyone else she held dear.

Determined to face the day stronger, to stop being an emotional wimp, she listened first to Armie's mes-sage. He wanted her to call him before she left the house today. Instead she texted her thanks to him, and told him she was fine. Then she listened to a message from Leese saying he was there if she needed to talk. She sent another text, thanking him.

Next was a message from Merissa that said, Rissy was here. It made her smile. Rissy seldom left lengthy messages. Her feeling was that people would either reply or not, but she didn't want to be a bother.

When she saw the note from Yvette, she hit the phone icon and called her friend.

"Hey," Yvette said before the phone had even fin-ished one ring. "Are you okay?"

For a second there, Vanity choked on her reassur-ances, but she cleared her throat, nodded and managed a credible, "Sure."

"Vanity." Yvette's tone chided. "What can I do?"

"There's nothing to do. It's over." Maybe, Vanity thought, if she said it enough, it'd get easier.

"No! That can't be. Surely—"

"It's okay. *I'm* okay," Vanity stressed. She hoped that would get easier, too, because right now she felt totally shattered, as if pieces of herself were missing. "In fact, I'll be leaving in a few minutes for the shop."

"No way! Take the day off. I'll work the shift."

"Honestly, Yvette, I'd rather do it. Moping around is for the birds."

Yvette hesitated, but she knew Vanity well, so she conceded. "Okay. I get that you want to stay busy. But count on lots of calls. Knowing the guys the way I do, they're going to take turns checking on you."

Vanity groaned. The last thing she wanted was sympathy. "Thanks for the warning."

Ready for some fresh air, she set the alarm, locked up the empty house on her way to the garage, and braved the cold to drive to the shop. On the way she replied to Merissa's text with a call.

Rissy, too, answered right away. "Hey, Vee. What's up?"

Going for the jovial route? Vanity found a smile. "You sound just like Armie."

Rissy groaned. "You take that back."

Vanity laughed. "Sorry."

"So… I just wanted to see how you are. You looked pretty shook up yesterday when you left the bar. I'm not sure what's going on with you and Stack, but—"

"It's over." The stunned silence surprised Vanity. "Merissa?"

"I'm here, I just… How can that be? Stack is crazy about you!"

Apparently not. "I did some stupid things, and I guess he couldn't forgive me. It's my own fault."

"Damn, Vee. I don't know what to say. I'm so sorry."

"Thanks."

Uncertain, Merissa said, "If you want to talk—"

"I appreciate that, Rissy. I really do." Sympathy would have her weeping again if she let it. "Right now I just want to stay busy."

"I understand. If you change your mind, shoot me a text. I promise I can be very distracting."

After agreeing that she would if necessary, Vanity got caught up on calls and texts. It seemed everyone wanted to talk to her, commiserate with her, try to make her feel better.

In different ways, they were each shocked that things were over between her and Stack.

One advantage to talking on the phone was that Vanity was able to ask for time. She didn't want visits, and while some of the guys were adamant that she needed them, in the end they agreed to abide by her wishes.

Though her heart remained broken, at least she knew that Stack's friends hadn't given up on her. They didn't know the issues, and they didn't pry, but they did care about her.

She felt better, knowing she wasn't alone after all.

Luckily, the resale shop stayed busy. She worked through lunch without a break, which suited her just fine. A few hours before her shift would end, things finally quieted down. Left with only her own unsettled thoughts, Vanity dropped to the stool behind the counter and propped her head on her hand.

Funny, because she usually didn't see Stack much during the day, but every hour, every minute, she'd missed him. The thought of going home alone didn't appeal at all. Maybe she needed to get a couple of dogs. When Norwood and Maggie had been there, the place had never felt empty. The dogs had brought a lot of energy and love to her house.

Her laugh sounded more like a sob. She couldn't replace Stack with pets. But what choice did she have?

She was thinking of going by a shelter when her phone rang and startled her. In a glance she saw it was Jack Woolridge, the PI she'd hired, and immediately worried that something might have happened to Stack.

Anxious, she slipped off the stool and turned her back to the front door. "Jack, hello. Did you have news for me?"

"Matter of fact, ma'am, I do." He gave a pause for emphasis, then announced, "I found Phil."

Thank goodness. Vanity might have blown things with Stack, but she could give him this. "Where is he?"

"That's the thing. I don't think you need to worry about him. See, I found him at this bar just outside of town. He was with a woman, and I got close enough to listen in."

Suspicions sharpened. "A woman?"

"Yeah. I pretended to be another drunk, so they paid no attention to me."

To Vanity, it seemed obvious who the woman might be. "What did she look like?"

"I can do you one better than a description. I caught her name when Phil greeted her."

"Whitney?"

"That'd be her. You know her?"

"She's friends with Phil and used to date Stack."

"Ah. Well, here's the kicker. Phil accused her of sending more goons to beat up your boyfriend. He seemed real put out over it."

Whoa, wait? What? "Phil thinks Whitney was behind that?"

"She didn't really deny it," Jack explained. "In fact, she laughed."

Oh, my God. Vanity hadn't figured on that twist. It didn't make sense. "Why would Whitney do that?"

"Phil asked her the same thing. From what I could hear, she's playing both sides. She said she learned from him, so I'm thinking Phil did send the first set of bully boys. Not to kill Hannigan or anything, just to stall him. Something about getting money from you."

Oh, God. Phil had deliberately held up Stack to ensure he wouldn't interrupt? New guilt stole her strength, and she backed up to sit on the stool. "Yes," she said in a croak. "He asked me for money the same night Stack was attacked."

"So that much is probably true. Now here's where it gets complicated."

Because it wasn't complicated enough already?

"I'm thinking Whitney told Phil to go to the apartment to get what he wanted. Then she tipped off Hannigan, making out like she was the good guy in all this. But really she just wanted them both there at the same time. See, she also sent two more thugs, and they were supposed to work him over good this time."

The thought of Stack being set up, ambushed, made her stomach churn. "Why would she do that?"

With a shrug in his tone, Jack said, "Heard her tell Phil that he'd caused the conflict between her and

Hannigan, so now he could be the solution. When the men attacked, Phil would get the blame, and she'd get to console Hannigan."

Things started to click into place, but it all still seemed very far-fetched. "So let me get this straight. Whitney convinced Phil to go to the apartment, then told Stack he'd be there, and *then* hired thugs to go after Stack, assuming he'd think Phil had hired them." *That bitch.* "She wants Stack to think she's confiding in him, trying to protect him, so they can get closer."

"She told Phil she wasn't done with Hannigan, so, yeah, that's how it sounds. While Hannigan healed up from his beating, she'd be there to coddle him."

"I think I'm going to puke."

Jack laughed. "Yeah, she's twisted. And that's why I'm calling. See, Whitney suggested to Phil that he might want to leave town. She doesn't want him around muddying up her plans by telling the truth to anyone. Phil threatened to go straight to the cops instead…and she told him he'd be next on the hit list if he did."

So many incredible threats. Vanity didn't know what to say, what to do. Her thoughts scrambled.

"After Phil charged off," Jack continued, "I decided he was the lesser of the threats, and I stuck with the lady."

"*Thank you*, Jack. Very smart thinking."

Jack cleared his throat. "I didn't know if you wanted me involving the cops or not, but Whitney made a call, told someone to go after Hannigan one more time."

Oh, no! *"When?"*

"Tonight I think, but I don't know where. What do you want me to do? Keep tailing her? Call in the police?"

"Tail her, yes. Let me talk to Stack, and then I'll call you back. Until then, don't let her out of your sight!"

"Got it covered."

Vanity disconnected the phone and immediately dialed Stack. He was probably still at the rec center, could still be working out. She hated to interrupt, but she had to get his input, and she had to warn him.

What if he was so mad, he ignored her call? If he did, she'd call Armie. Or Cannon.

Or…she still had the second phone for emergencies. If she had to, she'd use the blasted bat signal. "Vanity?"

Relief robbed her of strength. *He hadn't ignored her call.* That had to mean something, right?

Her relief was short-lived, because almost at the same time Stack answered, the shop door swung open, and Phil, haggard and breathing hard, stood there staring at her. Hatred and desperation darkened his eyes.

Vanity went temporarily blank.

"Vanity?" Stack said again, now with more insistence.

Oh, no, no, *no.* Phil looked unhinged. This wasn't a pot high, and this wasn't everyday anger. Alarm kicked her heartbeat into high gear.

Phil had a hand in his pocket…to conceal a weapon? If she told Stack he was here, would Phil lash out? With no time to waste, she settled on what to do, and prayed it was the right decision.

To keep Phil from catching on, she tried to sound pleasant instead of alarmed as she said to Stack, "Hang on, please," and laid the phone on the counter. Hopefully Phil would assume she'd put a customer on hold.

If Stack could hear her talking, he'd understand, so she said louder than necessary, "Phil. What are you doing here?"

WITH STACK'S KNUCKLES BRUISED, Cannon, Denver, Armie, Miles and Brand had all ganged up on him, refusing to let him hit the heavy bag. So he'd practiced kicks on it instead. Endlessly. Until sweat had soaked his body and his thighs felt like noodles.

Hadn't helped, so he'd gone for a jog. Hours long. He'd pounded the pavement until he couldn't breathe, and still a wild, turbulent mix of emotions left him unsettled.

No matter how he tried, he couldn't get Vanity off his mind.

It didn't help that everyone was so pissed. At *him*.

You'd think he'd beaten up a new fighter, the way they all vilified him.

Leese was the worst. If looks could kill, Stack would have expired that morning. A dozen times throughout the day he'd considered going after Leese, and Leese had looked to welcome it. But each time he took a step in that direction, Armie or Cannon was there, backing him off.

"Don't blame Leese for caring if you don't," Armie had said.

With no idea what that meant, Stack had ignored both men.

Later, when he'd found Leese mean-mugging him again, Cannon elbowed him and said, "You've got enough on your plate, Stack. Let it go."

He'd wondered why no one told Leese to let up, but

short of saying, "Leese started it," which would make him sound like a disgruntled schoolboy, what could he do?

He'd gone back to working out his frustration through physical exertion.

For most of the day Stack hadn't understood why everyone kept giving him ugly stares.

Then Yvette had showed up, storming past Cannon in a beeline to him.

Yvette never stormed, so she'd gotten Stack's attention right off. His first thought had been that something had happened to Vanity.

Fear had slammed into him, and he'd met Yvette halfway. "What's wrong?"

She stopped him with a poke at his chest. "You're a jerk, Stack Hannigan, that's what's wrong."

Whoa. Stack lifted his hands. "What'd I do?"

"Oh, my God, do you seriously have to ask?"

"Uh…yeah." Far as he knew, he hadn't done a damn thing to Yvette. He wouldn't.

Frowning more fiercely than he'd ever seen before, Yvette grabbed his elbow and pulled him toward the back wall.

Stack looked back at Cannon and saw his friend just standing there, arms folded over his chest, his expression…satisfied.

Well, hell. No help there.

Leese saluted him. Armie looked on the verge of laughing.

When Yvette stopped, they had a scrap of privacy—meaning no one could hear, but they could all *see*.

See him getting his ass chewed by Yvette.

Enough already. "Look," Stack started to say. "I don't know what—"

Tone feral, Yvette growled, "You made her *cry*."

Shit. Hating the thought of that, Stack asked, "Vanity?"

Yvette tucked in her chin. "Don't act confused. Yes, Vanity." And then with sadness, "How could you do that to her? I thought you were one of the good guys."

He thought he was, too. With the hairs on the back of his neck prickling, Stack explained, "We argued." That's all. An argument. How could he have known that would upset her so much? Vanity was the one who'd betrayed him with lies.

Although, now that he thought about their exchange, Vanity's side of the argument had consisted mostly of her yelling that she loved him.

Feeling a trickle of sweat track down his temple, Stack rubbed a forearm over his face.

By the time he'd left last night, Vanity had looked only pissed, not weepy. It twisted his guts to think he'd walked away when she might have needed him. "I'll talk to her." And somehow he'd figure it out, because lies or not, he cared about her.

"You should have talked before you told her it was over."

Stack took a step back. "I did what?"

Now Yvette looked near tears. "She's the strongest person I know, Stack. She *never* cries, not over anything." Going all angry Amazon again, Yvette stretched up to her tiptoes. "But *you* made her."

"We're not over. Jesus. Don't start rumors like that."

Yvette blinked. "You are." Confused, she'd dropped back to her feet. "Vanity said so."

Rage returning to the boiling point, Stack crowded in closer again. "She said she's through with me?"

Yvette stared at him, then behind him—and yeah, of course, Cannon had moved closer.

Stack knew he'd made a damned spectacle of himself.

No longer looking angry, Leese said, "Vanity got the idea that *you* were calling it quits."

As a warning, Stack told him, "Not even, so you can just back up on that shit."

"Glad to hear it," Leese said with his own black frown. "Maybe you should tell *her* that."

So Leese had been mad at him for upsetting Vanity? Maybe he owed him an apology.

Yvette touched his arm. "She's not as casual about relationships as most people might be. As long as I've known Vanity, she's never been serious about a guy, but she'd put everything on the line for a friend. I can only imagine how invested she'd be over the guy she loves."

The guy she loves.

And he'd accused her. Walked away from her.

He'd made her cry.

Looking less angry and more instructional, Leese said, "I tried to steer her in the right direction, you know? But she doesn't totally catch the cues. She wanted to get your interest when I knew you were already hooked."

Hooked, reeled in and happy about it. Stack drew a deep breath and released a lot of resentment. "She's mine."

"Well, hallelujah." Cannon smiled. "I think she's the one you need to tell."

Armie gave Stack a shove. "I'd say you should ice

those knuckles again, but it'd probably be better if you just grabbed a shower and got on your way."

To Vanity. Right. That sounded like a fine plan. And with that decided, urgency had replaced the anger.

He'd showered with haste, thrown on his clothes, and had just gotten into his car when she called. He'd been all ready to explain, to reiterate that he cared.

But a second after that, Phil had walked in on her.

So now, driving as fast as he dared, keeping the call on speaker, Stack listened in.

He could hear Phil talking but couldn't understand everything he said. Something clattered, and he imagined Phil moving into the shop, stepping around the space filled with a variety of items.

Vanity, who probably stood near the counter, came through loud and clear when she said, "You actually think I'd give you money again?"

More mumbling from Phil, and then, as if he'd gotten closer to her, Stack heard, "You have to help me. I don't have any other choice."

"You lied to me, Phil. You said you needed the money for a job."

"Yeah, a lie. Sorry 'bout that. This time I'll be square with you. Swear."

"All right." Vanity's voice faded, got stronger again. Was she moving around, too? Fear choked him when he realized she might be trying to keep space between herself and Phil. "How much do you need now, and why?"

"Two grand. I know, I know. It's a lot."

With a shrug in her tone, Vanity said, "Not really, but I don't have that much on me."

"I need it now." Phil hesitated. "How soon could you get it?"

Again Vanity moved away from the phone. Stack imagined Phil stalking her, and the visual made his entire body tense. *Hang on, darlin'. I'm almost there.* He wanted to call the cops, but he wouldn't disconnect the call. Hoping Armie would understand, Stack withdrew his second cell and used the bat signal. When Armie answered, Stack whispered, "Get the cops to Yvette's shop, stat."

No questions. "Done."

Stack disconnected with Armie and concentrated on the open call with Vanity.

Only a few more minutes and he'd be there with her.

"Get real, Phil. I won't give you a dime unless you tell me why you need it."

Knuckles going white on the steering wheel, Stack silently prayed that Vanity wouldn't push Phil too far. At this point, Stack didn't know what the man was capable of—but he kept remembering that gun in Phil's dresser, and his guts burned.

Phil no longer had that weapon, but had he gotten another?

"I'm going away," Phil groaned.

"Where?"

"I don't know yet." Something crashed, like a fist on a desk. "She's framing me!"

Soft, soothing, Vanity said, "Whitney. I know."

She knew? Stack checked the traffic, then blew through a yellow light. *What the hell did she know? What was Whitney up to?*

Stack's surprise was nothing compared to Phil's.

"You're working with her," Phil snarled with rage. "You fucking bitch."

"Phil!" Vanity's voice snapped with authority. "Don't

be more of an idiot than you've already been. I'm trying to *help* you."

Heavy breathing came through the line, and Phil asked, "Help me how?"

Convincing, calm, Vanity told him, "I hired a PI when I thought you were the one trying to hurt Stack. I know he can take care of himself, but not if someone sneaks up on him…although, I guess he handled that situation, too."

"He's a fucking wrecking ball."

"Yes, I know," Vanity said with pride. "Anyway, I hired the PI to find you." With satisfaction, she added, "He found you with Whitney. He heard everything. He's with Whitney now, keeping tabs on her."

Phil's breathing was so audible, Stack could hear it even through the call. He sounded desperate, and that made Stack desperate, too.

Finally Phil said, "I don't believe you."

Stack would agree, except in a twisted, illogical way, it made sense. Now Vanity just needed to convince Phil, to keep control of the scene.

To protect herself until he got there.

"Stay," Vanity cajoled. "Stay and I'll tell the cops everything I know. They'll understand that Whitney conspired a lot of this. Stay, and I'll give you the two grand to start over. But you have to talk to the cops, you have to tell them what you know."

She wanted Phil to help indict Whitney? Stack couldn't imagine Phil being a credible witness, but the PI she'd hired…yeah, that guy was going to come in handy.

In the middle of the turmoil, Stack felt pride. She was, by far, the most amazing person he'd ever known.

"Seriously, Vanity?" A different emotion influenced Phil's tone. "You'd do that for me?"

Uncertainty now sounded in hers. "Oh, um…yes. Yes, I would. To help *Stack*. Not to—"

"We've gotten along, haven't we?"

"No! I've tolerated you, Phil. That's all."

"You like me, I can tell. We clicked, didn't we?"

Just as Phil's voice went husky, Vanity's went shrill. "What are you doing? Get away from me!"

Stack screeched up to the curb, threw the car in Park, and jumped out running. He reached the glass door in time to see Phil corner Vanity. The bastard had one hand clamped on her arm, the other knotted in her long hair, and he was trying to kiss her.

CHAPTER TWENTY-ONE

IN A MURDEROUS RAGE, Stack stormed in...and saw Vanity bring her knee up to Phil's jewels. A direct hit. For that one second in time before the pain set in, Phil gaped at her and his hands loosened.

But Vanity wasn't done. As she'd been taught in the self-defense classes, she used the heel of her hand to bash Phil's nose. Hands to his balls, his head knocked back, and Phil staggered.

When blood sprayed, Vanity recoiled. "Eewww..."

Phil dropped to his knees.

Stalking in, Stack immediately drew him back up and slammed him against the wall. "You dared to touch her?" He slammed Phil again. "You miserable—"

"Stack!"

He stilled. Not Vanity's voice, but his sister's.

Groaning, Stack looked over his shoulder and there stood Tabby, her eyes flared, her mouth pinched.

She was going to be so badly hurt by all this.

Then he glanced at Vanity. She watched him warily, her eyes still red, her lips trembling. She'd been hurt, too.

By him.

Time for him to start mending things, instead of wrecking them. Opening his fingers, Stack released Phil and let him slump down the wall to the floor. One deep breath, then another, and he thought he just might be able to speak coherently.

"He had his hand in his pocket," Vanity warned. "I don't know—"

"Got it." Stack knelt down, frisked Phil and found a bag of pills but no weapons. Shit. He shoved Phil's face up, and only then did he realize Phil wasn't all there. "What did you take?"

"Don't know," he slurred. "I just needed…something."

"Courage?" Disgusted, Stack stood and tossed the pills on the countertop. His gaze met Vanity's.

"I'm sorry," she whispered.

And, yeah, that totally blew his cool all over.

Emotions combustible, he reached her in one long stride, drew her in, pressed her head to his shoulder while he gently hugged her. "You're okay?"

"Yes." She remained tense in his arms. "You heard everything?"

Over and over, he smoothed his hands along her back. "Yeah. Smart move, leaving the call open like that."

"I wasn't sure you'd answer."

Stack lightly kissed her. "You're unsure about a lot of things, I know."

Tabby elevated her tone in demand. "*What* is going on?"

Keeping Vanity close—something she didn't object to—Stack turned to face Phil. "We thought he was the one hiring goons to come after me, but it was only Phil the first time. After that, it was Whitney calling the shots."

Exasperated, Tabby rushed over to Phil with a handful of tissues. "I told you Phil wouldn't do that." She pressed the tissues to his nose as she took his arm, helping him to stand. "You're okay?"

Phil nodded, his cagey, bleary gaze on Vanity and Stack.

Stack was about to explain when Tabby gave them both a fierce scowl. "If it was Whitney, then why did you slug Phil?"

"Vanity did that," Stack said, unable to contain his smile. "Not me."

Vanity elbowed him, grumbling under her breath.

Brows going high, Tabby asked, "Why?"

Stabbing Phil with renewed anger, Stack growled, "He tried to kiss her."

"He…" Tabby's voice trailed off as she swelled with her own measure of anger. Slowly, she pivoted back to Phil. "You…you…" Then she slugged him, too. Her punch wasn't as direct, more like a wild haymaker catching Phil in the ear. He cowered, arms up, while Tabby kept swinging.

Pleased with his sister's reaction, Stack went to her, dodged a few flying fists, and corralled her by hugging her arms down to her sides. "Cops are on the way, sis. You don't want to be bludgeoning him when they show up."

Kicking out, Tabby said, "I'll do more than bludgeon him. I'll—"

The door opened again, and in stepped Detective Reese Bareden, one of Cannon's cop friends. At six and a half feet tall, the detective made an imposing figure. But at the moment, he only appeared curious as he looked around at each and every person.

"Armie called," the detective explained. "Said there

was a life-and-death situation. So, tell me, who's killing whom?"

Vanity rushed into explanations while Tabby slapped away from Stack's hold. She straightened her clothes, smoothed her hair, and hitched her purse up to her shoulder.

"Okay now?" Stack asked her. He knew his sister could be unpredictable.

"Yes." She flounced away from Phil and went to stand by Vanity, silently backing her—and in the process, filling Stack with yet more pride.

While still trying to explain to the detective, Vanity also tried comforting Tabby, and damned if that didn't make Stack smile, too. She kept him on a roller coaster of reactions but always, at the base, was love. He felt that now, an overload of it, settling the panic, soothing the anger, and ramping up the physical need.

He knew what he wanted to do; he knew he needed Vanity forever.

A second later a car pulled up to the curb across the street. Leese, Cannon and Armie all piled out.

Without missing a beat, Vanity gave Tabby one last pat, went to the door to hold it open for the guys, and then flipped over the Open sign to Closed.

To the detective, she said, "I can call my PI right now. I know it's a bother, and I'm sorry, but I really think you need to pick up Whitney. Especially since she had another attack planned against Stack tonight."

Phil groaned loudly. "She was going to blame me for that, too. I just know it."

Tabby threw a paperweight at Phil. "You deserve to rot in jail, you cretin!"

Phil cried out, his arms over his head. "It wasn't my fault!"

"You idiot, it's *mostly* your fault!"

Detective Bareden snatched a stapler from Tabby's hands. "Ma'am, if you wouldn't mind?"

Sighing, Stack said, "Reese, my sister. Tabby, *Detective* Reese Bareden."

"Oh, right." Tabby stopped trying to reach for the pencil cup.

After eyeing her to make sure she didn't go after another projectile, Reese smiled at Vanity. "You know, I do believe I should make that call. If you could share the PI's number, I'll get in touch with him right now."

While Vanity took care of that, Stack went to stand over Phil, once again slouched down to sit on the floor. He looked cornered, a bloody mess and very afraid. "You're lucky Vanity hit you before I could."

One hand to his nose, the other cupped over his junk, Phil said, "Don't feel all that lucky."

True. Vanity had held her own, and he was so impressed with her, he couldn't wait to get her alone. "If I had hit you, it'd be far, far worse."

"I know."

"You're doubly lucky my sister showed up when she did."

Phil slanted a look at Tabby, his gaze hopeful, speculative.

Not a chance. "You'll stay away from her."

"But—"

Squatting down before Phil, Stack repeated low, "You're done using my family. Stay away from Vanity, stay away from my mother and stay the hell away from my sister."

Phil quailed, ducking his face to the side.

Tabby touched Stack's shoulder. "If he crawled on bloody knees, I wouldn't have him." She, too, crouched down. "I'm done, Phil. Do you understand me?"

He nodded.

"You've cleaned out our accounts. You got your clothes. That's it. You can keep it all. The only thing I need from you is contact info, so the divorce papers can be delivered."

"I… I don't have any place to go."

Reese covered the phone and said, "I'm pretty sure I'll be able to help you with that."

Tabby nodded. "Perfect." Giving Stack a pat, she stood again.

A uniformed cop approached. "Let's go."

Phil's eyes widened. "But…they already told the detective. I didn't do anything!"

Reese strode over. "That's not entirely true, now, is it? Either way, you're coming to the station to answer questions. Until I have this sorted out, you're under arrest."

It took a little longer before the police left, the drugs confiscated and Phil in handcuffs. When Stack rejoined Vanity, he saw that Denver and Cannon were both on their cells.

Amused, he asked Vanity, "Checking in with their ladies?"

She nodded. "Yes." With a look at Armie, she softly added, "And he got a message."

Over Armie's shoulder, Stack saw the screen of Armie's cell.

Rissy was here.

Armie looked painfully undecided as to whether or not he'd text her back. In the end, Stack would bet on Rissy.

Needing to be alone with Vanity, he said, "You guys should go. Everything is under control now. Reese spoke with Vanity's PI, and he said they'll be picking up Whitney and charging her with conspiracy to commit a felony."

Vanity nodded. "Jack, my PI, overheard when and where Whitney arranged the next attack, so the officers will be watching. If things go off as planned, they'll arrest those men who, most likely, will share what they know about Whitney."

"And knowing Phil," Tabby added, "he'll be volunteering as many details as he can, especially if it'll help save his own butt."

Stack ruffled his sister's hair, and when she glared at him, he grinned and helped her smooth it back. Crazy as it seemed, he knew he'd missed her.

Thanks to Vanity, he was now reunited with his family. And just in time, considering there'd soon be a baby in the mix.

"Wow," Leese told Vanity. "You wrapped it all up nice and tight. Impressive."

Vanity blushed. "Not me. I just hired the investigator."

"A smart move," Cannon said. "If you hadn't, eventually Whitney might've gotten lucky."

"No," she protested, then took a deep breath. "Stack would never have let that happen."

He slipped his arm around her; her faith in him was humbling.

"Besides," she continued, "I don't think Whitney really wanted to hurt Stack." With a droll look at Stack, she added, "I think she wanted to create a situation where she could get back on his good side—meaning in his bed."

"And if he got beat up in the process...?" Leese asked.

"He wouldn't." Again Vanity glanced at him. "Stack can take care of himself."

Drawing her away from Stack, Armie enfolded her in a big bear hug. "Thanks to you, he doesn't have to, does he, Vee? Not when you're taking such good care of him."

Stack grinned and said, "True enough."

Quietly overwhelmed, Vanity accepted hugs from each of the guys. After Leese embraced her, Stack clapped him on the shoulder. "Thank you."

Leese nodded. "'Bout time you wised up."

"Also true."

Vanity frowned at each of them. "What are you guys talking about?"

"It's getting late." They had a lot to get straightened out, and Stack knew it'd be easier without an audience. "I'll help Vanity close up, and then we'll head home."

Vanity turned to stare at him.

"Your home." Brushing his knuckles over her cheek, he smiled. "If that's okay?"

She breathed a little faster. "Yes."

Damn, he loved her. "Good, because I need plenty of time to apologize."

Turning in a rush, she opened the door and tried to hurry everyone out.

Laughing, teasing her, treating her like a little sister, the guys finally left.

Now he just needed to get his sister on her way. "You need a ride?" Stack asked her.

"Nope. I have this awesome little brother who bought me a car that I stupidly let my soon-to-be ex-husband drive, but no more."

Vanity laughed.

"So." Tabby eyed them both, and the sternness of her expression sobered Vanity. "I heard this very nasty rumor that you two had called it quits. And I have to say, if that's true, if Stack is an idiot, well, Mom and I are keeping Vanity anyway."

Stack rolled his eyes. "Tabby, you *know* I'm not an idiot."

"If you walk away from Vanity, then you are."

"That would make me the biggest idiot alive."

"But…" Confused, Vanity started to speak to Tabby, then to Stack, then her brows came down, and she tightened her shoulders. "You were furious with me! You accused me of lying."

Gently, Stack said, "You did lie."

"Only about loving you."

Tabby used both hands to make a "time out" gesture, then rounded on Vanity. "Are you telling me you don't love my brother?"

"Of course I do. I always have. But he—" she straightened her arm to point at Stack "—wasn't interested. So I had to pretend that I *didn't* love him. I had to make him think all I wanted was… I…um…" She turned big eyes on Stack.

He smiled at her. "You want to finish that? No? Okay, I can pick up the slack."

"Stack!"

"She's family, honey. We don't keep secrets from family."

Vanity flushed again. Did she understand that she was family, as well? If not, Stack would soon make it crystal clear to her. He turned to his sister. "Vanity pretended we were having a casual hookup, so that I wouldn't get spooked."

"Yeah, right." Tabby didn't buy it. "That's hardly a reason to get bent out of shape."

Vanity bit her lip, her expression so guilty that it pained Stack.

Softer, with more gravity, he explained, "She also gave Phil money without ever telling me about it."

"Oh, crap." Wide-eyed, Tabby stared at Stack. "You thought Phil used that money to hire the thugs?"

"No. I already knew he hadn't." Hoping it wouldn't upset his sister too much, Stack explained what had happened, and how Phil had spent the money. "I got rid of the gun. I didn't want Phil to have it, and I didn't think you'd want it left in the apartment."

Tabby nodded, distressed, but taking it better than Stack had expected.

"I was trying to help," Vanity whispered.

"Because she loves me." Damn it felt good to acknowledge it, to say it out loud.

Vanity went blank.

Reaching for her hand, Stack reeled her in close, then tucked her hair behind her ear. "You do, right? Even though I was an ass?"

She nodded, her face pale. "I do. So much." Before Stack could return the sentiment, Vanity faced Tabby. "I'm sorry."

"For giving Phil money?" Tabby waved that off. "Believe me, I know. For years I did the same, trying to think of a way to get him motivated." She slanted a wry smile at Stack. "Much like Mom tried to motivate me. We both needed some tough love. Combined, we made my brother nuts."

Stack had hope for the future. "That's all behind us now, right?"

"Absolutely. It was bad enough that I let Phil screw up my life. I won't let him screw up a baby's life, too. If he gets his act together, if he gets a job and shows some maturity, then he can maybe be a dad. But if not, he can just stay away." Letting that go, Tabby tipped her head at Stack. "So you two aren't split up?"

Firm, Stack said, "No."

"Then how did that rumor get started?"

More confused than ever, Vanity said, "I thought we had."

"Why?"

She gestured at Stack. "He was mad, and I knew I'd really disappointed him and—"

"So?" Crossing her arms and cocking out a hip, Tabby said, "I make him mad all the time, and he's *always* disappointed with me."

"That's not true, sis."

Tabby grinned. "Close enough. And sometimes he disappoints me. More often than not he makes me angry. But Vanity, we still love each other. There will be plenty of disagreements. No one is perfect, so problems happen. It doesn't change anything, not if you don't let it."

Stack inhaled. "Damn, sis."

"Nailed it, didn't I?"

His sister looked very smug, but he didn't mind. "Yeah, you did."

Vanity bit her lip, but as Stack watched, she shrugged off the uncertainty and squared her shoulders. "So... you love me, too?"

Grinning, Stack hugged her right off her feet. "Darlin', I fell in love with you that night you propositioned me. You threw me for a loop, confused me, turned me on, and I've been obsessed ever since. My sister is right, we're not perfect. But I'm pretty sure, if you'll have me, we'd be perfect together."

Tabby squealed. "Stack! Is that a marriage proposal?"

Vanity gasped. *"Tabby."*

Laughing, hugging them both, Stack said, "At some point I'd like to get her alone, sis. So if you'll excuse us, maybe I can explain things to her properly."

Tabby squealed again, hugged them both too tightly, and then dug out her phone on her way out the door. Stack heard her say, "Mom, guess what!" before he got the door closed behind her.

Vanity watched him intently.

The love he felt for her filled him up, and he smiled. "You ready to go?"

"Oh." She looked around. "Yes, I just need two minutes to close up."

Stack helped her lock up the shop, then followed her home, and all along the way, he thought about loving her. Physically. Emotionally. In every way.

Forever.

They barely got in the front door, and he was on her. Vanity reciprocated in kind, her hands sliding up under his shirt, her mouth hungry on his.

Stack gently tunneled his fingers through her hair, held her still and looked into her beautiful blue eyes. "I love you, Vanity."

Her lips parted, trembled. "You do? Are you sure?"

"Very sure." Funny that everyone had realized it except her.

"I love you, too!" She hugged him tight. "Will you marry me?"

Stalling, Stack laughed and picked her up. "I should have led with that, huh? But damn, you make me hot, darlin'. I missed you."

"I missed you, too, even though it's only been half a day."

"That felt like a lifetime." Going down the hall and into her bedroom, Stack fell with her across the bed. "I want pets."

Vanity beamed. "And I can travel with you."

"And I love your house."

She laughed. "And me." Softening, her hand to his jaw, she whispered, "You love me."

Stack kissed her again. "So damned much, I can't imagine life without you."

She shoved him to his back and climbed onto him. "So, yes, you'll marry me?"

Laughing, loving her, Stack nodded. "Yes."

An hour later, when they could both breathe again, Stack trailed his fingertips down her spine. Vanity lay sprawled over his chest, her beautiful blond hair everywhere, her heartbeat in sync with his.

Quietly, she said, "I want to start out our new life right, so in an effort for full disclosure, you should know that I'm going to buy the building and lot behind the rec center."

Stack went still, then lifted his head to look at her. "Why?"

She shrugged. "The rec center is growing. You know it. Even Cannon said so." She inhaled. "It needs a separate shower area for the women."

Stack struggled to hide his laugh. He'd already guessed her plans, but he didn't want to steal her thunder. "Yeah, it does."

"I'm going to do it. Buy the property and sponsor the addition. Quietly, if I can. I'd just as soon everyone not know. And of course, Cannon and Armie can make the plans for it. I wouldn't have said anything, but you don't want me keeping secrets, so I just—"

"You're just wonderful." He gave her a squeeze. "I know Cannon will be glad to hear it. But are you sure the guy will sell?"

"Given enough money, yes." She toyed with his chest hair, then tilted her head back to see him. "I know because I already checked into it, and since I want a clean slate here, I—"

"Thank you." Stack smoothed back her hair. "It's your money, darlin'. You can spend it however you want, but I'd like it if you talked to me about it, if you didn't feel you had to keep things from me."

Beaming at him, Vanity said, "I'd marry you today if I could."

He liked that idea. "You don't want a big wedding?" It didn't matter to him.

"Not really." She wrinkled her nose. "I'd love it if it was just you and me, your family and our friends."

Laughing, Stack said, "That's a decent-size wedding. But I have an idea." Far as he was concerned, the sooner the better. But if the idea offended Vanity, he'd scrap it in a heartbeat.

Coming up to her elbows, she kissed his mouth and smiled. "I'm listening."

Damn, she was beautiful. Even more so now that she looked so happy. "We'll be at a fight in Vegas right after the holidays. The guys will all be there, and we can talk my mom and sis into going along." Especially if he paid their way. "How do you feel about getting married there?"

Face lighting up, Vanity squealed in a very Tabby-like way. "I *love* it. It's perfect."

Wondering how he'd gotten so lucky, Stack pulled her down for a kiss and turned so she was under him. "You're perfect," he told her. "In every way, but most especially…for me."

* * * * *

Look for Armie's story,
FIGHTING DIRTY,
coming soon from Lori Foster and HQN Books!

Meanwhile, read on for
BACK TO BUCKHORN,
a bonus novella in print for the first time!

CHAPTER ONE

SUNGLASSES SHIELDING HIS EYES from the hot afternoon sun, Garrett Hudson watched the front of the airport, scanning each female who strode out. He could have gone inside to baggage claim, but then he might've missed her. He stayed on the alert; people changed over time, and there was a good chance Zoey would look right past him. Though she'd had a few brief visits back to the area, they hadn't seen each other in years, and she expected his sister, Amber, to be her ride. But a busted pipe at the bookstore had sidelined Amber, and he got recruited at the last minute, which meant he was running late.

Would he recognize her? How much had she changed? He remembered her as the quirky girl from high school, the one who had danced without caring what others thought, who laughed at the oddest things.

Often the odd girl out, not that she'd ever seemed to care.

He remembered her being kind, always speaking up for the underdog, always befriending the other odd ducks, not because she minded going it alone, but because she knew they did.

What he remembered most about her, though, was her mouth. Full lips. Soft smiles. An easy laugh.

Not only did she have the sexiest mouth he'd ever seen, but she also talked a lot. Sometimes nonstop.

Back then, he'd been amused by her.

And he'd always wanted to kiss her. Badly.

For the tenth time, he checked his watch. When he looked up again, a new crowd of people surged out, dragging luggage along in their wake. He scanned each face, his gaze going past an older couple, a young mother with a kid, a bedraggled brunette—

His attention zipped back.

No way. Could it be? He'd think not, except for the way she zeroed in on him while biting her lip. That was a tip-off.

Zoey had always bit her lip when uneasy.

Damn. What the hell had happened to her?

She looked… Trying to be kind, he decided on *not good*.

Starting forward, he called out, "Zoey Hodge?"

She stared right at him, proving she did, in fact, recognize him. That probably accounted for the lip biting, too. He knew he'd always made her nervous…which was why he'd never gotten that kiss.

Anytime he'd made a move, she'd dodged him.

When he got close, she groaned and covered her face with both hands. And stood there. On the walkway in front of the airport with people forced to move around her.

"Zoey?" Pushing his sunglasses to the top of his head, Garrett bent to see her face. She stood several inches shorter than his six-two. Given the clothes she wore, he had no idea about her build.

But she smelled like throw-up. "Zoey." Why wouldn't she look at him?

"Can you just go away?"

He straightened. "Come again?"

She made a shooing motion with one small hand, then quickly covered her face again. "I'll get a bus. Or cab. Or…I'll walk if I need to."

Hands on his hips, Garrett considered her, but because he needed to be back at work soon, he decided to just take charge. In most instances, with most people, that worked.

He scooped up one bag, grabbed the handle of the other. "I'm taking your luggage." He stepped away… and waited.

Dropping her hands with an overly dramatic sigh, she said, "Fine! Suffer me."

Her makeup was everywhere, making her green eyes a focal point in her face, which was framed by badly tangled, dark brown hair.

But that mouth… Damn, it looked as good as ever.

Ignoring her comment—what could he say?—he started off. "I'm parked this way." She grudgingly followed.

Trailing behind him, she said, "I don't always look like this."

God, he hoped not. "Want to tell me what happened?"

As if she'd been waiting for him to ask, she started babbling. "There was a crying kid on the plane. He puked on me. I'd checked all of my luggage instead of carrying it on, so the mother gave me this—" she looked down at the baggy gray T-shirt "—this *thing* to wear. I think it was her husband's. Anyway, I got most of the mess washed off my face and chest, but there wasn't enough water in the tiny bathroom to get it out of my hair. I smell bad. I look bad." She pointed at him. "And *you* had to show up?"

His mouth quirked. Yeah, he'd always remembered Zoey Hodge as being different. Eccentric.

Original.

Off the top of his head, he couldn't remember any other woman screeching at him in accusation. "What's wrong with me?"

Her expression said it should have been obvious. "You're *you*."

"Okay." What the hell did that mean?

She bit her lip again. "That is…well, you know I had a crush on you in high school."

"You did?" News to him. Hell, *he'd* had a crush, but had never acted on it.

"Well, of course I did."

With no idea what to say, he just nodded.

"And," she continued with emphasis, "when you see an old crush after so many years, well, it'd be better not to reek, right?"

"You're fine," he lied. The baking sun amplified the smell, so he was glad when they finally got into the covered garage.

"I was all set to explain to Amber, to maybe even laugh about it—"

"Really?" He couldn't imagine.

"—and instead *you're* here, seeing me like this, making me even more humiliated and—"

"Amber had a small catastrophe. I was the only one available."

"Catastrophe?" She stopped dead in her tracks. "Is she all right?"

"She's fine. Her bookstore's a little soggy, though, thanks to a broken pipe."

She started walking at a fast clip to catch up with

him. "Oh, man." She pushed back her long matted hair. "Well...I don't mean to be ungrateful."

"You're out of sorts." Under the circumstances, she had a right to be grouchy, but she wasn't. More like frazzled, and plenty embarrassed.

They reached his truck and he put the bags in the back then went around to open her door for her. "We can leave the windows down and the smell won't be so bad." He hoped.

She groaned dramatically and got in. Poor thing. She even had stains on the top of her sneakers.

She noticed him looking and wrinkled her nose. "It's in my shoes. I can feel it squishing when I walk."

Sympathy kept the smile off his face.

One hand on the roof, the other on the door frame, Garrett watched her buckle up. Out of the blinding sunlight, he saw that no part of her had been spared. Her hair. Her face. Her jeans. Only the god-awful, too-big, men's gray shirt was clean, but it didn't add much to the getup. "The kid really hurled on you, huh?"

She turned to him, shading her eyes against the sun. "The little guy was so sick."

Even under the unusual circumstances, something about her had him analyzing all her features. Big green eyes, slightly upturned nose and that lush mouth. She had small hands and delicate wrists, so she was probably still slight of build. But under the clothes, Garrett couldn't tell for sure.

Yeah...and he should probably quit trying to tell. Forcing his gaze up to her face, he said, "That's rough."

Nodding, she said, "My heart just broke for him. Two years old and miserable on that plane. And his poor exhausted parents, they were doing everything

410   BACK TO BUCKHORN

they could. When he got distracted with me, I thought, well, good. Right?"

She didn't give him a chance to answer.

"Finally he wasn't crying. And I like kids, enough that I didn't mind entertaining him."

He remembered her as always being kind. Most people stuck on a plane with a noisy kid would gripe about it. Not Zoey. She'd tried to help. Nice.

"He was in my lap when he started retching." She wrinkled her nose. "Ever seen a kid projectile-vomit?"

"Uh, no." Thank God.

"I tried to...catch it." She held out a cupped hand to show what she meant.

The smile broke. "Yeah? How'd that work out?"

"It was like a shower of puke." She scrunched her face up more. "Who knew such a small kid could hold so much?"

Laughing, Garrett closed the door and walked around. As soon as he got behind the wheel, she continued.

"I didn't really think about it. It was like...reflex or something, ya know?"

"Sure."

"As a firefighter, maybe you'd have known how to handle it better."

He gave her a disbelieving stare—and her mouth twitched.

"That was reaching, right?" Humor made her eyes even brighter, a beautiful focal point of color in her face. "But firefighters are heroic and all that so I'm sure you'd have figured out something."

Definitely not his area of expertise. "Let's hope I'm never put to the test."

"He kept twisting around," she said, still trying to explain how she'd gotten covered, "and I was trying to keep him from spraying anyone else—and that's when he got me head-on." Leaning toward him, she whispered, "It filled my bra."

His gaze dipped to her chest again, but being covered in puke took the fun out of boobs, so he only made a noncommittal sound, then started the truck and backed out of the cramped parking space. "You seem like a natural. Do you work with kids for a living?"

"No. I work—*worked*—for a pet groomer. Now I hope to set up my own shop here."

"Planning to stay?"

She waffled…and then changed the subject. "Amber already told me that you're a firefighter. Do you like it?"

He nodded. "We're a small department. A mix of hired and volunteer guys."

"I'd love to see the station sometime."

"Sure."

"Do you do all that PR stuff, like visiting the school and teaching fire-safety classes and reminding people about their smoke detectors?"

"We do." He enjoyed interacting with his community, always had. "I like visiting the school the most." He slanted her a look. "That is, as long as no one is chucking."

She laughed—and damn it, he liked it. Her laugh could make him forget about the smell of toddler throw-up.

When he went to exit the airport lot, she scrambled for her purse. "I've got it."

"No worries." He had the ticket and bills already

handy, and reached out the window to give both to the woman staffing the payment booth.

The woman peered in the car, gave Zoey an odd look and lifted the gate for them to leave.

Groaning, Zoey sat stiff and straight in the seat. "What must she think?"

"You'll never see her again. Don't worry about it."

"This is awful." She held out her shirt, touched her hair. "I'm trying not to get your truck too messy."

"It'll wash."

"I'll pay you to have it done. And for the parking fee, too."

"Zoey?"

She bit her lip again. "Hmm?"

"It's not a big deal."

"Ha!" Her eyes widened over her own telling reaction.

"So it is a big deal?" Because she'd had a crush on him? Or maybe because she was still interested?

"No. Not at all."

He wasn't buying it. "Just take a breath and relax."

In a rush, she launched into more conversation. "So are your kids just incredibly healthy or do you not have any?"

"No kids." He steered onto the highway and headed home.

"Married?"

"Nope." He glanced her way, but didn't see a ring on her finger. "You?"

"God, no."

Such a heartfelt denial made him frown. Seven years ago, after she broke things off with her boyfriend, Gus Donahue, Gus had left in a rage.

Then crashed his car and died, leaving his parents with two children instead of three, robbing them of their firstborn.

For too many people, she'd been the undeserving girl, while Gus had been the all-star golden boy. He'd been viewed as perfect.

She was not.

The blame and accusations had rolled in, spurred on by the Donahues, unrelentingly cruel until, finally, she'd moved away to escape it.

Never had Garrett blamed her, but even long after Zoey had left, Gus's sister, Carrie, had done what she could to keep fueling the fire. And Cody, forever feeding the stories, had grown into a very angry sixteen-year-old, always acting out, probably doing what he could to overcome the distance of his parents' grief.

Garrett didn't want to get into all that old history with her. What kind of welcome would that be? Instead he asked, "Any serious relationships?"

She shook her head. "I take it you and Carrie didn't make it?"

Gently, assuming it had to still be a touchy topic for her, he said, "That was...what? Six years ago? Seven?"

Her expression turned quizzical. "Since I left, yes. That's when you and Carrie broke up?"

"Shortly thereafter." He couldn't abide the way Carrie and her family reviled Zoey. They'd taken every opportunity to run her into the ground. He'd understood their grief, and he'd also understood what a hothead Gus had been.

Most of all he'd understood that the Donahues had two children left who needed their attention.

"And here everyone thought you two were the 'it' couple."

"Not me." Carrie was as popular as her older brother, and that, more than anything else, had prompted him to date her.

Yeah, he'd been young and foolish, ruled more by testosterone than discretion.

Looking out the window, Zoey changed the topic. "I need to shower and change before I see anyone."

He was supposed to drop her off at the bookstore, but he could afford the time for a quick detour. "Where to then?"

"I don't know." She looked back at him. "My mom's in the hospital."

"I heard." Everyone knew everyone's business in Buckhorn, at least to some degree. "How is she?"

"She fell off her horse, broke her hip and a few ribs."

"Ouch." He winced in sympathy.

"The breaks are bad enough, but now she has pneumonia on top of it."

"The immobility probably helped that along." Garrett knew her mother had had Zoey later in life. Knowing Zoey to be around twenty-four or -five, her mom would be in her midsixties. "She'll be okay?"

"Yes," she said with absolute conviction, as if she could will it so. "But I'm not sure yet when she'll get to come home. They already did the surgery on her hip, but she'll go to a different floor for rehab before they release her." She repeatedly pleated and smoothed the hem of her shirt.

"Is that where you want me to take you?"

She shook her head hard. "No, not looking like this. I don't want to embarrass her." Her fingers curled into a fist. "She's been living with my uncle the last few years, but there's no way I can go there, either."

Her uncle had been the football coach when Gus died. Shit.

"I don't suppose you'd loan me your shower?"

Garrett shot her a look, but she didn't seem to think a thing of her request. Typical of Zoey. Trying not to be too obvious, he checked the clock on the console. "If we make it quick, I have enough time."

Relief took the tension out of her shoulders. "Thank you. I promise to be as fast as I can."

"No problem." But damn it, when he saw Amber, he'd let her know that her debt to him had just doubled.

NEVER HAD SHE met a man so hard to read.

Garrett Hudson, with his dark hair and incendiary blue eyes, didn't seem to react to anything. He'd seen her standing there in her vomit-covered clothes, smelling of it, and he hadn't blinked an eye.

He had to put her in his truck, and he just rolled with it. No fuss, no big deal. No censure or disdain.

Zoey should have remembered his even temper and iron control, but she hadn't been expecting him.

No, she'd been looking for Amber—and when she'd spied Garrett instead, she'd whispered a quick prayer that he would look past her so she could slink away.

She never had been the lucky sort.

Even though he hadn't let the appearance or smell get to him, he was her fantasy guy, her biggest regret, and he'd just found her looking as bad as any woman could.

Worse, she had to impose on him to use his shower. But good God, it was bad enough that he had to see her like this. She didn't want to face the rest of the town looking like she'd been regurgitated from an ailing giant.

Zoey was pretty sure things couldn't get any worse... until Garrett pulled up to an older Cape Cod and she saw two of his cousins in his driveway. It was all she could do to keep from groaning in agony.

Shohn Hudson was a year older, Adam Sommerville four years older, and they were both amazing specimens.

She tried to sink lower in the seat while Garrett quickly put the truck in Park and got out. "What's going on?"

Shohn said, "Not much. Just had a few quick questions for you. Since Adam and I were heading out to dinner, we just stopped by."

Hiding inside the truck, Zoey looked over the men. Amber had caught her up on all the family dynamics, so she knew Shohn, now engaged, was a park ranger. Seeing him in his uniform, his hair dark, his eyes darker, she'd be willing to bet a lot of women chose to get lost in the woods.

As a gym teacher, Adam stayed in amazing shape. A growing breeze teased his messy blond hair, and when he took off his sunglasses to see into the truck, she got stuck staring into sincere, chocolate-brown eyes.

Smile going crooked, Zoey waved.

"Who do you have in there?" Adam asked with a confused frown.

Only then did Shohn even notice her. He peered into the truck, too, and Zoey knew she had to quit being a coward.

Straightening the ugly gray T-shirt, she opened the door and got out.

Hands on his hips, head dropped forward, she knew Garrett resigned himself to explaining her unwelcome presence.

Nervousness always made her babble. "Hi. I'm Zoey Hodge." Gray clouds rolled in, which she appreciated. The bright sunlight only ramped up the smell and showed all the mess more clearly. "Hey, Shohn. We weren't in the same grade, but I knew you from school." She watched for signs of recognition, but he only stared at her. "No? Well, that's okay. I didn't really expect you to remember."

Shohn looked her over with doubt, and stayed quiet.

"But Adam, you're older, right? I mean, of course I remember you. Duh. All the girls knew you. But I doubt you ever noticed me."

Adam got his faculties working first and reached out to greet her. "Hi. Nice to—"

"No!" She held up a hand. "I got puked on."

Adam froze, then, as one, the two men turned to stare at Garrett.

He let out a breath. "On the plane. Sick kid she helped care for." He gestured. "Amber asked me to pick her up since she was dealing with that busted pipe."

They turned to look at Zoey again.

"Garrett's going to let me use his shower."

Eyes widening, their gazes shot right back to their cousin.

Flustered, especially at how she'd blurted that, Zoey continued, "He's been supernice, especially considering..." She gestured at herself. Unfortunately, the men were all downwind of her. It'd be best if she wrapped this up. "And Garrett, seriously, I appreciate it so much. I don't know how I can thank you enough."

"Not a big deal."

"Of course it is." Anxious to escape, she inched toward the back of his truck. "How about I take you to dinner sometime? It's the least I could do, right?"

Garrett shook his head. "No, that's not necessary."

"I insist." She bit her lip, saw that all three men noticed and quickly forced a smile. "I'll just…" Turning, she strode to the truck bed to get her luggage.

"I'll get it," Garrett said.

"It's okay." The last thing she wanted to do was be more of a nuisance. She lifted the heaviest suitcase over the side of the truck bed. "I have it—" But in her haste, she lost her hold and the suitcase hit the ground.

Then popped open.

A bra and two pairs of underwear fell out.

She snatched up the bra and one skimpy pair of panties with lightning speed, sticking both under the rest of the clothes.

She was reaching for the other pair of panties when a big breeze rolled them over the driveway and up against Garrett's shoes.

"Ground," she said with soft desperation, "swallow me whole, please."

Brows raised, Garrett picked up the sheer beige lacy scrap meant to dredge up pure male fantasies.

After grabbing the closest top and shorts, she slammed the case closed and hurried to Garrett. Holding out a hand, hoping to brazen her way through the uncomfortable moment, she said, "Thank you."

Looking more than a little stymied, he handed the underwear to her.

"Shower?" she prompted, hoping to get things going.

"Sure." He cleared his throat. To his cousins, he said, "You guys want to come in?"

They started making quick excuses, as if they thought he was entertaining her. She shook her head. They surely knew better but probably hoped to put him on the spot for fun. She remembered well how they all liked to tease each other.

"I'm just showering," she explained with a wrinkled nose. "That's all. No hanky-panky. I mean...look at me."

Shohn cocked a brow.

Adam tried to check his amusement, but she saw his smile.

"No, don't look at me," she corrected. Good God, the last thing she wanted right now was a closer scrutiny. "Look at *him*." She pointed at Garrett. "Clearly you guys know he and I aren't...well, you know. Right?"

Garrett was as gorgeous now as he'd been when she'd left. Possibly more so. Out here in the bright sunshine, his black hair glinted with blue highlights. And his eyes... She sighed. Sinfully gorgeous, as light as a summer sky but twice as wicked, with those incredibly long, dark lashes...

When she realized she was staring at him, and everyone else was staring at her, she demanded, "Make your cousins come in."

"You heard her." Garrett gestured. "A storm's rolling in. It'll be best if she finishes up before that."

"I'll hurry," she promised again.

As he unlocked the front door, Garrett said, "Soon as I get you settled, I'll move your luggage into the cab behind the seat in case the rain starts."

"Thank you."

With Adam and Shohn staying several feet behind her—probably to avoid breathing her in—they stepped inside the house.

Zoey stopped and stared. "Holy cow."

For the first time since they'd arrived at his place, Garrett seemed to relax. "Like it?"

Head back, she looked around at the cove ceilings, then down at the high baseboards. "It's incredible." Everything looked vintage, but also shiny and new.

He checked his watch, then said, "If you finish in enough time, I'll show you around."

Oh, shoot. She was holding him up again. "Lead the way."

As he headed for the stairs, they passed a cozy living room on the left, an impressive study on the right. Straight ahead she could see a beautiful country kitchen. Everything looked quaint and original, but in really good shape.

At the top of the stairs, immediately to her right, was the bathroom. Stopping at a closet he got out two big, fluffy white towels, a washcloth and a blow-dryer. "Shampoo, soap and all that is already in the shower." In the all-white bathroom, he lowered the toilet lid and set everything on top of it.

She could have guessed he'd be a neat freak. Men as controlled and contained as him wouldn't appreciate clutter.

Unfortunately, she was a messy, cluttered catastrophe.

"So much character."

He did a double take.

"The house, I mean."

He studied her as if he'd never seen a woman before. "I've always thought so." He looked around. "There's just something about an older building and all the extra detail put into it."

She nodded. The freestanding tub had a shower stand at one end, an oval curtain rod suspended from the ceiling. "It's just…awesome."

"Pipes are old. Might take a minute for the water to get hot."

"I bought an older house, too, but judging by the pictures I've seen, it's nothing like this."

"Pictures?"

"Your sister helped me pick it out."

"You bought it without seeing it?"

She shrugged. "Yeah. I needed a place." For herself—and her mother. Her house would need a year of work before she even got close to this perfection. "Maybe I can show it to you sometime."

Appearing curious, he said, "Sure."

Forgetting herself, Zoey put the clothes—panties on top—with the towels. The glossy subway tiles on the wall drew her fingertips. "This looks vintage, but can't be. It's in such great shape."

"I redid most of it using the same style. Salvaged what I could, but yeah, a lot is new."

Maybe she'd be able to get some pointers from him. About to ask him, she glanced his way and found him staring at her panties again. Taking one big step she put herself in front of the clothes. "Thanks again. I'll only be a few minutes."

Still he stood there, watching her in a funny way.

"I think I've got it from here."

His gaze went over her face, then he shook his head and started out. "If you need anything else, let me know."

AFTER MOVING HER LUGGAGE, Garrett walked into the kitchen, where he knew Shohn and Adam would be waiting to rib him. The second they saw him, he said, "Shut up."

Shohn laughed. "You gotta admit, it's pretty funny."

"Not from her perspective, I'm sure."

"Yeah, probably not." Shohn asked, "A kid really threw up on her?"

"Yeah." He relayed the story.

"Almost happened to me once," Adam admitted. "A fifth-grade girl came up, said she was sick and started gagging. I got a garbage can under her in the nick of time, and it was still gross. Felt really bad for her, too. The other kids teased her until I made them all run laps."

Garrett wondered how Zoey felt about walking through the airport in such a messy state. Had she gotten stares? Whispers? She'd put up with it in school. She shouldn't have to put up with it still.

"So..." Opening the fridge and searching around, Shohn helped himself to a cola. "Why's she using your shower?"

"Like she said, she just flew in."

"She's not from around here?"

He shook his head. "She moved away back when I was a senior. Remember Gus Donahue?"

"He's that guy who died in a car wreck, right?" Buckhorn rarely lost one of their own, and when they did, especially a kid, they remembered.

Adam frowned with the memory. "Jumped a hill and wrapped his car around a tree."

Distracted, Garrett pulled out a chair. "Upstairs in my shower is Zoey Hodge."

Shohn dropped into a chair across from him. "The girl who broke up with him?"

"The girl," Adam said with a frown, "who too many blamed?"

"One and the same."

The old pipes in the house rattled when the water came on. Both his cousins looked up at the ceiling as if they could see her showering overhead.

They looked with sympathy, but damn, even with the surprise of her wrecked appearance, Garrett was starting to feel a little differently. Maybe because no woman had ever used his shower.

Or maybe because she bit that full bottom lip the same way he'd always imagined doing.

Or it could be those hot little panties she'd soon be slipping into...

"She's moving back?" Shohn asked.

"Here for a visit, far as I know. Her mom got hurt pretty bad when she fell from her horse. Zoey will be helping out. But the mom had been staying with the uncle—"

"Who was Gus's coach." Adam let out a low whistle. "Surely he doesn't blame her?"

"No way," Shohn said. "Not after all this time."

Garrett shrugged at them both. "Don't know." But he remembered Coach Marchum being a real asshole. "She didn't seem interested in going there, though, and I couldn't see taking her straight to the bookstore without letting her clean up first."

The water shut off and they all looked up again. True to her word, she'd made it quick. And right now, she'd be stepping out.

Naked. Wet.

Knowing he needed to get his thoughts back on safer ground, Garrett turned to Shohn. "What did you need to talk about?"

Sitting back in his seat, his gaze speculative, Shohn sprawled out his legs. "Remember that damned fire at the lake? The one where everyone scattered before you could figure out who'd started it?"

"I do." What had probably started as a group of high schoolers roasting marshmallows and indulging in a little necking, got out of hand when a knucklehead decided to toss in some fireworks. They'd gone off and started a dozen small fires. No real damage, but next time could be different, so it wasn't something they'd entirely overlook. "We're still asking some questions about that, but you know how it is. None of the kids want to be a snitch."

"I was hoping you'd found a name or two because there was another fire like it at the park."

Garrett sat forward...until Shohn waved him back.

"The fire was already cold when I found it, and whoever set it did a good job of keeping it contained. But there were fireworks wrappers left around the area." He shook his head. "Bottle rockets and dry conditions do not mix in the woods."

"And we both know which knucklehead has a tendency to dick around with bottle rockets."

"I'll snoop around," Shohn said with a nod. "See if he was camping out that night."

Just what this situation didn't need. "Shit." Squeezing the bridge of his nose, Garrett fought off a headache.

"Not enough sleep?" Adam asked.

"I'm fine." But yeah, he'd been up most of the night with his shift, then had talked with a few Scout leaders about letting their kids come in for a tour. He still had a dozen things to do today, and—

He froze as he suddenly heard singing. Off-key singing.

They all grinned.

Garrett didn't mean to laugh at her, but wow, she sounded bad, maybe even worse than she'd looked. "She's probably using the blow-dryer and doesn't realize how loud she's being."

"Or," Shohn said, "she doesn't care."

Adam cocked a brow. "You think?"

"If I'm remembering right, she always was a little out there."

"Yeah?"

"A real free spirit," Shohn explained.

Garrett narrowed his eyes. "Thought you didn't remember her?"

"Not with how she looks now, no. But since you jogged my memory, it's coming back to me."

Adam watched him. "You going to take her up on dinner?"

Shohn scoffed at the idea. "No offense, but you saw her. He'll find a way out of it."

But how? Garrett didn't want to hurt her feelings.

When the singing suddenly stopped, he froze. They all listened. Hell, Garrett even held his breath. But she made not a single sound on the stairs.

And then suddenly she was there, striding barefoot down the short hall to the kitchen.

The air left his lungs in a low exhalation.

Without even realizing it, he pushed back his chair and stood.

Shohn and Adam did the same.

They all gawked at her.

Zoey held her dirty clothes wrapped in the gray T-shirt. Freshly washed long brown hair hung in soft waves, pulled over one shoulder to cover her left breast.

Supershort, white-cuffed shorts left her entire long, shapely legs bare, and the peach-colored halter emphasized the shape and swell of modest B-size breasts.

Her bare shoulders were lightly kissed by the sun, her green eyes bright with amusement, her mouth—*God, that mouth*—curved as she appreciated his reaction.

With a small curtsy, she said, "Better, right?"

They all nodded.

Adam got it together first, at least enough to say, "Incredible."

Zoey laughed.

"Hard to believe," Shohn murmured, "that you're the same woman."

Her small nose wrinkled. "Throw-up has a way of making everything pretty icky." She turned those big green eyes on Garrett. Her teeth sank into that plump bottom lip as she searched his face, then her smile widened. "What do you think?"

He thought he wanted that mouth, in about a dozen different ways. He cleared his throat. "Dinner sounds great. I'm off next Saturday."

CHAPTER TWO

TONIGHT SHE'D GET to take Garrett to dinner.

Zoey smiled, thinking about how nicely her first week back had gone, especially given how she'd dreaded it. She'd expected unfriendly reunions, awkward greetings and ugly stares of condemnation.

Instead, for one reason or another, she'd seen Garrett almost every day. The town was small, so every time she turned around she ran into him.

Each and every time he stopped to talk with her.

Each and every time her infatuation with him grew.

Never mind that he was a big, sexy hunk with an easy smile and a hero's personality. He was...well, everything else, too. Friendly, respectable, admired, liked—not just by her, but apparently everyone else, as well.

A few times she'd seen him at his sister's bookstore when Amber invited her for lunch. Amber didn't close the shop during her visit, but it was a slower time for her and few people stopped in.

Yet somehow, each time, Garrett showed up.

Amber also took her to dinner—at Nadine's house, with Shohn and Adam and some of the other cousins there, again, including Garrett. She loved Nadine's pet hotel, and she really enjoyed seeing Nadine and Shohn interact.

They all had pets, and all swore they'd be giving her plenty of business once she opened her grooming salon.

It seemed to Zoey that Amber's family went out of their way to make her feel welcome. It was so relaxing being with them, because she didn't have to worry about running into someone who might still blame her for what had happened so long ago.

She knew those people still existed in the town, just as she knew Amber's family had never been part of the hate crowd.

Because the invites always included Garrett, Zoey almost felt like Amber was playing matchmaker, but if so, Zoey enjoyed her efforts. It had given her a chance to see Garrett with his family, how he played with the animals, helped out in the kitchen, thanked his sister for a burger, carried Nadine a drink.

So attentive—to everyone.

She'd also run into Garrett at the hardware store when she bought a grill and needed supplies to fix up the house she'd bought. He'd chatted with her, lingering, making her self-conscious over her paint-stained T-shirt and ragged jeans—not that he'd been anything but pleasant.

The owner of the hardware store had slid many suspicious glances her way, but after Garrett came in, he spent his time bragging about Garrett's handyman skills, claiming he'd learned from his uncle Gabe. The owner's wife smiled at him as if he were her own son. They'd talked for maybe twenty minutes, and every minute or so someone new greeted him, including several women. But he hadn't been drawn away. She figured that was likely why the women gave her dirty looks, and not the incident from her youth.

So far, she'd run into him at the grocery, at the ice-cream shop, the gas station and Amber's bookstore. She'd even seen him during one of her many visits to the hospital. Her mother was doing better, but on top of the broken ribs her blood pressure was high and the pneumonia really left her exhausted. Zoey did her best to make her more comfortable, telling her over and over how much fun they'd have once she was well again.

Somehow, she'd make it so.

Garrett was there checking on an older woman who'd almost set her house on fire when she forgot her dinner in the oven. She'd inhaled a lot of smoke, but would be fine.

Such a great guy—and tonight she'd have him all alone, with the opportunity to talk beyond polite pleasantries.

Maybe he'd give her some tips on fixing up her old house, given the amazing job he'd done to his own.

Thanks to a recommendation from Amber, she'd bought the furnished two-story "fixer-upper" sight unseen. And she had no regrets. The second she'd walked across the squeaky wood floors, touched the crystal doorknobs, admired the stained-glass window in the stairwell, she'd fallen madly in love.

The aged, scarred and worn furniture still had charm. Everything—the house and the furnishings— needed a ton of work to spruce it up, and she looked forward to tackling it all. On top of pleasing her aesthetically, it also had a huge sunroom in the back that led to a fenced yard, making it practical for her animal-grooming business.

And when her mother was ready, the spare bedroom with a bathroom just across the hall would work out per-

fectly. After she'd set up her own bedroom, Zoey had
worked on the guestroom, tearing out old wallpaper,
using Spackle on the walls where needed and adding
fresh paint. She'd decorated with colorful throw rugs,
fresh bedding and privacy curtains at the windows.

Best of all, Zoey thought as she opened the gate at
the farthest part of the property, the land connected to
the lake. She could already smell the water, and filled
her lungs with the fresh scent. After moving away, she'd
missed swimming, boating, just lazing in the sunshine.

It had taken all of her savings to move back and set
up shop here, but so far she was on track to open her
business in a few more weeks, and then, with determination, she'd make it all work.

Laying her cell phone, towel and sunglasses in the
shade of a tree, she walked out on the rickety dock,
tested the water, found it nicely tepid and went down
the ladder. Until she knew the depth, she didn't trust
diving in.

After working on the house all morning and afternoon, scrubbing walls and floors, cleaning closets,
painting trim and making repairs, she needed to cool
off and relax her aching muscles.

Along the shoreline, frogs protested, splashing as
they jumped in. Once in, she closed her eyes, held her
breath and submerged herself in the green water, going
down as far as she could to try to reach bottom.

She came up for air, pleased that it was so deep.
The wide cove would accommodate a boat, but with a
farmer on one side of her, and woods on the other, the
area was quiet and peaceful.

Going to her back, she hooked one foot through the
ladder and floated, letting the hot sunshine caress her

mostly bare body. How long she stayed like that, she couldn't say, but somewhere along the way exhaustion took over and she might have even dozed.

A trickle of cold water on her belly brought her jerking upright with a gasp. She found Garrett crouched down at the end of the dock, his wrists hanging loosely over his knees, an icy bottle of water dangling in one hand. He wore a black cowboy hat tipped back, and a very intent look on his face.

Her foot was still caught in the ladder, leaving her awkwardly thrashing until she freed herself. She went under again twice before finally getting upright. Breaking the surface of the lake, she slicked her hair back and stared up at him.

Mirrored sunglasses kept her from seeing his eyes, but somehow she just knew he was looking at her body, not her face.

"Wanna tell me why you had yourself all hog-tied in the ladder?"

"To keep from floating away."

Voice low, he murmured, "Guess it worked then, huh?"

"Ummm…" Legs kicking as she dog-paddled in place, she squinted her eyes against the glaring sunlight. "What are you doing here?" He hadn't been to her house before.

"Besides taking in the view?"

"Were you?"

"Yeah. For a while now."

Her stomach bottomed out. *How long had he been there?* Had she looked at all appealing…or like a drowned rat? After seeing him so often in town, you'd think she'd be used to his impact.

Not so. He got close, and she went breathless, became anxious and chatty—just as she had in high school.

"Yeah." She cleared her throat. "Besides that."

Straightening, he set the water bottle aside, went for her towel and returned. "Come on out and we'll talk about it."

Zoey blinked up at him.

He stood right there, her towel hanging in his big hand, watching her. And waiting.

Shoot. "I had two suits to choose from," she told him. "A nice, modest one-piece and a bikini. I figured on being alone, so I chose the bikini. Now, though, with you here, I almost feel naked."

"Because you almost are." Unsmiling, Garrett stared down at her...or at least, she assumed he did. Those damned sunglasses hid so much.

Did he look flushed?

She chewed her lip, nodded at his shirt and said, "You could skin down and join me instead." As soon as she said it, her stomach tightened more. Would he? *Oh, she hoped so.*

The barest of smiles teased his mouth. "You trying to get me out of my pants, Zoey?"

What woman wouldn't? She grabbed the ladder for support. "You look—" *hot* "—too warm."

His smile expanded. "That might have more to do with you in that little bit of nothing, than the summer sun."

Her mouth opened, but nothing came out.

"Wish I had more time today, because I think we'd both enjoy it," he continued.

She knew she would.

"Why don't we make that another date? Maybe for my next day off?"

So…he considered dinner tonight an actual date? Not just a way for her to thank him? "Okay."

He checked his watch. "I gotta get back to work soon."

A hint for her to hightail it out of the water. "Right." Besides the hat, he wore a dark blue T-shirt with the fire station logo over the left side, matching uniform pants and a thick black belt with a pager attached to it. It wasn't a uniform, but on Garrett, it had the same effect.

Dropping the towel, he crouched down again and stretched his right hand down to her. "Up and out with you."

Leaving her no choice, she reached up and took his hand. He lifted her, caught her other wrist, too, before she could climb the ladder, and literally hauled her out and onto the dock.

Lake water pooled on the weathered boards below her feet and dripped from her hair, down her arms, her chest, her legs. Uncertain what to do, she stood there beneath the sweltering sunshine in an agony of expectation. When Garrett said nothing, did nothing except breathe deeper and look at her, she decided it might be best if she covered up.

He circumvented her effort to reach for the towel.

"I've got it." Keeping his attention on her, he absently, blindly, bent and snagged her towel before she could.

She waited, but he didn't offer it to her.

Fighting the urge to cross her arms over her chest, Zoey shifted from one foot to the other. Her dark suit wasn't different from what most women wore on the lake. It might even be less revealing than many.

So then why did he stare at her as if he'd never seen anything like it before?

"How long were you in there?" he asked, his voice a little rough.

She had no idea. "What time is it?"

"Three-thirty."

"Oh." She winced. They were supposed to do dinner in two and a half hours and here she was, waterlogged. "Over an hour I guess."

Keeping the towel in one fist, he reached out with the other hand and touched her shoulder, across her collarbone.

That touch made her shiver in reaction.

"You're turning pink. Did you put on sunscreen?"

By dinner she might be even pinker. Her plan had been to cool off, then get in the shade to relax for a bit before preparing for their date. But she didn't want to admit to him that she'd forgotten the sunscreen, or that she'd been so tired she'd all but passed out in the water. "Why did you say you're here?"

There came that suggestive smile again. "I hadn't yet." He moved closer and draped the towel around her shoulders.

Which meant his arms went around her, too.

Standing near enough that she felt the heat of his body, he held the towel closed under her chin. "I need to change our dinner plans."

Well, darn. Hoping to hide her disappointment, she nodded. "Okay." Would he have a good reason to cancel...or had he just changed his mind? "I understand."

"Don't know how you could since I haven't yet explained."

She couldn't think with him so close, his warm hands resting casually above her breasts. "Sorry. I'm listening." *And melting.*

Silence ticked by. "Do I make you nervous, Zoey?"

She shook her head hard in denial and said, "Yes."

Laughing, he released the towel and smoothed her wet hair over her shoulders. "Real clear, honey."

Honey?

Finally, his smile crooked, he gave her some space.

She almost collapsed with the release of pent-up tension.

Standing a few feet from her, he asked, "Better?"

Heck no. She liked having him close. It was just that close equaled weak-kneed.

Should she admit to being flustered by him when he clearly didn't have the same problem?

"Requires some thought, does it?"

"You don't make me nervous, really, I mean, not usually. But here like this—"

"With you showing all that sexy skin?"

"I…ah…" No way could she agree, because that would sound like she thought she was sexy. "I wasn't expecting to see anyone."

"Can't say I'm sorry I dropped in."

That dark, carnal tone made her toes curl against the rough boards of the dock. "I haven't been in a lake since I moved away. I missed it."

"It's good to have you back."

Like anyone had missed her? Not likely. "If you say so."

He removed the hat, then pushed the sunglasses up

to the top of his head, and oh, God, that was worse. Sweat dampened the front of his shirt so that the material clung to his chest. The hat left his dark hair more disheveled than usual.

And his eyes... His eyes could mesmerize, especially with the sun overhead.

She drew a deep breath and let it out slowly.

Motioning her closer, he said, "Let's move to the shade before you get burned worse."

"Okay." She'd follow him anywhere... Wait, what? Shaking her head, she muttered, "You're dangerous."

He gave a soft laugh, shook his head and turned to go to shore.

Zoey quickly readjusted the towel, wrapping it around her body under her arms so that it covered her from chest to midthigh.

He glanced back, and she gave him a bright smile, quickly following.

When they reached the makeshift bench just off the dock, in front of a ramshackle shed, he gestured for her to sit, then sat very close beside her.

He dropped the hat on the ground beside him with the glasses. "I was looking forward to dinner," he told her. "But I'm going to be tied up 'til eight now."

A hundred thoughts went through her head, and she decided to be straight with him. "You aren't just dodging me?"

Quirking a brow, he looked over her bare legs and shook his head. "Now, why would I do that?"

Relieved, she shoulder-bumped him. "So then... you'll have to eat eventually, right? You could just come by here. I don't mind eating late."

He glanced across the wooded property to her house. "You're sure?"

"Actually, I'd love it." He could come at midnight and she'd enjoy it. Knowing she'd sounded too eager, she added, "I was hoping to get your advice on a few fix-up projects anyway."

"Yeah?" He eyed the dock, and then the shed behind them. "You could start down here. I'm surprised either of these is still standing."

"I doubt I'll use the shed for much, and other than worrying for splinters, the dock seems fine." She had more pressing concerns, but she could explain all that to him later. "What's your preference for tonight?"

As he looked her over again, one of his eyebrows went up.

That heated scrutiny sucked the air out of her lungs. "I'm a good cook," she blurted. "Name it and I'll take care of it." God willing, he wouldn't choose anything too difficult.

"You have a grill?"

"That's what I was getting at the hardware store the day we ran into each other."

"The day you wore that messy shirt and had your hair in braids." He tugged on one dripping hank of hair. "You looked really cute."

No way. And here she'd been embarrassed. Feeling her face go hot, she mumbled, "Thanks."

"So if we have the grill, how about I bring some steaks? You can fix whatever you want to go with it. I'm not picky."

She bent a stern look on him. "This is supposed to be my treat so I can thank you."

His attention went to her mouth. "There are other ways you can thank me."

Whoa. Just like that, a porno played in her head. "Like…what?"

"Not what you're thinking."

"Oh." Disappointment brought her brows down. "How do you know what I'm thinking?"

Abruptly, he turned away.

"Garrett?"

He scrubbed a hand over his face. "I was never going to let you buy dinner."

Spine stiffening, she repeated softly, "Let me?"

Paying no mind to her indignation, he stood and took a step back from her. "Know how you could really thank me?"

Suspicious, she stood, too—and his attention went back to her mouth.

Heart thumping, she licked her lips. When he groaned, she bit her lower lip.

He drew his gaze up to her eyes. "Sorry." He worked his jaw. "I do get distracted by your mouth."

"My mouth?"

Abruptly he said, "You can thank me by going to the fireman's fund-raiser with me."

That was so far from what she'd expected that she blinked. "Really?"

"End of the month."

Plenty of notice. Would she not see him again until then? Cautiously, she said, "That's a while off."

"I know you're busy now getting your house set up for your mom."

"True." But that didn't tell her what she wanted to

know. "I had a lot of stuff shipped here, and I'm still unpacking."

As if he'd read her thoughts, he said, "My days off vary, but I wouldn't mind coming by to help you with the house remodeling if you'd like."

She opened her mouth, but didn't get a single word out before he spoke again.

"I enjoy fixing up old houses, so it'd be a pleasure."

He made it sound like she'd be doing *him* a favor. "I—"

"I work half a day next Saturday so we can get started then, and do a little swimming afterward."

He coordinated dates quicker than she could keep up.

Still looking all too serious, he asked, "What do you think?"

"Actually, I'd love that."

"Which part?"

"Any of it. *All* of it."

"Perfect." He released a pent-up breath and moved in close again. "Now, let's get back to your mouth."

Self-conscious uncertainty had her licking her lips again.

He made a small, hot sound of approval. "Will I be rushing things too much if I kiss you?"

Canting her head, she considered him. He wanted to kiss her, but instead of just doing it, he asked? "I…um…" *Yes, please.* But that'd sound awfully enthusiastic—which she was. "I suppose…"

His hand slid along her jaw so that his fingertips touched the back of her neck. "I haven't been able to think about much other than your mouth."

"Really?"

"Except for when I saw you in the lake." He angled his body near hers. "Then I was thinking about all kinds of things—only some of them having to do with your mouth."

He was so much bolder than she remembered, but of course, he'd been a kid back then.

And he was now a man.

After resting her hands on his shoulders, she hesitated. "I don't want to get you wet."

"Funny." He leaned down until she felt his breath. "I can't say the same to you."

And before she could react to that, he put his mouth to hers, his lips warm and firm, nudging hers open so that his tongue could touch just inside, teasing her own, easing her into things until he had both hands in her wet hair, their bodies pressed together, mouths moving in a hot, eating kiss that obliterated clear thought.

Overhead a crow cawed. Somewhere on the lake, a fish jumped.

When Garrett finally let up, she realized her towel had dropped around her feet. Slowly, he lowered one hand to stroke her naked waist, while his other hand curled around her nape, keeping her right where he wanted her.

She went to lick her tingling lips, but he kissed her again, capturing her tongue and making a sound of pleasure before pulling back.

Still very near her, he whispered, "Even better than I'd imagined."

"You imagined kissing me?"

His gruff laugh teased her nerve endings, but not as much as when he whispered, "I've been imagining it since way back when we were kids in school together."

That surprised her enough that she didn't even blink when he stole another kiss.

"And a hell of a lot more since then."

She remembered Garrett had always been nice to her, but she couldn't recall a time when he'd ever asked her out, or even asked for her number. "I had no idea."

His thumb teased over the corner of her lips. "Now you do." Smiling, he tasted her again, deeper, slower, before reluctantly ending things.

If he'd kissed her like that so many years ago, she wasn't sure she would have left town. "Wow."

"Yeah." He moved his thumb to the pulse thrumming in her neck. "I need to take off, but I'll be here at eight—and I'm already looking forward to it."

In a daze, Zoey watched him snag up his hat and glasses before heading across the yard, his long strides easy, the muscles in his shoulders shifting and moving with each step.

Without much grace, she dropped to sit on the bench again.

If she believed him…well, then, he'd been thinking about kissing her for a very long time.

Odds were, he'd want to kiss her again tonight.

She was naturally an upbeat person, but facing the town again hadn't been as easy as she'd pretended.

Yet now, after Garrett's sensual attention, pure giddiness stole through her, leaving no room for anything else.

For the first time in a very long time, she was flat-out happy. Needing to share, she snatched up her cell phone and put in a call to Amber, her only remaining friend in Buckhorn—even if she was Garrett's sister. By sheer force of will she managed to downplay the kissing aspects and instead focused on her excitement for the coming days.

After her chat with Amber, who was appropriately attentive, Zoey decided to take a quick shower and head to the hospital for another short visit. On her way home she'd stop at the grocery for salad and potatoes.

There were so many changes going on in her life right now, but it was thoughts of Garrett that put the smile on her face and kept it there.

GARRETT HAD JUST FINISHED his general check of the station, making sure everything was clean and orderly. He had a phone meeting in a few minutes, but wanted to grab a Coke before that.

His sister waylaid those plans.

Storming through the station as if she owned it—and sometimes the newbies thought she did—she snagged his elbow and tried to haul him along. There were times when Amber forgot her "little" brother was all grown up, a head taller and a hell of a lot brawnier.

Garrett felt everyone glancing their way, especially Noel Poet, the new hire who'd only recently moved to the area. The locals were used to Amber, but he wasn't sure Noel had ever seen her before.

To see her now, trying to boss him around, wasn't good.

When Garrett stood his ground, Amber's momentum brought her around until she almost slammed into him.

He caught her arm and eased her out of his space, asking calmly, "Problem, Amber?"

Fuzzed up about something, she smoothed her hair, gave a tug to her T-shirt and glared up at him. "I'd like to talk to you in private."

"If you ask real pretty like…"

Instead she tossed back her long hair—as dark as his own—and went on tiptoe, saying in a snarl, "It's about Zoey."

Curiosity ripened in the air.

Not wanting his personal business aired to the station, Garrett took her arm and now it was him leading her off for privacy. She had to double-step to keep up with him.

He took her into the office and closed the door. "Okay, what's the problem?"

Never one to hold back, Amber declared, "You're going to break her heart!"

His brows came down so hard that his head throbbed. "What the hell are you talking about?"

"Zoey!" She slugged his shoulder.

Garrett crossed his arms and propped that shoulder on the wall. "I hit flies harder than that."

The insult rolled right off her. "I didn't want to hurt you. You're supposed to be the good guy."

"I am a good guy." Hell, everyone told him so. "I got her from the airport for you."

"And?"

"And…agreed to let her take me to dinner." After she'd gone from looking pretty nasty to looking like a wet dream. He was still a little shocked by the transformation.

"And?"

"And what?"

"The fireman's fund-raiser?"

Damn, news traveled fast. "Yeah, so?" He had no idea why that had his sister spoiling for a fight. "I figured you'd be glad she had a date." Not that being noble had factored into his motives. "The whole town will be there."

"Right. The whole town—including the Donahues and all their friends."

He scoffed at that. "You aren't saying they'd cause a problem?"

"Oh, my God, where have you been? Living under a rock?"

"They're not that bad." He hoped. But now that she said it…

"When was the last time you saw any of them? They're *always* a problem."

If that was her big concern, she could relax right now. "I won't let anyone insult Zoey."

Rolling her eyes, she gave him a look that said he was hopeless. "Yeah, that'll make her feel better. To be insulted and then have you cause a scene about it."

"I don't cause scenes." He kept a cool head, always.

"Because everyone adores you. But if you'll recall, Zoey left because everyone does *not* adore her. And you two being together will bring up comparisons."

"To her and Gus Donahue?" He dropped his arms and his negligent attitude. "Damn, Amber, that was years ago."

Her attitude softened the tiniest bit. "She's been gone ever since. Her showing up is going to revive that whole nasty bit of history." She held out her hands. "For some, she'll still be the girl from the wrong side of the tracks who brought down the all-star golden boy. And brother, that's how they'll see her with you, too."

He shook his head in denial.

Pitying, Amber sighed. "You know this, Garrett. You know the influence our family has, how others view you as a hero, and how some people can be when it comes to Zoey."

Yeah, damn it, he did.

Even knowing he wouldn't do it, he asked, "Did you want me to cancel on her?"

"You can't. She called me about it because she was thrilled."

Thrilled? He scoffed. "Over going to a fund-raiser?"

"Over being with you."

Yeah, he had to admit—to himself, not his sister— that it thrilled him a little, too. "So she's glad to have a date." Though given how she looked, she probably could've had her pick of men. "It'll be good for her to get around the town if she plans to stay."

Arms crossed, Amber started tapping her foot. "And?"

He wouldn't talk about kissing Zoey. It was private, and none of his nosy sister's business. "And butt out."

Of course she didn't. He wasn't sure Amber could. His sister lived to control the lives of others.

It was one of the things he usually loved about her. She was good at it and could be a terrific resource when vetting dates.

But not right now. Not when it came to Zoey.

"You know it's tough for her to be here, that her mom is in a bad way, that she's trying to start up a new business on top of just buying a run-down house that needs a ton of work before she can bring her mom there. She has her hands full and then some."

Yeah, he did know it. That was one reason he'd offered to help her out—not that he'd tell Amber about it with her being so prickly. Besides, Zoey hadn't acted at all daunted by the pile of burdens. If anything, she seemed eager to take on each and every responsibility. "I saw her house." Then, in case Amber made assumptions, he said, "The outside, I mean."

"Reminds me a little of your place."

"Yeah. Hers could use some TLC, but it's nice."

"The inside is far worse than the outside. Livable, but in need of a lot of repairs."

"That's the way with most old houses." As he rubbed the back of his neck, he thought he saw Amber smile, but the flicker of amusement was gone too fast for him to be sure.

Suspicions gathered like storm clouds as he eyed her innocent expression. Amber was a matchmaker extraordinaire; she always had motives for what she did— including chewing out her brother. "Are you trying to manipulate me?"

She struck an appalled pose. *"Me?"*

What a laugh. "Yes, you."

Checking a nail, she said, "Actually, I put you with Zoey because I thought you'd be least likely to go overboard."

Lightning joined the thunderclouds in his brain. "Overboard…how?"

She dropped her hands. "Face it, brother, you're not Adam."

Insulted without even knowing why, he asked, "What the hell does that mean?"

"He skates through women like it's a sport." She flipped her hand. "And for him, it probably is. He's twenty-nine years old and hasn't once been in love."

Garrett backed up with very real alarm. "You expect me to fall in love with her?"

"Don't sound so horrified. I'm telling you *not* to fall in love with her."

"Wasn't planning to!"

"But you shouldn't sleep with her, either."

He put the brakes on his retreat. "Now wait just a min—"

"Since you're not Adam, who would probably already be in her bed—"

Over his dead body!

"—you should be able to handle that, right?"

No, damn it. He didn't want to handle it. He searched Amber's face, saw she looked dead serious and turned away with a muttered curse.

Since leaving Zoey earlier, he'd thought a dozen times about the way she kissed, how good she'd tasted, the small sounds she'd made, the way those full lips of hers felt under his...

"I can almost hear what you're thinking."

Jerking around, he pointed a finger at her. "Then close your meddling ears."

She pointed right back. "If you sleep with her, then you damn well better step up and be there for her!"

Just what did she mean by that?

Amber slung her purse strap up and over her shoulder and started for the office door. Hand on the doorknob, her back still to him, she paused.

Garrett felt the imminent doom.

"She's not welcome at her uncle's. I don't know if you knew that, but he blames her, too."

Son of a bitch.

"If you've heard the gossip, then you know a lot of people are hanging on to that old grudge."

"You don't," he reminded her. "I don't."

"No." She glanced at him over her shoulder. "You and I also know she deserves better than to be used after walking back into the line of fire for her mom. I hope you remember that, Garrett."

After that direct shot to his lustful intentions, his sister departed, now with less steam than when she'd entered.

Garrett watched her, noticed that Noel Poet did, too. He scowled, but with guilt sitting heavy on his shoulders he couldn't work up any real concern over it. God knew, Amber could take care of herself.

Talk about a turnaround. He'd wanted Zoey, was pretty sure he'd have had her tonight, and he'd figured on them both enjoying themselves.

But he didn't want to hurt her, or add to her burdens. Amber was right—Zoey deserved better than that.

His sister's visit had just changed everything.

Well, hell.

CHAPTER THREE

ZOEY SPENT MORE TIME at the hospital than she'd meant to. But her mom was awake, feeling more energetic and seemed to enjoy her company. She moved better now, without as much pain. She still had staples in place from the surgery on her hip, and she tired easily from the pneumonia, but she smiled and it gave Zoey hope.

They'd made plans, talking about how it would be when she moved in with Zoey, and for the first time since her return, her mother's eyes had glittered with anticipation instead of pain and defeat.

How could she leave in the middle of that? She couldn't, so she'd stuck around until the very last minute, then had to race to get to the grocery store so she'd be back at her house before Garrett got there.

Funny thing though, as she raced the cart down an aisle, she recognized his sexy butt in worn jeans.

He stood at the meat aisle checking out the steaks.

Zoey snuck up behind him, considered patting that fine tush, but decided against it with so many people around. Her rep was bad enough without adding fuel to the fire.

Instead, she gave him a hip bump. "Hey, stranger."

Garrett turned with a big smile that, for some reason, faded as he saw they had an audience. "What are you doing here?"

She could ignore the gawkers, if he would. "I was
visiting with my mom, so I'm running late. Sorry. Just
grabbing some salad and potatoes and heading home."

He snagged up a package of steaks, commandeered
her cart and steered them both back in the direction
she'd just come from. "How's she doing?"

"Much better, thank you. They'll have her up and
walking soon." She eyed the enormous steaks.

"I meant to hit the butcher's, but a meeting ran over
and they closed a few hours ago. Luckily the grocery
stays open all night now." He hustled her along as he
spoke. "You remember how they used to roll the side-
walks up at six?"

"Yes." She tried to slow him down. "Where are we
going?"

"You said you wanted salad."

"Isn't it back that—"

"Zoey Hodge."

Oh, God. That particular screech of outrage carried
the same effect as it had in high school. Zoey cringed,
knew Garrett saw her cringe, and belatedly realized
why he was taking her the long way across the store.

He'd hoped to spare her, but it was bound to happen
sooner or later.

Taking two seconds to compose herself, Zoey put on
a friendly smile and turned to face the unpleasant past.
It wasn't just Carrie. She had her younger brother—
Cody—with her. They both gave her venomous glares.

"Carrie," Zoey said with calm, polite regard. "How
have you been?"

As bitter as ever, Carrie crowded into her space,
narrowed her eyes and spat, "How dare you come back
here?"

As THEY STOOD by the grill, for the tenth time, Garrett asked, "You sure you're okay?"

His concern was sweet, but it was starting to get laughable. "Do I look broken?" She rolled her eyes, hoping he'd let it go. Yes, it had been ugly. Cody had watched her with sad, narrowed eyes. And Carrie had looked…haunted.

She felt a little sick being the recipient of all that ugly emotion.

But she hoped she'd handled it well.

Certainly, she'd handled it better than Garrett. She could still hear him saying, *High school is over, Carrie. Grow up already.*

The poor girl had stood there looking mortified, wounded and vindictive all at the same time, until Cody had quietly led her away. Clearly she'd expected Garrett to back her up.

That he hadn't made Zoey almost feel sorry for her.

His hand clasped her shoulder. "The Donahues are only a small part of the community."

"I know." In high school the Donahue children had been part of the elite society. But even before Gus had died and Carrie started openly hating her, Zoey had been an outsider. Her lower-income upbringing and the free-spirited way her mother raised her had ensured she'd always be different. She couldn't remember a time when she'd ever belonged.

Freaks, Carrie had told her, belonged nowhere.

Zoey told herself that most people were happy to move beyond a seven-year-old scandal. "A lot of people here have watched me with some uncertainty, but overall they've been nice." She stepped around Garrett to turn the steaks. "And your family, of course, is always awesome."

"Yeah, they are." He took the long fork from her and removed his steak from the grill, plopping it on a platter.

Distaste scrunched her face and her stomach curled. "You're going to eat it that bloody?"

"It's rare," he explained.

"It's still *mooing*."

He laughed, took in her aversion and paused. "Does it really bother you?"

"Yeah. I'm not sure I can kiss someone with blood on their teeth, and I really wanted to kiss you again."

As if someone had used the fork on his sexy butt, he jumped—then froze.

Case in point, Zoey thought, knowing she'd again spoken out in a way few would have. But darn it, she had no skills in tact or subtlety. "You don't want to kiss me again?" Because she was pretty darned certain he did. And she definitely wanted him to. Shoot, her lips still tingled from that earlier taste.

His gaze went to her mouth, held there, and he groaned.

Now what was that about? Did he regret kissing her? Hands on her hips, she frowned at him. "Is something wrong?"

"Not a thing." While muttering something about his sister, he put the steak back on the grill.

Unsure if that meant he would kiss her after all, she moved nearer to him. When he faced her, her heart tried to punch its way out of her chest. "Amber eats her steak raw, too?"

"Rare, and no. She's medium." He stroked her hair,

seemed to catch himself, and tucked a stray tendril behind her ear. "What about you?"

"I'm well-done. No pink at all."

He opened his mouth…then shut it again with a wince of guilt and focused on his steak, using the long fork to move it to the corner of the grill.

"What?" Zoey goosed his midsection, realized there was no give to the solid muscles there and opened her hand on him for a better feel. He felt *really* good under the soft cotton of his T-shirt. "What were you going to say?"

"Something I shouldn't." He caught her hand and held it.

"Okay, now I have to know!"

"It was…" He glanced at her, did a visible struggle with himself and gave up. "Suggestive."

"Suggestive?"

"Sexual," he clarified.

"Really?" Better and better. She leaned in and lowered her voice. "Tell me."

With a wicked smile, he gave in. "Something about me liking pink." When she just stared at him, he elaborated. "Pink. On you."

She shook her head.

And that made his smile widen into a grin. Bending to her ear, he whispered, "I think of pink, and I visualize all those warm, damp places on your naked body—"

"Garrett!" With a rush of heat—not all of it embarrassment—she stumbled back from him.

Amusement growing by the second, he shrugged. "You insisted."

When he had her blushing, he seemed more comfortable, like maybe her embarrassment presented a necessary barrier between them. "I don't understand you."

"I'm a guy. Easy enough to understand."

She snorted. Nothing easy about him at all. He teased and flirted, but was most at ease when she didn't return the favor. Did he flirt with every woman? Maybe she read too much into it. Maybe it made him uncomfortable to know she was equally—or probably more—attracted to him.

He lifted the steak. "Is that cooked enough that I can eat it without repulsing you?"

It wasn't, but she nodded anyway.

She didn't have a picnic table yet, or even any outdoor chairs. But it didn't bother Garrett. Before starting the grill, he'd gone to his truck, got a blanket from behind the seat and spread it in the yard picnic-style beneath one of the tall elm trees.

It was by far the most wonderful, romantic dinner she'd ever had.

By the time they started eating, the sun had sunk low, barely visible behind the hills, splashing the sky in inspiring shades of crimson, tangerine and mauve. The air cooled a little, making it more comfortable even as the nighttime humidity set in.

They ate in a cozy silence, watching as lightning bugs showed up by the dozen. Zoey plucked a blade of dewy grass. "I'd forgotten how damp everything is around a lake. I'm getting wet just sitting here."

This time when he grinned, Zoey knew why and she threw her napkin at him.

With a low laugh, he tossed it back at her. "Don't want me to visualize that, huh?"

"No!"

"Too late," he said softly. Reaching out, he caught her ankle and moved his thumb over her skin. "Are you this soft all over?"

At that brief, simple touch, her heart sped up. "I don't know."

Their gazes clashed and held as his fingertips trailed up her calf to the inside of her knee.

Her heart hammered and her toes curled.

Abruptly he released her, pushed his empty plate back and left the blanket to explore the fire pit a few yards away.

Staring after him, Zoey saw the stiff way he held his shoulders. Why the sudden retreat?

"Have you used this yet?"

"No." Quickly she finished up the last few bites of her own meal and joined him.

It felt very intimate standing beside him in the shadowy sunset. All around them insects chirped as twinkling stars pierced the dark sky.

Zoey didn't want the evening to end already. After clearing her throat, she asked, "Can we fire it up, do you think?"

He crouched down and examined the stones placed around the pit.

While he did that, she examined the breadth of his shoulders, the long line of his spine, how his thighs strained the denim of his jeans.

No two ways about it, the man was put together fine. But her draw to him was more than that. He'd always been friendly, a natural born leader, and now as a fireman he lived as a hero. He had an easy, comfortable way about him that proved he made up his own mind instead of being swayed, didn't judge others, but instead offered help when he could.

She thought of how he'd defended her in the grocery store, and it did funny things to her. Nice things.

Turbulent things.

For the longest time he remained in that position, his face turned away from her.

Tension mounted until Zoey doubted she'd be able to convince him to stay. "Garrett?"

He straightened again, and looked down at her for a heart-stopping length of time.

She smiled. "You okay?"

"Yeah." Almost against his will, he touched her cheek, then shook his head. "I'll gather up some kindling if you want to grab matches and maybe some old papers, too."

"All right." But to be sure, she asked, "You're staying a little longer?"

"If that's okay."

"It's terrific." Lighthearted now that she knew she hadn't chased him off, she collected their dishes on her way in and put them in the sink. Her ancient plumbing didn't include a dishwasher, so she'd take care of washing them later.

While inside, she hugged herself, anticipating more kissing.

Garrett kept her guessing, but she'd learned to live with optimism.

After locating an old magazine and the box of matches she kept with candles on a shelf, she hurried back out.

It pleased her to see that he'd rearranged the blanket and their drinks closer to the pit and had an impressive

stack of twigs laid inside it, with some bigger fallen
branches waiting to go on next.

"Will this work?"

"That's perfect." He tore out several pages, rolled
them tightly, and stuck them between the twigs.

Unsure what else to do, Zoey lowered herself to her
knees on the blanket.

And hoped he would join her soon.

While he worked, he asked in more detail about her
mother's progress and seemed genuinely pleased that
she was doing better. Because his work as a fireman
included paramedic training, he had a great understanding of what her mother's treatment would be.

"I should be able to bring her home by the end of
the month. Until then, I still have a lot of stuff to get
done inside."

"Before I leave, I could take a look."

"At what?"

He laughed. "Your house. That way I'll have an idea
of what we need before we get started next Saturday."

Sitting back on her heels, Zoey considered him and
his repeated offers to help. Was he just being his usual
terrific self, or looking for reasons to be around her?

Everyone knew his entire family was made up of
do-gooders who took large, active roles in the community, either through their careers, or plain goodwill.
Being that he was the same, maybe Garrett saw her as
a project.

She hated that idea.

Once the fire started, Garrett added a few of the bigger logs, waiting until they snapped and hissed before
sitting beside Zoey. Legs out, arms braced behind him,
he sat catty-corner to her, facing the fire.

She faced him, her knees almost touching his thigh.

"That shed is a fire hazard," he said. "I think we should just knock it down."

"I peeked inside there one day, saw a snake and haven't gotten anywhere near it since."

"I'll take care of it."

That made her frown. She put her shoulders back. "It's my shed, so I'll help. Even if there are snakes."

He gave her a fleeting smile. "All right."

Damn. She glanced at the shed in the dusk and shuddered. Maybe she should have kept her mouth shut.

"So, about your mom…" With noticeable caution, he asked, "Think she'll be up to joining us at the fundraiser?"

Thrilled at the suggestion, Zoey stared at him. "You're serious?"

"It's a big event. Most of the town will be there. I mean, it's not like it would have been…"

"Private?" The way this was.

"Yeah. There'll be competitions and dancing and raffles. What do you think?"

The firelight played over his face, putting blue highlights in his hair, emphasizing the cut of his cheekbones, the length of his dark lashes. She sighed. "I think you're wonderful."

That must have surprised him. His brows twitched with a puzzled frown. "You don't mind?"

That he was sweet enough to include her mother? "Of course not." Without thinking about it, she leaned in and gave him a quick, tight hug of gratitude. "Thank you."

She started to lean away again, but with his left arm around her, he kept her close. His hand opened on her back, caressing. He nuzzled her temple.

Relaxing, she sank against him.

Near her ear, he murmured, "You smell good, Zoey."

She loved hearing that particular husky tone from him.

The heat of the fire teased along their skin, combating the humidity. Down by the lake, frogs started a chorus of croaking that echoed over the yard.

When he did nothing else, she asked, "Are you going to kiss me again?"

"Do you want me to?"

She pressed back to see his face. "That's a joke, right?"

He smiled. "I'll take that as a yes."

Zoey held her breath…and then held it some more while Garrett appeared to struggle with himself.

Starting to feel insulted, she quirked her mouth. "If you don't want to, I won't pressure you."

"You can't pressure me." He held on to her when she would have pushed away. "And what I want isn't the problem."

"Then do it."

His gaze dipped to her mouth.

Exasperated, Zoey huffed, leaned in and smashed her mouth over his. That spurred him into action and he took over, slowly adjusting to make the kiss softer, deeper, nudging her lips to open so he could lick his tongue inside.

One hand tangled in her hair, the other curved low on her back, very near her behind.

Zoey wrapped her arms around his neck and held on. She wouldn't mind kissing him for, oh, a week? He tasted good, smelled good and felt even better.

Easing back, he kissed the corner of her lips, her jaw, up to her ear.

Zoey rasped, "See. No problems."

She felt his smile against her jaw. "You'll give me a tour of the house?"

Unsure of his motives, she measured her words. "I'd love to show you around." They'd be inside...near her bed.

Was she ready to go there so soon?

Once her mom came home, the opportunity might be lost, so...yes. She was ready, especially after that heated kiss. "Just keep in mind that relocating and buying the house and starting up the new business is straining my savings, so I'm doing things as—" *cheaply* "—affordably as I can."

"Not a problem. Labor is usually the biggest cost." He nipped her bottom lip. "But I'm affordable."

Would she need to pay him? And how would that work?

Another quick, firm kiss, and he sat back from her. "Stop fretting, Zoey. We'll work it out."

"I almost never fret. It's pointless." And thinking that, she dropped to her back on the blanket to take in the inky sky glittering with stars. "Look at that."

Garrett said, "I'm looking."

"It's such a clear night." When he didn't comment, she asked, "You don't enjoy the stars?"

She sensed more than heard him moving closer before he said, "I do."

"I swear they look different here than they did in the city."

"That's where you lived?"

"When I left here, I wasn't sure where to go. I just

wanted…out. But I ended up in Lexington, and it suited me. I had a cute little apartment, a terrific job as an assistant with a pet groomer, plenty of friends…"

"That you didn't mind leaving?"

What could she tell him? Lexington was great—but it wasn't Buckhorn. "As Dorothy would tell you, there's no place like home." And she'd missed home so very much.

He came down on his elbow beside her, near enough that she felt the warmth of his body and could breathe in his scent. "You should never have gone away."

Turning her head, she tried to see his thoughts, but the flames of the fire danced, distorting his features, making him look almost…apologetic.

But that didn't make any sense. He'd had nothing to do with her situation back then.

Quietly, she said, "You know I had to."

"I know the rumors. I heard the gossip. You broke things off with Gus Donahue, and he didn't take it well."

Her short, harsh laugh disturbed the quiet of the peaceful night, and she quickly apologized. "Sorry. It's not funny—but what an understatement. His reaction was so over-the-top, I didn't know what to do."

His gaze drifted over her, her face, then her body beneath the moonlight. "Would you tell me what actually happened?"

There had been few opportunities to talk about that wretched event. She'd confided only in her mother because there'd been no one else interested in the truth. "You really want to know?"

"If you don't mind telling me."

As if the words had been bubbling near the surface,

just waiting for permission, she blurted them out. "Gus wanted to have sex, I didn't, and he flew off the handle."

Garrett didn't seem surprised, and he didn't doubt her. "I can understand him trying. You were hot even back then."

She blinked at him. Garrett had thought her hot?

"But even a horny kid has to understand that no is no."

"He said I'd led him on and that the whole town would call him a fool if he couldn't score with someone like me."

Garrett was silent—but he touched her, first her wrist, the back of her hand. He traced her fingers, then laced his in hers, palm to palm. His big, strong hand engulfed hers, emphasizing the differences in their sizes and giving her an added thrill. "I'm sorry."

"About what?"

"How unfairly you were judged when no one had the whole story."

She shrugged it off; she'd long since grown used to the biased assessment of what had happened that day. Even so, it felt nice, really nice, having someone to hold on to. "It wasn't the first time that he'd gotten enraged over something ridiculous. I'd had enough of it, and I told him we were through."

"That's when he left?"

Remembering, she gave a slow shake of her head. "First he broke a few things. One of our lamps, my mom's music box." Her chest hurt with the memory. "It had been her grandmother's, and it sat on a shelf in our living room."

Garrett lifted her hand, kissed her knuckles.

That small kiss held encouragement and understanding, spurring her to tell it all. "He...he shouted and cursed, called me some vile names and punched the wall right by my head. He hit it hard enough to leave a big hole there, and his knuckles were bleeding."

Garrett went still.

"It terrified me, and that made me furious." To explain that, she said, "I always lose my temper when I'm scared."

"That's better than giving in to the fear."

"I guess." A damp breeze drifted over her skin; here, now, with Garrett, she felt exposed and vulnerable, but not in a bad way...which made no sense at all. "I pushed him away and told him to get out and never come back. It was like I flipped a switch. He went from furious to sorry and pleading." Her breath caught. "He begged me to forgive him."

"But you made him leave anyway."

"Yes."

He kissed her knuckles again. "That was the smart thing to do, Zoey."

"It didn't feel smart after he died." Her stomach cramped, remembering the devastating news, the guilt that had all but smothered her.

"What happened after he left wasn't your fault. *None* of it was your fault."

Seeking a measure of calm, she pulled away from his hold, folded both hands behind her head and focused on that big, star-studded sky. It was easier than looking at Garrett. "That's not how everyone else saw it. I went from being a nobody to being public enemy number one."

"That's not true."

"Close enough." Had he scooted nearer somehow?

He seemed to be looming over her. She kind of liked it. "It wasn't easy coming back here."

"You're strong and brave."

Laughing, she slanted him a look. Yep, definitely closer. "You like to see the best in people." The moonlight and firelight competed to emphasize all the most appealing angles of his face, the width of his shoulders, the bulge of his biceps. She sighed. "If it weren't for my mom, I wouldn't have come back. Ever."

"I'm sorry she's hurt," he whispered. "But damn, Zoey, I'm glad you're here."

GARRETT HAD DELIBERATELY chosen to eat outside with her, thinking it would be safer than being indoors…near a bed. But seeing Zoey like this, relaxed, sharing, with the stars shining above her and her clear enjoyment of nature, well, it was worse than having a bed nearby.

It was heated foreplay, and he felt himself reacting.

Filtered through the leaves of tall trees, the moonlight played with her body, slipping over the swells of her breasts, the length of her thighs.

It'd be so easy to lean down to her, to kiss her…and more. To let his hands explore all that warm, dewy skin.

Even while he fought with himself, his breathing deepened and his muscles tensed. The shorts she wore teased him, exposing so much and concealing so little. And that V-necked T-shirt, dipping low to her cleavage. Every so often when she moved, he saw the edge of lace on her bra and it drove him nuts.

Each time he saw her, he discovered something new about her, something nice, or enticing, or…lust-inspiring. Without seeming to try, she reeled him in with open smiles, silly conversation and her big heart.

In many ways she was such a dichotomy—strong and accepting, ready to tackle the past and future alike. But so soft, too, her hair, her skin, that peek of lace… and her attitude toward others.

He didn't want to be a sap, but her emotional generosity really got to him. He'd never known a woman like her—sympathetic enough to help care for a sick kid, understanding in the face of insults.

Even Carrie, with her nasty reception and hateful barbs, hadn't been able to dent Zoey's natural compassion. He'd been furious with Carrie and Cody, but Zoey had been calm and thoughtful.

"You're so quiet," she whispered. "What are you thinking?"

Her light brown hair, baby fine, fanned out around her head, drawing his fingers. "I'm having a hard time not kissing you."

"Oh." She dropped her gaze to his mouth. "You can, you know."

Encouragement was the last thing he needed, because he knew the truth even if she didn't. "Kissing will lead to more."

"Like…?"

Laughing a little roughly, he sat up and turned away from temptation. *Remember what Amber said, remember what—* "Like how I'd love to get you out of those shorts." The words left his mouth and he wanted to kick his own butt. From the moment she'd come downstairs from his shower when she'd arrived in town, every instinct he had as a man told him to go after her.

To get her.

He wasn't used to fighting himself. Before Zoey, it had never been an issue.

Zoey said nothing, and the silence condemned him. She hadn't been back to town that long, she had a full plate, and here he was pressing her for sex.

As soon as he got himself together he'd apologize.

Just the fact that he had to collect himself proved his reaction to Zoey was different. As a firefighter, he'd learned to stay calm no matter what.

As a man, that personality trait had come naturally in all relationships.

Now he felt far from calm. He couldn't recall the last time he'd been this physically and emotionally drawn in.

Yet his meddling sister had to go and spell out a dozen legitimate reasons why Zoey should be off-limits for casual sex.

He heard the rustling of her movements as she came to her feet, likely to call an end to the evening—not that he could blame her.

With the apology forthcoming, he turned—

And Zoey unzipped her shorts.

He froze, every muscle clenched tight as he waited, watching her, anticipation burning hot.

She pushed the shorts over her hips and let them fall to her ankles.

God, she was gorgeous.

She stood there with her T-shirt rumpled, her hair messy, wearing that same sexy pair of panties that she'd dropped in his driveway.

"Well?" Twisting her fingers together, she whispered, "Say something already."

He had no words. Scooping an arm around her behind, he tugged her closer and pressed his face against her, kissing the bared flesh of her belly between the bottom of her T-shirt and those minuscule panties that barely covered her.

She felt smooth and soft, smelled indescribably good. He opened his mouth against her skin for a gentle love bite, then soothed the spot with his tongue while tasting her warm skin. He wanted to devour her. Every inch of her.

Right here in the open yard.

Moaning out a soft sound of acceptance, as if that plan worked for her, Zoey sank her fingers into his hair and held him closer.

In that moment, Garrett had no doubts; right or wrong, he'd already reached the point of no return.

CHAPTER FOUR

SLIDING A HAND around to her shapely ass, Garrett cuddled her closer. He wanted to touch her everywhere, all at once, and he wanted more of her mouth.

God, her mouth.

He easily levered her weight, lowering her to the blanket again.

"Wow," she whispered. "You're strong."

"You're small. And sweet." He slid his gaze down her body, over her breasts to her belly, lower. "And so fucking hot."

Drawing in a shuddering breath, she watched him. "I've never heard you talk dirty."

"It's a wonder I can talk at all." Sitting back to look at her, he said, "I'm on the ragged edge here." Looking wasn't enough, so he opened a hand on her flat belly. Breathing deeply, he trailed his palm up to the dip of her waist, pushed the T-shirt up over her ribs, all the way to her bra.

Zoey surprised him by sitting up, grabbing the hem of her shirt and jerking it off over her head. "You, too," she ordered.

He obliged, stripping off his shirt and tossing it by hers.

With purring interest, she put her small, warm hands against him, spreading her fingers out over his chest.

He brought her in for another taste and, keeping his mouth on hers, lowered her to the blanket once more. He was aware of the crackling fire, the sounds of nature.

And Zoey.

Each small sound she made, each shiver and gasp, made him want more.

He was content to enjoy her mouth for a good long while, each kiss hotter, longer.

Damn, the girl could kiss.

When she pushed him to his back, he went willingly, enjoying the way she sprawled over him, how she stroked his shoulders and chest and down to his abs.

When her busy hands reached the front of his jeans, he went still. "Zoey…" he rasped in warning.

"Mmm?" Sitting up, she tackled his snap and carefully, agonizingly, lowered the zipper.

Like a sexy angel, she knelt beside him, the firelight making a halo of her tangled hair. Muscles pulled taut in anticipation, he watched as she slipped a hand inside his fly…and stroked along his length.

Groaning, he tried to think of all the reasons why he shouldn't let her rush things. But damn, with her hand working him, rushing seemed like a very good idea.

He was dying to see her, all of her, so while she stayed occupied making him insane, he reached for the front closure of her bra.

It opened easily, the cups parting to show soft, full breasts and tight, pink nipples.

Zoey removed her hand long enough to shrug off the bra, leaving her naked except for those sinful panties. Before she could go back to tormenting him, Garrett sat up to remove his shoes and socks, then stood to shove out of his jeans.

Still on her knees, now in front of him, Zoey said, "The boxers, too."

He had no problem with that and shucked them off, as well.

Like a living fantasy, Zoey gave another vibrating *"mmmm,"* and reached for him.

A smidgen of reality wormed in past the smoldering lust and Garrett caught her hands. "Hold up a second."

Staring up at him, her green eyes big and—*damn*—hungry, she whispered, "Why?"

It took a lot of fortitude on his part, but Garrett came down to his knees with her. Getting the words out wasn't easy, but for Zoey, he managed. "Are you sure about this?"

"Definitely."

Her answer came too fast for him to take it seriously. "You haven't been in town that long—"

"I'm ready."

"—and I'm rushing you."

Laughing, she toppled him backward so that she was on top again, her light brown hair forming a curtain around them. "Are you always this hesitant about sex?"

"No." God, no. He loved sex. Always. "I want you to know that you're different." As in special, damn it.

"Really?" Even though she sounded impressed by that, she squirmed on him, shattering his resolve. "That's sweet."

"Zoey." Garrett curved one hand to her jaw, the other to her ass, trying to keep her still. "I can wait if you need me to."

"Well, aren't you superhuman," she teased.

Damn straight, because that's what it took to be noble with her.

"The thing is...I'm not." Zoey lightly bit his bottom lip. "And it's been a long time for me." A sweet, barely there kiss on his chest. "And I'm ready now, as in *right now*." To emphasize that point, she moved against his straining erection. "Once my mom is here, I won't have much opportunity for stuff like this."

Was she already putting a time limit on their relationship? Like hell. Sure, her mom would need some help, but they'd figure it out.

"So please," she said, giving him another little nibble, "no more talking—unless it's to say something naughty or enticing. You know, to turn me on more." She trailed her hot little tongue along his ribs, and lower. "Not that I need it, because seriously, Garrett, I'm there."

When her mouth teased over his hip, he gave up. Again.

"Do you have protection?" she whispered.

He could feel her hot breath. "Yeah."

"I figured." She closed both hands around him, nuzzled against him and he knew, flat-out knew, if he felt her mouth on him, he'd never be able to hold out. They'd have to save that for later, when he wasn't coiled so tight.

Catching her forearms, he dragged her up his body so he could take her mouth again, then turned her under him. "My turn."

"But I wasn't done."

"Any more of that and I would've been."

"Oh." Satisfaction curled her lips.

Sweet, silly Zoey.

"I think I'd like that," she whispered. "Pushing you to lose control."

He cupped her breasts. "I'll look forward to it. Later

though, okay?" Lowering his head, he drew in one nipple, pleased with the way her back arched, how her breath caught, the clench of her fingers in his hair. He kept it light, suckling gently before moving to the other side. He drew her in, harder this time, and moved his hand down to her panties.

She lifted into his touch, her breathing ragged. Finding her panties already damp pushed him dangerously close to the breaking point.

Insane. He loved to tease, building the pleasure, but now, with Zoey, he felt consumed with the need to get inside her.

Hoping she was ready, he moved his fingers inside the material, stroking over her, parting her and finding her silky, wet and hot.

"Garrett, *now*."

"This?" he teased.

She held her breath when he slowly worked two fingers into her, pressing them deep, keeping the heel of his hand firm against her.

"Now," she insisted on a gasp.

"Soon," he whispered.

She clamped around his fingers, and he felt new moisture slicking his hand. "Now, now, *now*—"

Her urgency spurred his own. It took him only seconds to snag up his jeans and locate a condom. Eyes heavy, Zoey watched him tear open the foil packet and roll it on. He reached for her hips, snagging his fingers in the waistband of those sexy little panties.

With more haste than finesse, he tugged them off. She wanted him to rush, but he needed to take a minute just to look at all of her. "Damn, you're sexy."

"Flattery will get you everything."

It wasn't flattery, just truth, but she kept curling her toes and shifting, and he knew she was in the same shape as him.

He liked that she wanted him so much, that she felt the same chemistry.

"Garrett?" Her breasts trembled with her broken breaths. "Don't be a tease."

Smiling, he settled between her legs, then said, "Kiss me, Zoey," doing what he could to hold off, wanting it to last.

She did, but went one further. When her slim legs wrapped around him, her ankles locking at the small of his back, Garrett groaned his surrender.

He adjusted, positioned himself...and slid deep.

On that very first thrust, she cried out. Knowing sounds carried on the lake, he kissed her, and kept on kissing her even while riding slow and deep. She matched him in every way, countering with a roll of her hips, holding him tighter and tighter.

Given how quickly she started coming, she'd been even closer to the edge than him. Those sweet, internal contractions milked him, her heated scent enveloped him, and she arched hard, putting her head back on a harsh, high moan.

That did it for him.

Pressing his face against her neck, he gave in to release, still rocking into her until all his tension eased away.

He thought to keep his weight off her, but Zoey hugged him tight, so he carefully settled atop her.

Her long sigh of satisfaction made him smile—until he felt her stiffen. "What's wrong?"

"I think I heard something."

A second later, he heard it, too.

ZOEY HAD BEEN adrift in utter bliss, her limbs still tingling, the weight of Garrett's hot, hard body offering a very unique comfort.

Until a rustle in the bushes to the right pulled them apart.

She stared into the darkness. "What was that?"

Eyes narrowed, Garrett said, "I don't know." He pressed a hand to her shoulder. "Stay put."

"I'm *naked*," she reminded him in a panicked whisper.

"Not like I'd forget." He handed her T-shirt to her and pulled on his boxers and jeans.

She watched him. "What did you do with the condom?"

Even with firelight making the shadows dance, she saw the incredulity in his glance.

"Sorry," she whispered. "But I've never done this outdoors thing before."

Just as quietly, he said, "Tossed it in the fire."

"Oh." Ingenious. As he started to step away, panic set in. "What are you doing?"

Keys rattled when he pulled a key chain from his pocket with a small flashlight connected to it. "Checking on things."

She said, "Oh," again.

Garrett shone the low light over the tall weeds…and they both saw the movement.

Her heart hammering, Zoey quickly yanked on her panties. "Probably just a critter," she said hopefully.

"Not a raccoon or possum," he said. "Too big."

Too big? The weeds moved more, parted…and a pair of eyes reflected off the beam of the small flashlight.

She nearly swallowed her heart. "That's not a snake, right?"

"Stay still," Garrett told her.

She went one further and held her breath...until the dog came slinking out.

Oh, thank God.

"Hey," Garrett said softly to the animal. "Easy, boy."

Zoey almost melted. How could Garrett be so freaking awesome *all the time*? Few men could transition from incredible stud to stalwart protector to gentle caregiver without a hitch. Being so gorgeous was just overkill.

"He's limping."

Her heart softened more, this time in pity. "Looks a little rough around the edges, too. Poor guy." Very slowly she got to her feet and pulled on her shorts.

Watching them both, the dog held back.

"No collar," Garrett said, moving the flashlight over the mutt. "He's loaded with ticks, a few scratches—"

"And that limp."

"Yeah." He went down to one knee. "You okay, guy? How friendly are you?"

That Garrett didn't just try to run the stray off was almost enough to melt her knees. "Will you be okay here with him if I go get some food?"

"Yeah, but go slow."

"I know." She'd been around animals all her life. A hurt animal might take any sudden movements the wrong way. So she didn't run, but she didn't dawdle, either.

In the kitchen, she snatched a plastic bowl off the shelf and quickly emptied an entire package of bologna into it. On her way out, she turned on the back porch light. It helped only a little.

Garrett was now within a few inches of the dog, his hand extended.

If anything, the dog looked worried.

And desperate.

She was still a good distance away when he started sniffing the air. Smiling, she held the food out in front of her as she eased closer.

"Let me," Garrett said, reaching back so she would hand the bowl to him.

The big protective lug.

"I know what I'm doing," she reminded him. "I'm the expert."

"Groomer," he countered, but he didn't interfere when she very slowly set the bowl down in front of the dog.

"Does that mean you want to pick the ticks off him?"

"Want to? No. But I'll help." Taking her hand, they both moved back to let the dog eat.

He emptied the bowl in a few big, noisy bites.

Zoey studied him, the small, mostly tan body with black and brown markings, the floppy ears, the soulful eyes. "He looks like a beagle–Jack Russell mix."

"Still young," Garrett agreed.

Now that the dog had solved one problem, it inched closer, sniffing.

"No more just yet, sweetie." With apology, she said, "You'll get sick."

Garrett touched under the dog's chin, and he let him. As if that broke the ice, the poor little thing limped closer, his tail thumping with hope.

Tears turned Zoey's vision blurry. "I'm taking him in."

Garrett smiled. "I already knew that."

TRUE TO HIS WORD, Garrett stayed and helped. It was past midnight by the time they had the dog tick-free, bathed and a nasty thorn removed from between the pads of his front right paw.

Zoey put out fresh bedding, then put up a gate at the kitchen doorway. "Hopefully I can get a vet appointment tomorrow."

"My uncle Jordan will fit him in."

She'd forgotten that his uncle was a vet. "You don't think he'd mind?"

"He'll insist." Crossing his arms over his chest, Garrett propped a shoulder on the wall. "I can meet you there first thing tomorrow morning if you want."

So sweet. Smiling at him, Zoey stroked his biceps. She would never tire of touching him. Or looking at him. And hopefully more. Lots more. "If you're free and want to join us, that's fine. But if you're busy, I can handle it."

Now that the dog was clean, had eaten again and was given a fresh dish of water, he looked exhausted. After only a few cautious glances their way, he went to the corner of the kitchen where Zoey had made his bed, dug around, rearranged things, snuffled and kicked, and finally, after turning two circles, dropped down with a lusty sigh.

Garrett's grin pleased her as much as the dog's acceptance. She hadn't planned on taking on even more responsibility, but the dog was here, and she'd make it work somehow.

"I like your house."

Drawn from her thoughts, she looked around, seeing what he saw—cabinets that needed to be sanded and painted, cracked linoleum floors, watermarks on the ceilings.

His hands settled on her shoulders. "Every old house needs work. That's part of the fun."

She wondered if he really meant that. For her, it would be fun because it wasn't just a house, it was a new beginning. "I'm looking forward to it. But the kitchen won't be the first room." She took his hand and started down the hall. "I've already done some work on my mother's bedroom and bathroom, but I'd love your input on what still needs to be done."

The dog slept on undisturbed. He must have really been tired. Thinking of him wounded and all alone tugged at her heart. But never again. She'd make sure he had enough love to recover.

As they went through the modest house, Garrett offered nice compliments on every room she showed him. Like her, he focused more on the unique qualities of the older home, instead of what needed to be done. She loved that he felt the same as she did about it.

Midway through the tour he suggested she get a pen and paper so they could make notes and figure out what was needed.

"You're sure you don't mind?" Zoey didn't want to take advantage of him. He'd already put in a full day, then helped her with the dog. "It's getting really late."

He touched her cheek. "Tired?"

With him around? "Not me."

"Good." His thumb went under her chin, he tipped up her face and gave her a short, soft kiss. "Let's make a list."

For another thirty minutes they went over everything, and Zoey felt like she had a good handle on which updates were priorities and which could wait.

Even better, Garrett insisted he'd enjoy helping out as often as possible.

When they reached her bedroom, he stepped inside and looked around with interest.

Being there with him, near her bed, meant there was no way she could keep her thoughts on repairs. He'd already given her an incredible orgasm, but now...

Now she wanted more.

"The room looks like you."

That made her laugh. "Peeling paint and scuffed floors? Gee, thanks."

He nodded at the bed. "Soft blankets, everything tidy but colorful." His gaze met hers. "Inviting."

Such a wonderful compliment—though she seldom thought of herself as tidy. "Thank you."

"For?"

"Everything." Lifting a hand, she gestured at the house, at the pet hair and muddy paw prints clinging to his dark shirt. "For the kind words, the encouragement and advice, and for helping out with the dog."

He didn't move from his position near the bed. "Is that my goodbye for the night?"

"What? No." She closed the space between them. Unsure of how bold she should be, wary of chasing him off, she said, "I was hoping for more kissing?"

Humor lit his eyes. "Is that a question or a fact?"

"Both?"

Smiling, he shook his head. "You don't protect yourself at all, do you?"

"From you? Why would I."

Indecision took him across the floor—away from

her—but he came right back again. Determination stopped him in front of her. "You were phenomenal."

"Really?" She grinned and lifted a fist. "Go me."

"The thing is..."

Uh-oh. "What?"

"I can't be anything more than a friend."

They were already more than friends. Or, having had her once, was he satisfied? "You don't want me anymore?" She must not have been all that phenomenal after all.

His eyes flared, then narrowed. "Of course I do."

"Then what's the problem?"

"I'm not looking to settle down anytime soon."

Insult, disbelief and incredulity kept her staring at him for far too long. Should she laugh, be indignant? Or just be honest?

He stepped closer. "Zoey?"

Honesty won out. "Here's the thing, Garrett. I just got back to town, right? My mom is having *all* kinds of health issues. I'm trying to open up a new shop and make enough of a living to support not only me, but her, too. So far as I can tell, a third of the town doesn't remember why I left, another third remembers but doesn't care and that last third is still harboring some animosity."

"I'm sorry."

She waved off the apology. The last thing she wanted was his pity. "Do you really think I have the time or the inclination for a committed relationship?" He started to speak but she cut him off. "Because I *don't*. Actually, I'm pretty beat."

"I didn't mean..."

"And really. Sex once doesn't lock you into anything." She tried a cheeky grin. "Sex twice or three times still doesn't count as a promise, not to me."

This time when he started to speak, she put her fingers against his mouth.

"If you want to be friends, yeah, that'd be great—as long as it's friends with benefits because I'm too busy to clear my calendar just for an occasional chat or fast food. But sex? At my convenience, and yours of course, now that I can work out. So what do you think?"

He knotted a hand in his hair, looking a little frazzled. "About?"

"Weren't you paying attention?"

"I think so, yeah."

"So how about more kissing? And maybe more... everything else, too?"

CHAPTER FIVE

GARRETT BLEW OUT a breath. "Honest to God, Zoey, you make me a little nuts."

She pursed her lips. "Should I apologize?"

He laughed. He didn't mean to, but damn, she was about as unique as a woman could get. "Don't apologize, and don't change."

She eyed him. "I don't understand you."

"Okay, so understand this—I'd like nothing more than to spend the whole night kissing you." The *whole night*—what the hell was he saying?

"Yes."

He'd been about to retrench, to make excuses on why he had to go, but her unguarded enthusiasm made him feel like a coward. While he shied away from his emotions, she embraced hers without reserve.

He knew the truth; in a very short time he'd come to like her too much, think about her too often.

Want her in ways that were only in part sexual.

Would it be so bad if he let things progress naturally? Now that he'd had her, now that he knew how good it was between them, how could he walk away? Especially given that she claimed to feel the same.

And if they grew tired of each other...how could there be hurt feelings when right now, she didn't have the time or energy for more anyway?

"You're pondering things far too long," she complained. "I have my pride, you know. If you'd rather just go, I promise not to kick up a fuss."

That made up his mind. "It was dark outside."

"Just the firelight, I know."

"I'd like to stay. With the lights on so I can see you better."

Her eyes widened.

"And no threat of mosquitoes or echoes off the lake."

"Echoes." She covered her mouth. "I hadn't even thought of that." Then with a grimace, "Was I loud?"

"You were so damned sexy, I didn't get a chance to linger as long as I wanted. You started moaning all deep and hot and I lost it."

She beamed at him.

"Let's check on the dog, take him out one more time, then I could use a shower before we turn in."

"A shower—with me?"

"I was going to ask." Damn, she pleased him. For now, he'd put his sister's guilt trip from his mind and take things as they came.

One day at a time—starting tonight.

SEVERAL DAYS LATER, Garrett was outside with the guys on a quiet, sunny afternoon washing the engines when Amber came to visit him again. She and Zoey were friends, so no doubt she knew how much time he'd been spending at Zoey's house.

Was she here to give him another lecture?

He rolled his eyes at her purposeful, long-legged stride across the lot...until he realized Noel Poet had zeroed in on her, too.

Deciding now might be a good time to let the new

guy know of family connections, Garrett headed over to meet her halfway. "Amber."

She gave him a double take, then matched his formal tone. "Garrett."

Putting an arm around her shoulders, he led her to where Noel, shirtless and with his pants soaked to the knees, ran a soapy sponge over a rescue truck. Or more to the point, he held the sponge near the truck. With his attention clearly elsewhere, he wasn't doing much in the way of actual washing.

When they approached, Noel swiped a forearm over his face and then just waited until they'd reached him, his eyes narrowed against the sun.

He stood an inch or so shorter than Garrett's six-two. During a recent tour with the elementary school, Garrett had overheard two of the teachers whispering about Noel's dark blond hair and lean, muscular body. At the time he'd found it funny and had harassed Noel over it later.

Now, with his sister looking at Noel, Garrett wasn't sure how he felt about it, mostly because he'd heard other things, too.

Like how Noel got around, how he enjoyed variety and how he planned to stay single.

When they reached him, Garrett said, "Amber, this is Noel Poet. He's new to the station. Noel, my sister, Amber."

Surprise lifted Noel's brows. "You're intro-ing me to your sis? Seriously?"

Damn it, did the man have to make it sound like he'd just thrown Amber on the sacrificial altar?

Amber smiled and stuck out a hand. "Nice to meet you."

Smile slow and suggestive, Noel transferred the sponge to his other hand and swiped his palm along the seat of his pants before taking hers. "Might've been nicer if you weren't related." He kept the handshake brief.

Garrett worked his jaw. "I figured since she comes around often enough—usually to give me shit about something—I might as well introduce you."

Amber leaned in to Noel—which made both his brows go up—to say in a loud stage whisper, "I only give him a hard time when he needs it."

"Which she seems to figure is twice a week at least."

For one brief moment, Noel's gaze dipped over her before he caught himself. "The family resemblance is there," he told them both. "Wish I'd noticed sooner."

Amber's smile brightened more. "Hope you don't hold that against me."

Both men stared at her. Garrett because he'd never seen her flirt, and Noel, well... Garrett knew exactly where the man's mind had gone—and it had to do with holding body parts against her.

Frowning, Garrett took her upper arm. "I'll let you get back to it."

Noel nodded and murmured, "Guess I should," but he continued to look at her.

Uncomfortable for a variety of reasons, Garrett led Amber toward the garage and relative privacy.

"He seems nice."

No, he didn't want Amber thinking that, but if he tried telling her what to do, she'd do the opposite just to prove a point. "So what's up?" he asked, hoping to divert her.

She took the bait. "You and Zoey."

"Yeah?" He'd definitely been *up* that morning. The night before, too. But right now, here at the station, he had it under wraps.

That is, unless he started thinking about her too much.

"You didn't take my advice," Amber said.

"Advice?" His sister was never that understated. "You mean your order for me to leave her be?"

"Semantics." She walked over to a tool chest and seated herself. "Zoey said she's gotten more done on the house in the last week with your help than she would have in a month on her own."

"Yeah, so? I'm good at repairs."

"Sounded to me like you've been there nearly every day."

All but one, not that he'd give her details.

Amber stared at him.

"Stop it."

Failing at the innocent look, Amber asked, "What?"

"You're patiently waiting for me to spill my guts." In the past, that silent stare might have worked. But not since he'd hit his twenties. "My relationship with Zoey is none of your business."

"So it *is* a relationship?"

An awesome, hot, sexually inspired relationship, which he also enjoyed when they weren't having sex… but he didn't want to dwell on that too much. Things were happening fast. Mach-speed fast. He wasn't sure how he felt about that, and he had no clue how Zoey felt about it.

She loved sleeping with him, that much he knew. And she smiled a lot while they worked on her house.

He often found her watching him with a really sweet expression on her face.

But he didn't know what that expression meant.

Amber pushed to her feet in a rush. "I ask, because Zoey just assured me that it wasn't."

As usual, when he started thinking about Zoey, he got distracted. "Wasn't what?"

"A relationship."

Ire quickly replaced the confusion. "You were gossiping about me?"

Flapping a hand, she said, "Save that deadly tone for someone who intimidates more easily. I'm your sister and you know I would defend you with my dying breath."

Mouth twisted over that dramatic statement, he repeated, "Dying breath, huh?"

"Of course." Smiling, she added, "Because I love you."

Oh, hell no. "You're up to something."

That made her laugh. "I'm just trying to get a lay of the land."

Noel walked in to grab some dry towels. No one said a word, but Amber tracked his every step, making Garrett frown again. When Noel walked back out, whistling, Amber released a breath.

"So are you or are you not interested in her?"

Sneaky, jumping right back to the topic that way after she'd just ogled a fellow firefighter right in front of him. But how could he answer? He was far beyond interested. Bordering on obsessed. On the downhill slide to falling in love.

He knew it, but that didn't mean he'd share with Amber.

488 BACK TO BUCKHORN

"Never mind." She patted his chest. "I know you well enough that I can see for myself."

He caught her arm before she could leave. "What did Zoey tell you exactly?"

"That you guys were having fun in a no-strings-attached way that worked perfectly for her because—" Amber coughed "—the perks were awesome."

Nice. "She didn't go into the perks?"

"She enthused until my face was so hot I had to leave." After sticking her elbow in his ribs, she said, "A little brother should never be described as a stud. That's not a direct quote, by the way. Zoey was far more descriptive than that."

Garrett grinned.

Amber didn't. "So now, instead of worrying about Zoey, I have to worry about you." She shook her head. "A sister's job is never done."

"Why would you worry about me?"

"Oh, Garrett. You don't know? The bigger they are, the harder they fall."

He wouldn't fall alone, damn it. Zoey would come around. Right?

"If you're rethinking that no-strings-attached nonsense, you ought to clue Zoey in real soon. Once her mom comes home and her responsibilities double, she just might have to prioritize her time."

And Amber figured he wouldn't make the list? Or was she trying to manipulate him again? He'd bet on the latter. "We're taking it one day at a time."

"I know." She looked at him with pity. "And that means that tomorrow could be very different from today. You might want to keep that in mind."

This time when she started away, Garrett let her. Damn it, he'd been in such a great mood, and now...

Now he felt the need to make himself more invaluable to Zoey. He'd start on that tonight. If by the fireman's fund-raiser she hadn't come around, well, then he'd state the obvious to her.

The obvious being that they were good together, and that he fit into her life, whatever her life might be.

But until then, he'd rather give her a chance to tell him how she felt. He'd encourage her at least once a day...and every night.

LEAVING THE BED UNMADE—why bother?—she and Garrett repeatedly bumped into each other while dressing. It wasn't the limited space so much as she couldn't keep her eyes off of him. Fully dressed he was a visual treat. Naked...yeah. She wasn't missing that for anything.

While trying to step into her shorts, she tripped herself up and would have fallen if Garrett hadn't caught her.

"Let me." Going to one knee, he eased up her shorts... while kissing her thighs, her belly, each breast.

She braced her hands on his hard, wide shoulders and sighed.

Though they'd just finished making love, he murmured, "I need another hour."

Or a lifetime.

Her eyes popped open. Oh, no, where had that thought come from?

"Zoey?" He slowly stood, towering over her. "Everything okay?"

He'd spent the night again.

He stayed over almost every night.

And it was so wonderful that now she wondered how she'd ever be able to sleep again without him spooning her, holding her close. He worked with her, played with her, talked with her... He'd invaded her life in so many ways that now he seemed very much a part of it.

"Zoey?"

She tried to nod yes, but the answer was no, and she ended up sort of waggling her head in a totally indecipherable way.

Garrett grinned. "You are so damned cute." He kissed the end of her nose, then pulled her T-shirt over her head, smoothed her hair back and just held her face. "Are you worrying about your mom?"

"A little." That wasn't an outright lie. She worried about her mom all the time. "I want everything perfect for her when she comes here."

Garrett sat on the end of her bed and pulled her down onto his knees. "Can I ask you something?"

"You can ask me anything."

"What does your uncle think about your mom moving here? She's been living with him, right?"

"He's okay with it."

His big hand smoothed over her back. "Amber told me you weren't welcome at your uncle's."

Ducking her head, Zoey wondered how to explain. "He's still a little mad at me." As soon as she said it, she felt Garrett's anger. It was funny, but she could read him so easily. "He thinks I never should have left her. And he's probably right."

"Know what I think?"

She tucked her head under his chin and breathed in the warm, masculine scent of his big body. "Yeah, I do."

He tipped up her chin, forcing her to meet his eyes.

"Why didn't your mom or uncle back you up way back then?"

Seeing him like this, caring, concerned for her, well, she had to kiss him.

He didn't disappoint her.

Kissing Garrett would never grow old. But when she came up for breath, he said, "Will you tell me?"

There was really no reason not to. "My uncle wanted me to stay and defend myself."

That surprised him. "He didn't blame you?"

She shook her head. "Everyone assumes that. But he'd dealt with Gus and knew about his temper. He said he tried to help him work it out in football, but... he wasn't a very happy guy. It made my uncle furious that, as he put it, I was just going to turn tail and run. Especially since that'd leave my mom...alone."

As if he knew she needed it, Garrett hugged her tighter.

"Mom is the quintessential free spirit, always has been. She loves me a lot. Back then, I was her whole world. After dad died when I was twelve, she never dated."

"She just focused on you?"

"Pretty much." Zoey didn't want it to sound like her mother was weak, even if that was partially true. "She'd never worked outside the home, so she had a hard time holding down a job. That's why we were always so poor."

"Your uncle was counting on you to help her make ends meet?"

"And to be there for her." She opened her hand on Garrett's chest, toying with his chest hair, savoring the heat of his skin. "When I left, Mom just…gave up. That's why my uncle had to take her in."

"You were a kid, Zoey. Your uncle should have known you couldn't be responsible for your mom."

"That's the thing, though. I had been, ever since Dad died." She tipped back her head to see him. She needed him to understand. "Now I will be again."

"Now you're a grown woman and she's hurt. Family helps family, always."

"Yes."

"Which is why she should have been helping you back then."

The truth hurt, but she nodded. "Maybe, but she can barely help herself." As soon as she said it, she winced. "I'm sorry. A daughter shouldn't say something so awful about her—"

"Shh." Garrett pressed his mouth to her temple. "It's just me."

Just him—the only person she could really share with. Not to another living soul had she ever criticized her mother. "I love her."

"Of course you do."

He kissed her again—her ear, her cheek, the corner of her mouth—and she accepted the truth. Damn it, after all her assurances, she'd still fallen for him.

"So your uncle won't be a problem?"

"No." Loving Garrett…now that might be a problem. But not her uncle. "He's annoyed still and holding a grudge. But he'll come around because he'll want to visit Mom, and he knows he has to behave when he's here."

Rough fingertips glided gently over her jaw. "You're something else, you know that?"

"Yeah?" She smiled up at him. "Like what?"

He started to reply, but Ticket, as she'd named the dog given the number of ticks he'd had on him when she'd first found him, went into a barking fit.

The dog only barked like that when something scared him.

"You expecting someone?"

"No."

Garrett set her on her feet and started through the house.

She hurried after him. "What are you doing?"

"Seeing who's here."

She trailed him to the front door, where Ticket kicked up a fuss, bouncing up and down and howling like hell had come to call. "You think he heard someone?"

"Ticket is smart." As soon as he patted the dog, Ticket sat down and stopped barking. "See?"

"But I don't get any visitors." And maybe that's why Garrett looked so protective.

He opened the door...and there stood his father with his fist raised to knock.

The two men stared at each other, and Zoey felt her face go bright red.

After all, it was the butt-crack of dawn, she was badly rumpled, and Garrett wore only jeans. No way could his father misinterpret.

Trying to brazen out the embarrassing situation, Zoey said, "Mr. Hudson, good morning!" She peered around Garrett's bare shoulder. "How nice of you to visit."

Garrett choked.

Morgan, big beast of a man that he was, gave a slow

grin and clapped his son on the shoulder. "I'm not going away, so you might as well invite me in."

Silent, Garrett stepped back, opened the door wider and gestured for him to enter.

Ticket, the little rat, was the only one thrilled for the company.

GARRETT CALLED THE station to say he was running late, pulled on his shirt, socks and shoes and joined Zoey and his dad in the kitchen. He got there just as the coffee finished.

Giving one last pat to the dog, his dad gave him the once-over. "I was just telling Zoey how nice the place looks."

Garrett glanced at her, saw the high color in her cheeks deepen and had to smile. "We've been working on it."

"You don't say."

"Dad." He accepted a mug of coffee from Zoey and handed another to his father. "You're embarrassing her."

They both looked at Zoey, and she froze.

"Oh, no," she spluttered. In a too-high voice, she said, "I'm fine," and froze again.

Garrett pulled out a chair for her, urged her into it and bent to kiss the top of her head. "You remember my dad, Zoey?"

She bobbed her head hard. Reacting to her uncertainty, Ticket sat next to her chair and kept a watchful eye on things.

Yeah, Morgan Hudson had that effect on a lot of people. He'd been sheriff for a long time, and if the stories Garrett had heard were true, a badass longer than that. Few realized that overall, his dad was a big softie.

Not that anyone would believe him if he told them so. In his early sixties, his dad was still a brick wall of a man: tall, solid, unfaltering in his role as protector.

All in all, the best of dads.

"He used to be the sheriff back when we were kids," Garrett told Zoey. "Now he's the mayor."

She bobbed her head again. "I know. Amber caught me up."

"I knew you were a friend of Amber's." He nodded at Garrett. "Didn't know about this, though."

"Dad…" Garrett warned again—not that it would do him any good.

After sipping his coffee, Morgan asked, "You remember me as a fair man, Zoey?"

"Of course."

"Good. That'll make this easier."

Garrett wondered if they'd dealt with each other back when Gus died. Likely. For as long as he could remember his dad had been a pillar of the community. Whenever something happened, Morgan Hudson was there taking control and working out problems.

Was it a problem that had brought him here today?

Muscles tensing, Garrett put a hand on Zoey's shoulder. "Don't let him make you nervous."

"No, of course not." Her smile was about as nervous as it could get.

His dad gave him that look, the one that said all kinds of shit a son didn't want to hear, especially when he was full-grown and well past needing lectures.

"Did Amber send you here?"

Folding his arms on the table, his dad said, "No, why would she?"

"No reason." Interesting, that Amber hadn't told their

dad about him seeing Zoey. Maybe she still had hopes of him backing off.

If so, she was doomed to disappointment.

Garrett straddled his own seat. "So then why the visit?"

Instead of answering, he told Zoey, "I'm here on unofficial business. Do you want Garrett here, or would you rather talk privately?"

Stiffening from his toes to his ears, Garrett scowled. "I'm not going anywhere."

"Not up to you," Morgan told him.

Garrett turned to her...and saw her stricken expression. "Zoey?"

Eyes closed, she whispered, "Someone complained about me being here?"

"Complained—and made some accusations."

"The Donahues," Garrett growled. Damn it. What was wrong with those people?

Morgan ignored him. "I'm here as a courtesy, okay? To *you*, not them."

She nodded, swallowed. "Thank you."

"You're going to open shop?"

The switch threw her. "Pet grooming." Straightening her shoulders, she met Morgan's gaze. "Everything is legal, all my permits in order, everything to code."

He looked around again. "I assume you plan to live here, too?"

"With my mom."

Garrett had no doubt Morgan already knew about her mother being hurt, but he briefly filled him in anyway. "She should be able to come home by the end of the month."

"I'm glad she's doing better."

"Thank you." Zoey shifted with impatience. "I don't mean to be rude, but why are you here exactly?"

After turning his coffee cup, giving himself a moment to think, Morgan looked at each of them. "There was some trouble at the grocery?"

Dropping back in her seat, Zoey laughed.

Garrett didn't. "I was there."

"Really?" Raising his brows, Morgan said, "I must've missed that part."

"I don't want any trouble," Zoey said. "Not with anyone. I'm just here to take care of my mom."

Garrett felt a pang in his heart. Yeah, he knew that was why she'd returned. But hopefully she'd want to stay…for him.

CHAPTER SIX

INSULTED ON HER BEHALF, Garrett took Zoey's hand. "I can tell you exactly what happened." While explaining how well Zoey had handled the ugly confrontation, he felt incredible pride. "Because I knew it might be uncomfortable for Zoey, I was already leading her in the opposite direction. Carrie caused the confrontation, and she was damned nasty about it, too."

"I don't doubt it." Morgan finished off his coffee. "The Donahues aren't great at taking blame."

Zoey didn't understand. "Blame for what?"

Garrett shared a look with his dad. "Anything." A lot of people thought the Donahues needed to spend more time parenting and less time excusing bad behavior.

She shook her head. "If you didn't buy in to the accusations, then why are you—"

"To give you a heads-up that they might cause more trouble. I thought you were out here all alone." Now he looked at Garrett. "It's an isolated piece of land. Not far by car, but the nearest neighbor is a good two miles away."

"I have a phone," she reminded him.

"Storms knock out reception all the time."

Wearing an indulgent expression, Zoey asked, "Are you trying to scare me?"

"A little fear is a good thing."

She laughed. "It's not like the Donahues are psychos, or like Buckhorn is a hotbed of crime."

"No," Garrett agreed. "But we have had the occasional problem."

"And putting the Donahues aside, any woman alone in an isolated place has to use extra care." He looked at Garrett. "Until you get some security lights up and maybe an alarm system, it wouldn't hurt to have some company."

Meaning he should stick around and ensure her safety? Garrett had no problem with that. He wanted to be with Zoey, and no way would he let anyone hassle her.

But damn it, she'd spelled it out—her plate was full and she didn't have time for anything more involved with him. He was already pushing his luck staying over so often. If he got too intrusive, it might spook her.

As Amber had said, he could be the first responsibility she shook off.

His dad, though, didn't seem to have the same concern. "Should I take it you'll be around some?"

"Some," Garrett said through his teeth.

Which only made Morgan grin. "You know that youngest Donahue boy has a tendency to get in over his head."

"Yeah." He did know it. And in fact, he had some suspicions when it came to Cody Donahue.

"I personally think he's looking for attention, but—"

"I know. Tough to get through to Mr. and Mrs. Donahue."

"I can take care of myself," Zoey suddenly interjected with emphasis.

Garrett hadn't realized she was gathering steam until

he looked at her. Then he saw the stubbornness, and the independence.

She said she'd been looking after her mom since her dad died. By now she probably thought she didn't need anyone.

He'd have to find a way to convince her otherwise, but without being too obvious. "It can't hurt to take extra precautions."

Without looking at him, she said to his dad, "Thanks to the work Garrett's done here, the locks are all up-to-date. And of course, I have Ticket."

The dog jumped up to her lap, looked at Garrett and then at Morgan and let his tongue loll out.

Laughing, Morgan sent Garrett a look that said *I tried*. He pushed back his chair. "If anything comes up, let me know."

Setting the dog back on the floor, Zoey stood, too. With a lot of suspicion, she asked, "Is that the job of the mayor?"

"Around here, everyone seems to think everything is my job."

"I don't."

"Because you're new, I reckon." Morgan bent to give the dog a few more strokes. "But in this case, I head up the COCP program."

"Community organized crime prevention," Garrett explained. "Basically it's made up of residents and local agencies working together on crime, delinquency, vandalism, that sort of thing."

"You're part of it?" she asked him.

He nodded. "Shohn, too, since he's a park ranger."

"And Adam keeps an eye on things at the school." Morgan shrugged. "When everyone stays in touch with everyone else, things get figured out sooner rather than later."

Covering her face, she muttered, "The whole town is going to be in my business."

"Part of the charm of Buckhorn County," his dad told her with a squeeze to her shoulder. "Nice dog, by the way."

That got her to stop hiding behind her hands. "Thank you. He's wonderful."

As if he understood her, Ticket started wiggling all over again.

Morgan smiled. "I think you'll do a real nice business here, Zoey. Jordan already told me you have a way with animals."

His uncle Jordan had liked her on the spot. Anyone who took in a stray won him over, but Zoey was so sweet, who wouldn't love her? Sick babies, stray dogs… every guy with a pulse.

For certain, he wasn't immune.

Damn it.

While Garrett struggled internally, his dad started for the door, so he and Zoey followed with Ticket bounding behind them.

"The nearest groomer is a county over. You'll be more convenient, and the setup looks great—for a business. Living out here, though…" Concern still showing, he said again, "Be extra careful, okay?"

Before Zoey could answer, Garrett put his arm around her. "We will."

Amused at his obvious predicament, his dad grinned. "If you need any help advertising your grand opening, give a yell." He paused with the door half-open. "You'll be at the fireman's fund-raiser?"

"Garrett invited me and my mom."

"He did, huh?" His dad raised a brow. "Guess we'll all get to know you better then—if we don't have a chance to visit before that."

Which was code for *you should have brought her home for dinner already*, and *your mother is going to kick your butt if you don't take care of that real soon*.

"In fact, I'm betting the majority of the town will greet you warmly." His gaze met Garrett's. "The men are all real friendly that way."

When Garrett worked his jaw, his dad added, "The women, too, of course."

Nodding, Zoey said, "Thank you again, Mr. Hudson."

"Call me Morgan." He drew her in for a hug, winked at Garrett and finally left.

Garrett checked the time. He was going to be even later than he'd figured on, but he knew what he had to do.

He caught Zoey's shoulders. "We need to reconfigure our plan."

"Our plan?"

Meaning to keep it light, he kissed her—but yeah, that never worked with Zoey. Half a minute later, both of them breathing deeply, he said, "That whole business of taking it one day at a time?"

"What about it?" She pushed back from him. "Are you changing your mind just because your dad is trying to pressure you? I'm still fine with us just being friends."

He'd moved beyond the friend stage a day after meeting her. Now he just needed her to catch up. "Friends who have sex day and night."

She gasped in accusation. "You don't want to have sex anymore?"

Silly Zoey. Did she really think he could give that up? Give *her* up? "I want it to be exclusive."

She snapped her mouth shut.

Garrett dared another kiss, and managed to keep that one under fifteen seconds. "The longer you're here, the more people you'll meet." And his dad was right; guys would hit on her at the fireman's fund-raiser. "You and me," he said with insistence as he started away. "Friends with benefits, as long as we're only benefiting each other."

He gathered up his hat and his keys, and stooped to say goodbye to Ticket.

When he straightened, Zoey still stood in that exact spot. Did being exclusive scare her so much?

He tipped up her chin, and this time said more softly, "You and me."

Eyes huge, she bit her lip, and finally, *finally*, after torturing him with a long, searching stare, she gave a small nod. "You and me."

Progress, he thought.

One day at a time.

ZOEY AWOKE SUDDENLY, aware of Garrett sprawled beside her. Given the shadows in the room, it was super early still. They'd be doing the fireman's fund-raiser later, but they still had time.

Trying not to disturb him, she turned her head and took in the sight of his long, strong body. On his side facing her, his hairy thigh against her hip, his hand curved over her naked breast, he remained deeply asleep.

His long, thick lashes hid those incandescent blue eyes that never failed to melt her heart. Rumpled dark hair just added to his sexiness, as did the whiskers on his jaw.

She wouldn't mind waking next to him every day for the rest of her life.

Lately, things had been…surreal. Better than she'd ever known was possible.

After demanding that exclusive agreement—and really, who would she want other than Garrett?—he'd decided she needed to spend more time with his family, too. Not just the cousins, but his parents, his uncles and aunts. They were all so welcoming, treating her not as the town pariah, but more like someone very special.

He'd also made several trips with her to the hospital to visit her mother. Once he even stopped by without her, dropping off flowers that had put a smile on her mother's face for days.

Her house was now freshly painted, many repairs done and her business was ready to open. She still had some big projects to do, but thanks to Garrett—*oh, Garrett*—all the plumbing worked, the electrical was safe and the dock had been rebuilt.

He was just plain amazing. Tireless when it came to lending a hand.

Or sex. He was especially tireless then.

She didn't know how a guy could be more wonderful.

Ticket felt the same, always greeting Garrett with howls and a thumping tail when he got home from work. It warmed her heart, how much the dog loved him.

And it scared her a little, because she was starting to feel the same.

The hand on her breast moved, cuddling a little…and it was no longer just his leg she felt on her hip.

"You big faker," she whispered. "You're awake."

"I felt you looking at me." Still without opening his eyes, he brushed his thumb over her nipple, making her shiver. "What time is it?"

"I don't know." She twisted to see the clock…and instead found Ticket standing beside the bed looking at her.

She'd long since removed the gate in the kitchen, giving the dog the choice of where to sleep, but he repeatedly returned to the same spot where she'd first put him, what she and Garrett now referred to as Ticket's corner.

As soon as the dog saw her move, he barked.

Groaning, Garrett released her to stretch. "I take it he wants out."

Usually that would get a resounding yap from Ticket. Not this time.

He growled, reared back on his haunches and whined.

"What the hell?" Garrett sat up, looked at Ticket and threw back the sheet. "Something's wrong."

Having the same feeling, Zoey took only one second to admire Garrett's body as he yanked on jeans, without underwear. She grabbed for her housecoat, but Ticket was already racing down the hallway, barking in excitement, before she'd even gotten her arms in the sleeves.

Without waiting for her, Garrett followed him.

"Damn it." Zoey hastily pulled on panties then tied the belt to the housecoat. Figuring she was decent enough, she ran after them.

Gray dawn struggled through the fog, leaving too many shadows in the yard. The morning mist in the air kept the porch light from traveling very far.

With Ticket hooked to his leash, Garrett stepped out with him…and saw the smoke coming from her ramshackle shed.

He thrust the leash at Zoey, said "Stay here," and took off. Barefoot. Into the darkness.

And possible danger.

"Damn it," she said again, more meanly this time.

Ticket had a fit, jerking and pulling at the leash when she went back in for a flashlight and her phone. It took her less than a minute, but when she got back outside she saw her small shed engulfed in fire.

And there was Garrett, backlit by the flames, leading a reluctant Cody Donahue toward the house.

Oh, no. Just what she didn't need.

Her heart sank, especially when she got a good look at Cody's face. The boy was lost, and if someone didn't intercede, he could end up with the same needless fate as Gus.

Blowing out a long breath, Zoey knew she'd have to take on one more responsibility.

And it was going to be a doozy.

When Garrett reached her, he said in a voice as placid as the lake, "Don't let Ticket loose, okay? The fire should burn itself out, especially with everything still dew-wet. But we don't want him near it."

Straining away from Garrett's hold, Cody avoided her gaze.

She held the door open for both of them.

Like her, Ticket watched with quiet sympathy until they were inside, then he started sniffing the grass.

Zoey gave him plenty of time to do his business… while also giving Garrett plenty of time to do his. She assumed he'd call the sheriff, maybe the fire station…

she wasn't sure, but there'd definitely be some confusion going on.

When Ticket finished up, she went into the kitchen. With the phone to his ear, Garrett stood behind Cody, who sat at the table. He had a hand on the boy's shoulder, and to Zoey the touch looked more like reassurance than restraint.

When she caught part of the conversation, she knew it was Cody's father Garrett spoke to.

"This was a courtesy call, Mr. Donahue, that's all."

A raised voice came over the line. Garrett waited, occasionally giving Cody a squeeze.

"No, you may not come get him. He'll be at the sheriff's station." Garrett nodded. "Sure, call your lawyer if that's what you want to do. No, I'm sorry, but there's no mistake." Again he squeezed. "I caught him myself, Mr. Donahue. He still had the lighter in his hand."

Zoey unleashed Ticket, who decided to lay by Cody's chair, then she went about making coffee. She and Garrett finished up at the same time.

To give them some privacy, she said, "I'll go get dressed."

He nodded, and then to Cody, asked, "You drink coffee?"

"No."

"Want a cola then?"

Stubbornness and suspicion hunched his shoulders. "I guess."

"Don't run," Garrett said when he released him. "It'll only piss me off and this is bad enough already."

"I wasn't going to."

Feeling far too emotional, Zoey went on down the hall. By the time she'd dressed, the deputy had arrived, along with a fire truck and Morgan Hudson. The yard was busy, the kitchen busier. And all she could think about was how Garrett had handled Cody.

He hadn't bullied him, or hurled accusations. He'd been compassionate but firm.

God, she loved him. Like crazy, over-the-top, never-going-to-end love.

In for a penny, she decided... She'd do what she could for Cody.

And then she'd do what she could for herself...with Garrett.

THE MORNING WENT BY in a blur and Garrett stayed so busy he didn't get a chance to see Zoey after leaving the house with the deputy. He'd showered and shaved at his own place, and barely gotten to the fund-raiser on time. Now, behind a booth grilling corn on the cob, games all around him, a dance stage set up across the way, his thoughts divided a dozen different ways.

Number one, he wanted to throttle Cody's dad. The man had made a big production of insisting Cody was innocent no matter the evidence, no matter Garrett himself being an eyewitness. When his rude blustering got him nowhere, he turned on Cody, loudly complaining that he didn't have time to waste on nonsense.

Cody's dad was so opposite his own that Garrett couldn't fathom what it must have been like for him growing up. Losing a brother, having a father who made excuses, but didn't take time for him.

That led him to number two, because he wanted to take Cody under his wing and maybe help him see a better way. Cody needed to know he wasn't a waste of time. He could still make amends and get on a better path before he hurt himself or someone else. Though he thought for sure it was Cody responsible for the fire by the lake, and no doubt in the woods, too, he hadn't been busted on anything else. With a little guidance, he just might be able to get it together.

And thinking of better people led him to number three. Zoey. He wanted to cement their relationship, to have her actually commit to him. He wanted that bad.

A few minutes later, there she was, wearing a pretty sundress and sandals, her silky brown hair dancing in the breeze. Garrett set aside his tongs and watched her sway to the loud music blaring over the park. Did she dance?

He wouldn't mind holding her to a slow song when he got a break.

Her mother was in a wheelchair pushed by her uncle. They paused at a booth to get colas, smiling and taking in the crowd. Zoey bent to say something to her mom, smiled at some kids running past and pointed at balloons.

Garrett pushed back his hat, his heart already tripping. She had that effect on him. Every single time.

Moseying along with her mom and uncle, she searched the crowd. When she saw him, she stopped dead in her tracks. Color rushed into her cheeks and she sank her teeth into that plump bottom lip. Two seconds later she put her shoulders back.

Huh.

After saying something to her uncle, she started toward him.

Wondering what she was up to, Garrett nudged Noel, said, "Be right back," and left the booth.

He met Zoey halfway across the main entrance to the park. "Hey."

"Hey." Clearly keyed up about something, she stared at him. "Do you have a minute?"

The serious way she asked that left him uneasy. He searched her face. "Is something wrong?" Was she still upset over the fire that morning? "I can rebuild the shed, you know."

A smile flickered. "I know. It's fine." She poked him. "At least the snakes are gone, right?"

"You live in the woods, honey. There will always be snakes."

Wrinkling her nose, she said, "Thanks. Just what I needed to know."

"Forget about snakes. You're upset." And trying to hide it. "What's going on?"

She shored herself up with a big breath. "This morning, when I saw you with Cody Donahue, I made up my mind. About two things actually. And because you'll want to come home with me again after the fundraiser—"

"Damn right I will." Someone bumped into him. He glanced back and saw the line for the corn had grown. Noel looked harassed, especially with the music even louder now.

"Come here." He moved them both away from the growing line and noise and, to be clear, stated, "I *am* coming home with you."

She nodded. "I know. And I want you to. It's just—"

"If this is about the Donahues giving you a hard time—" Had she thought he went too easy on Cody? No, he couldn't believe that. Zoey was the most compassionate person he knew. She was also a woman wrongly targeted. "You know I'm on your side, right?"

"Oh, Garrett." She hugged him tight. "I loved how you dealt with Cody. That's actually one of the decisions I made."

"I don't understand."

Pushing back from him, she seemed to screw up her courage, then spoke in a rush of words that ran together. "I'm sorry because I know the timing is off and my mother is waiting and you have duties, but I haven't seen you since I made up my mind to do this, and if I don't do it now I might chicken out, so…"

"Hold up." This sounded serious, so maybe a little privacy was in order. Taking her arm, he steered her over to a park bench, out of the glaring sunshine. He ignored onlookers. He especially ignored Noel trying to get his attention. "Now." He wasn't entirely sure he wanted to know, but he asked anyway. "What's going on?"

She sucked in a very deep breath, then exhaled on a blurted, "I was wrong."

Uneasiness cut into him, tightening his jaw. "About?"

"Being friends with benefits."

Feeling lethal, and a little desperate, he reminded her, "You're the one who insisted on those benefits."

"I know!" She thrust out her hands. *"But I can't be just friends anymore."*

Getting a breath wasn't easy, so he just narrowed his eyes and waited.

"Garrett," she pleaded. "Don't look like that. I realize there's probably some right way to do this, but you know I was never any good at social etiquette."

"Screw etiquette." She didn't need to pretty it up

512 BACK TO BUCKHORN

for him. He wanted her to say it so he could get started convincing her otherwise. "Just spit it out."

"I'm messing this up so badly." She took his hand. "I *do* want you for a friend, yes."

Damn it. No way could he do that, not after being so much more.

"And sex, *yes*."

Okay, wait.

"But…"

With his heart suddenly thundering, Garrett nudged her. "But?"

She winced. "Am I being too bold?"

"No." *Be bold, Zoey.*

Behind them, Noel called out, "A little help here?"

He glanced back. Damn. Did everyone in Buckhorn want buttered corn? Looked like. Luckily, Amber strolled up to the booth just then. He saw Noel gesturing toward him, and he knew his sister would pitch in. When she sent him a thumbs-up, letting him know she had it covered, he nodded his gratitude.

Turning back to Zoey, he said, "Go on."

Uncertainty darkened her eyes.

"Hey." He smoothed her lips with his. "Remember, honey, you can tell me anything." And one way or another, he'd work it out with her.

"Right." Like a soldier, she came to attention and said quickly, "I care for you way beyond just being friends."

Now that was more like it. Satisfaction brought him closer, but he needed to hear her say it. "Tell me how much."

Her lips trembled. So did her small smile. She started to speak, but something beyond his shoulder caught her attention. She glanced there, then tipped her head for a longer look. "You know how I said I made two decisions?"

"Yeah."

She stood. "I'm sorry, but I need to take care of that second one right now."

No way. Halting her retreat, Garrett stood, too, followed her line of vision...and saw Carrie approaching. *Damn it, not now.*

Stiff and formal, Carrie stopped in front of him. She made a point of not looking at Zoey. "I knew you'd be here. I need to talk to you."

Sympathy weighed on him, but he had no idea what he could tell her.

Zoey knew. Smiling gently, she stepped around him to face Carrie. "I was hoping to see you here."

"I DON'T WANT to talk to you."

Though Carrie tried to turn away, Zoey saw the heartache in her eyes. "I know you're hurting." Talking over the music wasn't easy. The dancers had spilled from the stage to all around it.

Half urging, half pushing, she got Carrie to the bench they'd just vacated, then took her hand and didn't let go.

Scowling, Carrie strained away from her. "What are you doing?"

"I can't imagine losing a brother."

That stalled Carrie's animosity. "Gus is gone forever."

"I know." She'd been living with that fact for a very long time. "The thing is, Cody is still here."

"I know." She looked up at Garrett. "That's what I wanted to talk to you—"

"He's on the wrong path." Zoey regained her attention by saying, "And you know it."

She shook her head. "No, he just—"

"You might be the only family he has who knows it. He needs you, Carrie. He needs someone to care enough to not make excuses."

Carrie blanched. "I don't—"

"He needs you to start paying attention."

Taking that like a slap, Carrie said, "I'm not responsible for what he did!"

"Just as I wasn't responsible for what Gus did?"

When Carrie's bottom lip quivered, Zoey patted her hand.

"Believe me, I wish I had it to do over. I would have called the sheriff before Gus left. I would have called you. I would have…I don't know. Taken his keys."

At that, Carrie shared a tearful laugh with Zoey, because they both knew that hadn't been an option. For as long as she'd known him, Gus was a rage waiting to happen.

Taking the shared laugh as an opening, Zoey reached out for Carrie's other hand, too. "Unfortunately, we don't get do-overs. All we have is here and now, and your other brother, Cody, is here, *now*."

Carrie whispered, "I don't know what to do."

Looking over her shoulder at Garrett, Zoey said, "I bet you have a few ideas." She couldn't be wrong about that.

He looked surprised to be drawn in, but reassured her by agreeing. "I've been thinking about it."

Zoey beamed at him. "I knew you would."

"Yeah, you know me pretty well." He rested a hand on her shoulder. "I can't guarantee anything, but it's possible we could convince the sheriff to let Cody do some community time at the fire station. I wouldn't go easy on him. He needs to apologize to Zoey and rebuild the shed he burned. He needs to learn there are repercussions to the things he does."

"And," Zoey added, "he needs to understand the harm fire can do. It's not something he can play with."

Garrett nodded. "It won't be a picnic, but it'd be better than time in juvie."

Tears welled in Carrie's eyes. "You'd do that for him?"

So pleased that she almost couldn't contain herself, Zoey said, "Of course he would."

Garrett drew Zoey closer. "You'd have to convince your parents, and Carrie, we both know that's not going to be easy."

More resolute now, Carrie said, "Somehow I'll take care of it." She swallowed hard and admitted, "They mostly don't want to be bothered."

"He has you," Zoey told her. "Right?"

"Yes." Two shuddering breaths later, she managed a small smile and said to Zoey, "I don't understand you."

"You don't need to, as long as you understand Cody."

This time it was Carrie who squeezed Zoey's hands. "Thank you."

Content with how that had gone, Zoey watched her walk away.

Until Garrett tipped up her chin. "You were saying something about decisions?"

Wow, he'd jumped right back to that. "Yeah, um, decisions."

"I get that you decided to help Cody."

"Yes. That was one of my decisions. He's still young and his family is not easy—"

"And you know something about that, don't you?"

She did. "I knew you'd understand."

His smile seemed to touch her heart. "What else, honey?"

"I decided about you, too." If she didn't hurry it up he'd miss the entire fund-raiser because of her. "I don't mean to rush you, but I've decided that I want more."

He kissed her bottom lip, touched his tongue to her. "More with you? I like that idea."

Her heart stammered then stalled. "Not just sex." Then she amended, "Not that sex with you is ever *just* sex. That's not what I mea—"

"I love you, Zoey."

Her jaw dropped, but she recovered quickly. "That's what I was trying to say to you!"

Sinking his hands into her hair, he kissed her more urgently.

"You two are causing a scene."

They broke apart to see Shohn grinning down at them.

Garrett said, "Go help Amber and Noel with the damn corn."

"Right." He winked at Zoey, clapped Garrett on the shoulder and headed toward the booth.

Glad for the reprieve, Zoey rushed to say, "I'm not trying to pressure you. You have a house and I have a house and my mom is moving in and... Everything doesn't have to change right away. We could ease into things. Keep doing what we've been doing, because that's really working for me."

"Me, too."

"We could keep taking it one day at a time..."

Garrett hauled her close and kissed her quiet. "One day at a time works for me—as long as here on out each day is with you." Then he said it again. "Because I love you."

She squeezed him tight. "I am so glad I came back to Buckhorn."

"It's where you belong," Garrett whispered. "Here—with me."

AMBER WAS SO BUSY watching her brother, she kept bumping into Noel. Not a terrible thing at all.

When Shohn came around the booth and started tying on an apron, she said, "I love it when a plan comes together."

Shohn gave her a look. "Been scheming again, huh?"

Smug, she said, "Think maybe we could make it a double wedding?"

He glanced at Noel. "You getting married?"

Noel choked.

Amber felt her face go hot, but she ignored it. "I meant you and Nadine, Garrett and Zoey."

"Hey, I'm game. Nadine and I are ready to set the date anyway. But you'll have to corral the others."

"I can handle that." She smiled…until she saw Noel shaking his head at her.

So he thought she was a busybody? So what. She gave him a look of disdain and asked, "Want to dance?"

Shohn's brows went up.

Noel just smiled as he handed his tongs to Shohn. "Thought you'd never ask."

* * * * *

Enjoy a sneak peek from
A SEAL'S TEMPTATION
by New York Times *bestselling author Tawny Weber,*
another fun sexy story in the
UNIFORMLY HOT! *miniseries.*

Navy SEAL Shane O'Brian is on a mission—
to seduce Lark Sommers—
but neither of them realizes
this could be more than a fling...
On sale in September 2015 from Harlequin Blaze.

Prologue

"HEY, LARK. WE NEED two double-whipped, triple-caramel mocha lattes. And one of those passionflower tarts." Cassia Moore leaned over the counter, then said in a faux whisper, "You know, the ones your Aunt Heather makes. She told me the ingredients are enough to make a girl irresistible to any man."

"Heather said what?" Lark Sommers stopped in the act of ringing up the order to stare.

"Hey," Sara O'Brian hissed at the same time, smacking her cousin on the shoulder. "I thought you said that was a secret."

"Right, like Lark doesn't know what she's selling in her own coffeehouse," Cassia said, rolling her eyes.

Before Lark could admit that no, she actually didn't know what her aunt had her selling in the coffeehouse, Cassia continued.

"Besides, I haven't had sex in eight days. That's more than a week. At this rate I might forget my best moves." The redhead sounded as if she was about to cry.

And knowing Cassia, Lark Sommers figured she probably was. The only thing Cassia Moore loved more than herself was sex.

Still...

"C'mon, Cassia, you know better than to listen to Heather's crazy talk," Lark chided.

"Then they aren't real?" Cassia huffed. "But I need sex. Soon. Today. Now. Otherwise, I'm going to lose my mind."

"Oh, hush," Sara said. "Do you think everyone in The Magic Beans wants to know that you're desperate?"

"Desperate? You go a week without sex and see how you feel."

It only hurt for the first thirty weeks. But Lark didn't figure sharing that little tidbit would help. As the cousins bickered, she tried to remember what went into a double-whipped, triple-caramel mocha latte. And why wasn't regular coffee good enough for people?

Lark bit her lip, and as soon as she was sure that the two women were totally engrossed with their debate, she slid her cheat sheet out from its hiding place.

After a quick glance at the ingredients and steps, she began measuring, whipping, mixing and stirring. As she so often did over the past year, Lark felt as if she'd fallen down a very dark rabbit hole.

She pursed her lips, studying the only part of the café that felt like her—a wall of shelves holding ceramic cups, bowls, mugs and dishes. She'd made them for her mom when the older woman had decided to open a coffeehouse. Scattered around the place on high shelves and display cabinets were a few bigger pieces that she'd shipped from her studio in San Francisco. Guilt pieces, she called them, because she'd sent them instead of taking time out of her busy life and dream career to visit her mom's new home in Idaho.

"Lark, if you did believe in magic, would you think it was okay to use it to get a guy naked?" Sara asked as Lark filled the mugs with the mocha-caramel-caffeine mixture.

"Nope. I'm not getting between the two of you." Grabbing the whipped cream dispenser, Lark shook her head. When a single strand of hair, black and silky, slid out of her French braid, she blew it out of her way.

"Okay, fine," Sara said, shooting her cousin a sideways look. "How about this question. Do you think it's okay to talk about your lack of sex in public?"

"It depends," she said with a shrug.

"Depends on what?"

"On whether the discussion is between good friends or virtual strangers. On if it's held in quiet, considerate tones or put out there loud enough for the guy in the corner to hear."

The three women glanced across The Magic Beans. Seated in the corner at a table made of a tree stump was an older man. But he wasn't paying any attention to them, so obviously the sex talk hadn't reached his ears.

"But most of all," Lark added when the other two women turned to face her again, "it depends on if one of the friends is getting sex and the other isn't."

"Ha, there you go." Cassia poked Sara in the shoulder. "See, it's okay to talk about how devastating it is that I haven't had sex in over a week."

"Devastating?" Sara rolled her eyes. "I haven't had a date, let alone sex, in three months."

"Boo-hoo to both of you," Lark said with a laugh.

"I've been in dry dock for seventeen months, eleven days and—" she glanced at her watch "—nine hours."

"And you're not stark raving crazy?" Cassia eyed Lark as if expecting her to burst into maniacal laughter or run around the cozy café, screaming her head off.

Or worse, curl up behind the counter and cry. Which, Lark acknowledged with a sigh, was a possibility that grew stronger every day.

But not over sex.

Before she had to admit that, or react to the pitying look on her friends' faces, the door chimed.

"Well, well, what have we here? Three lovely ladies and coffee. What more could a man want?"

"Eww," muttered Cassia.

Sara pulled a face.

Lark barely managed to keep her smile in place as Paul Devarue approached the counter. The banker's pale gray suit did nothing to disguise his bulk, nor did his carefully styled hair hide the fact that he was balding.

Lark told herself not to hold any of that against him. Nor should she blame him for his ongoing campaign to convince her to sell her mother's coffeehouse so he could demolish Raine Sommers's legacy to put in a mini-mall. As he so often said, that was only business.

"Good morning, Paul," she said. "What can I get for you?" she asked. "Your regular? Black coffee, large, and a banana hazelnut muffin?"

"Coffee and a muffin sounds just right. The perfect start to the morning."

Lark glanced at the funky clock on the wall, a mosaic of coffee beans with spoons for hands, and gave a thought to the time in her life when she'd called 10:00 a.m. the start of the morning.

"Did you want it to go?" she asked, lifting the lid of the domed dessert dish and grabbing the largest muffin.

"Here is fine. With business so slow, I'm sure you can keep me company for a while."

Oh, goody. Lark filled a rich-purple mug with coffee and tried not to grimace. That sounded about as fun as being kicked in the gut by a scary clown during a tax audit.

Or barring that, having a pity party over her nonexistent sex life.

"I HATE THAT GUY. He's such a jerk." Her eyes narrow with suspicion, Sara watched the smarmy banker lean forward. "Look at how he's getting in her space."

"Quit worrying," Cassia said. "It's not like he's hitting on her."

"Worse. He's nagging at her. And if he keeps at it long enough, she'll sell him The Magic Beans. If she does, she'll move away. Then what?"

Misery was what.

Sara would lose her best friend. Lark was everything Sara wanted to be. She had a degree in Fine Arts; she'd owned a chic apartment in San Francisco and worked in a fancy art gallery and attended art shows there featuring her own pottery.

And she'd given it up for family. Lark had come to Little Lake, Idaho, a year and a half ago because her mom was sick. When Raine Sommers's flu had turned out to be cancer, Lark had stayed. First to take care of her mother, then after Raine passed, to take over running The Magic Beans.

Sara thought Lark was the strongest woman she knew.

"Well, she's not happy," Cassia pointed out. "She

puts on a good face and all. But she's working her tail off to keep this place going."

Sara winced. "She promised Raine that she'd keep it going."

"Lark shouldn't be miserable just because she made a deathbed promise." Cassia shook her head. "That's, like, medieval. And speaking of medieval, can you believe she hasn't had sex in eighteen months?"

"Seventeen months, eleven days and nine hours," Sara corrected. Then, frowning, she added, "Maybe ten by now."

"No wonder she's unhappy. I mean, can you imagine going that long?" Cassia gave an exaggerated shudder.

"Well, her heart was broken," Sara pointed out. "Between her mom and that jerk, Eric, she's had a lot to deal with."

Eric had been Lark's sexy San Francisco guy. They'd been practically engaged, and he'd cheated on her the first week she'd been in Idaho. Worse, Lark had found out when a friend posted New Year's pictures on Facebook—one of which was her true love with his lips plastered on a busty blonde's mouth and his hands on her butt.

"That's the answer," Cassia exclaimed, slapping her hand on the table.

"What's the answer?" she asked.

"Sex."

Sara blinked.

"Sex?"

"Yeah. You know, the horizontal boogie? "

"How is sex going to help Lark's situation?"

"Lark needs sex," Cassia explained patiently, pushing aside her coffee mug, only half-empty. "It'll give her a boost. If she's boosted enough, she'll be able to figure out what she wants to do with her life, and let's face it, she'll feel damned good."

"So you're saying if we get Lark some sort of date that she'll stick around? I mean, that she'll be happy," Sara corrected, not wanting to sound selfish.

"It can't hurt," Cassia said with a wicked smile. "Now, let's figure out who to hook her up with."

"Someone with a good sense of humor," Sara decided as she nibbled her bottom lip. "Lark's had it rough the past couple of years, so someone who makes her laugh would be nice."

"We want someone with stamina. A guy who can give her a dozen orgasms in one night, and still greet her the next morning with a breakfast boner."

"A breakfast…" Knowing her cheeks were turning pink, Sara shook her head.

"Yeah. Every woman deserves a once-in-a-lifetime guy. He needs to be temp, though. You know, transient. Otherwise Lark will get all emotionally involved and it could mess with her mind. "

"Good point," Sara agreed.

Lark's perfect guy, but temporary.

Sara's mind was racing. It could be one of those two-birds-with-one-stone deals. She'd help Lark, keep her best friend and fix a few family issues all at the same time. It was a crazy idea, but maybe…

"You thinking one of those online dating services?" Cassia asked.

"Nope." Sara waved a dismissive hand. "I've got the perfect guy for Lark."

1

The Present

"REPORT, O'BRIAN. DID YOU complete your mission?"

Petty Officer Shane O'Brian stood at attention. Shoulders back, chin high, eyes ahead.

"Yes, sir," he barked. "Completed with resources to spare."

"Is that so? And at any time did the target become aware of your mission?"

"Hell, no." Eyes dancing, Shane grinned. "He's as clueless as a newborn. Which, I've gotta tell you, is totally weird. Of all people, you'd think he'd be suspicious."

"Nice job." Shane's commander, Mitch Donovan slapped him on the back before dropping onto the couch. Resting his booted foot on the knee of his camouflage fatigues, Mitch laughed. "Gabriel's a wily SOB, but there's no way he'd expect an engagement party. Especially since the bride-to-be doesn't even know they're getting engaged."

"He's going to be so pissed," Shane observed, hand-ing Mitch the list of what had and hadn't been done so far.

"That you accessed his private information, evaluated his actions, went behind his back to report said information and actions, then compounded it by bringing multiple people into it in a way that will, when it comes out, be a huge slap in the face?" Mitch considered that, then nodded. "Yup. Seriously pissed."

"I can't wait." Laughing, Shane dropped into the chair opposite Mitch. Like most everything else in the apartment, the brown furniture was ugly, but it was comfortable. Shane figured that's all a person could ask for with base housing.

Both he and Mitch, along with their friend Gabriel— better known as Romeo to the SEAL team—had been assigned to the Coronado base a year ago. The three of them had bunked together until his buddies had hooked their perfect women. After they'd moved out, Shane hadn't seen any point in looking for other quarters— or in replacing the ugly furniture.

"You're sure he's going to propose?"

Shane simply raised one brow. They didn't call him Scavenger for nothing. There wasn't anything he couldn't find. Supplies, enemies, information.

"Right," Mitch said, shaking his head. "Of course you're sure. Which means he has no clue what you're planning."

"Oh, yeah, I'm sure." Shane said. "Nobody expects a party for getting engaged. Married, having a kid, okay. But for volunteering to hook on a ball and chain?" He gave a pitying shake of his head. Not over Gabriel landing Tessa, or that Mitch was newly married with a baby due any day. His friends had scored some great women.

But, Shane figured, the odds of military guys, SEALs especially, making it work long-term? Of finding a woman who got what they did, was okay living their life with a man who answered to Uncle Sam, put his life on the line on a regular basis and kept 90 percent of what he did to himself? Pretty much zilch.

Hell, he'd experienced issues himself in his family alone. His own mother was so pissed about his career, she refused to acknowledge it. To keep her happy, the entire family pretended he was a traveling salesman.

Shane frowned, taking the list from Mitch. He was better off without any more emotional crap in his life. Maybe his buddies would do better. But he doubted it.

Shane understood why his friends were making those choices. But those weren't the kind of choices he wanted to make.

So he'd make damned sure he didn't get himself in a situation that would call for them.

"Any thoughts on the ETA?"

"Not yet." Shane glanced over his list again. "He's bought the engagement ring, but you know Romeo. He's going to want to set the scene, make it something special. "

When the front door swung open, neither Shane nor Mitch had to school their expressions. They were experts at keeping their faces blank.

And in came Romeo, in all his glory. But if you knew to look, you could see a hint of smug terror in his eyes. Yeah, he deserved this party. Shane casually folded the list and stuck it in his pocket.

"Yo, Scavenger."

"Yo, Romeo?"

"Mail for you." Gabriel tossed a couple of envelopes

on Shane's lap on his way into the kitchen. "You got beer?"

Flipping through the envelopes, Shane waved to indicate he should help himself.

"Shit."

"What?" Mitch leaned forward.

"A letter from home."

Knowing Shane's family situation, Mitch gave a sympathetic grimace.

Shane stared at the flowery handwriting on the envelope, then tore it open. As he scanned his little sister's letter, his gut tightened.

"Well?"

"Huh?" He glanced at Mitch with a frown.

"The letter. What's wrong?"

"Drama. Sara's upset about the family rift. She wants me to come home for her birthday. Apparently she'll be miserable and her entire year ruined if I don't."

Shane frowned at Mitch's snicker.

"Go ahead, laugh. I have five sisters. If one blames me for her misery, they all will."

"So? You're what? Eight hundred miles or so away. They don't even acknowledge you're here. And it'd take a hell of a lot for them to storm the base and get to you."

"Maybe I can volunteer for a mission. Something far, far away," he muttered.

"Or maybe you can take some of that leave you have built up and go home," Mitch suggested. "Watch your sister blow out the candles, fix the mess with your mom."

"I'm already working on an assignment," he said defensively.

"An assignment that's on hold for the next two weeks.

Take a few days. Go home." Mitch waited a beat, then smiled. "Consider it an order."

"So, handsome... Wanna join the Mile High Club?"

Damning Mitch for making this an order, Shane peeled his eyes off the book he'd been trying to read. He slid a glance to his right in hopes that the whispered question hadn't been aimed at him.

But the big-haired blonde's hungry smile dashed those hopes all to hell. And in case he'd been too dim to catch a clue, she skimmed her fingers up his thigh.

Shane was a SEAL. He'd faced down terrorists, shot down enemy combatants and answered to cranky Admirals. He'd once jumped from a burning plane with a wounded soldier in his arms and a parachute on his back.

And he'd done it all with nerves of steel.

But faced with a predatory woman and he froze.

"I'm Barb, by the way." The lush blonde leaned closer. "Mmm, you have such an impressive body. I'll bet you work out a lot. "

"Whoa." Shane clamped down on the hand that was on the move. "Sorry. I'm going to have to pass."

"Now, why would you do that?" Barb gave him a wicked smile. "Don't you like adventures?"

Shane laughed. He couldn't help it.

"I live for adventures," he deadpanned. "I appreciate the offer, though."

As soon as the words were out, he cringed. *Appreciate the offer.* As if she'd just suggested he take the window seat and enjoy the view.

Shane didn't consider himself shy.

Shy was for girls and toddlers.

And it wasn't that he didn't know how to handle women. He was damned good when he put his hands on one. He was simply a quiet man who preferred to get the lay of the land, to get a feel for a person, before he opened up.

Barb the blonde took his refusal in good stride. Instead, she dived into a stream of chatter. Resigned, Shane tucked his book into the seat in front of him and gave her his attention.

But he was only half listening. The rest of him was making the mental adjustment from his life in California and his job as a SEAL with its military mindset to dealing with whatever was waiting for him when he got off this plane.

Since she hadn't returned any of the messages he'd left, he didn't know if Sara told anyone he was coming home or not. Either way, it wasn't going to be pretty. All warning would do was give his mom time to stew.

It'd been rough enough when his dad had died in a skydiving accident when Shane was seven. Then in Shane's senior year of high school his brother Mike, the oldest of the O'Brian siblings, had been killed in a drag racing accident.

Molly O'Brian was a strong woman. But the loss of her husband and her oldest son had devastated her. She couldn't handle the idea of her only remaining son, living in danger.

And Shane couldn't set his dream aside. Not even for his mother. When he'd joined the Navy right after graduation, she'd had a meltdown. But his joining the SEALs five years ago had been too much.

By the time he'd shaken off the blonde, deplaned and made his way through Boise Airport to baggage claim, he figured he should have argued harder with Mitch for a dangerous mission instead of this trip. Sara would have understood.

"Shane! You look so good. I missed you," Sara gushed as she hugged him.

Shane grinned back.

"Oh, Shane. I'm so, so happy to see you. You'll be here through next weekend, right?"

"What did mom have to say about my visiting?" he asked instead of committing himself.

He didn't need to hear her response. Her face said it all. Downcast eyes, a pouty lip and flushed cheeks.

"Sara—"

"Don't be mad," she said, her words spilling out. "I've got a place for you to stay until my birthday, then you'll pop in like the best present of my life. Mom will be so happy to see you that she won't have time to get upset."

He'd flown home. He'd met with his sister. He could pull a fifty out of his wallet, tell Sara it was her birthday gift and grab the next flight home. Technically, he'd followed orders.

And—he looked at Sara—he couldn't do it. His family ties were tenuous at best. He couldn't break them with the only person in the family who didn't pretend he was a traveling salesman.

LARK WAS PREOCCUPIED when she closed the coffeehouse at six.

As she cleaned the coffee and tea machines, she tried to imagine herself living back in San Francisco again. She was wiping down the last table when she heard a tapping on the glass.

"Sara," she exclaimed as she unlocked the door. "Did we have plans that I forgot about?"

"Nope. I'm here about the apartment. The one upstairs next to yours. You said I could put something in it this week, remember?" Sara's words were as upbeat and bouncy as her movements as she danced into the coffeehouse.

"Yeah, sure," Lark said, exchanging her sponge for the broom. The second floor housed two fully furnished apartments. Lark had taken one for herself. The other was usually rented out, but the tenants had moved the previous month. "What are you storing?"

"My brother."

Lark almost bobbled the broom.

"Your what?"

"Shane. My big brother."

"You want to put your brother upstairs? Why not at your mom's?" Then she narrowed her eyes. "Is he alive? Because I draw the line at storing dead bodies."

"Of course he's alive." Sara laughed, starting to help with the cleanup by grabbing a bag out of the trash can. "I dropped him at Sam's for a beer."

Lark glanced out the window toward the corner sports bar. She'd met all of Sara's family except the secret brother. This should be interesting.

"He flew in for my birthday," Sara continued as she emptied the rest of the trash cans. "Isn't that sweet? But I want to surprise my mom, so I need a place for him to stay until Tuesday."

"Is this your brother's first visit since I moved here?"

"Yeah. He's, um, super busy with work and stuff."

Lark could hear the tension in her friend's voice. It

took a second before she remembered that there were problems between Sara's mom and her brother.

Whenever she asked, Sara sidestepped, shrugged or sighed. Which was probably the issue their mom had. Maybe they were ashamed of his job. Lark frowned, trying to think of a job worth being ashamed of. But all she could come up with was male stripper.

Hmm...

"How long is your brother visiting?" Lark asked, grinning as she imagined Sara's reaction if she asked if her brother danced in a G-string.

"Only for a few days, but I'm hoping it'll be a week." Sara's shrug echoed her pouty tone.

"He has to get back to work?" Maybe he was a headliner at one of those fancy strip clubs.

"Yeah, something like that," Sara said. As if she were eager to avoid answering questions, the pretty blonde grabbed the tray of dirty mugs and carried them into the back.

As much to finish her chores as to tease Sara about her brother's stripping career, Lark followed.

"So," Lark said, loading the mugs into the dishwasher. "You never told me what your brother does for a living. Or is it top secret?"

"Um, yeah. Shane's job is sorta top secret, actually," Sara said, her voice carrying a fake edge. "He's not supposed to talk about it, so do me a favor? Don't ask him while he's here. He'd feel awkward, and it kinda upsets our mom."

Wow. He really must be a stripper.

Or worse.

Before Lark could figure out what a mother would

consider worse than a stripper, the chimes on the door tinkled.

Sara tossed the sponge at Lark and headed out of the back room. Figuring it was the stripper—no, no, the brother, she corrected—Lark took her time finishing up before heading out to meet Shane and decide if he had the body to justify her stripping theory.

Oh, my.

He was gorgeous.

She thought so, but the room had taken a nice, slow spin, which she was sure accounted for the sudden dizziness filling her head and the odd tightness in her belly. Lark blinked a couple of times so she could see him more clearly.

And oh, boy, was she glad she did.

Tall, close to a foot over her own five-four, he had a swimmer's build. Broad shoulders, a slender waist and long, long legs. The kind of body that would look mighty sweet naked but for a gleaming coat of oil.

His dark brown hair was cut super short, the top spiked in a way that looked as if he'd run his hands through its thickness while it was wet and left it at that.

"Lark, hey," Sara said, her arm hooked through her brother's as she pulled him across the room. "I am so excited. I finally get to introduce you to my favorite person in the whole world."

Lark hurried over to the checkout counter, hoping it'd be enough to prevent her from jumping him while his little sister was in the room. Jumping a guy before they were actually introduced was just rude.

And, she remembered as her stomach sank into her toes—taking a good chunk of her happy lust with it—jumping friends' brothers was against the rules.

Dammit.

But her body argued that he was hot. Easily the sexiest guy she'd ever met. She was single; she hadn't had sex in eighteen months, two days and—she glanced at her watch—twelve hours. He was single and he had a great smile.

Besides—her mind tossed with a victorious glee—he was probably a stripper. Sex with a stripper was all kinds of tacky.

To hell with the fact that he was only here for a few days, that he was her friend's brother and that he might make his living wearing a tear-away cowboy costume.

All she wanted was that body.

Pick up
A SEAL'S TEMPTATION
by Tawny Weber,
on sale in September 2015
from Harlequin Blaze.

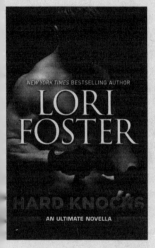

Blaze
Red-Hot Reads

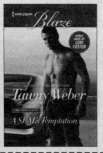

Save $1.00
on the purchase of
A SEAL'S TEMPTATION
by Tawny Weber,
available August 18, 2015, or on
any other Harlequin® Blaze® book.

Available wherever books are sold, including most
bookstores, supermarkets, drugstores and discount stores.

Save $1.00

on the purchase of any Harlequin® Blaze® book.

Coupon valid until February 25, 2016.
Redeemable at participating outlets in the U.S.A. and Canada only.
Not redeemable at Barnes & Noble stores. Limit one coupon per customer.

52612813

5 65373 00076 2   (8100)0 12075

® and ™ are trademarks owned and used by the trademark owner and/or its licensee.

© 2015 Harlequin Enterprises Limited

HBLFCOUP0915

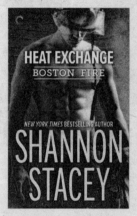
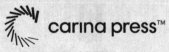

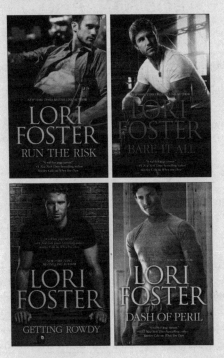

LORI FOSTER

78905	WHEN YOU DARE	___ $7.99 U.S. ___	$8.99 CAN.
77961	HOLDING STRONG	___ $7.99 U.S. ___	$8.99 CAN.
77904	NO LIMITS	___ $7.99 U.S. ___	$8.99 CAN.
77857	DASH OF PERIL	___ $7.99 U.S. ___	$8.99 CAN.
77816	HOT IN HERE	___ $7.99 U.S. ___	$8.99 CAN.
77806	ALL RILED UP	___ $7.99 U.S. ___	$9.99 CAN.
77779	GETTING ROWDY	___ $7.99 U.S. ___	$8.99 CAN.
77761	BARE IT ALL	___ $7.99 U.S. ___	$9.99 CAN.
77708	THE BUCKHORN LEGACY	___ $7.99 U.S. ___	$9.99 CAN.
77695	RUN THE RISK	___ $7.99 U.S. ___	$9.99 CAN.
77656	A PERFECT STORM	___ $7.99 U.S. ___	$9.99 CAN.
77647	FOREVER BUCKHORN	___ $7.99 U.S. ___	$9.99 CAN.
77612	BUCKHORN BEGINNINGS	___ $7.99 U.S. ___	$9.99 CAN.
77582	SAVOR THE DANGER	___ $7.99 U.S. ___	$9.99 CAN.
77575	TRACE OF FEVER	___ $7.99 U.S. ___	$9.99 CAN.
77444	TEMPTED	___ $7.99 U.S. ___	$9.99 CAN.

(limited quantities available)

TOTAL AMOUNT	$ _____
POSTAGE & HANDLING	$ _____
($1.00 FOR 1 BOOK, 50¢ for each additional)	
APPLICABLE TAXES*	$ _____
TOTAL PAYABLE	$ _____

(check or money order—please do not send cash)

To order, complete this form and send it, along with a check or money order for the total above, payable to HQN Books, to: **In the U.S.:** 3010 Walden Avenue, P.O. Box 9077, Buffalo, NY 14269-9077; **In Canada:** P.O. Box 636, Fort Erie, Ontario, L2A 5X3.

Name: _____
Address: _____ City: _____
State/Prov.: _____ Zip/Postal Code: _____
Account Number (if applicable): _____

075 CSAS

*New York residents remit applicable sales taxes.
*Canadian residents remit applicable GST and provincial taxes.

HQN™

www.HQNBooks.com

PHLF0915BL